SWITCH

ISBN: 978-1-64456-827-9 [Hardcover]
ISBN: 978-1-64456-828-6 [paperback]
ISBN: 978-1-64456-829-3 [Kindle]
ISBN: 978-1-64456-830-9 [ePub]

Library of Congress Control Number: 2025909912

INDIES UNITED PUBLISHING HOUSE, LLC
P.O. BOX 3071
QUINCY, IL 62305-3071
indiesunited.net

For Lee
Your love lights the way forward, every time.
I'll follow you anywhere.

In the universe, there are things that are known,
and things that are unknown,
and in between them,
there are doors.

William Blake

Also by Lisa Towles

Specimen
Codex
Terror Bay
The Ridders
Salt Island (E&A Series)
Hot House (E&A Series)
Ninety-Five
The Unseen
Choke

And published under Lisa Polisar

Escape: Dark Mystery Tales
The Ghost of Mary Prairie
Blackwater Tango
Knee Deep

SWITCH
A Thriller

Lisa Towles

INDIES UNITED
PUBLISHING HOUSE, LLC

Prologue

December
British Virgin Islands

We walked the beach together, Tortola's Little Apple Bay, carefully positioned an arm's length apart, me occasionally crossing my arms or clasping my hands behind my back to avoid touching him. The pristine, Caribbean sand and aqua water were a snide offset to what should have been poignant. I sensed we'd both prepared a script of gratuitous banter to fill what would of course be awkward space. *How have you been, what are you painting,* instead of the heavy stones that had burdened my heart all these years: *where have you been all my life, why did you leave us?* I couldn't come out and just ask that, could I?

I was a grown woman now of six feet and he was still tall. As a little girl, when I looked up at him, he was a giant. A little older, when I looked up *to* him, he was a different kind of giant. A powerful force of intrigue and surprise, which later turned to words like enigmatic, shadowy. The words that came from my mother were less charitable. Absent, deceitful. He betrayed her in a thousand tiny deaths, I realized only now as I recalled her anguished face with my toes burning in the sand. Burn then. Burn away a layer in my heart and bring me closer to the truth from which I can't stop running.

1

Earlier, he said he needed time to put away his paints and change clothes before dinner, the first meal we would have together in over twenty years. A painter? Seriously? Preposterous as it seemed, it was a perfect cover for an ex-CIA operative.

Maybe not even ex.

I looked off the balcony of Sebastian's on the Beach, a lovely hotel with rooftop dining on Tortola, BVI's largest island. I'd stayed here before on two occasions – looking for him and I'm sure he—or one of his associates—had watched my every move. Now it was me watching, wanting to be anywhere else, dreading the conversation and resenting that I'd had to ask for it. I mean, what was there to say after all this time that would have any meaning to me?

"Did you see what happened?"

I jerked my head toward the sound of my father's voice, more instinct than a conscious action. "They pulled a dead diver out of the water."

Yes of course I'd seen it. The beach had been crawling with police, EMTs, and an ambulance for the past hour.

"We said 6:30." I looked down at my iconic watch, a touchstone of comfort and a reminder of all I'd lost. "You're early."

Same impish, sideways grin with a dimple on one side. "Element of surprise?" He leaned down and kissed my right cheek before asking if it was okay. Gutsy move.

"I saw a throng of divers walking up the beach before I saw you earlier. I wonder if the victim was part of that group."

"People die all the time," he quipped with all the emotion of ordering a cocktail, then sat across from me. My eyes widened at the sight of a crisp blue suit - summer weight, white shirt open at the collar, the same aviator glasses he'd worn all his life. In his late sixties, he was still as dashing as I remembered. Richard Ellwyn, son of a bitch.

But it was me who had gotten here early, an hour in fact, giving me time to decide whether I was even still willing to meet. I forked through the untouched bits of shrimp and greens on a tiny appetizer plate in front of me and chuckled.

"What?"

"So. You're a painter now."

"I do actually paint, you know. And I'm not half—"

"You're good. I've seen your work. At...Flora's." The name came out cattier than I intended. Flora his other wife, his Virgin Islands wife.

Maybe he'd call her part of his tradecraft. Was he even capable of love?

A server came. My father ordered some kind of drink. Music floated up from the cantina on the bottom floor. My mind was elsewhere.

"You're a spy," I said finally, in a voice loud enough for anyone to hear it. "Why would you eat here of all places?"

Single shrug. "Well, plain sight of course. I'm not active, anyway. No one cares about me anymore."

There it was. More manipulation, always vying for leverage, pulling things from people they didn't want to give. I sure as hell didn't care about him, or that was the story I told myself.

"A spy ceases to be active when he's dead," he added and winked.

I peered at him behind my dark glasses. He couldn't see my eyes; I liked it that way. It was the kind of leverage I learned from him — micro power moves that looked innocuous but were carefully planned, psychologically strategized to the finest detail, like showing up for a negotiation dinner twenty minutes early. Your opponent arrives flustered, while you smile with a half-full martini glass. They're already late to the party. I'd used that one many times.

"Are you glad to see me?"

"You're a bastard," I said. He recoiled an inch but recovered instantly. I loved this moment. I ordered a second gin martini and maintained my distance, still observing him observing me. Such theater.

"What do you want from me?" he asked, reaching up to loosen his collar, realizing it was already unbuttoned. I made him nervous. So he cared about something after all.

I wanted to say my childhood back, the one he missed and wasted while he was off doing whatever spies did back then, pretending to be a simple businessman from a State Department corner office. "What do I want from you? I have no idea."

"Really?" he asked. "Like you haven't thought about it? Come on."

"I'm curious why you came."

"You're my daughter, that's why. Now answer the question."

I wanted to ask him about Jacques Martel, my nemesis. Maybe he was his nemesis more than mine. And I wondered if he'd ever loved me or my mother at all. If I lowered his aviator glasses right now, would his eyes be wet after seeing his only daughter again? I felt a vibration on the floor, his foot tapping. Ah, his signature tell, and the only manifestation I'd ever seen of fear.

"Never mind. We can talk about anything you like." He wiped his mouth, but there was nothing on it. "Anything."

"You're a liar."

"Yes. I am. What of it?"

"You are still active."

He puckered his lips, deciding.

"And I don't believe in fairy tales."

Chapter One

Late March
Ventura, California

Blue lights, grinding metal. *What day is it?*
"Lift her. Hold her head. On three."
A strobe bleeding through my crusted eyelids.
"What have we got?"
"Ellwyn, Marissa. Head injury, possible broken ribs, left hip impact."
"Where's the car that hit her?"
"Took off."
"Well that's it then, we'll never find it."
But I remember. Dark SUV, no headlights. We were almost out. Seconds.
"Who found her?"
"There."
"You, sir. Your name please."
Gloved hands groping my shirt, cold rubber things stuck to my chest. Shouting. Smells like antiseptic. Trying to save—
"Suction."

"—not breathing. Oxygen. Again."

"Better intubate her. Sats 98, tube going in."

Probing my neck, fingers down my throat. Please no. Don't do this.

"She's in."

"BP cycling. Pulse 92."

"Internal bleeding, likely concussion."

Two voices.

"How long?"

"Five minutes out."

I hear you. All of you. I can't talk and can't see, but I know Duga's near the ambulance, dying inside, blaming himself. The air feels cold in my nose, but I can't smell. Why don't I feel pain?

It rammed me in the left side and pinned me to a metal railing near a cargo loading ramp at the warehouse. But that was hours ago. Wasn't it? Was my mother here? Jada? I swear I smelled her Alfred Sung perfume. Come to think of it, a hospital was the last place I saw her, before she was abducted from her room. Are you okay Jada? Send me a sign. Wherever I am, I feel your presence here in a way only a daughter would.

The bed linens are scratchy, but my arms can't move. Can I walk? Have I had surgery? I'm awake but can't open my eyes. It must be anesthesia. Phone ringing. Somewhere.

"ICU 3, Jessup. Yes, Doctor. She's just arrived."

A TV, somewhere. A news story. Serial killer.

"Not yet."

Nurse Jessup will walk over to my bed again, lift my eyelids and flash a light in them, snap her fingers, looking for a response. I see you. Yellow teeth. Smoker.

"Ma'am. Marissa, can you hear me? Blink if you can hear my voice."

I'm here! It's Mari, no one calls me Marissa. Can't you see me blinking? At least I think I'm blinking, but I can't feel my eyelids moving. Is this what dying feels like? Or am I already dead?

Chapter Two

One Week Later

It felt like all I did was sleep. A spill of milky moonlight split open the velvet curtains, dragging me from another Caribbean dream, this time the warm sand near Long Bay Point in Capoon's Bay. My father's gravelly voice was fading now, from BVI where my half-brother Jaden had orchestrated an elaborate plan for us to meet again and start rebuilding our relationship, the one we never had to begin with. Howling wind seeped in through the hundred-year-old windows of the lofty Ellwyn family estate in the Santa Barbara hills, shaking me back to reality.

I still hate this house.

A shapeless noise woke me, echoing up from the foyer, through the cold air and empty hallways that never felt like home, even when I'd lived here. I was probably dreaming; these days so hard to tell. My training as an intelligence operative proved that anything closed could be opened with enough planning and strategy. Now, all I could see were doors. Closed and knobless, a nightmare I had to find my way out of. I'd done it before.

Dozing again, I stared down from some imaginary pier, my eyes glassing the water for movement that wasn't there. Two geese glided past on their surreal escape to the sad sun obfuscated by clouds and lies.

There, again, a faint knocking. Back in my Santa Monica house, that knocking would have meant the wobbling of a kitchen chair when my Great Dane, Trevor climbed to reach the cookie jar containing his maple frosted treats. But this was Santa Barbara, and I was now in my mother's house, the family mansion in the middle of nowhere surrounded by nothing, with Trevor down the hall in his two-hundred-dollar doggie throne meant to make up for this change of venue. Welcome to hell.

"I'm fine," was the last thing Jada had said in her cryptic voicemail, preceded by, "I don't want you to worry."

When did I ever not worry about my mother? Were her words coerced, someone standing over her with a gun promising violence if she revealed any details of her captor and whereabouts? Or maybe she just didn't want to be found.

Aggravated kidnapping events involving high-net-worth victims were usually straight forward. In the past year, my partner Derek and I had investigated two of these, both resulting in the successful recovery of the victims through a tight collaboration between my team, Robert Francone's extraction team, and Ivan Dent's hand-picked team of LAPD professionals.

The demand for money almost always came via phone within the first 24 hours, closely followed by delivery details the next day. Family abductions accounted for nearly fifty percent of all kidnapping cases, most of which involved a child and custody disagreements. But this— six months later, I had no more clarity on whether Jada had been abducted from that hospital bed at all. Had she gone willingly with Mason Middleton, maybe to address their unfinished business from thirty years ago before she married my father? Or had he waited till she was too incapacitated to protest? I had to be here at this estate when she returned. Not when, if.

The knocking sound again.

"Trevor?" I counted back from five, four, three, two, then the clicking of his paws on the hardwood floors. I would have normally invited him up on the bed with me, but my body was too fragile right now for 130 pounds of muscle. I pulled myself up and stroked his head gently. "What was that noise? I heard it too."

I laid down again out of breath, Trevor beside me on the floor, and someone outside with urgent business in the middle of the night. For years, Jada had a gardener, Tran, who ended up living here most of the time with her. Cooking, maintaining the grounds, it was a sweet arrangement in exchange for the five thousand dollars a week she paid him. Sometimes I called Tran for things like appliance repairs, but no gardening and certainly no grounds maintenance. I can barely walk, someone's outside, and I'm here alone. I'd dealt with intruders before. But feeling too weak to defend myself made me want to scream.

Bang bang bang, this time more of a pounding than a polite knock. My clock read 3:13 a.m. What would have taken me a second was now a series of carefully planned micro-movements that would strategically avoid pain: carefully peel back the bed covers, a quick check for nausea and dizziness, stand and hold onto the bedpost, slippers one at a time. I'm fucking eighty years old.

"Come on." I snapped my fingers, Trevor trailing me to the staircase. My father tried to install an elevator, but my mother thought it too modern for our historic home. Their standard struggle. I got halfway down the stairs and heard it again.

Four bangs.

"Ms. Ellwyn," I heard this time.

My spine vibrated. One of the bottom floor windows must be open. I stopped mid-step, shaking. I know I'd closed them all last night. No wonder it was so cold down here.

Trevor barked, glued to my side while my eyes locked on something. What…was that?

I touched Trevor's head, staring at something I'd never seen before in this house. Not growing up, at no time when I came to visit Jada and not since I'd moved back. An opening in the wall, or more like a separation between the wall and the millwork covering it. It was something you'd expect to see after an earthquake, when a tectonic shift pulled corners apart so they no longer matched. From this angle, it almost looked like a large, wooden drawer without a pull or handle. But in the wall?

"Ms. Ellwyn, I'm from the County Coroner's Office. My apologies for the late hour."

Trevor started barking for real, followed by growling. A man's husky voice, stressed, out of breath. Had he been traveling on foot and running from someone? I hadn't heard a car, but how could I from upstairs?

I wanted to flip on the staircase light but didn't want to risk being seen. Trevor followed me, watching my cues as we slowly approached the entrance. I saw my dim reflection in the mirror. Despite my six feet of height, I looked hunched over. My vibrant red hair looked almost brown, eyes sunken. Trevor resumed his aggressive barking and stretched his huge paws up the large foyer door. I heaved it open and heard the glass on the chandelier over our heads tinkle from the whoosh of cold air. The door to the Ellwyn mansion belonged in Downton Abbey. Even now, it took both hands to move it. Ridiculous.

There was no one at the front door. "Hello?" Where had he gone?

My father said things that happen in the middle of the night were out of time. I never knew if he meant they were intended for an earlier time of day, or out of alignment with space-time. Was I ready for what awaited? And in what version of space-time did they exist?

He kept a diary I wasn't supposed to know about. I knew because I memorized his movements, his daily patterns. Growing up, I made a study of him, being home as infrequently as he was, maybe as another way of clinging to him to make him stay longer. He wrote in the basement bathroom in a leather journal with a blue and silver fountain pen, only short messages at a time and never more than a page or so. And he set the journal each time in a locked box that he kept under a crumpled pile of towels in the laundry hamper. It impressed me how my mother never knew about the false bottom. I pulled it up once and saw the locked box underneath. I resented him enough to spy, but I guess I respected him enough to not look for the key. Was it still down there? How is it that I only remembered this now after living here again for the past six months? An opening in the wall...in this house? It had to have something to do with my father, and that journal.

Chapter Three

My phone vibrated in the pocket of my bathrobe, but I didn't remember putting it there. The doctors said concussions could do this.

I pulled it out and pressed the green button.

"Are you in position?" My partner, Derek Abernathy, with in his reassuring voice.

"You mean laying down in bed…that position?" I asked, retreating as quickly as I could back to the bedroom so I wouldn't need to lie. I mentioned nothing about our mysterious visitor.

"Come on, partner," he begged. "I know this stakeout's been twenty hours. Can you hold it together for a couple more?"

And that right there was the beauty of Derek Abernathy, demonstrating his inherent understanding of the human psyche and deft maneuvering of language to reach his goals. He asked instead of demanded. Inquired instead of whined at my audacity. Staying here holed up in this house, on this bed with three computers had been his idea, while he and Duga took point on an extraction with a high failure probability, and the potential to get them and an innocent target killed. E&A Investigations. This was our world, the path I'd chosen.

"I'm getting there." Out of breath from climbing the stairs, I pressed my palms into the mattress to force myself upright and crossed my legs under me, the only things on my body that didn't hurt at the moment. Though that could change. I tried to ignore the visitor downstairs and forget about the unlikely crevice in the foyer wall. It wasn't working.

"How ya doing?" Derek asked, no doubt hearing my gasps and grunts. "Dizzy?"

"Not bad."

"I still wish they taped your broken ribs."

"They restrict breathing and can cause pneumonia."

"I know, but they also immobilize you." Short pause. "Why are you out of breath? Were you out of bed? Bad girl. I'm gonna call Ivan—"

"Don't even think about it. Give me a minute."

"We've got just about that," he said emphasizing the last word, quietly reminding me of our ticking clock and the narrow window through which my team might possibly be able to capture the perp who had eluded us and the LAPD for nearly a year, wasting thousands of law enforcement dollars, time, energy, and technology. All in the interest of (what else?) money.

"I'm still online, I only slept for a few minutes," I argued, but he knew.

"Did you get sick again? How much water have you had?"

"Yes, and none."

"People die of dehydration you know, and you need food to help metabolize the painkillers you're on."

"Dude, gimme a break, I'm walking to the bathroom right now to fill a glass." I hated lying to Derek, of all people.

"You're doing nothing of the sort, and that's fine. Ivan will be there shortly to check on you."

Damn him. Now I really was filling that glass.

⁕ ——— ⁕ ⁑ ⁕ ——— ⁕

The five sips felt like rocks going down my throat, still raw from intubation, and I forced down three micro-bites of the cracker I'd left on the sink before throwing up for the third time. It would be a miracle if I didn't end up back in the ER tonight. But the tall bouquet of long-stemmed yellow roses gave me temporary respite. How could no one know where they'd come from? I asked everyone at the hospital. All they said was *a well-dressed man.*

Fortified by the meager hydration and calories, I remembered the lonely bottle of orange-flavored Vitamin Water in the door of my fridge. Could I hold it down? I could cut it with water. I calculated the time it would take to get down there and back in my condition.

"I'm heading to the bathroom. I'll be back online in three minutes," I told Derek.

"Roger that."

I woke Trevor by creaking across the wood floors and now heard his paws behind me, no doubt thinking I was getting him a snack. He stopped at the top of the stairs, reminding me of our vanished visitor. I need to go back down there.

"In a minute, sweetie," I said, and touched his head, my trusted chaperone. When I got down there, I poured half the Vitamin Water into my glass and filled the rest from the tap so it didn't shock my system. I took three gulps, rechecked the foyer and front room and crawled back upstairs one agonizing step at a time. Other than a hole in the wall that may or may not exist, I felt reassured the downstairs was intact. But someone was here. Where did he go?

I tuned my radio to the team channel so I could hear everyone's movements. "I'm online," I announced.

"Good to hear your voice," Duga said. Something pulled tight in my chest. He's denied it already, but I still heard grief in his voice, blaming himself for not protecting me.

He and Derek were tracking our suspect to a warehouse at 103rd and Compton in Hacienda Village. It's not that I was afraid of working in Los Angeles. As a private investigator and the intelligence field before that, I'd been in tight spots and plenty of bad neighborhoods. But we'd attempted a stealth mission already. It failed and I ended up in the hospital. So now they knew we were coming and I was their weakness.

They, in this case, meant James Traeger and his three "handlers", two of which were responsible for my hit while walking out of the warehouse. After months of planning, Duga and I tag-teamed the installation of audio surveillance on the tailpipe of their van, two of their trucks, and in two strategic locations inside the warehouse that stored their six-month supply of cash taken from a string of smalltime banks up the California coast. We left from different doors in near darkness. Somehow, I was seen by one of Traeger's goons, who ran me down on the sidewalk. Poor Duga, I'm sure he thought I was dead. The ambulance got there quickly but I'd lost a lot of blood. Could have been worse, they said. Way worse. But in my semi-consciousness, I heard one of the EMTs say another two minutes and I would have been a goner.

I had a theory about James Traeger, an unpopular one. My team, LAPD Detective Ivan Dent and his team, and the feds all wanted Traeger. But I knew he had no rap sheet, no prior crimes whatsoever. The prevailing thought was that he'd fallen into the wrong crowd and knew too much to get clear of them. I'd seen it before and had compassion for the guy. He and his goons weren't killers—just thieves who had, by now, swiped nine million dollars from California's economy. How? They were slick, each of them and together as a group, and they didn't make mistakes. As a former CIA Operative, that to me meant a clear head under pressure, which was a skill that was born not developed. Of course white-collar criminals were way harder to track than starving, drug dealers. And having a stash house in Watts suggested Traeger's team had friends in low places and weren't so greedy that they wouldn't give a cut to whoever was guarding it. I appreciated the value of high intelligence, but Traeger needed to be stopped. My accident was no accident. So I knew I had to be the one to stop him.

"Got anything?"

"I see you," I replied to Derek, "all of you. It's quiet on the other side though."

I stared at my three monitors, seeing the color-coded dots corresponding to Derek's, Duga's, and Traeger's movements in the warehouse, along with two other dots that had to be Traeger's men. Our mission's backup team consisted of Robert Francone, my security expert and friend from college, who was planted outside in a parked, beat-up car with a bug hidden in the cupholder that can detect clear voice audio up to five hundred yards while filtering ambient noise. That's some serious tech. Then there was Ivan's team of four officers, and Jazmin Jones, my newest and youngest employee running IT support. I half expected the knock at my door tonight to be her, but remembered I'd given her a key when I came home from the hospital.

Why hadn't I told Derek about my visitor? Maybe I didn't completely believe I'd heard the knock at all.

"Jazmin there yet?" Derek asked.

"She said within the hour and she's monitoring en route. You know her though - she'll be running surveillance while driving eighty on the freeway, backing up her root server, and eating a burrito."

Ivan now. "A car just pulled up to the dock," he whispered.

"Describe it," I replied, knowing, somehow, it was the same vehicle that ran into me. "Black?"

"Black or dark gray, I can't tell, an SUV. Male driver, female passenger, talking, not getting out yet. The man has binoculars trained on the back of the building around the left side."

"Team 2, you catch that?" I asked Derek and Duga.

"Confirmed," Derek answered. "Duga's heading around the back of the building."

"Team," it was Ivan. "Tell me again how certain we are the stash is here."

"Ivan," I sighed, "we went through it twice already at the station. What's the matter? Missing your favorite TV show or something? What else have you got to do tonight?"

"I'm still wondering why you're involved in this case to begin with. You're private investigators and this is a bank robbery."

I sighed and paused a beat, knowing this conversation should have been happening in private. "We know the bank manager of one of the banks Traeger hit, and he asked us to investigate it for him. We informed you right away, as an act of good faith. Didn't we?"

"Yes, you did. I still—"

"Quiet, you two," Duga chimed in. "Four confirmed drops."

"How long after the robberies though?" Ivan probed in his whiny voice. "How can we—"

"Within eight hours, each time," Duga said. "I've got them on camera heading into a warehouse—"

"This warehouse?" Ivan cut him off.

"That's right. Carrying a duffel bag and walking out without one."

"Doesn't that seem unlikely, though? Taking the chance that someone's watching their movements?"

Why would Traeger's team assume someone would be watching them here? Then recalling my history with Ivan and his unrelenting suspicious nature, of course he would wonder. Whether too few painkillers were causing my irritability or Ivan just being an old lady, it had been a mistake to bring him in on this mission. Sure, it was a police matter, and of course the feds were interested at this stage. Derek was always reminding me that bringing Ivan in on a case was a sort of insurance policy for us. But truth be told, he was right to question

15

Traeger's motives. The man was freaking Teflon. An automaton with a boyish face, who thus far had never made a single error in timing, judgment, or preparation when carrying out four armed bank robberies.

"I think that's the point," I said after a moment. "He wanted us to see, making the drop in this warehouse, multiple drops."

"You think it's a setup?" Duga asked.

"She's right," Derek said. "Think about it. With all the fire power we've got on this building, multiple teams and technology out here, what if he's counting on that to keep our attention off something else?"

I watched the dots on my screen move slowly, evenly, toward the back of the building.

"Duga, you got 'em? Two are headed your way," I said.

"Yep. The car's in sight and two are coming out the back entrance now. They're heavily armed."

"I'm right behind him," Derek confirmed. He and Duga were in the back of the building. Shit.

"Ivan, you have backup out front with you?"

"Are you worried about me, Mari?"

"Your sense of romance is misplaced," I said, but liked him saying it. "Answer the question."

"Backup team's fifty feet away, and I'm not gonna need them."

I studied the screen in front of me. "He's got his underlings leaving out the back to divert us," I said. "He knows we're here. Keep watching the front."

No sooner did the words leave my mouth than I saw one of the dots on the screen moving rapidly inside the cavern from the back entrance towards the street out front.

"He's headed out now. Ivan, you're in position? And you're recording this?" I asked.

"Yes and yes," he said.

"Still photography?"

"Backup team's taking care of that."

"We're letting him leave, right? That was the plan," I said.

"That's the plan." Ivan sighed. "We'll use the tape, photographs, and the report I'm gonna write up to get a warrant to search the building. But not tonight."

"How long will the warrant take, and who's gonna sign it?"

"Judge Biehn, probably. Leave that to me."

"Two men just got in the car, driving away slowly toward Front

Street. I got the plate number," Duga said.

"Nice. You get a picture of it?" Ivan asked.

"My camera flash would have gone off, so I made note of it and just texted it to you," Duga replied.

"Duga, stay down," Derek warned. "There's another car pulling up now. A different car."

I searched my screen, following the heat signature dots, but only one was showing inside the building now. That had to be Traeger waiting for the right time to exit. I reminded myself to breathe.

So who was at the back of the warehouse?

"One guy, tall, blocky build, military haircut, just got out of a black van, and he's headed into the building," Duga said.

"No visible weapon," Derek added. "Dark blue jeans and a black t-shirt. Doesn't look like the others."

"You've never seen him before?" I asked Derek.

"No," he whispered. "Duga, watch your ass, brother. Shit's going down here, I can feel it."

"I'm inside a metal drum so I'm good. Smells like gunpowder."

From the other room, Trevor's paws against the wood floor in the hallway startled me.

"Bang bang bang," sounded from the foyer downstairs again. Jesus, my heart nearly stopped. Not a gunshot, I reminded myself. Just someone at the front door again.

At four in the morning.

Maybe it was Jazmin, but she had a key. So my visitor was back.

17

Chapter Four

I muted myself on the radio to call Jazmin. She'd come to us two years ago via Ethan Webb, a former client, while we were investigating his wife's disappearance. Derek and I agreed that her intrepid field work approach plus technical acumen made her a perfect addition to our small team.

"Hey there. Are you close?"

"Why? Is everything okay?" she asked with her annoying habit of starting every sentence with why. Good for investigative work, I admit.

"Traeger's making moves, and we're monitoring on all sides." I paused.

"But that's not why you're calling."

"Okay, you're right. Someone's been knocking at my front door downstairs. Can you check the entrance and the yard on your way in? See if there's a car parked and tell me what you see? He said he's from the County Coroner's Office."

"Needing to talk business at four in the morning? Is he there now?"

"The knocking stopped for a while, but I just heard it again."

"Sit tight, I'll call you right back. Almost there."

Twenty-five years old, barely a 100 pounds, Jazmin Jones inspired this odd feeling of safety and protection in a way I never thought I'd feel for someone her age. Stealth, agility, discretion, and hacker-level IT chops were the four-way punch that made her one of the most sought-after consultants in the industry. Ivan and several members of his team had been trying to woo her into law enforcement. But she'd chosen our team and since then, we'd developed a mutual trust.

"Team 2, report," I said, and set my phone on the bedside table, next to the full water glass.

"Military Haircut just walked in the back entrance," Duga whispered. "Derek, see him?"

"There's some…hold up."

"What?" I asked.

"Some kind of argument," Derek continued. "I hear shouting, someone referring to 'T', which must be Traeger. Phrases like 'leave it, this isn't what we signed up for'. And there's a third voice, saying 'it's not that complicated', someone standing closer to Traeger. Military Haircut is still inside but at the back entrance now."

I waited, listening closely.

"I think they're planning to take it all with them tonight, and leaving in Military's van," Derek surmised. "Duga, where you at?"

I counted to five and took a deep breath, picturing him crammed inside a gunpowder drum. This was too close.

"6GW519, Ivan you got that?" Duga's voice was low-pitched and calm. "That's the tag on the van. I put a tracer under the rear bumper."

"Jesus, Duga." Seemed too risky for the situation, but now we might have a chance to trace them.

"Nice job," Derek replied, reading my mind.

"6GW519 got it," Ivan confirmed. "Anything further, Derek?"

"I'm hearing heavy bins or maybe bags being dragged around. Wait…Military's gonna back his van up to the loading dock. Duga, get outta there now," he urged. "Confirm."

I waited, we all waited… ten seconds, now fifteen. My forehead felt wet, and I was barely breathing. "Jesus Christ, Duga. Reply," I said too loud. Duga had become like family. No, he was family. I'd known him far too long to lose him now. Not like this.

I heard a faint, "All good here." My shoulders dropped, my chest relaxed.

"Okay. Everyone, stand down at this point," Ivan said in his command voice. "Let's assume Traeger and his team are gonna load their stash onto that van and no one pursues. Everyone copy that?"

"Let's make sure Mari's seeing the van on her monitor," Duga suggested.

"Got it," I answered. "It's a new, blinking dot outside the rear entrance of the warehouse. It showed up just before Duga said he planted that tracer so I know it's the right one. How far will you let them go before following?" I asked Ivan.

"Let's give them two minutes," Ivan replied. "They'll be watching with binoculars for any movement behind them or in any direction."

Two minutes seemed too soon, like we should give him five. But we could lose them. My dull headache had changed to a slow throb over my left eye now. Luckily, Jazmin would be here and could take over. Shoot, my phone buzzed a minute ago and I'd ignored it waiting for Duga to show signs of life. I muted my radio and picked up the phone.

Text from Jazmin: *Nobody's down here. I'm in the driveway, I just walked around the perimeter and it's all clear. Why in the hell don't you have motion detectors out here?*

I wanted to say it wasn't my house, but wasn't it, though? I spent most of my childhood here, and now so many years later here I was again. So, our intruder hadn't come by car, or maybe he parked in the woods to allow for a stealthier approach. That said something about his agenda.

They're on my list of home improvements, I wrote. *I need to rest now. Be right there.*

* —— • • • ━━ •

Assuming Ivan's team didn't botch the timing, we had about a fifty percent chance of apprehending Traeger, and the urgency had never been higher. The press had been cooperating with Ivan's pleas to suppress any public story, as it would no doubt make the PD look like bunglers, but with fed eyes on the case there was no escaping it.

If Traeger and his team caught even a glimpse of pursuit, they'd run, which brought our success likelihood down to thirty percent, factoring in other variables like tossing the stash, dropping someone off with it, or any of the other myriad possibilities of capture avoidance during a high stakes mission. So many of the shootings I read about seem preventable. Derek and I attended a law enforcement seminar on this last year, having drowned in statistical analysis of criminal behaviors for two days. Even so, I still relied as much on gut instinct as quantitative data. Traeger was going down, I could feel it. Hopefully none of us would go down with him.

I let Jazmin know via text to come in with her key, then Trevor and I moved down the creaky staircase together stopping at the first landing. There was no time for this right now and I shouldn't be away from my computer. But there's a hole in the wall paneling that I swear wasn't there before. I gripped the rail and took a few quick breaths to steady my swirling head. Dizziness, I'd been warned, could continue for weeks on and off, as well as the nausea that seemed to hit me two or three times a day so far, enough to remind me that I'd been struck by an SUV a week ago—*on purpose*. I think my heart still needed to respond to that violation, and so far there hadn't been time to process it mentally. The harm humans could do to each other hung like a shadow in my brain. And it would probably get worse.

Derek thinks I still haven't properly processed getting shot three years ago, or my kidnapping the following year. Joke all you want about occupational hazards, the truth of my vulnerability and my fears of appearing fragile to others came home every time I looked in the mirror. Especially now.

Trevor nudged my hand as if to say, "Come on, I'm here." Bless his heart. Okay, keep moving. Eight more stairs then we rounded the corner to where I'd first seen the glimpse of lightness where lightness shouldn't be—in the wall. What had been visible an hour ago now looked like a completely normal part of the paneling. I moved to the bottom step and slid my fingers over the wood. Had I dreamt it? My stomach clenched, inviting an unbearable possibility. Had my perception been altered from the concussion? If so, the doctors had omitted that important detail.

"Oh!" I slapped my hand to my chest. Jazmin came through the front door and hurried through the foyer to meet me.

"Sorry, I was in stealth mode." She locked the door behind her. "No one's out there. I checked all over," she said.

We stared at each other for a beat.

"When was the last time you heard a knock?"

"Twenty minutes a—"

Trevor lunged suddenly toward the door to the outer foyer. "Trevor, step!" I shouted, our code for halt.

"What is it? What does he see?" Jazmin jumped to reach the foyer behind Trevor. "I just came in and there was nobody out there."

"I think you mean who," came a voice from behind the door, followed by agitated barks and growls. The heavy, inner door opened in slo-mo. Trevor catapulted to the opening, standing tall on his hind legs with his big-boy bark.

"Trevor, step! Now." He ignored me and dragged his paws down the wood door over and over, trying to wriggle his body behind it through the crack. This meant he recognized the intruder as non-friendly.

"Stay back," Jazmin commanded to the intruder. "Unless you wanna be immobilized by a—"

"I don't. I'm unarmed," a man's voice shouted. "I just want to talk." A calm voice in the midst of mayhem. Good indicator of character. Hopefully Trevor doesn't tear him apart.

For a few seconds, I paused to observe the voice. Did I recognize it? Not specifically, but maybe. I knew my mind wasn't trustworthy right now.

"Jazmin, let him in. Trevor, we're fine."

Trevor heard me this time, turning his large head and wide eyes to assess my demeanor. If I looked calm, that was a visual tranquilizer for him.

"Come." I pointed to the floor beside me asking him to sit. Trevor death-stared at the intruder, then moped up the stairs to stand behind me, upset that I hadn't let him complete his interrogation. I was not turning my back on this guy, calm voice or not. Meanwhile, Jazmin entered the foyer where I heard a verbal exchange.

"We're cool," she said, motioning the man inside. "Always do business in the middle of the night?"

"I apologize for the lateness of the hour. I needed greater discretion than was possible during daylight hours." The voice was low, even, confident. The body solid, stocky, hair light and thinning, eyes… trustworthy at a first glance. Sometimes I was wrong. Okay, more than sometimes.

Jazmin stared the man down. "Ever hear of a phone?"

The man shook his head.

"Library?" Jazmin asked me, pointing.

I nodded, chuckling to myself, leaving Trevor at the foot of the stairs. The bookless room my mother ridiculously deemed "The

Library", only because she'd watched a hundred old movies with old manors and butlers that took guests into a holding pen for private conversations. I'd spent half my childhood in libraries, dropped off by my mother in the mornings during summer vacations while my father was off chasing, interrogating, doing whatever he did back then. Left to my own devices for often ten hours at a time, my eight-year-old self created a community of beings inside the library. There were these great statues of lions at the bottom of each staircase, my protectors who shared secret ways of getting into the forbidden stacks in the Archive room, and the reference librarian was the evil villain, of course, dragging me out by one arm.

Jazmin crossed her arms, her feet spread apart outside the closed door, watching me descend three steps to the foyer. I needed water, wishing I'd drank what I said I had earlier. And I needed sleep even more now, but the sky was already starting to lighten. That meant I was up for the day. My phone buzzed with a text from Derek. I looked down to read it. Shit.

"What?" Jazmin asked, watching my face.

"Traeger's on his way back to the warehouse."

She shook her head.

"Can you log onto my console and check the surveillance board for activity?" I asked her.

"Here first. After you," she said and held the door open. I liked that. She wasn't leaving me alone with this guy. What the hell was he doing here?

Chapter Five

"There are no books in this room," the man said, looking around.

"Thanks for the commentary. How'd you like to go to jail?" Jazmin postured her tiny frame beside him. I felt reassured having her here but often wondered if I relied on her too much. Especially now.

"Who are you?" I asked, wondering why I wasn't more rattled by the disruption.

"And how did you get in here?" Jazmin added.

The man looked at the floor, then pointed to the foyer. "Your windows don't lock and you left one of them open slightly. I climbed in and waited in there."

Climbed in. When he was knocking earlier, he was already *in* the house. Jesus. I'd checked and locked those windows. Even in my compromised state, I took every safety precaution. That meant he was lying.

I fixed my gaze on the roundish face, ignoring a sort of charm to the haphazard fringe of hair plastered to his forehead. We were all standing around the door, Trevor six inches from me, poised for the right moment.

"Linus Hagen," he said finally.

"You said County Coroner's office. Which county?" I asked.

"This one. Ventura."

Would be easy enough to verify. I gripped the back of one of the East Lake parlor chairs positioned on each side of the door, knowing there was a critical stakeout going on, and my monitoring the team's activity could be the difference between life and death. My mother hated these chairs. I remember my father sitting in this one by the door, smoking. His thinking chair.

"Have a seat, Mr. Hagen," I suggested, and hung back in the entry in response to Jazmin's gaze.

"Do you want Trevor?" she asked with a sick smile.

"God no, he's too agitated right now. I'll be alright. Let me know what's happening with, you know. I'll be up shortly."

I knew she wouldn't leave me down here alone with a stranger. The man stood in front of the sofa staring at the door. "Do you mind if we close—"

"Yes. I mind. You have two minutes."

He lowered himself onto the very edge of the sofa, wiping his palms on his knees, shoulders hunched. He looked like he'd had less sleep than me. "I think you know my boss," he said.

"Oh? Who?"

"Camille Bota?"

"Camille? She's—here? In Ventura?" My concussion-altered brain spun backwards to high school. My God. Camille had been my best friend growing up, and for a while in college. "Yes, I knew her," I admitted. "Once."

I watched as the man rubbed his face with open palms. "Look, I shouldn't be here," he lamented. "I had to take every precaution."

I sat in my father's chair, looking through the open doorway up the stairs. I was sure I could summon Trevor with the blink of an eye.

"Something's going on at the Medical Examiner's Office."

"And your role there is what?"

"Chief Forensic Pathologist. Camille Bota, my boss, was recently appointed to the role of Medical Examiner for the county because our former ME disappeared." He drew a breath and waited.

I remembered the old drama with Camille, knowing I had enough drama in my life right now already. More than enough. "Meaning he, or she, stopped coming to work?"

"I can't share any additional details of that with you, not at the moment."

It was getting better by the minute. I rolled my eyes while typing shorthand notes on my iPhone. "So you're here because," I waved my hand in the air, "you want me to investigate Camille's predecessor? And let me guess, she doesn't know you're here?"

"I'm here because something strange is going on. I know about your work as a private investigator."

"From Camille?" How would Camille have known that?

He shook his head and smirked. "I play tennis with one of your associates. Duga?"

It's funny how things worked sometimes, funny that in all this time I never even knew Duga played tennis.

"Okay." I nodded and smiled, acknowledging that a friend of Duga's moved Linus Hagen to a different category in my head. "What happened?"

"A John Doe. Young guy, bookish looking—"

"Where? The morgue?"

"Yes."

"Walked or wheeled?" I asked.

"Wheeled, I'm afraid. No ID on him. I wasn't able to establish either cause of death or manner of death. In eighteen years of experience." He shook his head. I could see the weight of that failure. "First time for everything I guess."

"Ego bruising aside, Mr. Hagen, you—"

"Doctor, actually. Dr. Linus Hagen. My friends call me Lin."

"Oh so we're friends now? Definitely ding me on your title after you've broken into my house." Asshole. "You must get John Does on a regular basis."

"Some of my examinations start out that way at least, but many have identification on them when they arrive. If not, they could be identified by family. Fingerprinting of course comes first, then next is dental records, DNA, which can be lengthy processes. We start with an investigation of the scene and an external examination of the body, followed by establishing the time of death, cause of death, then the manner of death. Sometimes an autopsy is performed," the man chuckled to himself. "And there's a whole world of politics involved in that decision."

I knew the process already and his two minutes were up, Traeger's team could be driving off the premises by now. Anxiety buzzed in my palms. "I'm still trying to understand why you're here and what the fucking urgency is. It's late. You broke into my house. I'm busy right now. What's the goddamn fire drill, and what have I got to do with it?"

He blinked back, but said nothing.

"I'm running a critical investigation that I need to attend to. I'd suggest meeting in my office in downtown Ventura later this morning, with my partner. I trust you can see yourself out? And through the door this time?"

"Can I have your assurance of discretion? That you won't contact Camille, or the PD, or anyone else until I've explained what I think is going on?" the man pleaded. "This case requires absolute secrecy, and delicacy, I might add. It's not appropriate for the police at the moment."

Interesting way of putting it. "You have my word. For now." I motioned for him to follow me to the foyer, where I kept a stash of business cards in the console table. Without taking my eyes off him, I opened the drawer, reached in, grabbed one, and held it out.

He glanced at the print. "E&A Investigations. This is your office address?"

"If you're resourceful enough to have found this place and confirmed that I'd be here, I'm sure you know that already, Mr. Hagen."

"Doctor."

"Meet me there at ten o'clock. I'll have Derek Abernathy with me. Then we'll hear your story and get back to you." I started up the stairs, got to number eight. I could tell the man hadn't moved. Jazmin was at the top of the stairs staring down, one hand on Trevor's collar.

"Doctor—" I turned and sighed.

"Something's going on there." He looked so small at the bottom of the grand staircase, hands crammed in his pockets, like something was eating him alive.

"Where? At your office? You mean Camille?"

Single nod. I descended one step. "Would you say that a crime has been committed?"

"Crime?" He laughed. "I honestly wouldn't know where to start."

I took one more step toward him. Meantime, James Traeger could be eluding both teams and headed out of state with millions of dollars stolen out from under us. Again.

"Something's going on with the John Doe case. The normal

procedure with a John Doe is to work with the PD and use evidence from where the body was found along with cooperation from the local community to aid in identification if we can't find a family member. We advertise on the County website that we're looking for the public's help in identifying a victim. There's a lot more to it than that, but—"

"That's not what happened?" I cut in.

He shook his head slowly. "Camille refused to authorize posting it on the County website, made everyone in the office sign an NDA about this individual, and she won't tell me anything more about it. She's new and we don't know each other very well, but our close collaboration on findings and results is critical to keeping the wheels moving, keeping our funding in place, maintaining our regulatory compliance. So many things." His face looked, of all things, sad.

I descended two more steps while trying to picture this well-fed middle-aged man lumbering in through a half-opened window. It didn't seem plausible. So, had he somehow gotten a house key made? But the alarm would have gone off. And, for that matter, why didn't my alarm alert me to the open window? Nothing makes sense tonight. I thought about the sound the windows made when you raised them. His story wasn't adding up and so far lacked the level of impact that would justify such premeditation. I'd asked him to come to the office because the Traeger investigation was more important. But now he'd roped me in, and I was curious. Camille Bota, wow.

"What do you suspect is going on?" I asked him.

"That's essentially what I was hoping you could find out. It's possible Camille has some kind of connection with John Doe and doesn't want him identified. Or she's being silenced by somebody else. Clearly she's afraid of something, and she's acted so uncharacteristically irrational lately."

"Uncharacteristically," I repeated. But he'd said he hardly knew her. "Can you be more specific?"

"Secretive, really. And suddenly. Like eating alone, taking phone calls from her office with the door closed instead of in the common area. One time I saw her answer her phone, ask the caller to hold, and walk out to her car and continue the conversation inside with the door closed."

"You've confronted her about this?" I asked.

"I was pursuing the open questions about cause of death and running down a trace to get an identification."

"Doing your job, in other words?"

"What I thought was my job. But Dr. Bota told me flat-out to drop any research into this case or she'd put me on an indefinite leave of absence."

I noticed he'd just shifted her name from Camille to Dr. Bota, formalizing their relationship, creating a separation between them. My early profiling training was sometimes hard to turn off.

"So did you?" I asked, standing awkwardly at the bottom of the stairs. "Stop your research?"

"No."

"And where is Dr. Bota now?"

"Missing, for the past two days."

LISA TOWLES

Chapter
Six

I agreed to meet Hagen in our office tomorrow morning and left Jazmin to make sure he actually left this time.

"Get his plate number," I said from the doorway.

She looked up with stern, dark eyes and mouthed the words, "No car."

Great. And now I'd need to decide whether to tell Ivan about what I just learned. Was Dr. Camille Bota—someone both Ivan and I knew well—a missing persons case, or had she voluntarily gone into hiding over their John Doe? I honestly didn't have room in my head for a another problem.

I returned to my perch on the bed and plugged in my headphones.

"Doing okay over there?" Derek asked.

"Fine," I said, not mentioning where I'd been.

"You got my text?" he asked, his voice betraying his exhaustion.

"Yeah. He's headed back to the warehouse. Which probably means he's onto us."

"Yep. He's almost there, I'm three cars behind him."

Derek three cars behind who he assumed was Traeger, headed back to a warehouse where Traeger had supposedly hidden millions of dollars. A lot of assumptions, and in law enforcement, even one was too many.

"How do you know you're actually following Traeger?" I pressed.

"I don't. I'm on one car, Duga's on the other heading in the opposite direction, which supports your theory that they're just driving around to confirm we're following."

"And maybe to see how big our team is," I added.

"Actually, I do think it's him," Derek said.

"Why?"

"His sunglasses."

"You're funny. Did you even see him last time?"

"I saw him," he argued. "Gray aviators, that's who I'm following. Don't believe me, that's fine. But don't you think they'd be directing us away from where they stashed everything?"

"Listen," I said. "Traeger's successfully pinched almost ten million from four banks in two months, without an arrest, and here we are spinning our wheels, no pun intended. Where's Ivan's team?"

"He's got one following Military Haircut, and two more staked out at the warehouse ready for their return."

I knew full well the level of destruction that could ensue at that warehouse. But our teams would be ready for them. My body was weak, and my head felt swimmy. So there was no way my joining them made any sense. Still, being holed up here in my robe and slippers was driving me insane.

"I need to rest," I said, hating the way it sounded.

"Sorry, who is this?"

"Shut up."

"I don't know who you are," Derek joked. "But I like your sensibility. You're paying attention to something you don't usually pay attention to."

"I can't help it, I'm dizzy again. Dammit."

"You sustained a concussion barely a week ago. You shouldn't even be on this mission at all—"

"—except that you didn't have anyone else to run com."

"Why don't you try to sleep a few hours. We got this covered at the moment."

I felt my energy waning in the same pattern it had since the accident: one hour high energy, next hour low.

"I'll check in with you at eight. Be safe." I hung up and punched in

Jazmin's mobile.

"He's gone," Jazmin said of our visitor.

"You watched him walk off? Which direction?"

"A dirty blue Rav, actually."

"I thought you said no car."

"He parked way down the street."

Not surprising. "Plate?" I asked.

"I got a photo but there was a tree limb in the way. Sorry. He's gone, for now."

I went downstairs one last time to check that all the windows and doors were locked. Trevor, in our special telepathy, seemed to know what I was doing and waited for me at the top of the stairs. He looked down like a sad soldier.

"We're fine. No more surprises for now."

I forced my limbs up the staircase, again passing the opening in the wall I'd seen earlier, when the moon was at the right angle and my eyes were fixed correctly. The house had two dumb waiters, which provided years of entertainment growing up. One off the kitchen and another in the dining room, both leading to the vast basement that still haunted my dreams. As if the uncovered, concrete floor down there hadn't been nightmare-inducing enough, my mother had kept my grandmother's collection of legless, headless dressmaker mannequins, called forms, arranged in a row along one of the back walls like a macabre chorus line. A winding, narrow walkway lined with large, industrial equipment had no lights installed and ended in a tiny room with a platform, a carpentry bench, and stacks of shelves holding coffee cans filled with nails, bolts, washers, and charcoal pencils. A creepy wonderland.

And keys, I just remembered. Tiny keys, skeleton keys, odd-sized equipment keys, safety deposit, child's diary, serrated, double bit, punched. Jada and I would empty out the key can, usually a vintage 1940's Folger's three-pound size, and once we found something called a flat steel key with an outline that looked like a silhouette of Sedona. It was beautiful. Maybe it was still there.

Four hours of semi-sleep and three cups of coffee later, Traeger, Derek reported, was back at the warehouse.

"Anyone with him?" I asked.

"Two other cars parked behind him, same as before they left."

"No arrests?" I asked, incredulous. It would have been Ivan's team making the arrest. What were they doing? "In four hours?"

"No."

"What the fuck are they waiting for?"

Derek sighed. "The right moment, I assume. Traeger's slippery. How many times now?"

"I know. Where are you right now?"

"Out front," he said. "Duga's back there and we're in text contact. Radio's too risky right now."

"Please don't tell me Duga's actually in the warehouse."

"Eyes on the ground," Derek said, reminding me. Shit. "Ivan's been gone for over an hour. I bet he's getting a court order to enter the building."

"Hundred bucks he's at a pancake house," I said. "You haven't heard from him?"

"No."

I knew what he was doing and it was a sound approach. "Rather than asking a judge who could say no because of lack of evidence, I bet he's waiting for a more hospitable hour to ask a more hospitable judge."

"Crafty. So he's good for something after all?"

"Those are your words."

"How are you feeling?" he asked. "I heard you had some interesting nocturnal activities."

Jazmin must have told him. "Not the kind I would have liked, either," I joked. "I asked my visitor to come by the office this morning so you could join me and we could have a longer conversation."

"Sleep when you're dead, right? That's fine. What time?"

"Ten."

"I'll be there."

I hung up and smelled breakfast wafting up from the kitchen.

"Jazmin?" I called. Trevor came trotting in from the other bedroom. "Where's Jazmin?" I asked him and kissed his forehead. Trevor looked at the door. My stomach growled at the scent of eggs and toast, and more coffee. God bless her.

In what felt like two hours, I shuffled to the bathroom, raked through the tangles in my hair, twisted it into a quick bun and followed the smells, checking the wood panel on the wall on my way down. Naturally, no visible crevice or opening, and when my fingers pulled at

33

the wood, nothing moved or cracked. I must have dreamed it. No more *Stranger Things* before bed.

Trevor escorted me from the bedroom to the kitchen. Why wasn't he moaning and cooing like he always did on the way to the food location? Oh lord.

"Did Jazmin feed you already? But she doesn't know where we keep your special food," I said, scratching him behind the ears, realizing the minute I looked up who had infiltrated my morning.

"Hello, sunshine! Have some coffee, you look like you need it."

Ivan Dent, at eight o'clock in the morning, wearing my Sur La Table apron. God help me. I snatched the cup from his fingers, prepared exactly the way I like it of course, and barely a nod before I sat at the end of the long table.

"Come onnnnn," he said, arms outstretched. "What's the matter?"

"You're the second person to enter my house uninvited today."

"Wait. What? Who do you mean?"

"Never mind."

"You're sulking. Do you want me to go? After I've made us such a nice breakfast?"

"I'd just like you to knock," I argued. "Or ring the bell, or call me first. We don't live together anymore." I hated hearing those words as they came out of my mouth. Too late, that's where I was today. More coffee sipping.

He sat beside me. "I'm sorry."

"No you're not. Does Derek know you're wasting time in my kitchen while he and Duga, not to mention the rest of your team, are still on a twenty-hour stakeout? These are your priorities?"

He stared. "Judge Carr is not likely to sign the court order. I'll ask her and present it of course, but I'm not holding my breath."

"We gather more evidence, then." I was undaunted. "That's the issue, right?"

He shook his head. "I can't keep my team on him 24/7. You know I don't have the resources."

"That's what you came here to tell me?" I asked, like I didn't know already.

"No. I came here to check on you. You could have died in that accident. It hurts to even say it."

"It was no accident."

"Yeah, I know. Thanks for reminding me."

"You look good in my apron, by the way."

Chapter Seven

Duga's heading your way, Derek texted me. *Says he has information for you.*

> *You're still on our subject?*

Pause. *Four cars behind.*

He left? Why the fuck didn't they arrest him? Are you're driving and texting right now?

> *Stop light.*

Liar.

I barely picked at the breakfast Ivan made me, after which I moved one agonizing step at a time upstairs to shower and dress. Frustration buzzed in my palms as I shuffled around this huge house in slippers like an elderly shadow. It didn't feel like living. It didn't feel like me. Still, I knew enough from prior injuries to give my body the time it needed, or else. Right? That meant no running for probably two more weeks, no exercise at all and most of all, no stress.

I heard the doorbell and my stomach clenched, thinking again of my visitor. Duga had his own key but I liked how he still rang the bell. Jazmin jogged across the tiled floor to let him in. I heard his voice echo from the foyer. He took the stairs two at a time.

SWITCH

"Are you decent?" he shouted.

Duga felt more like my brother than either of my actual brothers. "Come on in," I said from the edge of the bed and motioned him to my new Willa Arlo tufted chaise.

He sat, rolling back and forth on the cushy surface. "Is this new?" He gave a sly smile, like he'd caught me.

"Not really."

"Are you settling back in here after all?"

"No way. You know I hate this house." But if my mother returned and I intended to wait for her, I could at least do it in comfort.

"Uh huh. Anyway—" He took off his jacket and shook his head.

"What's the matter? I know that look."

"I don't know."

"You think it's a setup?"

"Yeah, obviously."

"Why?".

"Because - they're driving normal speed, taking normal roads. They're not evading us."

"Traeger's smart, I told you. I've been studying him. Take everything we know of criminal behavior and turn it on its side. We can see how Ivan does getting a warrant for the warehouse."

Duga tipped his head. "You don't sound optimistic."

"Depends on the judge of course, but we've got a pretty good story for probable cause."

"You've got an affidavit from law enforcement, which is a good start."

"Plus, all the surveillance tapes showing him and his team going in and out of that place over the past two months. But again, it's all about the judge." I also knew Ivan was very charming, as he liked to constantly remind us.

"Well, I've got something to add to your mental dossier." Now he sat for real and crossed his legs.

"About him?" I asked.

He nodded slowly, fumbling with the phone in his pocket. It was ringing. "Duga," he answered. "Yep, okay, right."

"Traeger?" I asked.

"No, but I gotta go."

"What about—never mind," I said. I needed to get to the office to meet my midnight intruder, Dr. Hagen anyway.

Duga slid his feet into his shoes again and stood square in front of me, checking me out. "You know if you overdo it and exert yourself or move too fast, there's an 80% chance you'll end up back in the hospital."

I pushed out my lower lip to make a frowny face.

"And you hate hospitals, don't you?"

"See you later," I said, waving him off. "Be careful."

I heard two sets of footsteps on the staircase going down.

"Sorry Trevor," Duga said. "Not today, buddy."

Chapter Eight

I ordered a double shot mocha cappuccino from Beacon Coffee on Olivas Park Drive on my way to the office, and a teaspoon's worth of it sputtered from the cup onto my pants when I dropped it into my cupholder. Dammit. That reminded me; I still needed to coordinate with Tran to have him look at the spare washing machine in the basement since the cycle water wasn't draining properly from the main machine. I prayed Dr. Hagen was late. I needed thirty minutes to drink coffee in peace.

Our Ventura office was originally a townhome built as a standalone structure and later turned into condos. Its two best features were designed by architect Frank Gehry, who lived here for two years before creating our prized, wrought-iron spiral staircase and a wall-sized bookcase. I placed my desk deliberately in front of it, which created a wonderful power-seat when clients walked in. Then, to offset the modern décor, we put a warm, burgundy Hamedan Persian rug over the stark, white floor. Derek chose it, I wouldn't have, but I discovered that giving Derek his way, on occasion, had many benefits, mostly to me.

I went into the kitchen to fill my water bottle and emerged to find a slightly more disheveled version of Dr. Lin Hagen standing inside the door, still looking sheepish.

"Try this again, shall we?" I jibed.

"Good morning."

"Can I get you something?"

"Sorry again to have disturbed you last night."

"Has something else happened since then?" I asked.

"No. Well, not really." He sat tentatively on the sofa, looking back at the door. "Tell me about your business."

I sat at my power desk and folded my hands. "What would you like to know?" I positioned my laptop so I could take notes.

"Your practice, I mean. What types of cases do you investigate? Every day a different crime type of thing?"

I squinted my eyes down to slits, scrutinizing the odd comment and the mismatch between his B&E stunt and this very ordinary looking man across from me. Balding, overweight, bad teeth, and something genteel in the way he spoke, almost apologetic. Maybe too much so. I wasn't buying it.

He'd planted himself in the center of the too-hard sofa. What kinds of cases did I really want to be investigating these days? Jacques Martel and his Inspector Moriarty crime ring had gotten me shot. Three years later now, we're chasing a high profile, sophisticated bank robber. I was starting to believe Traeger might not even be a bank robber, that maybe he was chasing a much bigger prize. I still needed to hear what Duga was going to share about him.

"I guess there's some kind of regularity to the irregular cases we take," I admitted. "The human brain's always searching for order in the chaos, right?"

"I don't know. Some people prefer chaos."

I laughed, more at the smirk on his face. I suspected Lin Hagen ate dinner at the same time every night and kept his cloth napkins neatly folded in a drawer. Chaos? Doubt it. But maybe that was a cover, too.

"Well, we investigate all kinds of crimes. Some of them aren't even crimes."

"Domestic? Cheating husbands and the like?"

"Sure, though they're not my typical cup of tea."

"Missing persons?"

I sat back and my pants felt too tight around the waist. I couldn't remember the last time I'd gone running, and by now I'd missed so much of my workout time from my medical recovery, it wasn't even worth tracking. "Dr. Hagen, this is sounding like a job interview. Weren't you going to—"

"Sorry," palms up. "Camille, Dr. Bota, has been following your career and has mentioned you several times in the short time we've worked together. You're old friends. You're lucky."

"In what way?"

He shrugged, choosing his words. "Friendships are a luxury, especially when people stick around for a while."

I didn't need to mention that I hadn't seen Camille in decades.

"I'm just trying to understand what you do so I can better understand what she admires about you."

"Sorry to be blunt, but why do you care?"

"I don't know. We have a complicated relationship and I guess I want to understand her better."

Was it five o'clock somewhere yet? I needed to steer this conversation towards a measurable outcome. Complicated relationship. Understand her better. Clearly, he had some connection to her beyond the professional. Camille Bota, the wily party girl I'd gone to high school with, was now Chief Medical Examiner in Ventura County. She was certainly smart enough, but I was still trying to picture it.

"Complicated how?" I asked.

He shrugged, and in that moment I saw a lonely man with an attractive boss. The roll of his shoulders spelled shame.

"Are you provincial in your thinking, or progressive would you say? Because from what I remember about Camille, I imagine she'd be very cautious, to say the least, of any man standing in the way of her career." I read his face, asking himself why he'd come here.

"I would never do that," he said softly. Did he have feelings for her? Love, even? I nodded to myself and made a mental note.

"Why are you here, doctor?"

"Because she's missing and I'm concerned."

The metal pop from the door handle interrupted us. I hated that thing. Couldn't be Derek, who always knocked before he entered. Polite to a fault. The door thrust open.

"Dr. Bota is most certainly not missing." I heard the booming voice first. Ruddy face, sweaty forehead like a tired bureaucrat squelched by years of lost battles.

Hagen's eyes were shut tight. I closed my laptop. Here we go.

"Can I help you, Mister—"

"Declan Fergus." The two names came out quickly like bullets exiting his mouth. And he raised the last syllable, for effect. "And it's Doctor, not mister."

Lord. Would it be impolite to laugh right now? The man's jaw was clenched tight after he said it, obviously accustomed to landing zingers in the laps of his audience. I was tired of him already.

I stood but didn't extend my hand. "Well, Dr. Fergus. What can I do for you? I'm Marissa Ellwyn."

"I know who you are. So does he." The man pointed to Lin Hagen, my presumed new client, whose face had turned gray.

Hagen sat upright. "Let me explain. Dr. Fergus has temporarily taken over Dr. Bota's role. I was just getting to that part."

"So he's your boss." I paused to read the room. "I understand. Dr. Fergus, I don't take walk-ins. If you'd like to have a conversation with me, please take a card and make an appointment. Now, if you'll excuse us?" I moved around the desk to stand in the center of the room.

The man smirked, unbuttoned his jacket, and sat in one of the four blue chairs I had lined up by the lobby door. "I'll wait."

"I don't think you heard me, so I'll be happy to go over it again. You need to—"

The man crossed his legs and folded one hand over the other, obviously practiced in the art of making others uncomfortable. "Let me make this clear." Chin raised, eyes half closed. "I will not permit Dr. Hagen to share any details about Dr. Bota with you or anyone else."

"About how she's apparently missing?"

"That's right," he said too quickly, caught himself, and squirmed.

"As far as I'm concerned, Dr. Hagen's free to share anything he wants with me."

Hagen hung his head.

I backed down, lowering my feathers. My eyes shifted from one man to the other. "Then do we have anything further to discuss?" I asked Dr. Fergus.

Hagen's eyes widened. I felt his frustration, dying to share with me important details. Another time.

Fergus rose with a flourish, getting his ill-fitted trench stuck in the crease of the chair in the process. "Not with you, Ms. Ellwyn. This is purely an internal matter."

"Well, not exactly." For once in my life I felt grateful for my six feet of height. Was it my imagination or was Fergus an inch shorter than me? I was going to get a lot of mileage out of that…and I was wearing flats. Even better. I stepped slowly, careful to clomp my soles on the wood floors and enjoying Fergus' face respond to my tactics.

He opened the door with one hand and half-turned back. "Oh? What interest could you possibly have in an ME-related matter, Miss?"

For the second time, Hagen's frame sort of collapsed into itself, no doubt hoping to disappear entirely, maybe wondering if I'd mention his break-in at my estate. I kept my eyes on Fergus, already seeing his lack of experience with both tall and strong women.

"Before you so rudely interrupted us, Dr. Hagen informed me of his concern that Dr. Bota might be missing. Since I've known Camille for twenty years, I've now got an interest in her well-being. So really, Dr. Fergus, this is sounding more and more like a police matter and I'll be contacting them as soon as you leave." I paused to give my words legs. Hagen wore a spark of jubilance in his eyes.

Chapter Nine

Alone again finally, I refilled my Beacon cup with some French press coffee from our office mini kitchen, remembering that Carrie, our Admin, would be returning from vacation on Monday. That meant someone would be able to sift through everything I'd ignored since my accident. I returned to the desk, holding my hands around the warm mug when the front door opened. Derek poked his head in first. He didn't knock but paused to check the space. What was he looking for? Hair messed up, collar on his jacket turned in on one side. I smiled, enjoying an opportunity for comedy.

"Sleeping in today?"

Our office downtown was too far from Derek's house in Glenwood. Sometimes he came up three times a week, other times he'd stay in one of the guest rooms at the estate. Trevor loved when Derek stayed over because he took him for longer walks and gave him more treats. The spoiler.

"I had a—"

"One night stand? A bender?" He knew I was joking.

"Rough morning, okay? Some coffee would be nice."

I handed him my mug and watched him take two long sips, then I filled another cup from the kitchen. I came back and stood opposite him, both of us sipping in silence for a moment. "What happened?" I asked.

"Nothing happened. Last night was supposed to be my first full night's sleep since we first took on the Traeger case. I slept about ten minutes the whole night." While he told me about a dog barking down the street, I was deciding how much to tell him about Hagen.

"Where's your visitor?" he asked. "And why do you look so happy? It's morning."

I raised a brow.

"A new case?" He sat on the sofa with a satisfied grin.

"Unofficially anyway."

"Your visitor showed up I take it?"

I nodded. "With his boss, no less."

"Looks like I missed all the fun."

"A little drama, a lot of posturing, both of which I could've done without."

He set his briefcase on the floor. "Are we even able to take on another case right now?" he asked. "Traeger's taking up 75% of our team and our resources, and we've got—"

I nodded. "Fair question. But we got payment on the Myers case, so that's done, and the two new cases that haven't launched yet."

"What are we waiting on there? One of them had a partner in another country, I thought," he said of a corporate corruption case I was still only considering.

"Until they get back and can come in to meet with us, I'm not investing any energy in preliminaries."

"You don't trust what he told you so far?"

I shrugged. "I just don't see where there's necessarily a case. So no, I guess I don't." I sat opposite him.

"Things change, I guess," he said, but it was a question.

"What, you think before my accident I would have taken that meeting?"

"Would you?"

"Maybe it's more like shit happens and *we* change."

Derek's phone buzzed with a text. "Did you hear about that serial killer case?" he asked. "It was in my Twitter feed again this morning."

"It's called X now," I corrected him. "Do you read any actual news, like subscribe to any news channels or apps?" As I talked, I had a vague memory of a serial killer news story on TV, but I hadn't watched TV in weeks. Maybe when I was in the hospital? The memory was more about the creepy feeling I'd had when I heard the story. Derek's voice pulled me back to the room.

"…found bodies in Santa Monica, Redondo, and one other place. I don't remember."

"Do they know anything yet?" I asked.

"No and it's surprising it's made it into the news circuit. Normally the potential panic is offset by facts, which they don't seem to have yet."

"You think the press leaked it?" I asked.

"Maybe someone did."

"You-know-who's back on Monday." I smiled and crossed my arms, changing the subject. "Are you ready for that?" I asked of Carrie, enjoying how Derek's features changed without even saying her name.

"No. I mean, there's nothing to say. Next subject."

"That's fine. You're off the hook, for now."

Head shaking, a look of disgust. I knew he liked Carrie's adoration but he made a science out of pretending.

"Traeger?" I asked.

"Yeah. Traeger. Okay." He reached into this briefcase, thumbing through files. "Shit. I don't know where my head is today. Be right back, the file's in the car."

The pain in my back and hips when I got up reminded me that no, I wasn't recovered yet from getting rammed into a metal grate. I slowed my pace and managed to water the two ferns Carrie had placed in each corner of the lobby. Only a half a coffee mug worth of water each, no more. No overwatering, as was my tendency. Then my phone chimed. I'd just upgraded to an iPhone 14 and loved the new ring tones and alerts. It was one of my favorite things about upgrading, offset of course by temporarily losing all my contacts despite how I'd backed them up beforehand.

The text was from a number I didn't recognize.

It's Lin Hagen. 6607 Bristol Rd in Montalvo. Go now, or you'll miss it.

I read the text. *Miss what?* I wrote back.

It's Camille.

Chapter
Ten

I showed Derek the text from Dr. Hagen and locked up the office.

"You drive and I'll navigate," I said in the parking lot.

"I haven't had enough caffeine yet."

I paused and gave a long sigh. "Fine, I'll drive."

"Can you?"

"Sure," I said and took his keys, carefully climbing in the driver's side.

"Are you okay?" I asked.

"Not really, no."

"What happened this morning?" I started the engine.

"He's driving us around in circles, It's been going on all night."

"Who's at the warehouse now?"

"No one's inside, three cars parked out back and get this, a kid, like a twelve-year-old boy standing out front right around where you got hit." Derek put his hand on my arm and squeezed. "Sorry, bad memory I know."

I'd always loved Derek's coloring: light blue eyes and a slightly worn, ruddy complexion which, despite its red undertones, always looked nicely tanned. Today his eyes were ringed in white circles with sagging skin. Nothing a good night's sleep or two wouldn't cure.

"101 South?" I asked, ignoring his reference to my attack. Whoever drove, the other would navigate. He was pulling up Waze on his phone.

"Yeah, keep going to Montalvo. Exit 63, Johnson Drive. Off the exit, left on Johnson, right on Bristol."

"Okay." Now I wished Derek had driven, because for some reason my back and hips throbbed. I reminded myself that pain was normal right now. I'd take a lavender bath tonight before bed to help restore myself back to balance.

"The street address is 6607 and I assume it's a residence, but Dr. Hagen didn't tell me much. Just that we didn't have much time and there's something we needed to see."

I turned at the Johnson Street exit, followed it to a light, then another light. "How far to Bristol?"

Derek held up his phone, then plugged it into his charger. "1.8 miles. Did he say what we might find here, or did you get any other information?"

"No and no."

He widened his eyes in the WTF look.

"Hagen's undermining a direct request," I explained. "Though that's too mild a word. His superior, acting Chief Medical Examiner Dr. Fergus, said that Dr. Bota is absolutely not missing. So I suspect Hagen texted me from the bathroom or something wanting to ensure discretion."

"So I think we can safely assume that she *is* missing."

"Well, what I assume is that Fergus has something to hide."

Derek rubbed his face and combed his fingers through his hair. "Um, wait, sorry," he stammered. "Back up a minute."

I slid my foot to the brake pedal and simultaneously checked my rearview mirror. "What?"

"No no no, sorry. Not the car, keep going. Did you say Fergus?"

"That's right."

"Declan Fergus?"

"Do you know him?"

"Nobody knows a man like Fergus," he grumbled. "I mean, I do but I don't, not really."

"I'm sensing some personal history here maybe," I said.

"Let's leave it at that for now."

"Fine."

"You think he might be involved in her disappearance?" Derek asked, wide awake now. Apparently, the name Fergus was all the caffeine he needed.

"Or something," I said. "He's definitely threatened by anyone looking into her whereabouts, so much that he followed Dr. Hagen to the office and barged through the door like a Texas Ranger. He's got something to hide and that's enough reason for me to try to find someone from my past." And yours, apparently.

Chapter Eleven

Something about Ventura had always intrigued me. You could stand at the end of its 1600-foot pier and look out into the wilderness of the Channel Islands, a remote ecosystem so far untarnished by the modern world. It had been an easy choice for where to open our new E&A Investigations office, such an improvement over the salvage yard trailer in LA's Fashion District, where Derek and I had first met. The family estate in Santa Barbara worked well for the moment, roughly 27 miles from the office.

In the last mile leading up to what I assumed was Camille Bota's home, I took in every detail. Quiet, almost too quiet for the height of the morning, healthy palm trees, manicured lawns. Orderly, tidy, a perfect picture of suburban American life, but for the shadow in my heart warning me to beware of this case. Was it her? Camille? Sure, we had baggage, I could admit that to myself. Knowing it could also be fatigue reminded me of all the lies I'd told my doctors to get them to discharge me. My body ached everywhere. I knew the relationship between pain and irritability. No, it wasn't Camille. But Dr. Fergus was preventing me, trying at least, from looking into her disappearance. As a Medical Examiner, she wasn't an elected official like the coroner, but more of a trusted, community pillar helping a city or municipality with its most important work of all—dealing with the dead and uncovering the truths nobody wanted to hear.

Police homicide detectives uncovered the who and why leading up to a death. But the ME had the more important job of uncovering the how. I'd foolishly thought, early on, that determining the method and manner of death was a straightforward process. Now it seemed even more convoluted than the who and why. Suffice it to say that Fergus' obstructionism had activated my defiance. Where was my friend Camille, and what had she been about to expose? A crime within a crime, within another crime. There, a new theory. One born every minute.

As was our custom, I passed by the address to get an initial look, then circled around the block parking five houses away. The neighborhood had few trees and was completely sunny, which was a bummer. Normally we'd return after dark, but Hagen's text implied urgency.

We'd both seen the car—a pristine, white Lexus in the driveway parked haphazardly with the driver's side door open.

"Looks like trouble," Derek said. "I'd be shocked if the neighbors haven't called this in yet."

"Gloves?"

Derek pulled two pairs out of the console compartment between the front seats.

"Hagen said it was urgent," I said, biting my lip.

"An abandoned car with the door open? Seems so."

I nodded, taking in the scene, my stomach tightening. "We can't assume it's necessarily her car."

"Could check the mailbox, but we're too conspicuous."

"Here's what I suggest. I'll walk up. Less suspicious if it's a woman coming to see her."

He snickered. "This ought to be good."

"I could be her friend picking her up for lunch, or a co-worker wondering why she didn't show up for work," I explained, seeing the error. "Okay, okay, so could you. I get it. You go then."

"What's the play?" he asked.

"Walk up like you're surprised to see her car, walk entirely around it, go to the front door, ring the bell, wait ten seconds, and come back. Gloves on for the doorbell, please."

He cocked his head to the side and nodded. "Not bad. Performing a play for the neighbors so they can report it to the cops later?"

"No. When you get back to the car, we'll report it to the Ventura PD and we'll both stand in the driveway on our cell phones with gloves on, looking like investigators, gathering as much data as we can without touching a single surface before the PD gets here."

"That'll also give us at least thirty minutes to check out that car. You're good," he said.

"I know."

Chapter Twelve

Derek approached 6607 Bristol Road on foot. A well-kept, modest ranch with a garage on the left, weathered white paint and evenly spaced boxwoods leading to the front door. The home of a busy, no-nonsense person. Could this be Camille's house? Sure. Maybe. I could see Derek's exhaustion from the Traeger all-nighter, mental and physical, in his slower gait, wrinkled jacket, and slumped shoulders. Fucking Traeger, he'll be the death of us. If we can ever catch him.

The actor performed his part flawlessly for any old ladies peeking through living room blinds. I watched with binoculars from his car across the street. He paused in front of the white sedan with the driver's side door open, lowered himself a few inches to peer inside, then turned for a 360 view of the street. He returned his gaze to the car, looked at his watch, and shook his head, hands on his hips. Perfect. Now he headed up the slate walkway to the covered front door. He rang the bell and peered into the home from the frosted glass on each side. I hated those things. While appreciating the design feature and obvious curb appeal, frosted glass created a security vulnerability you wouldn't find on a steel door with a peephole and no windows.

When no one answered, Derek made it back to the car as a cluster

53

of dark clouds gave some needed shade.

"No answer, obviously. No noises that I could hear inside either. I'm hungry."

"Of course you are."

Eyeroll. "Want me to call it in?" he asked.

"Yeah. Ventura PD. Ask for Abel if he's available."

Derek stood outside with his hands on the roof of his car, pointing at the other car in the driveway. He approached it, crouched down and peered in the driver's side without touching anything. I stayed in the passenger seat of his car watching the display.

"Abel's off today," he said of Officer Mike Abel, literally the nicest guy I'd met here in Ventura. We'd worked with him on several other cases so far. "They're sending a unit out, twenty minutes or so."

He climbed in the driver's side and closed the door, eyeing my notebook. He nodded.

"So?" I asked.

He looked in my eyes first and sighed. "White sweater on the driver's side seat," he paused. "There's a red smear on the top."

"Top of what? The sweater? Where?" I asked.

"Collar."

"What kind of smear? Lipstick?" Please be just lipstick.

He pinched his lips.

"Shit." I recorded the detail in my observations list. "What else?"

"Not much. The keys are on the floor of the driver's side."

"Keys on the floor. That's odd," I added.

"Nothing noteworthy at the front entrance of the house and I can't see anything through those frosted windows."

"Nothing else visible in the car? No other clothing, shopping bags, food wrappers?" I asked, certain there had to be something. I remembered Camille, when we had been close years ago. She was a pack rat, always finding reasons to keep things, to reuse them, and her ingenuity in always finding innovative ways of avoiding waste. I admired her sense of conservation, but it was an annoying habit.

"Not that I can see, no. Looks like a very clean, tidy car. I'm gonna take a quick walk around the back of the house."

"Maybe the sweater's not hers," I suggested, dying to look at her registration. While Derek was gone, I stayed in the car but turned all the way around to scope out the neighbors. Without anyone visible in the windows, the house diagonally across the street had a perfect view of

Camille's driveway. He jogged around the far side of the house toward me shaking his head.

"Access points?" I asked.

"There's a slider, it's locked and the curtains are drawn. No other back entrance and a small, grassy yard. Nothing out of place."

Waiting for the Ventura PD officer to arrive gave us a few minutes to start a report, even though we hadn't been retained by anyone and technically shouldn't have been there. That meant carefully avoiding all the legal pitfalls.

"Do you want to call the DMV?" Derek asked.

I considered this.

"I know you don't want to."

I checked his expression. "You know me so well, do you?"

"You don't want to call it in because it makes whatever happened to her more real. And that's okay, we don't need to do that right now."

"Especially because an officer's on the way. Let them do their job."

"Agreed," he said. "What about texting Hagen to ask him about it?"

"He's got enough problems right now, I suspect."

I got out and we walked around what we presumed was Camille's car. I typed notes on my phone while Derek narrated.

"Lexus ES, looks like two or three years old by the paint, four-door, off-white leather interior. Women's white cardigan sweater half on the seat and half on the floor with a visible red stain on the collar."

Impressed as I was by the word cardigan, I stopped him. "Collar? Most cardigans don't have those."

That look, the comical frown always on the right side of his face. I cracked up. "Fine, how about neckline?"

"Thank you." I winked.

"Continuing on, the mailbox is empty, no lights on in the house, and there appears to be no timer," he added.

I looked out at the yard. "I don't see a mailbox."

"It's mounted to the wall near the front door."

"Be right back." I moved back to Derek's car and reached below the driver's side seat for the full-sized Maglite I knew he kept there. I crouched low. My hips, my ribs, maybe a bad idea.

"What are you doing? I would have done that for you."

"Quick," I said, handing it to him. "They'll be here any minute. Shine this inside Camille's car and see if you can see anything."

I waited while he aimed the light all over the interior of the front seat, back, then the same thing from the passenger side windows. He slowly returned to the driver's side and raised a brow.

"What?"

"Look." He pointed at the sweater. "There's an earring stuck to the collar, I mean neckline."

"Good catch, I never would have noticed." My stomach sank at the implication.

"Do you read that the same way I would?" he asked.

I sighed and slid my hands in the pockets of my suit pants. "From the blood and the earring, I might conclude that the abduction went very quickly, that the abductor or abductors surprised the driver, whoever it was, and that the sweater had probably been draped over her shoulders when they dragged her into the other vehicle." Camille. What have you gotten yourself into?

"There's something else," Derek said, Maglite shining under the passenger seat again.

"What now?" I asked.

"There appears to be a notebook. I can see it when I shine the light in the back from the driver's side door."

"Let me see."

He handed me the flashlight. I aimed the beam on the floor behind the front passenger seat and saw something shiny on the floor. "Looks like a leather folio, the kind you can stick a legal pad in. That what you were thinking?" I asked.

Derek searched my face, asking me his telepathic question about whether it was okay to remove something from this car.

We both felt the weight of the moment, knowing the owner of this car was likely in danger and possibly dead. The question was, why? If it was Camille's car, did she know something that she shouldn't, or had she threatened to tell something to the wrong person? I felt a little nauseous, my eyes locked on a classic, fine gauge cotton or possibly cotton and silk sweater, just the kind she always wore, its beauty offset by a blood smear near the top button. Had someone held a knife to her throat while she had the sweater on, forcing her out of her own car and into another?

"Now or never. I'll do it but you need to give the word. You know her, I don't."

"Do it," I said. The driver's side door was already open, which gave us an easy in.

Within thirty seconds Derek had leaned through the driver's side and reached into the back with gloved hands and pulled it out. I snapped a few gratuitous photos of the driver's side, paying close attention to the sweater, a separate closeup of the red smear and another of the pearl stud earring stuck in the fabric.

Right there standing in the open doorway of the driver's side of what we believed to be Dr. Camille Bota's Lexus, I nodded to my partner for him to open the cover of the notebook. Without even leaning down, I zoomed in with my fingers and snapped a photo of the first page.

"Flip."

Derek flipped the page, checked to see if there was writing on the back, there wasn't. Three paragraphs of scrawl filled the second page, and I got a photo of it, along with two more, and a table on the fifth page.

"Good. Return it just like you found it," I said.

Within one minute, we were both sitting back in Derek's car with the door closed, Camille's car in its original state like when we'd first pulled up. My heart pounded in my chest. Blue police lights reflected on the street.

Chapter Thirteen

"You talk to him. I want to read the contents of that notebook," I said.

Derek got out and walked around the car to stand outside the driver's side window.

"What's the matter, detective?" I sometimes called him that, because at one time he was a homicide detective working with Ivan Dent with the LAPD. I knew what he was thinking so I answered the question myself. "Trespassing? Is that the issue?"

"Isn't it?"

I took a long breath, framing my defense. "No. I don't think so."

"And why not?"

"We have no intent to harm, steal, or otherwise interfere with the ownership of the vehicle. But more importantly, if we have probable cause to believe her vehicle contains evidence of a crime, and the vehicle is available to search without improper breach of privacy, we *can* search it without a warrant."

"This is likely to end up as a crime scene," Derek argued, crossing his arms. "The squad car just parked and that officer's gonna be asking us these same questions, so we'd better get it straight."

"I've read the Cali Code of Ethics," I sighed. "We're fine. Besides, if you were so uncomfortable with it, why didn't you make me fish out the notebook myself? I would have."

He bent low and leaned in. "You're recovering from an accident. I didn't want you to injure yourself. That reach into the back seat might have undone your stitches."

Damn him for being so thoughtful. "I can never stay mad at you."

"Hurry up, we don't have much time. Why wasn't that trespassing, in your opinion?"

Long sigh. "Okay. Vehicle Code Section 10852 is tampering and 10853 is about climbing into a vehicle." Derek knew I had these references taped to my desk. "Without an intent to commit injury or malicious mischief, as it's called, there's no issue. Furthermore, the door was not only unlocked but it was wide open. And besides that..."

"This ought to be good." He backed up a few paces.

"I'm here as a private citizen asking the police to do a welfare check on my friend Camille, who didn't answer her door and hasn't shown up for work in two days. I saw her car door open and of course looked inside because I was worried about her."

"Sorry but I already identified us to the police as E&A Investigations."

"Derek, the driver's side door is wide open. Stop being ridiculous."

"Have you confirmed that she even lives here?" he pressed. "Do you know conclusively that's her sweater?"

It was the kind of sweater she would wear; I'd seen this style on her before. Thin, tall, delicate bone structure. Camille Bota was a stunning woman who made any clothing look like it had been designed specifically for her.

"I don't know either of those things," I admitted. "But the door was open, we have no malicious intent to steal or harm her property, and we suspect that my friend lives here and she might be in danger."

"Okay. You're the boss."

Dammit. He only said that when he thought I was wrong.

• —— • • • —— •

I could hear Derek talking to the officer. It surprised me that he gave up Dr. Hagen, that he'd tipped us off as to the car in the driveway. Did he not know the impact this might have on Hagen's job when Fergus found out? He knew Fergus, too. So maybe he wasn't that thoughtful after all.

A text vibrated my phone. Tran, thank God. He wrote *Busy lately, sorry. What do you need?* I'd called and left him two voicemails. I dialed his number.

"Tran, finally," I said when he picked up. "How are you doing? I'm working and only have a minute. Will you have time to come by and look at my washing machine?"

"Which one?" he asked, typically getting right to the point.

"The main one, the one on the left. You still have your key, right?"

"I have it. Later this week or early next week, not sure yet. What is it doing?"

"It fills up with water but doesn't cycle," I said in a monotone, eyes on Derek and dying to get off the phone to look at those photographs of the notebook.

"Is there water in it now?" he asked.

"Yes," I said, knowing that wasn't the answer he wanted.

"Hose problem. I'll come this week. Just leave it."

"Thank you, Tran, take care."

I kept Lin Hagen in the back of my mind while I zoomed in on the first photo from the notebook in Camille's backseat. Then, distracted by another thought, I texted Derek suggesting he ask the officer's permission to check the car registration.

I had to admit, without having looked in the mailbox or seeing the registration document, it looked like what I remembered of Camille's handwriting. She was a lefty and the slanted script showed it. Not only that, she'd been writing quickly, maybe under duress. Now my mind was running away from me.

Derek waved from his position outside the squad car, standing beside a young male officer. He gave me a thumbs-up and pointed to the car. I nodded, telepathically saying *you do it, I'm busy*. Or maybe I was just afraid of the confirmation that it was her car, knowing the grave implications. Now, time to focus.

The first page was the beginning of her report of a John Doe. Interesting that Hagen hadn't mentioned anything about this. Did he not know? I scanned the page, all hand-written but the kind of detail that would normally have appeared on a form.

- Sex: Male
- Race: East Indian

- Date of Death: Unknown
- Estimated Age: 30-35 years
- Eyes: Brown
- Hair: Dark Brown
- Height: 6 feet 0 inches
- Weight: 152 lbs
- City of Death: Ventura, California
- Condition of Body: Well-nourished adult male, evidence of dehydration, possibly due to extended outdoor exposure, ligature marks on neck *
- Death Manner: Appears to be asphyxiation by strangling (see page 2 comments)
- Features: Red mark on shoulder and right side of collar bone (ink?)
- Physique: Athletic build
- Clothing Description: Jeans, light blue dress shirt, black socks, tennis shoes
- Scars or Tattoos: No tattoos, surgical scar on right forearm
- Jewelry: N/A
- Teeth Condition/Restoration: Two fillings, not recent

Other non-categorized features:
- Small torn piece of paper in victim's mouth. Faded writing but still visible: "ST9".
- Positive ID: N/A, no one has identified body, nothing posted on ME website
- Place of Death/Place Found: East bank of Lake Piru, Ventura, California
- Found or Pronounced: Body discovered by hikers: Gorman, Mr. and Mrs., Santa Barbara, California. Left phone and address but did not provide a statement to police
- Transported By: Gold Coast Ambulance Services
- Suicide Note: N/A

I was about to flip the page, when I heard Derek's footsteps approaching the car. I turned to the opened window.

"Deep in thought? What have you got there?"

"Interesting. I'll tell you later. What about the car?" I asked.

"Registered to Camille A. Bota. It's her car."

"Amadi."

"Sorry?"

"Her middle initial," I mumbled. "Stands for Amadi. She's Nigerian."

Derek must have seen my face change. He reached in through the window to touch my shoulder and squeezed. "Hey, let's not assume anything here."

I nodded.

"We know nothing so far except that she's missing. And that she's missing a very nice sweater."

I half smiled, knowing he was being logical but feeling a darkness spread through my heart. Because I no longer wanted anything to do with this case.

Chapter Fourteen

I'd been up too long without sleep and was gonna pay for it. I made Derek drive back to the office, at least, while I scoured the other photographs of Camille's legal pad. He stopped at a Starbucks on Victoria Ave on the way to 101, then a Subway a half mile in the other direction. We ate and coffee'd up on the way.

"Who were you talking to before?" he asked.

"Tran."

"Your gardener?"

"He's technically a landscaper," I said, reading. "And a licensed electrician. And a major appliance repair man. He's a find. Not big on social skills though."

More chewing, less talking. My mood had turned dark at the almost certain indication of Camille's abduction, plus my body had been getting sore in the late afternoons since the accident.

"We need to contact Hagen," Derek said between bites. He wasn't asking this time.

"I know. I'll text him."

The asterisk next to the ligature notation under "Condition of body" on the previous page appeared again on the top of page 2. It was a short paragraph in the same hand as page 1, in parentheses, and the lettering was lighter. Had Camille changed pens, or was she nervous about what she was putting on paper and tried to obfuscate her text? This detail made me wonder if she was writing these notes to transcribe to her official report, or something else.

  * *Ligature marks on neck – Looking closer with a magnifier on the victim's neck, the ligature marks are false and were likely made with some kind of staining agent to the skin. Upon cursory external exam at the location where the body was discovered, there was no apparent damage to the larynx, hyoid, arteries or veins, no petechiae, no ischemia. Victim did not die of strangulation. The purported assailant took steps to simulate strangulation, suggesting a high level of premeditation and likely homicide.*

  ** *Round, filled in, red dot the size of a pencil eraser on the neck lateral to the Adam's apple, at the carotid artery, and on the shoulder. Appears to be the same type and color of ink on the false ligature marks across the front of the throat.*

  *** *ST9?*

  **** *AEI?*

  ***** *Tox, standard, non?*

Tox likely meant toxicology, but there was no indication in this document that she'd sent samples out for testing. She had to, though. So where were those results, and was that why she was missing? I slid my thumb to the left to show the image of the final page of the notebook, depicting the crude drawing of a male form. Camille had circled the areas she referenced on Page 2 with arrows pointing to the front of the victim's throat, the dots on his neck and shoulder, and his mouth.

"Are you gonna tell me what you're reading?"

Derek's voice pulled me from deep inside my head. I hadn't even noticed we were almost back to the office.

"Time to call Ivan?" he asked.

"Hell yeah, but first I need to talk to Dr. Hagen." I turned off my phone and lowered it into my purse. My eyes felt overused, and my heart heavy for Camille. Derek pulled into the parking lot of our building. "You mentioned Hagen to the officer," I said again.

He turned off the engine. "Well yeah, he tipped us off to the car. You wouldn't have?"

"Not immediately."

"What's the issue?"

"What's the issue?" I let out a loud sigh. "We need something from him. Information, and we need it urgently because he's about to be completely shut down to us."

"By the PD?"

"Yes, by the PD because he'll most certainly be taken in for questioning. But even more than that is—"

"Fergus," we said in unison.

"Right," I confirmed. "Once Fergus finds out Hagen tipped us off about Camille's car and that he's talking to us, he'll be a brick wall, not to mention fired."

"You think the cops are gonna pick him up tonight? We could call Ivan and get him to intervene, at least long enough for—"

I shook my head, irritation rising through my body. "Please I beg you, don't make me deal with him right now."

Derek sat back and studied me with the same smirk that always accompanied this type of resistance. "Okay," he said softly. "Tell me what you want to do."

"I want to get a burner phone to Hagen so we can communicate with him tonight, share what we found out, ask a few questions before the brick wall is completely constructed."

"Do you know where he lives?" he asked.

"No. I'll call Robert," I said. The very thought of our security specialist, Robert Francone, concretized the danger surrounding my old friend.

"I'll call him. I want you to go home. This has been a longer day than you expected and you're only at half capacity right now."

"If that." I opened my mouth to raise a protest, which was met by Derek's palm.

"Do you want me to drive you?"

"I have my car, I drove here."

His brow was raised. I knew what that meant. I was exhausted. It was definitely time to rest.

"Fine," I said. "You'll call Robert then?"

"Doing it right now."

I grabbed my laptop and locked the office. Twenty minutes later, I unlocked my front door, never so happy to see Trevor's face. He needed to be fed, and I felt dizzy from over-exertion. Or maybe just emotional overdrive.

"Trevor, ready for dinner?" It was Jazmin's voice that made his ears prick up to two fine points at the top of his head.

65

"Go eat, sweetie, I need to lay down."

He blinked his beautiful dark eyes at me for a second longer than usual, which told me he understood the nuances of vulnerability. Trevor knew I was injured and weak. I bent down and kissed his head, then started up the gigantic staircase when my phone buzzed.

Robert's got Hagen's car, his address, and has a burner phone for him, Derek typed.

Robert Francone, an old college friend, was ultra-fast when it came to jobs like this. I never knew how he secured his information, but there were two intrinsic truths about him—an unimpeachable character and he knew absolutely everybody. Literally a mole in every corner of the state, both high and low. I liked how I didn't need to worry about how Francone would deliver the burner phone to Hagen, and what excuse he would use to get him to actually use it. Why? I trusted him. He'd find a way.

Chapter Fifteen

I crashed hard, slept for two hours and woke disoriented. Now 4:00 p.m., it seemed more like eleven. Did I even want to get out of bed? My head felt like it was three times its normal size, a throbbing over my right eye. I reached a hand outside my duvet cocoon and snatched my phone off the bedside table, but it slid onto the floor. Shit. That meant sitting completely up, using my sore-as-hell ab muscles to move to the edge of the bed, and crawling around on the floor. Fuck it, I thought, flinging back the covers. I needed to get up anyway. I opened the blinds and used a tactic I'd used before as an operative: I simply pretended I wasn't tired. While I was at it, I pretended I wasn't recovering from a near-death accident, concussion, and two hairline rib fractures. I ripped the phone off the floor and fell back in bed propped by two extra pillows, hoping for news about Dr. Hagen.

Three texts, the first from Francone.

Hagen burner: 805-566-9787.

Ah, thank goodness. I added a heart emoji. That didn't take long at all. Robert Francone did it again.

I brought up the keypad on my phone and paused. My head still felt swimmy after my mega-nap and dehydration was likely the cause of my headache. More than water, I needed a strategy. I slid my feet into the slippers beside the bed. What did I need to know from Hagen? And what was I prepared to tell him about what we found today?

I paced from the chaise to the bedside composing the initial text to Hagen in my head, knowing I had one chance to set the bait correctly. Time was running out, and that's assuming the police hadn't gotten to him yet.

Derek picked up on the first ring.

"Hey."

"Did you sleep?" he asked.

"Did I ever. Listen, I'm getting ready to text Hagen. I just got the burner phone number from Francone."

"And he's delivered it, successfully I mean?"

"Presumably. Did the officer today mention anything about bringing Hagen in for questioning?"

"Of course they'll bring him in, he's their only lead. Besides us, that is. What are you thinking?"

"Just working out the timing. We've got a ticking clock."

"I doubt they've gotten to him yet, if that's what you're wondering. By the time that officer submits his report and gets authorization to follow up, it'll more likely be morning. Or later. Besides, Robert suggested that Hagen make himself inaccessible."

"Unless," I said thinking out loud. "I mean, if someone's filed a missing persons' report on Camille, the higher urgency would necessitate moving on anything they could. I'm gonna text Hagen now. Call you back shortly."

"Right."

"Any news on Traeger?" I asked.

"Still waiting," Derek said, then hung up.

I punched in the burner phone number and started typing a text.

Dr. Hagen, it's Mari Ellwyn. We found the car you led us to, and I'll be happy to provide details of what we found if you'd like to meet somewhere or call me back. Primarily I need to know about the John Doe. Are you available now for a call?

I watched to see if he was typing a reply. Nothing happened. I resumed my pacing, realizing it was almost Trevor's dinnertime. Checked again, no dots. But now I got the message on my phone that my text message had been read. So he'd seen it, good. If he wasn't writing back immediately, was he going somewhere more private to call me? I needed more details on whether the burner phone had been delivered to him at home or at work, and under what circumstances. Dots, finally. Here we go.

Stearns Wharf, he typed. *Waterfront running path in 30 minutes.*

I knew that path well, .8 miles of open ocean and one of Santa Barbara's more Instagram-worthy spots. Since moving here, it had substituted for my primary running path, sometimes with Trevor. But I still missed mornings on my beloved Santa Monica Pier. And now, God knows I haven't been running anywhere. Not for three more excruciating weeks. I felt desperate to extract as much intel as I could from Hagen, but the idea of bending down and crawling into an uncomfortable car wasn't appealing.

Hagen seemed to read my thoughts. *Are you at home, I can pick you up if you'd like. I'm nearby.*

If he was using a burner phone, why couldn't he just call me? I didn't understand the purpose of the in-person visit. But after being at Camille's house all afternoon, now I felt more invested in an answer.

Sounds good, I wrote. *I'll wait outside.*

15 mins, he wrote back.

Here goes nothing.

Chapter Sixteen

The sky had turned to slate while I slept too long, and now a low ceiling of clouds darkened the neighborhood. Maybe I needed the rest. I'd dreamt of the flowers that used to grow in this garden. Bird of Paradise, clematis, poppies. It was almost April, wouldn't be long now. The tops of the Italian cypress trees lining the western edge of the property made a silhouette of silent soldiers looking over my shoulder. I liked them there. Especially tonight. Something told me the clock was running out on Lin Hagen.

"Get in, quickly," Hagen said, through the opened passenger window.

I did my best to crunch my six-foot frame into a small Volkswagen hatchback—a different car than the Rav he was driving last night. Did he own two cars, or had he stolen it? Hagen sped down Holly Road, then turned onto Tunnel Road which took us out to 192. At the freeway onramp on the edge of Mission Canyon, he pulled to the shoulder and stayed there idling, looking left and right. I watched him, grateful I had my gun in its holster in my bag, glancing in the side mirror to spot a tail. Only darkness followed us.

"What's going on?" I asked, already sorry I agreed to the trip. For backup, I texted Derek and let him know Hagen had picked me up and described his car.

"Someone followed me home from the ME's office," he said, pulling onto the road behind another car heading toward the freeway entrance.

"On foot or what? Did you see them?"

"No. In a dark green mini van with a gun in clear view on the dash when they were behind me at a red light."

"Not very discreet, which probably means they're not very experienced."

"Or sending a stern warning."

"Do you see them now?" I asked him.

He checked the mirror again and shook his head.

"Nevertheless, if someone is following you, your office and this car could be bugged, for that matter. I suggest a detour."

"Agreed."

I tapped him on the arm and lip-synched "downtown".

He nodded once, telling me he was accustomed to sensitive operations, clandestine research, and suppressing vital information from interested stakeholders to protect larger agendas. Maybe he'd make a good operative, if he wasn't one already. But my gut reminded me that I didn't know him yet and I still needed to maintain objectivity in case he was, in fact, the one behind Camille's disappearance. Both noted in my mental journal.

I had a client three months ago who took me to a dingy dive bar on State Street called Whiskey Richards, nice and dark inside. Hopefully I could still remember where on State Street. Without talking, I used hand signals to direct him, and shook my index finger when he was outside a parking garage. Too risky.

We parked on the street four blocks away, so I could check shop window reflections to see if we were being tailed. So far it didn't look like it.

"Here we go," I pointed. "There are some booths in the back."

The bar was huge and U-shaped. He pointed to an empty booth near a pool table. Unfortunately, it was also loud. He ordered two Coronas, which would normally have been fine, but I was still on pain meds. Luckily, he was driving.

I sipped slowly forming my questions. "Oh my God, I love beer," I moaned, feeling the cold bite on my throat.

Hagen grinned. "That's a strong testimonial. So do I. Do you not drink it often?" He was glancing around the place, paranoid.

"Not really. I'm more of a martini aficionado." I gave him a few scant words about my accident without revealing anything that could jeopardize our Traeger investigation. You never know about people. Dr. Hagen could be Traeger's silent partner, for all I knew. I took another few sips to help me relax, giving Hagen time to digest what was happening in his world.

"I need to ask you a few questions," I said finally.

"I know."

"Are you and Camille lovers?"

The tired eyes widened, forehead rising an inch. His shoulders pulled back.

I tended to do that during witness interviews. Derek didn't like my gut punch approach. It was true that it sometimes worked against us. But I had a feeling about Hagen, and I sensed I didn't have much time to validate it.

"Wow. You don't—"

"No, I don't."

Slight nod. "Well, no. I mean—" He took two long sips, rolling the bottle around with nervous fingers. "Not lovers."

"You're obviously in love with her though."

Hagen turned to look at the door, probably gauging how many steps it would take to exit, knowing I'd be slow to pursue in my current condition. Now he shook his head, rubbing his finger tips on the shabby wood table. Next, he tipped his head to the side. Not just to the side but to the left, which according to tradecraft psychology sometimes meant acquiescence. The tradecraft checklist was visible in my mind's eye, a pen already checking boxes.

"I have nothing concrete on which to base this, but I sort of felt there was something between us."

"Meaning she felt the same?"

His palms came up, then waved me off. "I don't know. I guess you could say that I'm in love with her, at least in some sense of the phrase."

I had to be careful with my next few questions, careful to not try to impersonate a police officer or imply that I suspected him of any wrongdoing. I took another blissful sip forming my thoughts.

"What was your impression of how her car was left in her

driveway? And how did you come to see it like that in the first place?" The second question was by far the more important but positioning it as an afterthought made it seem slightly less calculated.

I watched him collapse into the uncomfortable wooden booth, tapping his fingernail on his glass. "I thought it looked like she'd been taken. Why else, right?"

I nodded, waiting for more.

"I was there this morning because I live nearby and sometimes we drove together to the office. She was supposed to pick me up this morning and we usually stopped to grab coffee at a—I don't know the name. This little place."

"Beacon," I said.

"That's it."

I loved Beacon Coffee. He was slowly redeeming himself from breaking into my house.

"I'm an early riser," he explained. "I don't even need coffee to wake up. It's more of a social thing for me."

"For you and Camille?" I asked.

"Me and anybody. Coffee sort of binds people together. Don't you think?"

I found binds to be a peculiar word in the context of coffee. I added it to my mental checklist. "What time did you plan?" I asked.

"Seven-thirty was the usual pickup time, for either of us."

"So what happened when she didn't show?"

"I waited, not sure if maybe she was just getting a slow start. At 7:50 I texted her. No response. I drove to her house, parked at the curb, texted her again that I was here and asked if she was okay. No response. I called her, no answer. So I texted you and drove to the office. I locked the door to my office and…I don't know."

"Was her car in the driveway at that time?"

"Yes."

"And did you walk up the driveway and ring the doorbell?"

He nodded. "No answer. Then back at the office, I just sort of sat there, thinking."

"About what?"

Hagen stared now, more intently than before. "About what I didn't get a chance to share with you yet because we were interrupted by Fergus."

"What's that?"

73

"The body's been moved. And not by me."

Chapter Seventeen

My father thought assumptions were the bane of success. So I learned a long time ago that gut instinct should still be put through the rigors of validation. When the thought forced itself into my brain that Declan Fergus could be behind the disappearance of John Doe's physical remains, I knew proving that would be a long path. The fact that Fergus was an asshole worked against my theory, of course, because now my feelings for him were influencing the facts of what had now become an actual case. If nothing else, it was a welcome distraction from Traeger.

If Fergus was behind John Doe's disappearance, he'd be motivated to remove all forms of evidence, like the body itself, and to prevent Camille, his Chief Medical Examiner, from revealing what he was working to suppress. But why would he want to suppress evidence, unless he would be somehow implicated by it? This didn't feel like the usual tug of war in murder cases—evidence discovery and suppression. The path to this case was tangled to begin with, and the most disconcerting part was how several of these strings undeniably led back to me. I had a personal connection to Camille. Hagen too had a personal connection; he was Duga's tennis partner which, again, led back to me. I was starting to think of our John Doe as the tip of an iceberg with three hundred feet of secrets beneath the surface.

No one followed us from Whiskey Richards back to the estate, or not that I could see from the side mirror. I clipped Hagen's door closed with a quick goodbye and an eerie feeling in my belly. He would almost certainly be picked up by Ventura Police tomorrow morning in connection with the condition of Camille's car, which had by now most likely been impounded and brought to police headquarters to be taken apart by crime scene investigators. Surveillance footage was not likely in her neighborhood, but they would definitely find signs of a struggle, which will kick it up in priority. Camille, what on earth did you find?

I never got the chance to open the topic of Camille's notebook with Hagen, nor did I have any reason to believe he even knew about it. The fact that it was still wedged under the passenger side seat led me to believe Hagen hadn't gone through her car and had instead sped off to his office like he described to me in the bar. Did that mean he was a trustworthy witness after all? Or was he hiding as much as everybody else in this case?

I considered Camille's handwritten pages as I unlocked my front door, consciously turning the deadbolt behind me, then ensuring all the bottom floor windows were locked. Again.

Her first postscript bothered me the most. She hadn't said but certainly implied that ligature marks had been somehow inked on the victim's throat to simulate strangulation. If that were true, it would imply a level of premeditation that might not have been considered otherwise. Manual strangulation often precluded premeditation, implying a sudden, uncontrollable rage on the part of the assailant. Ligature, meaning strangulation by way of some kind of instrument, like rope or twine, did imply premeditation, or at least enough to make a first-degree homicide arrest. But simulating ligature marks would have been done to conceal the real cause of death, which wasn't apparent to Hagen despite his years of experience. And it required a qualified tattoo artist willing to perform the procedure on a dead body, which narrowed the list even further.

The red, round dots on the neck and right shoulder were noted in Camille's notes but also on the drawing she made of the body, indicating the ligature marks, and the paper found in the victim's mouth bearing "ST9". The killer hiding the truth, but leaving us a clue. So odd.

An hour later I was lounging in my favorite dark blue silk pajamas,

Trevor on the floor at my feet, wondering why I didn't just move to one of the bedrooms downstairs but remembering my pillow top mattress and how badly my body still hurt. A call from Derek interrupted me. I said I'd call him when I got home from my meeting with Hagen. Dammit. He was such a worrier, too.

"Do you ever call me when you say you will?" he whined.

"Sorry," I said and sort of meant it, my post hospital discharge excuse already overused. I gave him the skeletal details.

"Do you suspect he's right, that he's being followed?"

"Something's going on at the ME's office. Camille's missing, and now so is our John Doe."

"Inked ligature marks," he mused. "If she means a tattoo, that would be difficult."

"We can certainly check it out. What's the Traeger update?" I asked.

Long moan. "He's a fucking phantom. He's got different shifts of crew with him and it's looking like a much larger operation than we originally thought."

"You're still watching him though, right?"

Pause. "I'm not even sure who we're watching anymore. Duga's got someone on him, but I didn't get the chance to connect with him today. He said he'll come by here tomorrow. How about you and John Doe? Any thoughts about Camille's notes?"

I desperately needed a glass of wine. "I've researched references for ST9, so far only getting as far as a tax form and a Star Trek film. As for AEI, I haven't gotten to that yet," I said. And that's exactly what made research one of the most interesting parts of my job. Too bad it was almost always under the cloud of murder.

After we hung up, I laid my head back and must have fallen asleep with the light still on. The mark of a good pillow. I awoke from a dream at 3:05 a.m., disoriented and freezing because I'd also left the bedroom window cracked. I got up and fumbled with the drapes to crank the hundred-year-old, single pane, louvered window closed, another point of contention between my parents. Jada always fought to preserve history just as it was, not to change it to fit newer standards because they were easier to maintain.

I pulled the chain on the bedside table lamp and collapsed on the chaise to latch onto my dream imagery before it completely faded. Camille, a younger Camille, and me, but at my current age, helping her, grabbing her arms and pulling her away from someone. I think she was screaming, though I wasn't sure if it was at me or at someone else. Large hands were holding onto one side of her, pulling her hair, and I remember the word "Never" repeated as I continued pulling her out of some dark crevice. A garage, or some kind of tunnel? It had seemed lower in elevation than street level, but I knew dreams couldn't be trusted. I rubbed my eyes. Come on brain, give me more. Please. Then I realized it, like a tablecloth had been yanked out to reveal an antique beneath it. Her attack—not this one but the one when we had lived together years ago during college. Someone broke into her campus apartment and stole her purse, but not without a struggle that left her with a broken rib and a knock on the head. They never found the guy. How could I have forgotten it all this time, and then all day as I've been working on the case of her disappearance? Could it be related? Another part of my past I would have liked to leave behind.

Chapter Eighteen

Wake up. **Derek's text pulled me** from another fitful sleep, after tossing and turning all night.

Better be good, I typed back. *Too early.* I could almost hear the snicker on the other end.

Lead in Camille's disappearance.

Fine, one minute.

My head felt heavy from the weight of my dream. Could it be a coincidence that Camille had been attacked years ago and was now missing? Of course, two unrelated incidents could coincide with the same person. Previously shot, abducted, then rammed into a metal grate, I'd considered this about myself more than once, if trauma begets trauma. Could one event predispose you to attracting similar disturbances? It was circular logic and, as my father would say, a waste of otherwise useful mental energy. I slid my legs to the floor and sat upright, slowly, loving how the silk pajamas made it easier to move around in bed, temporarily forgetting my injuries. I heard sounds from the kitchen. That was the worst thing about this place. Thirty-seven stairs and nearly an eighth of a mile stretch from my bedroom to that side of the house. Ridiculous. Derek tried to get me to put a Nespresso machine up here. No of course not. That would make too much sense.

"Sounds like you're up." Jazmin clinked her always-blue fingernails on the railing up the stairs to announce her arrival. I loved her for that.

I smelled the coffee from the hallway. "God bless you a thousand times. Did you stay last night?" She'd taken over one of the guest rooms since I got home from the hospital, no doubt a promise she made to Ivan or Derek, or maybe Duga. My hapless bodyguards, they tried hard.

"I like it down there," she said. "There's no TV in the room so it's quiet."

"I bet you also like all the wifi boosters all over the house," I said, and happily took the mug from her hands.

"Hell yeah, I installed them." She smiled and searched my face. "You have another rough night?"

"It shows?" I took two blessed sips. Hot, very hot.

"Why are you up so early?" she asked.

"A lead from Derek that he felt the need to tell me about at six o'clock. I need to call him back. Might have a job for you today. What's your schedule like?"

"I'm free until noon. Just let me know."

As she headed back downstairs, I noticed she'd done something different with her hair. Still long with thin dreadlocks but they were clipped back off her forehead in a different way today. Looked good on her, showing more of her sculpted bone structure. There was only one reason why a woman changed her hair.

I returned to the chaise for a few more sips of the strong brew. This seat had a fantastic view of the woods behind the estate, which bordered the Santa Barbara Botanic Garden property. I heard owls here late at night, and usually a cacophony of birds upon waking. This morning held nothing but crickets and an occasional mourning dove. I finally called Derek back after brushing my teeth.

"Hey partner," I said when he picked up. "Where are you right now?"

"Impressive. Your one minute only took forty-five today. Driving north, and there's no traffic. Are you awake enough for a report?"

"Jazmin brought me coffee after I got your text so I'm getting there. She must have heard the floors creaking up here. What's the lead?" I asked, getting down to business.

"Someone called in a missing person's report."

"Our John Doe?" I asked, hopeful.

"Meets the description."

"Really." I nodded, reminding myself how I've gotten my hopes up on missing persons reports in the past, only to discover later that the person either wasn't missing at all or was missing on purpose. "Hold on." I pulled on yoga pants and a t-shirt, drained the last sip, and headed downstairs to refill it. I popped in my AirPods and put my phone in my pants pocket so we could keep talking. "Young East Indian male?" I asked. When I got to the bottom step, I looked up at the wood paneled wall and squinted my eyes, remembering the opening I'd seen. Too many pain killers apparently.

"Yep."

I poured more coffee from the stainless-steel carafe. "Interesting, but hardly suggestive. Who called it in?" I asked.

"The caller left only a mobile number, refusing either a street address or email, as was requested."

"And you're thinking there could be a connection to Camille?" Please don't be dead, Camille.

"I wasn't thinking that specifically, but let's keep it on the table."

• ——— • • • ——— •

I met Derek at the office at 10:00 a.m., where we'd call that mobile number, hoping for an interview.

He'd already planned to drive up from Glenwood and stay at the estate for the next two or three nights to monitor Traeger and get traction on our new case. Trevor will be thrilled.

I used the speaker phone on the office land line to make our call. Hard to believe anyone had a land line at this point, but the office came with it, so I used it and saved my iPhone battery and data usage. The phone rang four times.

"Mornin." Female voice, hint of a drawl.

"Kelsey Kramer?" I asked. "My name is Marissa Ellwyn."

Pause. "My mama's Kelsey Kramer," she corrected me. I guessed South Carolina. "I'm Kelsey *Jo* Kramer. You can call me Jo. What can I do for you?"

"I'm a private investigator. I was wanting to ask you a few questions."

"Val," she said.

"Sorry?"

81

"Guess I should've been prepared for this call. Didn't realize it would come so soon."

Val could be our John Doe. "I'm not calling from the police department and no I don't have any specific news about the man you reported missing. We'd like to ask you a few questions about your missing person's report."

"We?"

"My partner and I."

Another pause.

"Would you be inclined to meet so we can talk?"

"Sure, come now if you can. I'm leaving for work soon," she replied without a second's hesitation, noteworthy. "I'm in Ventura Keys in Pierpont Bay. My daddy's got a house here he lets me stay in. What's your number? I'll text you the address."

Quick, no-nonsense, nothing to hide. Maybe. I gave her my mobile and within moments the text with her address came in. I drove us in my car heading south.

"Take East Main," Derek said, climbing into the passenger side of my car. "There's construction on 101 this morning."

"What a surprise."

The traffic on East Main could be just as bad. "What did you think about how quickly she agreed to meet with us?"

"Urgency? You know I don't put much stock in first impressions. What do you think?" Derek asked.

I felt curious about her relationship to John Doe. Was she a family member? If so, she seemed a little too composed about whether we'd identified him or not. Boyfriend? Same thing. My guess was a neighbor or a coworker. Either way, I had a feeling Kelsey Jo Kramer could be the missing piece in this case, or at least someone to lead us to that piece. No assumptions, though. Time will tell.

Chapter Nineteen

"Knock or bell?" Derek asked standing outside the door.

It was this thing we did when interviewing witnesses. If one of us knocked three times and no one answered after thirty seconds, that, according to Derek, was a sign that they would fail as a witness. But the bell-ringing prompt was no better. If the doorbell was a traditional "ding-dong", that meant the person would be a successful witness. And a single tone or a buzzer: bad news. I stood back, eyeing a polished mahogany door.

"She's in a hurry and probably getting ready for work, so she'll answer right away. Knock."

Three knocks. The lock clicked and the door opened two seconds later. Derek smirked.

"I was waiting for you. Sorry for the smoke."

A young woman with pale blonde hair and a slight gap in her front teeth smiled easily in the entry, almost like she was pleased to see us. She opened the door fully pressing her back against it. Early twenties, she was dressed in the sort of tech company uniform of jeans, button-down shirt, and tennis shoes.

"Come in," she coaxed, waving cigarette smoke out of our faces.

83

"A nasty habit. I'm working on it."

"I rarely see anyone smoke cigarettes these days," Derek commented and followed the woman into the living room, where we stood in a circle.

She extinguished her cigarette and offered her hand to me. "Jo Kramer."

I shook her hand. "Mari Ellwyn and this is my partner, Derek Abernathy."

"Life partner or business partner?" she asked.

Derek's cheeks flushed. Hilarious.

"Business," I said.

I took one of the armchairs. Jo Kramer and Derek sat on opposite ends of a tan sofa, which looked like an expensive microfiber. The house was beautifully appointed, like Architectural Digest furnishings without the slightest hint of human occupancy. No clothes on the backs of chairs, papers, mail, clutter.

"You said this was your father's home?" I asked, waving my finger around the room.

"That's right," she said, gently. "My daddy's an oil man and he travels all the time."

"Where are you from?" Derek asked. "The Carolinas?"

The woman tapped her leg with her fingers, no doubt wishing she hadn't extinguished her cigarette. "Alabama. Mostly Montgomery but my sister lives in Mobile. My family's lived there for generations. I'm the only one who ventured out." She was proud of her independence; I could tell by her raised forehead and the slight smile on her lips. Well, as independent as one could be living rent-free in your father's luxury condo. Something, though, a darkness behind her eyes hinted that she was more than the sum of her parts.

"I don't want to keep you, you mentioned you didn't have much time," I started. "Derek and I are private investigators looking into a John Doe who was discovered recently, which the Ventura County Medical Examiner's office is trying to identify."

"A dead body?" Jo Kramer nodded.

I tried to just talk and act natural, but it was like I was incapable of turning off the profiler part of my personality. So far, she was sitting and listening. I didn't see any obvious tells either way. "One of the ways they do that is by mapping a description of the body with known and recently filed missing persons reports. Your name came up as reporting a missing person." I paused to let that sink in, which was also my cue for Derek if he wanted to add anything.

"Do y'all work for the police? I mean—" she crossed her legs— "I gave a lot of information to the officer when I filed the report."

She meant why was she being questioned. "No," I assured her.

"What can you tell us about the missing gentleman you reported?" Derek asked. So smart. I knew exactly why he used the term 'gentleman', too. Jo Kramer was a Southerner. And Derek was hoping to soften her defenses by appealing to her old-world sensibility with a word that conjured safety.

She smiled. "Gentleman," she said, then angled her head down and wiped her right eye. "I'm sorry. His name's Val Sharma. A lovely young man I work with. Worked."

Unless they were crocodile tears, this woman felt loss for that man, and maybe some anger. I pulled out a tiny notepad from my purse and wrote down the name, hoping I could get Ivan to get me a copy of that missing person's report to see all the details.

"Where do you work?" Derek asked in a more casual tone.

"AEI."

Ah, from Camille's report. Bingo. I kept writing and let Derek take the lead, more confirmation that Camille's disappearance was related to John Doe.

"What do you do there?" he asked. "And what did your friend Val do?"

"I'm a software engineer, in training really. I've got a degree but not much experience yet."

"Val was training you?" he asked carefully, knowing the word could backfire on him. But it also had the potential to reveal the part of their relationship she might not want to talk about.

Her face expanded in a grin. "Oh no. He's not an engineer. He's the Marketing Director. We became friends because we sit in the same part of the office. I started as an intern, so they put me in one of the cubicles in the Marketing Department because it's all they had available."

"I see." Derek nodded. "Are you concerned about him?" he asked now. That was an interesting turn of a phrase. I wouldn't have used it, but I trusted his instincts.

"Well, yeah. He's been gone for over two weeks," she replied, this time changing positions on the sofa, shifting her weight.

"Can you remember when you last saw him? Was it at work?"

The woman nodded, then looked at her watch. "I don't mean to be rude, but I've got ten minutes. Happy to talk later if you'd like. I'll do anything I can to find him."

"I think we can wrap this up by then," I jumped in. "But you've got my mobile number if you think of something else. What does AEI stand for, and what kind of company is it?"

"Abacus Enterprises," she said, moving to the edge of the sofa like she was about to get up. "It's a research consulting firm."

"Mathematical research?" Derek asked. "Applied mathematics?"

"That and other types of research. Sort of depends on the project," she said. "Statistical, and some more, well, esoteric things."

I could tell Derek was forming another question. "Thank you, Jo, that's very helpful. Do you have the reference number of the report you filed with the police?"

"I'll text it to you when I get to work. Okay?" She rose.

"That would be great."

When I shook her hand again at the door, I saw fear in her eyes.

"Do you know someone named Camille Bota, by any chance?" I blurted without thinking. Derek jerked his head in response.

"I don't think so. Does she work for AEI?"

"Never mind. We'll be in touch."

Chapter Twenty

Kelsey Jo Kramer texted me her Ventura Police Department Reference Number twenty minutes later, as promised. That meant AEI was in Ventura. We had plenty of time to investigate them. For now, I wanted that report.

"Are you gonna call him or do you want me to?" Derek asked on our way back to the office.

My shoulders caved at the thought. "You do it. I had to see him yesterday. That should exempt me for at least a —"

"I heard he made you breakfast," Derek smiled. "Not even that can endear him to you?"

Derek knew the long history between Ivan and me, how we'd lived together, how badly the relationship ended, and now Ivan saved face by saying he was the one who moved out. I guess I let some things go with Ivan because I believed in the long game. Him as Chief of Detectives, and Derek and I as private investigators meant we had a tricky relationship and sometimes needed each other.

"If you want to call the Ventura PD," I said, "ask for Scotty. Leave him a voicemail that he'll never listen to and you'll have to follow up with him in a day or two."

Derek pressed the speed dial in my car for Ivan's mobile, which showed how often we were in contact with him. "Hey, it's Derek," he said as I hit the freeway, choosing Highway 1 this time.

"Hey!"

"She's driving. You're stuck with me for the moment." Derek explained that we needed access to a Missing Person's report and gave him the number we'd gotten from Jo Kramer. Derek turned to me and held out the phone to see if I wanted to speak with him. I rolled my eyes. "Okay thanks, man. Later."

"Does he have it?" I asked after he hung up.

"He said he'll take a look for it shortly and will email it if he finds it."

Now my phone chimed with a text. "Can you check that?" I asked. "It's in my purse."

Derek reached into the back seat and pulled out my phone. "It's Duga. Says he's got a lead on Traeger."

My Bluetooth had my phone connected. I pressed Duga's number on the console.

"That's literally the fastest response to a text I've ever gotten from you."

Duga's voice always helped me ratchet down my stress level. "Well, your text was provocative, what can I say? Let's hear it. Derek's with me."

"Morning, Sir," Derek said.

"How's it going?"

"Hungry for restitution. What have you got on our friend?"

"He works out at one of the dojos I teach at." Duga paused to let that sink in.

"Traeger does martial arts?" Derek thought about this.

"Sorta fits the profile," I commented, smiling in a way. Fucking Traeger.

"Is he taking a class?" I asked Duga.

"And how'd you find out?" Derek interrupted.

"He's enrolled in an intensive Jujitsu program. I wasn't sure it was him at first. But I recognized him, pulled our casefile photo, and confirmed."

The arrogance of plain sight. Reminded me of my father.

"But that's not what's most interesting," Duga went on. "He's apparently also studying 1:1 with a teacher who provides instruction on

SWITCH

a very controversial technique. I don't know conclusively that that's what Traeger's studying with him, but seems like kind of a coincidence."

"Do you know the schedule of his classes?" I asked. "I mean, how likely is it that we could get a team in there and, what, get him when he's walking out to his car? The guy's a fucking phantom."

"You should know," Derek joked. "You're pretty elusive yourself."

"Ah, I try," Duga said.

I waited during an awkward silence. He was holding something back.

"Duga." I said his name because I knew what he was doing. "Spill it. What are you not telling us? Do we need to talk in person?"

"For this? Yeah. Because if I'm right, he's got more going on that just a string of bank robberies."

"I definitely want to hear this," Derek sighed. "What's your schedule today?"

I cleared my throat. "And I still need to talk to you about your tennis partner, Lin Hagen. Remember?"

"All your questions will be answered in due time."

"Thank you, wise Master Yoda. Seven o'clock tonight."

As we got back to the office, the manicured walkway to our building was a good distraction from the idea of Ivan. I could see it from the end of the street. Installed by one of Duga's associates, the smooth, stone pavers and white quartz stones were offset by something that sparkled, probably mica.

In our typical division of labor, I ran down the missing person's report from Ivan, while Derek worked on the AEI angle from Jo Kramer. But his first thought upon walking through the door, of course, was food. He ordered Bagelicious and got me their Crazy Turkey sandwich, which was way too much food but I was hungry. I watched him, camped out on the main sofa in our waiting room, briefcase open, sandwich half eaten, water on the coffee table, laptop on his lap.

"You know, you have an office. With a door, two windows, and a wet bar."

"You're still mad about that, aren't you? Do you need some privacy?" he asked, then with affect he sniffed his armpits. "I did take a

89

shower this morning."

"You're a partner here. Just saying."

"Did it ever occur to you, who likes efficiency so much, that if I want to talk to you it's easier if we're in the same room?"

I smiled. "Laziness is not why you work in the waiting room."

He sat back and put his feet on the marble coffee table. "This ought to be good."

"Never mind." I went to my desk, took two bites of a sandwich that I could barely fit my mouth around, and realized I wasn't that hungry after all. My mind, it turned out, was still preoccupied with a detail. One single detail that had been hiding in my subconscious, only visible now. This was how my investigative mind worked, I'd finally realized. I see something, or hear something, and it flows in through the grates and sometimes takes a little while before it floats down to the bottom of the well, where it can then be properly analyzed, dissected, observed, allowing a tiny kernel of truth to emerge. Somewhere. I must have been tapping my pen on the desk, an absent-minded habit. Derek was staring.

"Sorry. Just thinking about the car."

"Whose?"

"Camille's." I rose from my chair and walked around the desk, then moved to the spiral staircase to stare out the east window. "There was a smell in there. I noticed it at the time but couldn't put my finger on it. Then I forgot about it until now."

Derek set his laptop on the sofa cushion and crossed his legs. "Can you describe it?"

I searched my mind for smell-oriented words, thinking immediately of perfume. Floral, fruity, spicy, sweet. None of those.

"Did you notice anything?" I asked him.

Derek shook his head. "Not in the backseat anyway, where my head was when you made me dive under it to get her notebook."

I smiled. "Such a whiner. How about when you reached in the front to check the registration?"

"Nothing that I noticed, though the door had been open. It wasn't windy, but that would still likely vent most of the smell. You must have a keen nose."

"I do," I said. "There have been many times I detected scents other people haven't."

"Go with it," he said, and got up from the couch. "Scent is often related to memory. If you can't remember or place the scent in Camille's car, did the smell trigger any kind of—"

"Oh my God." I stood there frozen by the windows, eyes wide. "Yes, actually. My grandmother's basement, where my grandfather's art studio was."

"What did it smell like down there? Art supplies? Chemicals?"

I shook my head. Camille's car, for some reason, had triggered an instant image of the black, red, and white Sir Walter Raleigh pipe tobacco can that my grandfather kept paint brushes in. He smoked cigars while he painted. I nodded, certain now.

"Camille's car smelled like pipe tobacco."

Chapter Twenty-One

Sluggish from the carb-overload in that sandwich, I felt like a nap. The doctors had recommended them at least once a day in my stack of hospital discharge paperwork. Fat chance.

"Definitely not cigarettes?"

"No. It's a totally different smell," I said, like it was obvious.

Derek and I argued back and forth like this for a few minutes, me telling him tobacco was sweet, nostalgic, almost inviting, all the while my brain forming itself around the thought that Camille's abductor was an old man. Maybe it was a woman. Maybe it was a non-smoker. Assumptions again, the brain at its worst.

"Have you ever smoked a pipe?" Derek asked.

"Funny."

"You'd look good with a pipe."

"Whatever."

"What's your theory then?"

I moved to the couch and took off my shoes, reminding myself my legs weren't ready to sit cross-legged yet. "Well, the theory is that Camille was abducted from her car shortly before we got there. That's why the tobacco smell was still detectable to me even though the door was wide open. Low wind that day."

"Is Lin Hagen a pipe smoker?" he asked.

I tipped my head. "No idea. He was there that morning and was the one who saw the car and told us about it."

"What about Fergus?" he asked, watching my eyes. "You're thinking about it."

"Maybe. He certainly might have wanted Camille out of his way. But I don't think so."

"Hunch?"

"Personality, more like. He's not the right profile for a daylight abduction. He'd get an underling to do it."

"What would Richard Ellwyn say about this?" Derek asked.

Risky, he was probably the only person on earth I'd allow to ask a question about my father. I smiled, picturing him here on the other side of the couch, the permanent smirk on his lips sizing up the world, and not even minding that it never measured up. He would love Derek and I'd wished many times that in some parallel universe they could know each other.

"He'd say what I just said was circumstantial, at best. I know that. He believes that when you make an assumption, a door in your mind closes and you're no longer open to other possibilities and viable details that could lead you to the truth."

"What about gut instinct?"

"Of course. He was a spook most of his life. In fact, he still might be now. He just doesn't believe in a hunch being a substitute for verifiable evidence."

Derek peered at me and crossed his arms.

"What?"

"Just thinking that I like how you shifted into the present tense just then, about him."

Despite our doomed meeting in Tortola a few months ago, my father was still off grid and unreachable through normal channels. Last year, my half-brother Jaden orchestrated what seemed like a chance meeting, on that same beach. I knew how to reach Jaden, and he knew how to reach our father, if the need ever arose. But why would it? At any moment, my father could just as easily be in Morocco or camping out in my garage.

I reached down and tapped the old, worn, scratched watch on my wrist with my index finger, and winked at Derek. Belonging to his father, he'd given me the watch on the two-year anniversary of my father's disappearance, I'd thought at the time as a symbol of hope. But now knowing him better, knowing he had no siblings and no family he saw regularly, I think he gave it to me to sort of invite me to be a part of his family and him a part of mine, to deepen our connection. Whatever his reason, most nights I slept with it on, allowing the metal to warm my wrist, reminding me that I was never completely alone in this world.

"The question is, was he there to pick her up for work, like he told you, or was he there to force her into his car and take her somewhere?"

I shook my head. "Doesn't feel right."

A half-laugh emerged. "What, Hagen seems like a nice guy to you?"

I knew what he was doing—exactly what I paid him to do. Challenge me. "Yes." I shrugged. "Doesn't mean anything in particular but I don't know the guy yet."

"So he seems safe?" he asked, more earnestly this time.

"Well, aside from the fact that he broke into my house?" I shut my eyes and went through the facts again. "I mean, intellectually the idea of him abducting her doesn't fit. They worked together. He just about admitted to me that he's in love with her. There was blood on her sweater. Why would he want to harm her?"

A phone chimed with a text notification. "Yours or mine?"

He picked up his phone from the coffee table. "Yours."

I went to the desk to rummage through my purse.

"It's here." He waved me over to the sofa where he held my phone out to read the message.

"Is it from Ivan? Did he send the report?" I asked of Kelsey Jo Kramer's missing person's report.

Derek turned and glared with mock horror. "Does he do that? That would be a complete breach of protocol, not to mention—"

"Personal favor."

"For you, what wouldn't that man do?"

I sighed. "Are you done now?"

He stifled a laugh and looked down at the phone. "Looks like it was filed five days ago at eight in the morning, which suggests she might have gone to police headquarters before she went to work."

"Why would she do that?" I asked. "What if the man was at work? Wouldn't she need to go to work first and then leave from there if he hadn't shown up?"

"The person who she reported missing was a Val Sharma, East Indian male, early thirties—"

"Both of those details jive with Camille's report," I added.

"Weight estimated to be about 150 pounds, clean shaven, black hair, brown eyes, roughly six feet tall. She said he was wearing black pants and a white button-down shirt the last time she saw him and that was at work, AEI, where they've both worked for the past five years."

"Right. She said she started as an intern and now is working as a junior software developer. Does it say what position the man had?"

"Marketing Director," Derek read, which coincided with what Jo Kramer told us.

"I've started looking into AEI," but so far there's not much, other than an agricultural company."

"Keep digging."

"Bet your ass I will." Iceberg.

Chapter Twenty-Two

Somehow, we'd missed a voicemail on the office land line from Duga. I phoned him back after collapsing into my ergonomic desk chair. It was late afternoon now, which meant my body hurt everywhere. I slid my feet into the slippers hidden under my desk and watched Derek creep into his office. The huge, metal file cabinet did its usual thunk when he opened the top drawer.

"Can you—"

His door closed with a quiet click. Thank you.

"Hey there." Duga always picked up on the first ring, making me feel like he was waiting for my call.

Derek almost never answered calls directly. I'd let his devil's advocate game about Lin Hagen irritate me, which was an irrational, emotional response to standard investigation work. Question everything and then question it again. He knew it too, the way he'd slinked into his office giving me space. I liked the fact that we knew each other well by now. In fact, he would probably make me a latte in the kitchen, knowing coffee was my key to any kind of distemper. I shuffled to the kitchen and poured water in the Keurig.

"I'm so sorry," I said. "I know we were supposed to meet. We got delayed."

"No worries. Hungry?" Duga asked through the phone. I could hear the banging of metal in the background.

"Duga's cooking," I shouted into the crook of Derek's closed door.

"Indian?" he asked, opening it. "Are you making coffee? I was just gonna brew you some."

I snickered to myself. "Derek wants to know what you're making." I put Duga's call on speaker.

"Fish tikka masala, chana masala, and samosas, if they cooperate this time."

"Family dinner?" Derek asked, eyes wide.

"That's up to the boss," Duga said. "Do you feel up to having the whole crew over tonight? I know you run out of gas before sundown lately."

I thought about it. He was right, but it was always a good opportunity to talk shop and share information.

"I'll bring everything, just need your nice plates."

"Of course. That sounds great!" Maybe I added too much enthusiasm and wasn't ready to host yet. Derek knew it too, narrowing his eyes at me. "Are you taking us through your sting proposal?" I said into the phone.

"What sting proposal?" Derek asked.

"Traeger," I mumbled. "He's got an idea."

"Have Francone and Jazmin there, if possible," Duga said, which answered my question. He wanted our security and IT staff to provide a feasibility analysis to whatever risky business he had in mind. Sure, fine. Espresso would keep me awake.

"I can't wait to hear what you've got up your sleeve," I said and meant it. I took Duga off speaker and went to my desk so I could sit. "Hey, I need a favor, and it's urgent. I know you're busy right now but hoping you might have one of your minions available?"

"Sure. What do you need?"

"We need to get another burner phone to Dr. Hagen."

"We just gave him one."

"You know I'm paranoid about surveillance. Besides, he's likely being watched and if they've seen him talking or texting with a phone they don't recognize, they'll just tap it and clone it anyway. We need to stay a few steps ahead."

Short silence. "Good idea actually. I've got another one ready to go.

Do you know if he's at work today?" Duga asked.

"I think so."

"Text me the number of the burner we just gave him. I have it somewhere but don't have time to look right now. I'll get someone on it."

"Will do," I said. "And tell him to text me when he gets that phone and give him my number again. I've got an urgent matter to discuss with him today."

"You got it."

"Thank you. See you tonight, chef."

"Seven. Ish."

I heard the milk frother and the clang of dishware in the tiny kitchen. Derek set a latte, complete with a shake of cinnamon on top, on the glass-topped desk, then sat in the chair across from me. "You need to extract what you can from Hagen before either the police or Fergus completely shut him down."

I slurped the first sip, mostly cinnamon froth. "Delicious." I wiped my mouth. "What I can't figure out is why they haven't picked him up yet. It's been almost two days."

"Heavy workloads?"

"Maybe. Maybe not."

"Are you sure you're up to this tonight?" he asked.

"I can make my own coffee," I said, this time gulping down the well needed caffeine.

"You know, sometimes letting people take care of you is a way of taking care of them."

Before I could respond, he went back to his office and pushed the door mostly closed. Dammit.

* ————— • • • ————— •

We worked independently for a couple of hours in the office, as the light from the west windows turned from yellow to orange and drew long shadows across the light gray tile. I texted Derek a picture of my empty mug, but my independence was a constant sore subject for us. At 5:25 p.m. my phone rang, breaking the long blanket of silence. I didn't recognize the number.

"Dr. Hagen?" I answered.

"Are you guys gonna change my phone every week? I'm not even sure anyone's following me anymore."

"Blue Hyundai, about ten years old with a dent in the rear left fender," I replied.

Silence. "You saw them? So that means you've also got me under surveillance? For God's sake."

"Look, doctor, you came to me," I replied. "A different burner phone to protect our conversations from being heard is just a good security measure. Your John Doe is missing, your boss is missing, her boss has threatened you if you do anything about it. Seems like a bit of caution would be prudent right now."

He exhaled slowly. "Okay. Fine. I'm in your hands."

"Good. Have the Ventura Police been to talk to you yet about Camille?"

"No," he said. "I'm sort of surprised be—"

"Me too," I cut in. "And that's good because I have a few things I need to talk to you about, and there's an urgency about them."

"Did you find her?" he asked in a lowered voice.

"No. But I did find her notebook wedged under her passenger seat. Were you aware that she kept a legal pad in the car?"

"Yeah. I saw her writing on something a few times when she picked me up on the way to work. I usually kept her waiting for a few minutes." He sounded embarrassed.

"Look, I need to tell you about what I found in that notebook, because I think it has everything to do with her disappearance, and it means that you might be in danger as well."

"I'm listening," Hagen replied.

I debated telling him about Kelsey Jo Kramer, wondering about need-to-know and if that detail could help me get what I needed out of him. Probably not. I opted for an overview of page one of Camille's notes. I cleared my throat and read through the highlights.

"Sounds like the standard list of questions on the initial ME's intake form," he said, then paused. "Nothing unusual there, that is unless her answers on the legal pad differ from the official report."

I so wished he hadn't used the words *official report*. It just made my next question even more inappropriate. I wondered if Derek had been listening so far, always feeling like he was the Ethics Director in my head questioning every decision I made in our cases together. Of course he was listening. How could he not? I went on to give Hagen the description of page two of Camille's notes, the one that had an outline of a man's body and had been annotated with arrows in the margins.

99

One for the marks across the neck, the red dots on the throat and shoulder, another for the "ST9" notation. A chilling addition.

"That sounds like the information I remember from the official report."

Thank God for small miracles. "Did you write that information, and make that drawing?" I asked, not meaning for it to sound like the third degree.

"No. I assumed Camille created it and I read through it as part of my process."

"Where is that report now?"

"You know where it is, Ms. Ellwyn," he challenged. "It's missing along with everything else. Paper copies, digital copies of reports, lab results, not to mention the body in question."

"Who performed the initial exam?" I asked.

Short pause. "I did."

"What about photographs from the external exam?"

Longer pause. I could hear the rubbing of clothing, like he was changing positions or removing his jacket. Maybe he was hot and sweating. And maybe he was sweating because he was lying. Oh the tangled webs. "They're still here," he said finally. "I saw them yesterday."

"You went looking for them?" I pressed.

"Yeah, to see if they were still where I'd last seen them. Everything else disappeared from this case. I wondered if Fergus, if that's who sanitized everything, had found them."

"Why weren't they taken as well?"

"I don't know," he said, defensively. He was lying.

"Doctor, I need to see those photographs."

"No way." His voice went down in pitch when he said it, then I heard the click of a door closing.

"Look…" I started. "You broke into my house, climbing through the window in my foyer and lying that I'd left the window open—which I hadn't—because you needed to see me so desperately that you couldn't wait till the next morning." I was yelling now. I couldn't help it.

My eyes caught the shape of Derek in the doorway of his office, watching me. He said, "What the fuck?" with his eyes. I'd told him about it, but it was after he'd been up for twenty-four hours chasing Traeger. I'd fill him in later. Now he was lip-synching 'Jo Kramer'. I nodded.

"Doctor, have you had any dealings with a company called AEI? Your John Doe may have worked there."

"No, not that I recall." Hagen stayed quiet after that, giving me tacit permission to make my most persuasive case.

"Someone's going down, and I think you know that. Camille knew something about your John Doe, and now she's missing along with the body. Fergus, if he wasn't involved in her disappearance himself, will probably stop at nothing to protect his dirty little secret, whatever it is. And you could be next."

I paused to breathe. Derek moved to the chair across from my desk, not liking what he was hearing.

"Don't you want to know what ugly truth Fergus is protecting? The truth Camille was protecting?"

It was a good try. I'd done my job, stated my case. I retreated to my perch, as Derek called it—the window under the spiral staircase, resting my head on the wrought iron. Not very comfortable but a spectacular view.

"Alright." Hagen had lowered his voice even more. "What do you want to know?"

I wanted to put him on speaker so Derek could hear but didn't want to spook him. I moved to the chair beside Derek, turned the volume all the way up and leaned in so he could hear Hagen's responses. "I want to verify what Camille wrote in her notebook about the ligature marks on John Doe's neck."

Pause. "What about them?"

I sighed, loudly this time, not caring that my frustration was showing. "You conducted the initial autopsy report but said you couldn't conclude either the manner or cause of death. That's why I want to see those photographs."

"To do what?"

"To compare them with what I read in Camille's notes."

"To what end, though?" Now he was annoying me.

"In particular, whether you and Camille saw physical evidence consistent with ligature strangulation, manual strangulation, or something else."

"Well, I can tell you that now. It looked like neither of those, but I don't know what."

"So, he wasn't strangled?" I pressed.

"Not from my examination of the eyes and throat, no."

"So how do you explain the marks on his neck?"

"Lots of possibilities." His voice was calm. Too calm. "It's possible the man was attacked and strangulation was attempted but the victim got away. Even from attempted strangulation, though, there would still be evidence in the larynx and in the eyes. The blood vessels don't lie. And no such evidence was apparent to me. Or to Camille."

How about to Declan Fergus, I thought. "You discussed it with her?" I asked.

"Once, over the phone. It was late."

So, they spoke on the phone outside of work. Interesting. "When was this?" I asked.

A pause. "Two days before she disappeared. And that was the first time she told me she was assigning me, all of us, the staff, to another case. John Doe, or this John Doe, she said, was now entirely off limits."

"Alright, thank you for that. Onto an administrative matter. We've now spent enough time on this case that we need to talk about my fee."

"That's fine. I'm happy to pay a retainer," he replied, almost too quickly.

"I was about to say that we charge $200 an hour and—"

"Do you take PayPal or Venmo?"

"Doctor, I didn't necessarily mean right this minute."

"All the better. Text me an invoice and I'll send it tonight."

"And those photographs?" I pressed.

"Will send them too."

Chapter Twenty-Three

Preparing for our family dinner, I allotted more time than usual so I wouldn't have to rush. I left Derek working in the office a while longer and went home to lay down for a spell. These dinners typically included my whole investigation team of Derek, Duga, Robert Francone, Jazmin, and sometimes Ivan or Bobby Bishop from our old office in LA. This was intended to be a working dinner to hear Duga's idea about a Traeger sting operation, since so far all other methods had failed. Miserably.

I didn't bother changing clothes, just laid on top of the bed and drew the curtains. An hour later, I woke to the chime of a text. Ah, Lin Hagen. Right on time.

I feel them. They're not here yet but they're coming.

Who? I typed back.

The police. I keep seeing blue police lights outside thinking they're going to stop here and charge through my door.

A sixth sense didn't fit his profile. Still, he might be right. *Let me know if they show up. Just write PD*, I typed. *I'll know what it means and one of us will meet you at the police station, assuming they bring you to Dowell Street.*

And that car is still following me, he wrote. I wasn't sure if he'd read my previous reply. *I can see there's only one person in it.*

Blue car?

Yes, for the past two days. As promised, 9 images are coming, poor quality, best I could do. Number four should give you the close-up you were looking for. I'd be drawn and quartered for this breach or, at the very least, fired, which may happen anyway. It demonstrates overt ethical compromise, which I'm fine with under the circumstances. Did I tell you they're making us sign another NDA about John Doe now?

I wasn't surprised. Realizing the room was dark and I'd need my glasses to see the pictures, I moved to the chaise and clicked on the crystal pendant light hanging over it – the best light in the house. *Nothing's come through yet,* I typed.

Keep an eye on your phone, I have slow wifi here. They'll be there in a minute.

Did you take these photos today, or are these from your original external exam when you first saw the body?

Original exam. I wouldn't be able to take photographs of them now.

You mean legally? Or maybe he meant because the body had been moved, or so he'd reported two days ago. I sat perched on the edge of the chaise feeding my feet into my slippers, wondering how to ask Dr. Linus Hagen to breach protocol again. *Why not?*

He's gone.

What do you mean? I wrote. *You told me the body had been moved by someone other than you.*

Yeah, to another morgue, I was told. And now it's missing from there, too.

Chapter
Twenty-Four

6:15 p.m. now, I had 45 minutes left to prep the house. Based on our past dinners, Duga would get here in about fifteen minutes with his two main dishes already hot and ready to serve. I set the dining room table using my mother's Noritake white china edged in platinum. I always hated those dishes growing up. We only seemed to use them when either someone had died or at formal dinners with grownups smoking and talking in harsh voices. I'd planned, after I moved back here, to invest in a new set of china that had a more colorful pattern…and no baggage. Still on the list.

I think because I'd actually slept during my brief nap, I felt recharged even before I drank another cup of reheated coffee. Still, an unexplainable itch tugged at the back of my brain. A shadow floating through my dreams, almost like it intended to remind me of something, pulling me somewhere I didn't want to go. I sucked in a deep breath and shook it off.

Though I still wasn't myself, I always felt alive in the kitchen, moving effortlessly around the space in one of my Sur La Table aprons steaming fresh kale with shallots and garlic, setting the table, opening bottles of wine and setting out a pitcher of filtered, room temperature water.

My efficiency was coming back, too. My body felt strong and fluid for the first time since the accident. I lit candles and adjusted the lighting, turning the heat up to 72, which time had proved was perfect for this time of year in a drafty, century-old house. I also brought out the apple pie I'd defrosted to the kitchen counter and lifted the lid, allowing the warm air from the room to get inside the box. When had I last baked a pie from scratch?

I stood back in my apron, arms crossed, pleased with how my table looked. Call it old fashioned, but I inherited my grandmother's hospitality skills, and from her I learned the importance of order and decorum when it came to fine dining. That meant a smiling host when guests walked in, cloth napkins on the table, wine decanting, and gleaming cutlery. In other words, making your guests feel like you're ready. Jada, on the other hand, would have served my brother and me frozen fish sticks our whole childhood if we'd let her get away with it. She had her redeeming qualities. Quite a few, actually. Hospitality wasn't one of them.

Duga came through the front door when I was in the pantry. He drew two gigantic serving dishes out of insulated bags, the kind used for pizza delivery.

"Hey," I said, and half-hugged him. "Let me look at you." He was wearing a dark blue, silk mandarin collar shirt with the sleeves rolled up, and white pants, typical for his attire.

He leaned over to kiss me on the cheek, pulling out serving utensils, standing back to size me up.

"Alright fine," I said. "Have at it. How do I look today? And before you start, I'll have you know I took a nap and actually slept."

"How do your bones feel today? And how does your head feel? Concussion symptoms can last six months."

I knew that, because in the hospital the medical staff had rammed that fear-mongering down my throat day and night. I leaned against the counter and decided to give his thoughtful questions a moment of consideration. "Well, I do feel better this week than last week. My head seems a little less, I don't know, swimmy? I'm less forgetful, and getting in and out of cars isn't as painful. I think that counts as progress."

"Naps are good too," he replied. "More of those please."

"Thank you for preparing this bounty for us tonight. What's the occasion? There must be more to this than unveiling a plan. Are we celebrating?"

Duga hung his head, pausing his process of stirring the large lumps of fresh salmon in the tikka masala tomato cream sauce. Oh my God, the smell. "You know me, I do my best thinking when I'm cooking. And Indian food is complex and labor-intensive. So it's perfect."

"Hello hello," someone bellowed from the front door.

Derek and Jazmin entered the kitchen, followed by Robert Francone. Ivan texted that he couldn't make it but appreciated the invite. And I knew he did, just like he felt wounded anytime he wasn't invited to something. An eight-year-old in a forty-year-old body.

I made my way around my beautiful table, gushing with pride, making small talk. I didn't think I was ready for this but it felt good to be hosting again. I was getting there. My mind was elsewhere, though, desperate to see those pictures from Dr. Hagen. They still hadn't come.

Duga lifted his gigantic platters of chana masala and fish tikka masala onto the dining room table. The samosas were arranged like lumpy, perfectly-fried potato and pea triangles on a long, skinny, white plate—two per row. The cilantro and tamarind chutneys were in white porcelain cereal bowls set beside them. I never understood how he didn't dribble on the floors of his car when transporting food. I'd never learned how to do that properly. I probably should, to add it to my hospitality playbook.

"Are you sure you're not Indian?" Derek asked Duga while biting into a samosa. "Your last name is, I never pronounce it right—"

Derek, seated now, clutched the plate of samosas to his chest and said, "Mine."

"Hey, no hogging. Over here." Jazmin snapped her fingers.

"Come on, it's only two syllables," Duga quipped of his name. "Puri."

"No, there's another name in there I thought," Derek said with a finger pointed in the air, then he spooned some of the cilantro chutney onto his half-eaten samosa.

"Acharya," Duga said with a nod. "Tibetans don't really recognize surnames. But my mother was Tibetan and my father was a Sikh from northern India. Acharya came from my father's family, and Puri is a village I'm named after."

"Golden Temple," Francone piped in. "Punjab, right?"

"Very good." Duga smiled. "Have you been there?"

"Amritsar, yes, I've been there. I've been all over India," Robert smiled. "A long time ago."

Duga had shared his birth name, or names, with me, but it was something I never spoke of because it was private to him. When Derek, or even Ivan, had asked me in the past, I dodged the question and often changed the subject, one time suggesting they ask him directly. And of course they'd forget about it before then. There was something about Duga that felt sort of holy, like I'd be betraying some kind of spiritual code by talking about it. He was never Duga Acharya Puri to me. Just Duga. And there was only one Duga on earth.

Jazmin was seated beside Francone. I was glad because they didn't get to spend much time together. Jazmin, being in her early twenties, had so much she could learn from a security veteran like Francone, but Robert could learn a lot from Jazmin's tech prowess and IT acumen. They were talking shop about two-factor authentication as it related to small business cybersecurity. Everyone was finding seats, nodding to me at the beautiful table, commenting on my apron, and I wasn't really listening to any of them. All I wanted right now was to sit in a room alone with my phone and my reading glasses so I could dig into every detail of those pictures, which would no doubt supply some direction in the case of our missing John Doe, a/k/a Val Sharma. Hagen had said slow wifi. Maybe that was true. Or maybe he was playing some kind of game.

I sat back watching the scene play out, these people around my table, whom I both knew and cared for. Some of whom I loved. I ate a few bites of the fish tikka, samosas with tamarind sauce, all the while disconnected, or maybe in the process of disconnecting from the case of James Traeger. It's not that I lacked interest. In fact, Traeger had so far proved a worthy adversary. His evasive skills were impressive and he was quickly going down in history as one of California's most notorious bank robbers still at large.

I knew Duga was excited about the sting operation he had in mind, finally getting a break in our unsolvable case. I think a part of me knew we'd never catch someone like Traeger the usual ways. Maybe Duga's extraction at the dojo, where Traeger trained, was a sound method. I nodded, laughed at the right times, spooned more food into my plate, ate a few bites here and there, poured wine when glasses emptied. But by and large, Indian curries were too heavy for my digestion. Besides, I was literally dying to check my phone. Derek's green eyes blinked back, telepathically saying *I know you're not okay.*

"Is Traeger taking a group class?" I asked Duga.

"No, not right now anyway. He's booked a series of 1:1 sessions with a specific instructor. My teacher." He smiled. "Jordan Banfield. He's impressive, to say the least."

Duga's face beamed while he talked about his teacher's credentials, his combat neuroscience center, his Ph.D., multiple certifications, and a retired government agent.

"How'd you find out about this? He's obviously not using his real name. Right?" Derek asked.

"J.J. Banks."

"Banks. What a comedian," I said, rolling my eyes

"Seriously?" Jazmin now.

"He's still playing us," Derek commented. "What's your idea, Duga?"

"It's very simple, and simple is good in this case," he admitted. "Having an undercover cop working out, sparring in the same room, and he walks over and handcuffs him, then displays his badge and says he's under arrest. We'll have cops in both doorways. Doesn't need to be fancy or complicated. We just need access and enough of our wits to determine the right timing."

"Sounds—" I started, then shook my head. "It sounds easy enough, which means too easy."

Derek raised his fork to Duga. "You've seen this guy. How do we know he's not on to us already?"

"We don't. I'm open to suggestions if there's a better one."

"Here's my problem with this," I said. "A guy this smart, wily, and elusive, is willing to be seen in public? He could probably afford to buy the whole dojo and put it in his house. Why work out here?"

"Young, cocky, and full of himself," Derek suggested. "We already know this."

"Can we coordinate it with his instructor?" I asked Duga. "Your instructor?"

"I don't know," he said, thoughtfully. "It already feels like betraying a trust, in a way. I'd have to think about that. Under the circumstances, I think the urgency is sufficient to investigate that. I'll get back to you."

"What's the timeframe?" Derek asked.

Duga poured himself more wine. "Tuesday afternoon's his next class. We have three days to plan logistics."

"Duga, it's your idea so you're running it," I said. "We're here to support. Just let us know who and what resources you need. I assume you've talked to Ivan?"

"Where is he by the way?" Derek asked. "I've never known him to say no to free food."

"Oh that's rich coming from you," I laughed.

"I mentioned I had an idea but I haven't shared the details with him yet," Duga answered. "I wanted to bring it here first," Duga said.

I liked that answer. "Anything else about Traeger? Questions, comments, concerns?" I asked the group.

"Duga, let me know if you need security backup at the dojo," Robert said. "I can provide two people to help. We've worked with slippery characters like him before."

"Like Traeger? No offense but I doubt it." Derek this time, calling out Francone. Not this again. Nobody moved, eyes wide around the table.

I watched Francone finish chewing food in his mouth then slowly take a sip of the Zinfandel. "Martel. Jacques Martel. My team was brought in to suss him out…and we got him."

"You arrested Jacques Martel?" Derek asked, almost laughing, looking back at me sitting beside him, trying not to look mortified by the name that would haunt me into the afterlife.

"We did bring him out, yes. A while ago now. We arrested him." Francone cleared his throat and wiped his mouth. "Then we lost him."

Derek sat back and crossed his ankle over his knee. His face was flushed. I put my hand in the crook of his elbow and pulsed it. "Let it go," I whispered.

"If this was before 2019, your losing him might have gotten Mari shot! Hadn't heard that story I guess?"

"Derek. Cool your jets," I said in a calm voice. "He knows. I told him about the Martel baggage. It's not his fault."

No one moved or spoke. Derek sat back and breathed. "No, it's not," he said now, staring right at Francone. "I'm sorry."

Francone looked at me, then Derek, and back and forth, like he was putting something together in his head, something that wasn't there, had never been there, or maybe I'd just failed to see it. Derek was protective over me, too protective. I just hadn't realized what a wound that left on his heart.

I rose and grabbed a wine carafe, then made my way around the table to refill glasses. Jazmin did the same with our water glasses, the two men glowering in our midst.

"Martel took something from you that you never got back," Derek said, softly.

"Yep, he did. I got too close, he shot me, my career got derailed and my father went missing." I looked at Derek. "Then I got my PI license, hung a shingle." I nodded at him. "Hired a partner."

"All's well that ends well?" Derek smirked.

"Getting shot was a turning point, and Martel gave my life a reset." I looked around the table. "I like where I've ended up."

Duga cleared his throat, returning to Francone's original offer. "Thanks Robert, I appreciate the offer and might take you up on that."

"What about IT support?" Jazmin asked Duga.

"Not sure about that yet, but I want to talk to you about something else. After dinner."

"Cool. I'll be here."

"I'd actually like to hear more about Lin Hagen," Derek said, when no one spoke up.

"My tennis partner," Duga grinned, lightening the mood. Thank God.

My face felt oddly cold; my forehead was wet and I felt my blouse sticking to my chest suddenly. Why was it so warm? "Is it hot in here?"

"I'm fine," Jazmin said. "And I'm always cold."

"I forgot you were working with Lin," Duga replied. "He mentioned he was looking for someone to help him investigate something in his office and I recommended you guys." Duga looked at me when he said it, studying my face.

"What did he say about what was going on there?" Derek asked, watching Duga watch me.

I felt my belly and chest expand with the breath I drew in, but with more sensation now. The room got quiet, like pin-drop quiet. My neck and the tops of my shoulders, also the back of my head felt warm and sort of fuzzy suddenly. Numb. Something's not right.

I reached my hand down to the pocket of my long sweater for the hard shape of my phone. I had to see those pictures. Everything was riding on the John Doe case for some reason. Why did I care so much about it? I think this was part of the restlessness I'd been feeling lately. Not falling asleep right away, waking up early, dreaming of shadows. Ever since Hagen broke into my foyer, it's like he or his case was pushing me onto a different path. I don't know why but I had to see those photographs, I had to understand what connection they had with the rest of my life, or my future. I had to find out what happened to Val Sharma, Dr. Lin Hagen's John Doe. Or was he Camille's John Doe? Fergus? I didn't know who he belonged to, but somehow Val Sharma was tied to my destiny.

I roved my eyes around the table listening to the conversation. Something weird was happening in my body. People's mouths were moving but in slow motion, yet I couldn't hear any sound. It was like I was being pulled somewhere else, a fog of cotton surrounding my head. And why was it suddenly so dark in here? I...wait...where's the...

Chapter Twenty-Five

God no. Not again. That smell. The acrid, chemical-laced air in my nose, polluting the back of my throat. It smelled like a perfect mix of feces and ammonia. The familiar fluorescent lights hurt my eyes when I opened them. I was on a crackly, papery bed that felt like lying on potato chips.

"What happened? What day is it?" I blurted, peeled open my lids and saw Derek looming over me, and the outline of Duga's head in the doorway behind him. Doorway to where? This wasn't my house.

"Did she say what day is it?" Duga's voice.

"Monday, April 20th," Derek answered with his warm palm on my forehead. "Do you remember anything?"

Another hospital. Give me strength. My chest caved and my eyes filled. They already felt wet and hot. Was I turning into my mother, the way she had cried uncontrollably that night after her stroke? Had I had a stroke? A heart attack? Derek reached his torso over my face to grab a tissue on the table near the bed and dabbed my right cheek.

"You're okay. Do you remember passing out during dinner?"

I nodded. "What the fuck is wrong with me?"

Derek turned to Duga for guidance, but Duga left and closed the

113

door behind him.

As soon as the door clicked, it opened again with a nurse coming through to a woman lying in a bed to my left, completely ignoring me. Maybe I wasn't on her rotation? Derek sat on the edge of my bed and leaned close.

"Sir, please don't sit there," the other patient's nurse said. "I realize this is not ICU, but we're watching her very closely right now. Five more minutes then you'll need to wait outside."

"Understood." Derek popped up and stood awkwardly beside me.

"Someone will be coming in shortly for her next test." I wasn't sure if the nurse meant me or my roommate.

Derek stood close to the bed, eyes on the unfriendly nurse, hands in his pockets.

"Are they saying I mismanaged my recovery so far?" I asked Derek.

"Not to me. You passed out and hit your head on the dining room floor. So that's considered a post-concussive head injury. You might be here a while."

More tears now. Maybe this was some kind of penance, punishment for previous transgressions, relationship mishaps. I went back to the dining room in my mind. Had I eaten something, or maybe the wine? "I feel okay now but I'm so tired. Did they sedate me?"

Derek looked up at the nurse before answering. She came over to the other side of the bed. "I'm Jen. How are you feeling right now?" the woman asked. She wore her light brown hair in a cheerleader ponytail and looked like she hadn't slept in about three days.

"I feel like I've been sedated. I was in here several weeks ago for a concussion after an accident. I thought sedatives were a bad idea after a concussion."

The woman nodded, and drew her large, dark eyes to the ceiling. "They can be, yes. The psychopharmacology of post-concussive treatment is very tricky. You were confused and agitated so we gave you a very mild sedative to calm you down while you were in transit in the ambulance and getting you checked in up here."

Sounded reasonable enough but still didn't explain what I was doing here. Eating dinner one minute, waking up in the hospital the next. I was tired of feeling subpar, and now the clock had just reset itself back to zero. Just kill me now.

"What's the plan and when can I get out of here? I have urgent work to do."

The young woman smiled in a way that meant to mask an eye roll, ridiculing my sense of self-importance and my cluelessness about the dangers of my condition, no doubt. "MRI. We need to determine the cause of the symptoms you experienced last night, take a look at your brain scans to be sure there aren't any lesions."

Brain lesions? No wonder I was crying when Derek came in. I could almost feel the war within my body, the rising panic welling up in my chest and the substance running through my veins blocking that sensation to keep me fluidly calm.

"Are there any indications of brain lesions so far?"

She shook her head. "It's a precaution we need to take with any patient who returns to the hospital after a concussion. Brain injuries, even extremely mild ones, are unpredictable. You can manifest concussion symptoms right away, or for others they might not manifest at all for a month or two. There are a lot of variables and every patient's different."

Derek was holding my hand, not squeezing it tightly, just reassuring me with his warm flesh and comforting touch, which reminded me of the tension at dinner between him and Francone. Another thing I'd need to deal with.

"I'll be back shortly. Your MRI is in about thirty minutes." She looked up at Derek, then out into the hall. "Your friend can come in," she said of Duga. "You can move some chairs over to her bedside. Just don't close the door, and please don't upset her in any way. Five minutes." Nurse Jen swooshed out of the room like a gust of cold air.

I felt Derek's horror at the insinuation that he might upset me. Poor Derek. This might be harder for him than for me. But I couldn't move my thoughts off the idea of brain lesions. I just wanted to be alone right now, to look at the photos from Lin Hagen and keep my mind occupied with the more mundane details of this case. Derek dragged two chairs near the bed where he and Duga sat editing their thoughts.

"Hopefully I can get out of here tomorrow," I said, breaking the silence.

"Do you want me to wait on the operation at the dojo?" Duga asked.

"Much as it pains me to say, don't wait on me. I know you've got a lot of logistics to work out. Really, you guys don't have to stay. I'll be fine here. I'm so sleepy anyway."

Duga took that as a cue. He kissed me on the cheek and left silently through the open doorway.

"Am I banished too?" Derek pushed out his lower lip.

"Why would you want to stay here? It smells like a hospital. There are sick people everywhere."

"What's the matter?" he said, standing so he could look in my eyes. He touched my hand gently and folded his fingers around it.

"Besides the obvious?" I shrugged.

"And it's not Traeger. You've had this way about you lately, like you're off somewhere else. I can't put my finger on it, and the fact that you're not telling me is a concern."

I sighed. My mouth was dry. I sipped from the plastic cup near the bed. "I'm tired of chasing ghosts. Not many people in my life would understand that, but you do."

Raised brow, slight nod. Of course he knew. I loved that about Derek. He was smart. Educated, sure. But he was also street smart, which had its own intrinsic value, a keen observer of human nature. "I'll bet you are. It must be exhausting. Do you consider Jacques Martel one of them?" he asked.

I went back to the dinner table. Francone. Martel. How had I not known that? "Certainly him, yeah. And my parents. Val Sharma, the John Doe in Camille's office, has this sort of, I don't know, hold on me. I don't really know what I mean."

"Is he one of the ghosts?" he asked, leaning in.

"Lin Hagen told me last night that the body's missing."

"Missing, really."

"Well, I don't necessarily suspect someone stole it, seeing as it would be difficult to do so. Just that it's no longer where they expected it to be."

"Does Hagen know where it's been moved to?"

I wasn't sure even Hagen knew that. "What I do know is this. I need to track him down and find that body, because Val Sharma has something related to him that I need in my life right now."

A tiny grin crept into Derek's lips. "Did you get a tarot reading or something?"

"Ha!" It felt good to laugh out loud. "I don't know how I know, I just know. I need to track down the whereabouts of a dead man and find out why he died. Are you in or out?"

"In, of course. I don't know how much of my time or expertise is needed in Duga's sting operation, but I'll talk to him about it. Where do you want to start?"

"AEI, where Val Sharma and Jo Kramer worked. Let's pull Jazmin in on this, I want to see what she thinks. Let's see what she can track down."

"Okay, I'll take care of it. And your job," he pointed a finger, "is to rest tonight. That means sleep and not on your iPhone. Agreed? Where is your phone actually?"

"You're not taking my phone, so don't even think about it."

"Geez. I'm just asking where it is."

"No idea. Maybe back at the house," I lied. He knew it too.

"Give me the phone."

"I'm feeling agitated, suddenly. Maybe I should call Nurse Jen."

"You're forcing me to resort to drastic measures. Ivan should probably know that you're here."

"You wouldn't," I gasped.

"Wouldn't I?"

"I'm pressing the call button."

"Ivan's right," I said. "We're like ten-year-olds."

Chapter
Twenty-Six

As soon as I no longer heard Derek's footsteps down the hall, I pulled my iPhone from the tissue box on my bedside table, but slid it under the covers and waited five minutes just in case. I was proud of my ingenious hiding spot, knowing someone would likely try to take it from me. It was getting dark, and the overhead lights were terrible. I turned up the phone brightness all the way and found new texts from Dr. Hagen with what I hoped were the pictures he'd promised.

They were here, thank God. Ten of them. The last was a photograph of a handwritten note done in a black sharpie on a plain, white sheet of printer paper. Something about handwritten notes in Sharpies made my stomach clench, reminiscent of ransom and suicide notes.

On the page, Hagen had written, "Things bad here, Fergus knows, no one talking to each other, people scared to come to work. Fergus having me followed, everyone knows the body's missing now, it's a mess."

The next part was double-underlined. "Delete the pictures I just sent after you get them. Email them to yourself or even better, to your partner. Do not save them to a cloud server like Google Drive or iCloud. Text me on burner phone to confirm after the pictures have been deleted. I won't sleep tonight until you do."

I found myself eyeing the hallway, making sure no one was monitoring me. If I wasn't attached to wires, I would have gone into the bathroom for the next steps. Okay, I can do this. Without looking at the pictures, I emailed them to an old Yahoo email I never used anymore. I attached all nine of Hagen's photos to the same email, put the word "Pasta Primavera recipes" in the subject line, and waited till it was sent. Okay, good. Now I opened my old Yahoo email app and waited, refreshed my browser, waited again and refreshed again. Finally, there it was. I opened it, saw the pictures attached, and I clicked on one to be sure it opened.

Next, I closed the Yahoo email app. Then, come to think of it, I moved the Yahoo email message into my Trash folder and left it there. I could dig it out later on a laptop when I got home. I went back to my Gmail, found the email I'd sent to Yahoo, and deleted that message, then deleted it again from the trash. And for the last step, I opened my text messages again and deleted all messages from Hagen's burner phone. Whew. I needed a drink after that.

So now, if someone managed to hijack my phone, there was no visible trace of Hagen's text message to me, and no trace of those pictures saved anywhere on my phone or in my primary email account. Even in Yahoo, that message was in the trash. I don't think anyone even knew I still had a Yahoo account.

I texted Hagen on the latest burner phone number. I typed the word, *Done* with a check mark.

You followed all directions? he shot back.

Yes.

Where are you now? I want to bring you something.

St. Francis Hospital, 3rd floor, Room 317.

Long pause. Was he reconsidering? *I'm sorry to hear that*, he wrote finally. *Are you up for a quick visit?*

If you get here soon, I typed back. *I'm about to have an MRI.*

I'll be there in twenty minutes. If you're not there, I'll wait.

I liked how he asked if I was up for a visit, though now I was wary of my exposure to whoever was following him. I didn't have my gun with me and Derek took off knowing I was about to have an MRI. I smiled as a spark of hope lit up in the center of my chest. Duga, my guardian angel, was no doubt camped in a car in the parking lot, or he'd sent someone to keep an eye out. It was worth checking anyway.

Hey, are you anywhere near St. Francis? I texted him.

Very close. What do you need? he typed back.

A broader smile spread across my face. Somehow, I didn't feel quite so alone. There was still a woman in the bed next to me, asleep.

Lin Hagen will be here in a half hour. He said he has something to bring me. I'd explain the thing about the pictures when I saw him.

This late? he typed. *I'll text you when I see him.*

Keeping my eyes on the doorway, I flipped on the bedside light and scrunched my bed pillow to sit slightly upright, so I could see Hagen's photos. I knew enough about autopsies from my prior research to know that the pre-autopsy phases included an external exam with details of the body's outer appearance, including clothing and any accessories on or near the body at the time of death. Then the body was photographed. I expected to see several images of the face and head, images of the front and back of the body clothed and unclothed, and then closeup photographs of anything of interest. According to what I'd read on the legal pad in Camille's car, there would hopefully be at least one image of the man's neck and throat area. There may also be photographs of any surgical scars, birthmarks, tattoos, piercings, or any other physical abnormalities that could point to details that could help determine cause or manner of death, which was apparently still undetermined.

I looked toward the doorway again. Why wasn't anyone here for my MRI? Come to think of it, I hadn't heard anyone on my floor in several minutes. That seemed strange for a busy hospital ward.

I opened the email and touched the first picture. As expected, it showed the face of a brown-skinned youngish man, dark hair, clean shaven, front view. I decided to do a quick scan of each picture and then come back later for closer scrutiny.

The first photo, Image 2, was the left profile of the face, and Image 3 the right side.

I opened Image 4, remembering that he was found at Lake Piru in the Los Padres National Forest. This mattered because the fourth image was a front view of the man's entire body with his clothing on. What looked like it had originally been a white Oxford, button-down shirt—I could tell because the collar was white—was now brown in some places but mostly tan from dirt and dust, almost like he'd rolled down a sandy berm during his last hours. The shirt was half-tucked into dark jeans, which looked normal and in good condition. Bare feet. Image 5 was a back view of the man with clothing on, showing an interesting stain or wrinkle pattern on the back of the top right shoulder.

Images 6 and 7 showed the same front/back view but without clothing, showing a slender but well-built, adult male with no apparent injuries or visible wounds. I checked the doorway again, thinking I'd seen a shadow. Then a hospital worker rushed past my room carrying a pillow and blanket.

Images 8 and 9, the ones I was most interested in seeing, were close-ups of the man's neck and throat area. Image 8 was chin to collar bone, and 9 was just of the marks on the neck. At a quick glance, I was more curious about Image 8 because of something I saw in Camille's drawing. A small dot was depicted on the figure's neck and right shoulder. Red, small, round, in the middle of the right side of the throat. But more curious to me was the dark discoloration under the dot. Was it a bruise of some kind? Was the dot intended to draw attention to or away from that discoloration? So far, I couldn't tell.

After another paranoid glance toward the empty hallway, I opened the long-awaited Image 9, zooming into the throat area, but I could tell right away it was too dark in the room to see the coloration closely. I needed more light. First, I reached left and angled the bedside lamp to face more toward my direction. That didn't work. I tried zooming even closer, but needed my reading glasses, which were likely in my purse or at home. I went to my iPhone settings and increased the display brightness all the way. Slight improvement.

Now I could zoom out a little bit too. From this view I could gauge the general size, width, and overall shape of the neck marks. It looked like – or was made to look like something the size of a narrow rope around the neck. The top and bottom edges of the mark were mostly smooth, with some points and stray edges as if the implement had rubbed or moved up and down on the skin. Wow. If this was a tattoo and not an actual mark, that was some detail. I couldn't help but marvel at the significant level of premeditation and planning something like this would require of the assailant. So, if the assailant hadn't killed this man, that raised a few questions. Why would someone go through the trouble to conduct this procedure on another human being? Why, and how much sedation would be needed to force the victim still for 7-8 hours – if he'd been alive when it was done?

Would the tattooing process be any different when applying ink to a live human as opposed to someone already deceased? And if the ME's office failed to assign "homicide" as the conclusive cause of death, where did that leave us? *Undetermined* was definitely one of the other manners of death in addition to accident, suicide, and natural causes, but often carried the most potential for political fallout. Though the manner was perfectly legit based on inconclusive evidence or conflicting information, I'd seen it carry the optics of an incomplete autopsy or steps left out of the process. In other words, an implication of incompetence or mishandling.

If Val Sharma had been an otherwise healthy young man with no underlying morbidities, how did he die, and what was the meaning behind the marks on his neck? Lin Hagen had already confirmed the absence of laryngeal skeleton fractures, soft tissue hemorrhages, conjunctiva of the eyes, tongue swelling, and any other of the more common signs of fatal strangulation. I hadn't asked about latent fingerprints on the victim's neck. I zoomed in again, blinking the image into view. There was an area of what medical examiners refer to as petechiae "showers" or tiny hemorrhaging marks that can cluster on the eyelids and parts of the ear in response to lack of oxygen flow to the brain during strangulation. Image 9 clearly showed Val Sharma's right eyelid with petechiae below the dark, bushy eyebrow. I looked at it again to be sure.

Why had Lin Hagen covered this up? Now that just evoked another swarm of questions. My head had started pounding, probably from the bright lights and intense viewing. I turned off the bedside light and set the phone back in the tissue box, taking a long breath. I knew I shouldn't be doing this. Derek would kill me, and justifiably so. I needed to rest both my body and my brain if I was to recover fully and properly from what had been an attempt on my life. Where was the medical team that was supposed to take me to get an MRI? But now another panicked thought creeped into my consciousness: where was Dr. Hagen?

Chapter
Twenty-Seven

New question: Who could have benefitted from Val Sharma's death?

Anything yet? I texted Duga about Lin Hagen.

Nada. Slow night.

That's weird. Hagen said he'd be here in twenty minutes, I typed back, then checked my watch. I'd spent thirty reviewing the images he sent to my phone. I thought about pulling up that last image with the hemorrhage marks on the eyelid. No don't, I told myself. I've done enough work for tonight.

Cops pick him up yet? Duga asked.

Maybe that's why he's not here.

We're looking at Thursday for Operation Dojo btw, Duga wrote. *And before you ask, no, you can't be on scene.*

I started a protest when I saw Dr. Hagen's head and shoulders in the doorway. He swooped into the room and wound around to the inner side of the bed. *Thursday, got it. Hagen's here. You didn't see him?* I typed then slid the phone back into the tissue box before I read Duga's response.

"Hey. Sorry. I had to run up here."

123

"Why? Is everything okay?"

Slight smile. "Sure, except someone's still tailing me, and it is definitely not the police. Where's your purse?"

I pointed to the chocolate brown, large, pebbled leather Alexander Wang handbag crumpled on the floor at the foot of the bed. Why would he need that? I remembered when I'd bought that purse right after I moved back to the family estate in Santa Barbara. So much had happened since then.

Hagen eyed the door, crouched low, unzipped and thrust his hands around the inside of my purse.

"Um, what the hell are you doing?"

His eyes never left the doorway. I felt his fear and tension. Must be a reason.

He rose, finally, coming awkwardly close on the left side of my bed. "I want to get a soda." Then he walked out of the room, vanishing as abruptly as he'd arrived.

What just happened?

Okay. So, the problem now was that I was stuck in this bed with wires attached to me, an IV drip in my left arm, and my purse was too far away to reach. Shit.

Sorry to bother you. Any chance you could come up here? I typed to Duga, hoping he was still in the parking lot. Of course he was. He wouldn't have left. Would he? I counted. Five seconds. Ten. Twelve.

On my way, he wrote.

I pressed the brighter setting on the bedside lamp and inspected the IV needle in my arm while I waited. It had tape over it to hold it in place. I probably didn't even need it anymore, I thought as my fingers picked at the edges of the tape.

"What do you think you're doing?" Duga's voice boomed from the hallway, pointing at my hands.

"Jesus, you scared me." I swallowed the lump in my throat. Duga moved closer and pulled out his phone. "Lemme show you something." He scrolled through his texts and displayed his phone screen.

"What?" I whined.

He moved to the other side of the bed and pulled my reading glasses from his pocket. "Put these on and read it out loud please."

I sighed. "Why? Fine, give it to me. It's from Derek. It says," I paused to read it trying not to crack a smile. *DO NOT let her leave the hospital. I suspect about now she'll be scheming for some reason to leave. She's there*

SWITCH

for a reason and now they suspect she might have a brain lesion. Please. You know all her tricks.

And Duga had replied with, *Roger that.* He put the phone back in his pocket and folded his arms across his chest. "You were saying?"

I nodded. "Can you pass me my purse?"

"You called me up here for that?"

"Yeah."

"Explain why you need it."

After a twenty second standoff, he pulled the purse from the floor and set it on the bed beside me. As I opened it and looked around, I told him about my strange encounter. I found the change purse in my wallet. Hagen had gone into my purse to supposedly take money for a vending machine, before he just up and left. So odd. Something small and white caught my eye. I peered inside and saw a half-folded, crumpled piece of paper. I pulled it out and stared.

"That wasn't in there before?" Duga asked.

Still staring. "I don't think so. I don't store notes in my change purse. I don't even use it. I rarely even carry cash." I unfolded the page and leaned left to hold it up the light. "What the hell—"

Duga leaned into me to read it. "Looks like a shopping list, and it's not your handwriting."

"What's that on the back? Turn it over. There's something on there."

"Looks like he was writing in a pen that was running out of ink," he said, squinting at the page. "Amtk lostate A457."

Come on, Mari, use your brain. Amt usually stood for amount, but with the k on the end, it seemed obvious enough. "Of course," I said. "Amtrak. The Amtrak here in Santa Barbara is on Lower State Street."

"That's impressive. Is it a storage locker or something?" he asked.

"That's what I would guess." I reached back into the purse and pulled out the wallet again, unclasping the change purse. I looked down and, sure enough, there was something silver in there that wasn't round. I pulled it out. "And this looks small enough to be a locker key." I raised a brow and smiled.

Duga watched a thought form on my face. "Don't even think about it."

"Duga, listen to me."

"Seriously? You're gonna do this? You collapsed in your freaking living room and hit your head. Derek's right, you're here for a reason."

125

"I'm fine. I honestly feel fine; I don't have time to be here right now. The clock is ticking."

"What clock?" he argued. "Traeger? I've got that covered."

"No!" I exhaled, then made myself take some slow, regular breaths sitting back against the pillows. "Val Sharma is our John Doe. He's connected with the reason why—no, he is the reason my friend Camille Bota has disappeared. And now someone's following Dr. Hagen, your tennis partner I might add. Not only that, Val Sharma's disappeared from the ME's office."

"The body's missing? Since when?"

"Well," I clarified. "Not sure missing is the right word, but Hagen told me he'd been moved, though no one knew where."

Duga walked to the doorway and looked out into the hall. "What do you think we're gonna find in that locker?" he asked.

I was so happy to hear the word 'we're' that I almost cried. Okay, so it was decided. Duga was going to break me out of this hospital room. The question was how.

"I have no idea. See anyone out there? It's been a dead zone for the past two hours. Someone was supposed to collect me for an MRI, but they never came."

He looked at me again, this time appraising me in a more medical manner. "Can you even walk?"

I tried to swing my legs to the side of the bed. My IV tugged on my left elbow. Dammit.

"You'd need to be able to walk out of here like you're visiting someone and look normal. We have to go past the nurse's station."

"Can you help me remove my IV without setting off alarms or buzzers?"

Duga stood back, closed his mouth, and crossed his arms. His expression looked sad, or maybe just disappointed in me. Damn him, I didn't need a lecture right now. "Sure, after I read you something." He brought up something on his phone and took two steps toward me. "Things that can result from an untreated brain lesion."

"Duga. Please."

"Personality changes, neurological and cognitive impacts, including," he paused for emphasis, raising his brows high. "Seizures, paralysis, coma, or death. Now. What were you asking?"

"I seriously feel okay now. I think it was maybe low blood sugar."

"Fine, but I'm telling Derek. If you don't mind incurring his wrath,

I'll do it. Extend your arm," he said, grasping my elbow with one hand. With the other, he pulled the tiny needle out of my arm then re-taped the bandage over it. He set it on the bedside table. "I think we're good. Do you need help getting dressed?"

"No, I'll go slowly." I still had spare yoga pants in my purse. My thin, rumpled t-shirt would have to do for now. "Can I wear your jacket?"

"Sure. Make haste." He stood at the door while I slid my legs into the pants, his expression tight and strained. I'd have to pay for this later, in more ways than one. I put on his jacket and reached to coil my purse handle around my shoulder.

"Ow, ow, ow."

"I'll do it," he said.

My arm was killing me from the IV and would likely be bruised by morning. I stepped in bare feet around the room before putting on my ballet flats, just to gauge my dizziness.

"You good? We should go now."

"Duga?"

"Don't bother. You know this is a terrible idea. Derek's gonna kill us both."

I nodded. But I was certain whatever Lin Hagen had to show me would have a material impact on the case of Val Sharma's killer.

Chapter
Twenty-Eight

My long legs wobbled under my weight, swaying me side to side like a tall ship. Duga's arm slid around my waist, hiked up under my ribcage to steady me.

"Ow. Broken rib, broken rib. You're punishing me."

"Sorry. Sort of."

Ten steps later, I was fine. But why was the hallway completely empty? Not a single person in front of the elevators or lobby on the way out to the car.

"I'm getting as paranoid as Hagen. Where is everyone? He said he's been tailed for the past few days and not by the police."

A few more steps and I could see normal activity in the lobby, foot traffic, people talking, an old woman waiting by the entrance, probably for a ride home.

By the time we got to the parking lot, my body had found its normal gait. I tried not to be obvious scanning the surroundings, certain someone from the hospital staff would call out behind us, reminding me of health risks and discharge paperwork I hadn't signed. And even with Duga here, I felt vulnerable. When we got to his car, he held out his phone. "Either I tell Derek what's up or you do."

"Fine, I'll do it." I pulled out my phone and texted Derek about where we were headed. "I told him it was your idea and you said to stop being a wuss."

"Yeah I'm sure he'll believe that."

I always loved the Santa Barbara Amtrak station, reminiscent of the San Juan Bautista Mission, where Hitchcock's *Vertigo* was filmed. That Mission Revival architecture, with its arched openings and heavy pillars created the most sinister shadows. It made me wonder if I was being watched right now, someone pressed against the stucco hiding in a dark pocket.

"Key." Duga held out his palm. I knew that look. It meant there was no room for conversation, and he would be the one opening Hagen's locker. I handed it over. He thumbed it into his pants pocket. "Can I borrow my jacket back?"

I wriggled out of it, curious about the request. He put it on, then reached into the side pocket of his driver's side door pulling out a crumpled pair of green rubber gloves. Smart.

While he was gone, I ran through a list of what could be in there. Why go through the trouble of putting it in a railway locker? Because obviously it was related to either Camille or Val Sharma, it was something that had intrinsic value, and maybe something other people were looking for.

The car door opened and startled me. "Do you have any kind of little bag in your purse?"

When I shook my head, he climbed inside, locked the door, carefully held the small, dark object in his gloved hand and used his other hand to peel off the glove with the object concealed inside.

"What is it?"

"Cell phone," he whispered.

I don't know if he saw someone on his way in or out, but his eyes told me to wait to either inspect the item or discuss it.

Duga arranged for us to meet Derek back at my house to face my reckoning. When we got there, I looked in the mirror and realized how scary I looked. I changed clothes and did what I could to look presentable, then came downstairs a half hour later and found both of them sitting at the kitchen table, hands folded, in silence. Shit. Trevor was chilling in his downstairs doggie bed, which meant someone had given him treats already.

Something smelled amazing. Maybe Jazmin had made something

after I collapsed at the dinner table, still so hard to believe. Duga had made coffee, and there was a plate of something on the counter covered with one of my dish towels. I lifted it off to find a neat pile of what looked like black currant scones, good enough to have come from a bakery. I pointed to the plate then looked at my house guests, who shrugged.

"Jazmin," we said in unison.

I peered down to examine them. "These belong on the Great British Baking Show. They're freaking perfect."

"Ethan Webb told me she lived in the UK till she was ten," Duga said, reminding me of that earlier case.

"And now she's on our payroll as the best investment we've made in the past two years," I commented and sat across from them, appreciating how my table was wide. Derek was tight-lipped and fuming.

"Fine," I sighed, my palms on the table. "Let's get this over with, shall me?"

Derek shook his head. Duga bit into a scone.

"I'm very sorry if I worried you. I would never want to do that." At least that part was true, but he wasn't having it.

"I think you have a death wish and you're blaming yourself for all kinds of things that you're aren't responsible for." He bit his lip. "It makes it hard for people who care about you and count on you."

"I said I was sorry." I lowered my forehead to the table. "And I was joking about Duga, he had nothing to do with it, other than trying to scare me into staying in the hospital."

"You're a grown woman."

"You noticed?"

Now a smile cracked into his lips. "How are you feeling?"

"Not terrible. I need to know why this happened, but I suspect if I really did have a brain lesion, I'd have other symptoms."

"Well now we'll never know. Anyway," Derek picked up a mug and sipped.

When the pot of coffee was empty, we moved into the dining room —the same room where we devoured Duga's Indian feast when I suddenly keeled over—with rubber gloves on to examine the cell phone.

Derek was asking me if I was okay, but where had his outburst come from last night, when he verbally attacked Robert? Clearly, we had some unfinished business. Duga had put the phone he retrieved from the locker on the dining room table.

"Doesn't look like an iPhone," Derek said.

"Samsung Galaxy, couple versions old," Duga said. It was charging now. "Camille's?" he asked.

"My guess is Val Sharma, our John Doe. Camille's purse wasn't in her car when we saw it yesterday, so she's probably got it with her. Dr. Hagen would have had access to Val Sharma's personal effects because he works for the ME's office."

"Except you said his body had been moved," Derek said, reminding me of that complication.

I nodded. "That's right." I pressed the power button to turn it on. Without knowing how long Val Sharma had been dead before he was discovered, it would be miraculous if the phone even turned on.

"You're kidding," Duga said when the backlight blinked on. "No password? For a tech worker?"

"Lucky break," Derek said.

I rose to pull three scones off the platter, cut them down the middle, added a small pat of butter and put them in the microwave for thirty seconds. I grabbed some raspberry jam while they warmed and brought everything to the dining room, setting out three napkins.

Trevor appeared at my elbow. "No, not for you, sweetie."

Derek was right. It was unusual that Val Sharma didn't have a system password on his phone. Maybe he needed instant access to everything he stored in there and anything confidential was internally password-protected. Maybe he didn't have anything worth protecting, or maybe he had a second phone.

I texted Hagen's burner and confirmed that we had the item from the locker.

"Hagen's texting back now. I asked if he could call us." I gestured toward the plates with my hospitality smile. "Dig in, boys."

Derek bit into his scone, while Duga kept his eye on my phone. A second later, I expected it to ring but instead it was the doorbell. Derek and I looked at each other. Hagen?

"Lemme put Trevor upstairs, actually. To him, Dr. Hagen's an intruder and he won't be okay with his visit right now."

Duga got up and pulled open the ever-clunky foyer door, then the outer door. After a brief exchange, I heard two sets of footsteps and the word 'game' mentioned. Duga and Dr. Lin Hagen stood in the dining room doorway as I came back downstairs.

"Where do you guys play tennis?" I asked them.

"Camino Real Tennis Center mostly," Hagen said with a sort of embarrassed half-glance to Duga.

"Please, join us," I said, and stood. My legs felt weak. I definitely shouldn't have left the hospital.

"My partner, Derek Abernathy," I said. Hagen leaned forward and shook Derek's hand. I got up, went to the kitchen to prepare another scone for our guest. "I'm surprised to see you today, Doctor," I said, my way of asking what the hell he was doing here.

"The two men who've been following me, for days now, have changed from driving to foot surveillance. They chased me around downtown today, no doubt looking for this—" he held out the burner phone Duga had given him— "and that," he added pointing at the phone we'd retrieved from the train station.

"I take it this belonged to Val Sharma?" I asked.

Dr. Hagen nodded, soberly staring at the plate of scones. He sniffed the air. A sly smile traced his lips. "Someone British made these. I can smell the sour milk."

"I told you, GBBO!" I laughed.

"GBBO?" Duga asked.

"Great British Bake Off. Anyway, how did you come to receive this phone?" I asked Hagen. "I assume you're now more than just slightly exposed if anyone, like Declan Fergus, knows you have it."

Hagen shook his head and took off his jacket, hanging it on the back of the dining chair farthest from me. He pulled a scone off the plate and bit into it, letting crumbs fall all over the table. "No one at work knows I have it. The men chasing me, yes, probably."

"Remember the earthquake last Monday?" he asked. "Wait, no it was Sunday, very early in the morning."

I remembered reading about it on one of my social media feeds, but I hadn't felt anything.

"It wasn't a big one, but it was the Oak Ridge Fault, which is right near the M.E.'s office."

"Why is that significant?" I asked.

"Ah," Duga smiled. "I'll bet some things in storage could have shifted from the movement or something?"

Hagen's eyes widened. "Bingo. This phone wasn't stored properly in a sealed, manila envelope like it should have been. It was just loose in a file folder. My guess is it slid out the side of the folder, then to the back of the file cabinet. It got left behind when all of Sharma's hard copy files were removed two days ago. And before you ask me who moved them, I have no idea."

"What made you go looking for it?" Derek asked. I could tell more interested in this case now.

"I was looking for something else, another report kept in that same file drawer, and the drawer contents just looked funny. All the files were pushed to the back of the drawer. I looked in and saw something black sticking out on the bottom. That's the only way it would have been visible. I knew what it was immediately and pocketed it, mainly so no one else would find it." He raised his eyes, then lowered them. "I know what I did. I knew the risks when I was doing it and I no longer care about protocol. Anyway, Val Sharma is apparently a hot commodity."

Yes. The question was why.

Chapter Twenty-Nine

After Dr. Hagen left, Duga took off to get ready for Operation Dojo and Derek stayed and made us dinner while we combed through the details. And honestly, our relationship needed some attention so the alone time was necessary.

"Why do you always love cooking in *my* kitchen so much?" I asked. "As I recall, you also loved cooking in my other kitchen in Santa Monica."

Somehow, I was glad he stayed. Something about being alone in this big house, since the accident, just didn't sit well in my heart, even with Trevor here. I think it was why I'd been waking up in the middle of the night lately, not knowing what woke me other than some kind of unrest. Like the house was trying to tell me something.

"Maybe I don't like living alone anymore," he said, wincing as he heard his own words. "Or not as much as I used to."

"Honestly, I don't think you've had time to feel lonely lately. How could you? Your mean partner has you working like ten hours a day, doesn't she?"

"She is mean, isn't she?"

His back was turned now but I felt his smile.

"What are you doing so studiously back there?" he asked. "So much for your no phones at dinner rule."

"That's your rule." I'd been scanning through Val Sharma's most recent calls, looking for repeats and patterns. I long-sighed and reached back to stretch out my arms and shoulders. My skeletal system felt more susceptible to pain than it used to, yet I never seemed willing to actually take the pain meds I'd been prescribed.

I held up the phone. "It's Val Sharma's. No calls but lots of texts back and forth between him and our friend Jo Kramer."

"Oh?" He half-turned. "Of what nature?"

"Nothing scandalous, just work." I did another quick scan before I spoke too soon. "Mainly things like 'where are you, you're gonna be late for a meeting,' sometimes they linked up for lunch, some pretty funny banter, actually. They were friends."

"Friends plus?"

"No, I don't think so. Then recently there were a lot of calls, often late at night, from someone named Wallace, saved in his contacts. Often the calls were very short."

"Interesting," Derek said, and turned toward me. "How short is short?"

I checked. "Thirty seconds. I know what you're thinking."

"No last name?" he asked.

"It says Wallace Journ," I said and spelled the unusual name. "Other than that, looks like calls and texts to and from family." I kept scanning without knowing what I was looking for. "I'm not seeing anything that's obviously shady here, other than the Wallace fellow."

"You gonna follow up with that?" he asked, plating what looked like scrambled eggs and toast.

"I love breakfast for dinner."

Derek winked. "I knew that about you."

"I'm gonna call the number, yeah, but first, I want to look at something." I took the plate and set it in front of me, then turned back toward my laptop and did a Google search on journalists named Wallace. Derek walked behind me to view my screen.

"Journ, journalists, of course. Good thinking. Mind if I eat?"

"No please, I'll join you in just a—ah, now that's interesting. There's a Wallace McCoy who's a technology writer with the San Francisco Chronicle, also written for the London Times."

Derek sat across from me as I poured two glasses of one of my favorite red wines ever.

"What's your latest martini concoction?"

"Lemontinis lately. It's a lemon drop martini." Truth was, I hadn't made one in a while.

"Sounds delicious. I love anything lemon."

"Sweet, tart, perfect. Go ahead, try this," I said and held out a glass. Derek swirled the dark red wine around in circles. "Is this Tamarack?" he asked, surprised. "I thought you couldn't get them anymore."

I'd picked up a few Tamarack Cellars Firehouse Reds the last time I was in the Bay Area. The Columbia Valley winery for some reason didn't distribute this far south.

I nodded, sat, and took the first sip. "Doesn't even need to breathe. Stunning."

"I wouldn't normally drink wine with eggs but who could say no to such a great bottle? Company's not bad, either."

"So I'm not in trouble?" I asked.

"Hell yeah you're in trouble. I'm just eating right now."

"I see." I touched glasses with him. "Can you guess the blend? They're not always the same."

"Well," he said, then paused to swallow a mouthful of eggs and toast. "Aren't most of their Firehouse Reds predominantly Syrah, Cab, and Merlot?"

"In varying degrees. Then they've got Cab Franc, Mourvèdre, Grenache—"

"Petit Verdot?" he asked.

"Yep, Sangiovese, and one more I'd never heard of before."

"Are you still on pain killers though? Should you be drinking?"

I stared back and winced.

"You're not taking them?"

"Actually no."

"Why the hell not? You know you're in pain, I can see it when you walk. What's the issue?"

"They make me feel foggy," I argued. "And honestly, I already feel foggy enough from the concussion and the trauma. I'm fine without them, if I'm careful."

"And that's the problem. You're not."

I sighed. "I feel like an eighty-year-old woman and I'm barely middle-aged."

We ate and sipped silently for a while, with the sound of crickets from the open kitchen window. "No word on Camille?"

"No, and Hagen's continued to evade the police, or else they're just not interested, which is even more suspicious."

"Other than Duga's sting operation, what's next?"

I sat back feeling full, or maybe I'd just eaten too fast. "Well, I fear there's gonna be an Ivan reckoning pretty soon."

"Have you told him about—" He stopped and laughed. "Of course you haven't."

"Val Sharma? Why would I? I did get the missing person report from him, though not sure he'll put two and two together," I said with a defensive tone. "That case has nothing to do with him. Besides, it's not even a case. We brought in the Santa Barbara PD, and that was the right thing to do."

"I meant about Duga. Project Dojo."

"Oh." I widened my eyes. "That."

"You're still touchy about Ivan," he said, with a disarming smile.

"He's annoying, that's why. It's nothing more than that."

"I don't disagree. What's your plan?"

"Duga needs to coordinate that with Ivan's team, and sorry to say it but that will likely jeopardize the chances of success. Too many cooks, you know?"

"I can talk to Duga about that and work with him if you want."

"That'd be good. As for me, I'm going hunting tomorrow for Val Sharma's tattoo artist."

"Remember our back up rule."

We didn't exactly have a rule, but I knew he was worried about my doing something risky without considering the consequences, which was what had gotten me in trouble so many times before. "Of course. It's just research," I lied.

137

Chapter Thirty

Every minute, it seemed, was a war between strength and weakness. There must be a name for this condition. The next morning, I decided to walk Trevor around the neighborhood, exploring the east Santa Barbara hills. I was sure my malaise-bordering-on-depression was due to the sudden lack of activity after decades of being a runner. My medical team would call this reckless and advise more time recuperating. But my muscles were desperate for exertion.

Most of these roads we knew by now, and it was the easiest way to get Trevor, and me, some well needed exercise. But our neighborhood was no substitute for Arroyo Burro Beach. An oceanfront beach and county park, it had a lovely grassy area for dogs to roam off leash and for me to run till my lungs couldn't take it anymore. Only three miles from here, every day that place felt farther away.

I had two conversations planned with potential clients this morning, so I wanted to get back to Holly Loop. Trevor inched his nose in the air when we reached the driveway, telling me there was still more walking to do.

"Really?" I sighed. "Okay, just down the street again and back. That's it."

I used the time to breathe in more fresh air and force myself into sales and marketing mode, by far the worst drudgery of business ownership, even for extroverts. Trevor kept angling his head back vying for eye contact, always knowing when I was distracted and hating emotional distance – just like all the men in my life. When we reached the top of the hill, my hips were talking to me.

I was practiced at using car windows as mirrors to see behind me. I guess I had a feeling all of us were being monitored. The vista from here was fodder for a painting. I used it to calm my thoughts, remembering this same walk with my father so many times early on.

"Stop." I tugged once on Trevor's leash when he was moving too fast for me. Often one tug turned into three or four, accompanied by an elevation in my voice. He is a Great Dane, after all, with a typical strong personality. Today he skidded to a halt, sensing the tightness in my grip. From our vantage point, I caught the familiar shape of the back of a white car protruding from an outcrop of shrubs in front of a fire hydrant. Did they not see the hydrant, or did they park in haste and not care? The more important detail was that this looked like Camille's white Lexus. But the cops had taken it. So how could it be?

"Stay." I stroked Trevor's head and stood right beside him while I watched glimpses of a woman's bare legs moving in and out of the trees. She had on a light top, short hair. Camille, my God. What are you doing here? Trevor and I made our way slowly down the hill, monitoring the car. I tried to make sense of these facts, while alternating my gaze from the ground to the outcrop of bushes ahead. Camille rose next to the driver's side door watching me.

I saw her retreat as Trevor and I drew closer, not an unusual response considering his size. Her palm went up as we edged to the corner. "I didn't want to put you in danger." Her voice was hoarse and she looked like she'd fought her way out of a bar brawl.

She moved around the front of the car and took a few steps up the hill, still partially concealed by the tall shrubs and low trees lining our neighborhood. I met her gaze, appraising her appearance. Tan skirt, black slip-on shoes, and an off-white, short-sleeved crepe blouse knotted in the front. The knot was blotted with dark stains and smears, the hem torn on the left side, and on that same side, her face, neck, and arm were bruised, likely the side that got pulled during her abduction from her driveway.

"I'm looking for Lin. He told me he's been talking to you." She looked down, apologetic almost. "I thought he might be here."

I shook my head. "Camille, you need help."

"Some men took me from my driveway and kept me in a closet in some house not far from here." Her eyes looked hard and hollow. "I haven't had food or water in…" She waved her hand in the air and used it to cover her eyes.

"I live just over there."

"I know. That's why I'm here."

"Please, let me bring you something."

"No. Thank you." She bent over to take a few breaths. "I broke out last night, or maybe they let me break out. It seemed too easy. I half expected them to follow me, but I haven't seen any of them this morning. They had my car parked next to the apartment they took me to, and the keys left on a ledge by the front door. So, I just—" She cut off her own words to laugh, which quickly turned to a momentary cry. She didn't move her hand to wipe her tears, instead just letting them roll down her cheek.

"Didn't the police impound your car from your driveway?" I asked.

"Maybe, but it still ended up here. Catch my drift?"

I stared. "Santa Barbara Police?" I knew those people. I'd worked with them.

"I'm just giving you the facts."

It was interesting that Derek and I had been unable to reach Abel, and he still hadn't called either of us back. He was young, but trustworthy. I had a feeling someone else had intervened.

Trevor sniffed the air. "I know," I mumbled. Dogs don't miss a trick. "What do you need?" I asked Camille as she took two hesitant steps closer to the street.

"They think Lin took John Doe's body and now—"

"We think his name is Val Sharma," I said.

Her eyes teared up again. She stared back. "They're gonna kill Lin."

Lin told us that he had nothing to do with that body going missing. Even though Camille and I had history, right now Lin was the one I believed more.

"Who's they?" I reminded myself to stay neutral, another tradecraft trick used to further unglue a witness. And Dr. Camille Bota was most definitely that.

"Declan's men," she answered quickly.

"Camille, what's going on here? At some point someone's gotta tell me the real story or I can't help you."

She took a long breath in and out. "I was offered fifty thousand dollars to keep John Doe's real name anonymous."

"You mean even after Kelsey Kramer identified him?"

She shrugged. "I don't know who she is, but another fifty to rule it as accidental."

"Was it?" I asked, watching her dark eyes scan up and down the street.

"Did you see the throat?" she asked, without meeting my gaze. "I assume Lin showed you the pictures? I know he contacted you."

Okay. So, this told me Hagen had contact with her *after* she was abducted. Interesting.

"I saw the notebook in your car with logs about the external exam, where you suggested the marks on the neck could be tattoo marks."

"They were," she confirmed, and lowered her eyes to meet mine.

"Do you know why?" I posed.

"Just another layer of whatever they're covering up."

These eyes no longer looked like the carefree Camille Bota I'd known years ago. She was self-directed back then, ambitious, but still a free spirit. This was a different face, a tougher, colder Camille in the same runway model package, maybe the kind who might take a payoff.

"So, John Doe was killed by someone who made it look like he was strangled," I said, pulling the threads together. Trevor was quiet, matching my vibe.

"Yes. I believe so."

"But you don't think he was strangled? What about the petechial hemorrhages?"

She looked at me now like I was a stranger, maybe wondering how I could know forensic details like this. "Lots of things besides strangulation can cause that manifestation. Electrocution, craniocerebral trauma, even extreme intoxication. No," she shook her head. "He wasn't strangled."

"Could his death have been accidental, though?"

"Possible. Not likely."

"Can you prove that from the external exam and the autopsy you performed?"

She shook her head, fast like excising a painful thought from her head. "Lin did the autopsy. I did the external exam. Sometimes we arrange it that way." She looked at her shoes. "I can't prove that it wasn't an accident without being in the lab with access to his body fluids. Or at least *a* lab."

Interesting. Was she asking about using Ivan's crime lab down in LA? She bit her lip like she was waiting for an answer to the question she didn't ask.

Sure, I'll bite. "Even if we could find another crime lab where you could review the findings and lab results, could you get access to all your case data?"

She smiled. "I have it. It's in the cloud. Well, I should say accessible by like five levels of encryption and firewalls, but I have the access, yes."

"I'm confused. So then why do you need a crime lab? Just log in from home and review the lab results, review the case notes. What am I missing?" I pressed. Trevor started pacing around me. I needed to get him home. Time for his snack.

"I have the autopsy and external exam results, and all the case file notes, intake report, things like that. But I don't have the lab results on his body fluids and toxicology because they weren't back yet by the time the body was moved. I have no proof, but I think it was the toxicology results that caused all this."

"What did you test for? Were these tests standard?" I asked, remembering something from her written notes.

"Standard, yes. Blood, urine, liver, testing for alcohol, drugs, other toxins."

"Would the tests be done by now?"

"They should, yes. But the request needs to come from the pathologist on record." She smirked. "And now, currently, that's Lin. And I don't know where he is."

I nodded, getting it now. "And that's what you're doing here? Does he come to this area or something?"

"No, but I knew he was talking to you and thought he might be here. I didn't want to risk bringing danger to you, so I parked a few streets away and have been looking out for Lin's car."

"He's been followed for the past three days. I think he's been borrowing other peoples' cars to get around."

"Jesus." She shook her head.

"You didn't take the money obviously? The fifty thousand?"

She closed her eyes momentarily and paused, maybe a little too long. "No, of course not. I refused."

"I don't know where Dr. Hagen is right now, but I can give you the number of a burner phone we gave him."

"We?" she asked.

"My team," I said like it was obvious. "My partner, Derek, and a few associates. I don't have my purse with me, but I need to bring Trevor home. I can come back in about ten minutes and give you that number."

Camille nodded, then shook her head. "Okay, but not here. I'll drive my car to the next street corner." She was looking east to the corner of Santa Clara and Las Posas Road. "I'll be parked, the passenger window will be open, I'll be in the driver's side seat."

"Ten minutes," I said, only half expecting that she'd actually be there.

Chapter Thirty-One

Trevor tugged at his leash rushing to get home, no doubt unsettled by our strange encounter. Pain jabbed at my right elbow, shoulder, and hip as I resisted his weight, nearly jogging ten steps behind him. Exertion, maybe. But I wasn't ready for jogging.

"I know I know," I said, rushing us into the house. "It's snack time, isn't it?" His big brown watery eyes looked up at me, not asking for food but if everything was okay. God, that face.

I put an extra generous scoop in his dish and texted Duga. *Need backup.*

Are you okay? he typed back with barely a second's pause.

Yes.

Are you home?

Yes.

I can't break away right now. Jazmin's here, I'll send her.

Roger that.

I texted Jazmin asking her to meet me down the street in her car and be ready for anything. Hopefully Camille wouldn't see her and get spooked, but that would be easy to explain, if needed. I'd already given Jazmin a heads-up about a trip to a tattoo parlor in Venice so I could research the marks on Val Sharma's neck and have them looked at by an expert. Plus, it was a great excuse to get breakfast at my favorite place on Venice Beach. Too bad Derek wasn't here to join me this time. Those were the days.

Okay, what would Camille need most right now? I gathered some cash, bottles of water, peanut butter chocolate granola bars, then thought a moment. Camille was an attractive woman in a skirt and a short-sleeved shirt, and she was visibly injured, which made her even more conspicuous. I climbed the stairs to my bedroom and pulled out some cropped workout leggings, knowing Camille was about six inches shorter than me, along with a thin t-shirt and oversized black hoodie.

The sky was dark gray but there was still enough light to detect a six-foot-tall woman walking down an empty street. I left through my back entrance, going through the gate to Mr. DeMello's prized rose garden, careful to avoid the landmine of his motion detectors, which I'd triggered once while chasing Trevor. One more yard and I ended up on the sidewalk of Holly Court. I couldn't help thinking that if Camille had contacted me, whoever abducted her would be looking for me now, too.

I saw her car parked strategically close to the curb, which had a nice berm on the driver's side. I approached the front and tapped my fingernails on the hood as I walked up so I wouldn't scare her. She was alert and waiting, sitting up tall. She nodded as I crouched low and sat back on the dirt slope while she rolled down her driver's side window, putting me about a foot away from her.

"I leaned forward, holding out the bag. "A few supplies."

"That's kind of you." She grabbed it and put it on the floor of the passenger side.

"I've missed you, Camille."

Another curt nod, and she closed her eyes this time. Was she remembering the times we'd spent in the past? Was she sorry for not contacting me sooner? I was guilty of the same sin. "Missed you too. Glad you're doing so well."

How would she know anything about me? Did she know about my intelligence background and that I'd been shot by one of Europe's most dangerous offenders? Or that I was abducted at gunpoint a few months after opening my PI firm? My most recent accident included, no one could say I was doing *well.*

"So, who is Val Sharma and why was he killed?" I asked.

Slight smile. "I was told the same would happen to me if I spoke to anyone about him. Declan says that—"

"I don't give a rat's ass what Declan says, Camille. Declan's a punk in a cheap suit and your life is in danger. So is Lin's, and it looks like you've survived so far by a hair's breadth and through wit and grit. Hagen's been on the run for the past week, probably because they think he knows something."

"You're right. He's trying to protect me," she said, sniffing.

"Don't you want my help? I mean, how else do you think you're gonna get out of this jam?"

"I don't know. Once the body's been recovered—"

"Camille, you're not thinking straight. They're gonna find you and kill you because of what you know, regardless of your intentions about what to do with that information. I want to help you, but I need to know what's behind all this. Kelsey Jo Kramer, Val Sharma's coworker, said he was a software engineer at a research firm. Not exactly your typical hit target."

Camille raised her eyebrows but sat frozen in the front seat, her dark eyes deliberating. Would it be worse for her to absorb the burden of her knowledge alone, constantly hiding and on the run, or was my support worth the cost? She looked at the sky, maybe surveying the darkening clouds as a barometer of risk.

"Okay." She turned her head toward me. "He works for a company called AEI. They do—"

"I know that," I moaned. "They offer consulting for corporations on mathematics and statistics. Special projects, type of thing. We learned that from Jo Kramer."

She shook her head, turning her body to lean her elbows on the open window. She motioned me to move closer. I slid down the hill, now crouching low with my body weight on my ankles, which felt uncomfortable. But I wasn't moving now, not for anything.

"Not a consulting firm?" I asked.

"Special projects, you could say that," she said with a sneer. "They're a subsidiary of a larger shell corporation. Called Praxis I think, run out of the Cayman Islands."

"What kind of company?" I asked in a whisper.

"I don't know. But what I gathered from overhearing Fergus' phone calls, and some from my two abductors, is that AEI's work and operations have nothing to do with that parent company. They're just a small division."

"A CIA front?" I recalled one of my handlers sharing the voluminous list of CIA front organizations, some more surprising than others, and how the agency had a whole division that invested in cutting edge startups that could have potential global impact.

Camille bit her lip. "That would certainly explain some things. Maybe Fergus got roped into this through coercion. Maybe he didn't have a choice."

"But he's your replacement, right? Couldn't he be a part of something like this?"

I looked up and down the dark street, thinking, then shuddered as if my brain had been turned off for the past twenty minutes: where was Jazmin's car?

"Or maybe he's part of the parent company. Did that possibility occur to you?" I asked.

"Maybe you only think you know people," she replied softly.

"What can you tell me about your abduction?"

"They weren't your average thugs, for one thing. Two guys, trained professionals, slick, even tempered, organized. So, I wouldn't be surprised if you were right. The work the parent company is doing is highly classified, and from what I could gather, they've been able to hide all their financial transactions from the feds, including billions of dollars coming in and out over the past ten years."

"Which would further validate my theory," I added.

Camille raised her brows and nodded.

"So, I think we can be pretty sure that Val Sharma knew what the parent company was doing," I said.

"Not only that but what they were hiding. And whatever that is, it's obviously a secret worth killing for."

"Whistleblower," I mumbled. "His phone."

"Whose phone?" She turned sharply to me.

Shit. I answered with my eyes instead of words.

"You have Val Sharma's phone? How the hell did you get that?"

I shrugged. Camille was no fool. "Let's just say it was given to me. Anyway…" I stood and pointed toward my street. "I need to get back."

I hadn't had time yet to investigate the journalist listed in Val Sharma's phone contacts. Thinking of Val as a whistleblower certainly changed my ideas about his death. And probably Camille's as well. "I wrote my number down for you, it's in the bag. Is there a way I can get in touch with you?"

Her finger was on the window mechanism, about to roll it up. "Not at the moment."

"Be careful," I said.

"You too."

My head, now throbbing at the temples, ached with information overload, with Val Sharma and what he was about to reveal about Praxis before someone stopped him.

Chapter Thirty-Two

My phone showed a text notification from Jazmin when I picked it up. *Sorry I couldn't make it today,* it read. *Dojo. Are you okay?* Dojo meant Duga's Traeger sting was going down now. Why hadn't there been a dry run? That would be typical for something at this level of impact, and typical of our team. I felt it in my chest before it even reached my brain - they didn't want me on this op. And my presence on the Sharma case was even more precarious. Nothing about it was typical, and whoever was following Hagen could eventually target me. Maybe my pattern of recklessness had cost me the trust of my team. If so, it was my own fault.

I had a day's worth of research to do. I like research, the solitude of it, the silent discovery late at night in the dark, drinking coffee like I shouldn't and, in that empty quietude, allowing new facts to coalesce as new possibilities in my brain. Too often, though, the reality of research was drawing conclusions when I was stressed, running, out of breath, and doing five other things.

After a miraculously quiet afternoon, my phone chimed with an incoming call – Jazmin. About time. I'd call her back. My shoulders and neck were wrecked from hunching over my computer reading all day, so I stood out on the front porch stretching under a dark orange dusk. The beauty of Santa Barbara was unmistakable, despite my displacement.

"Hey," I said to Jazmin, returning her call. "Everything okay over there?" I asked casually, awaiting an explanation of her no-show.

"You first, you're the one who called for backup."

Maybe it was a lapse in protocol on her part, but I already leaned on her more than I would have liked lately, and only because of my injuries. "I'm fine," I said finally. "I spoke to Camille."

I gave her the background on how I'd seen her earlier, while my eyes tracked a large, shiny SUV driving right past me a little too slowly. My brain flashed back to my accident, but it was a different color. The windows were tinted, but it seemed like the passenger turned to watch me as they drove past. What the hell was that? I stepped a little further onto the sidewalk, now on the street looking in their direction. I shouldn't be out here alone right now, but I was twenty steps from my front door. Even so, my hand felt an empty spot on my hip, my piece was inside.

"You okay?" Jazmin asked in a moment of awkward silence.

"Um, yeah. This car just drove by very slowly. Probably nothing. What's happening over there?"

"Where are you?"

"On the street."

"Take cover. If a car's monitoring you, you shouldn't be standing outside."

She was right. "What's the dojo report?" I asked, changing the subject.

"We've talked through some details and have a plan in place. Traeger's in class now for the next two hours."

"Is Ivan's team there yet?"

"Hold on," she said, mumbling something to another person.

While I waited, I came out further into the street. The SUV had driven off. I stepped back onto the sidewalk to sit on a concrete slab that lined the driveway. I should be able to get at least a partial plate number if they come back.

"No, Ivan said they won't be here tonight. The actual operation is planned for Thursday," she said. Two days from now.

So there had been a dry run after all and Duga hadn't asked me to join. Maybe he thought I was bad luck.

"Did you see the tattoo guy?" I asked her, sad that I hadn't gotten down to Venice after all.

"Yeah, I'll give you a full report later tonight when I get there."

"Quick preview?" I pressed.

She sighed. "You can do it, but it's harder."

"Why?"

"I talked to Manny, he said you can certainly tattoo a corpse. It's just more challenging, not to mention fucking morbid."

"Agreed. Why more challenging?"

"Apparently gas builds up in the body and can change the shape, texture, and firmness of the skin. Rigor mortis, decomposition are some others, just depending on how soon after death the tattoo is applied."

"Did you show him the picture I sent you?" I'd sent her one of the two close-ups of Val Sharma's neck from Lin's autopsy images.

"He didn't say much. They could have been applied before death or after. He doesn't know of a conclusive way to determine that."

Shit.

· —————··•·•—————— ·

It was Tuesday, the night Derek and I usually had dinner to catch up and go over cases. While I was with Camille, he'd left me a voicemail that he was bringing Chinese food over in an hour, probably from Mama Lu's, always opting for his favorite foods instead of mine. That gave me time to do yoga before dinner, the first time in weeks.

Starting with some stretches, I noticed a new text from Tran that my broken washer was unfixable and needed to be replaced. And he just happened to have an extra, brand-new, never-used unit he could *give* me. Um…what? I'd just need to pay his labor charge. My mother told me if something seemed too good to be true, it probably was. But so far Tran had been trustworthy, and with the expense of my medical bills, that unit could be a godsend.

I let Trevor climb onto the cedar chest at the foot of the bed, staring me down with those big eyes as I rolled out my yoga mat, like he was telepathically reminding me that naps were a medical directive upon discharge. Yes, I understood their value, that they'd let my body and mind rest and encourage my concussed brain to heal correctly. Instead, I managed two rounds of sun salutations, pleasantly surprised by my strength and balance. When I got to the final pose, I remembered the recurring number from Val Sharma's phone. Here goes nothing.

It rang once, twice, obviously he was looking at the unfamiliar number and deciding.

"Hello," a man's voice answered as a statement rather than a question. I always tried to reserve judgment, but I liked this voice.

"Wallace McCoy?" I asked after a short pause.

"Who's asking?" Now I heard an accent I couldn't place. Not British. Something else.

"I'm a private investigator working on a case and have a question you might be able to answer."

I visualized Robert Redford and Dustin Hoffman in my mind as Woodward and Bernstein from *All the President's Men*, wondering if Wallace McCoy wore a tattered corduroy jacket or chain smoked. He could dress like a corporate banker for all I cared. I just needed him to tell me why he'd spoken to Val Sharma thirty times before his death.

"Would I be inclined to answer your question, do you think, especially since we don't know each other?"

So, this was how it was done. Leading questions, evasiveness, innuendo. Reminded me of my days as an operative, when I was always acting a part, being someone else. I didn't miss that.

"I was sent by Dr. Lin Hagen. Do you know him?"

"I don't think so," he answered quickly, which indicated he was telling the truth. "Look, private investigator, I don't mean to be rude, but I don't have much time now. What's this about?"

"I think you might know someone I know."

"I doubt it." A slight snicker. "Try me."

I bit my lip, remembering a similar case I'd worked on. "Kramer. Kelsey Jo Kramer."

"The name's not familiar. Is she dead?"

"What an interesting question," I commented, trying not to laugh at the poker game I'd inevitably started. How many of my cards was I willing to show? "No, but her coworker is."

"Dead?" he asked, this time in a softer voice, probably getting up to go into a conference room with a door by the sound of footsteps. He sounded surprised.

And that was the problem with impulsive moves like making a sudden phone call that otherwise required preparation. Derek would have preferred me to wait till he got here before I made that call.

"I think you know who I'm talking about."

Nervous laugh. "What exactly is it that you think I know?"

"Kelsey Jo Kramer's dead coworker. And that's not all. I think you might know how and why he died."

"It's possible. Who's her coworker?"

I paused but only for a brief second, to add to his anticipation. "Val Sharma."

The line went dead.

Chapter Thirty-Three

The bulbs should have emerged by now. I looked down at the neglected garden from the bathroom window, with the last spill of sunset on a dark blue background. The flowers here growing up were magazine-worthy. Daffodils and tulips, different colored poppies, now just dirt and weeds. Fitting. I kept reminding myself that I was here for a reason, maybe just not sure anymore that it was a good one.

Derek showed up late, so I had time to shower before dinner, but it took longer than expected. My bones and muscles ached from overdoing it today, or maybe it was my heart that hurt, knowing someone had harmed me on purpose. I understood it – we got too close to Traeger and the walls were closing in on him. Attacking me, especially by car, had been a great distraction diverting all our attention and resources to me and Duga instead of our target. The question now was whether any of Traeger's men saw Duga the last time we moved in on the warehouse, and if they'd recognize him at the dojo. Seemed like not enough time had been spent on that question. I'd ask Duga about it later tonight.

I opened the front door just as Derek was ringing the bell. His eyes lacked their usual sparkle, lined with dark bags.

"Hey, Partner," I said and slid my arm around his waist. "Thanks for dinner. What'd you get?" I said, laughing at the two giant bags.

"Szechuan Restaurant this time, Kung Pao 3 for me and Imperial Shrimp for you."

"And three times as much rice as we could possibly eat?"

"You betcha. I like leftovers."

I was grabbing plates and cutlery, when he shouted from the dining room. "Everything's already on the table."

Eating with chopsticks out of cardboard containers like nomads, an old debate and I was too tired and sore to argue. Derek talked about the dojo operation, logistics, and orchestration of our team, like where, when, and placement, which would end up being of tremendous importance if we wanted to pull this off.

"You're not really listening, are you?"

"Sorry, no." I wiped my mouth. "I was thinking about Camille."

"How did she look?"

"Bad," I shook my head. "She's tough and she found a way out, but she knows they're coming for her. I think she feels hunted. That can't be a good feeling."

"But even so, she sought you out...you, after all these years," he said. "That says something about trust. Don't you think?"

I nodded. "I guess so. Let's talk about what's on my list over the next few days. I know you're on Traeger so I can pick up the slack on our other cases."

"Actually, Duga's organized a pretty big team, so I can be here if you need me."

"What I need to know more about right now is this shell company Camille told me about, Praxis. That's the first thing. And I'm gonna start with Jo Kramer."

"Do you think she even knows about it, and will she talk to you?" he asked.

"About that?" I took another bite. "Depends on my approach. Jazmin did some tattoo research for me and didn't come up with anything conclusive about Val Sharma's throat tattoo."

Derek chewed and considered this. "So, what does that mean, exactly? You told me Camille and Hagen were unable to conclusively identify Sharma's cause of death. What were you hoping for with regard to the tattoos?"

"If the tattoos were applied post-mortem to try to simulate

strangulation marks, who was the tattoo artist and, more importantly, what was the real cause of death they were trying to hide?"

"And of course, who's *they?*" he added.

"Right. What I want to know about is the red dot on his throat, and the piece of paper they found in his mouth. Whoever did that wanted us to know how smart they are, and that they're ten steps ahead of us. Sound familiar?"

Derek nodded. "You're assuming another person, or party, put the note in the victim's mouth to throw the ME or law enforcement off track? Remind me what was on the note again," he said, as my phone buzzed with a call. Duga.

"Hey, Duga. You're missing Kung Pao from Szechuan Restaurant." I smiled at Derek and heard static in my ear. "Are you there?"

Derek stared, awaiting my answer. "Sorry, what was that?" he asked me.

"The note."

"ST9, and I have no idea what it means yet. Camille didn't either."

"Hey sorry," Duga said into the phone finally. "I'm downtown Santa Barbara. Cell service is bad here. What's ST9?"

"Still working on that," I replied. "There was a piece of paper inside Val Sharma's mouth, our John Doe, that had ST9 in red letters."

"Didn't you say there was a red dot visible on his throat, too?"

"Yes. Do you know what it means?" I asked. "I'm putting you on speaker so Derek can hear."

"Bro," Derek said into the phone after scooping more rice onto his plate.

"Where on the neck was the red dot, specifically?" Duga asked.

"I'm trying to remember Camille's drawing," I said, wondering why he was asking. "Right side, about halfway between the chin and collar bone. Why?"

"Interesting."

"In what way?"

"Well, there's a powerful Chinese medicine point for acupuncture or acupressure, ST9. It's a stomach point."

I stopped chewing to stare at Derek. "A stomach point on the neck?"

"Yes," Duga replied. "Is that relevant?"

"You bet, I appreciate it."

"It answers a question that leads to a hundred more questions,"

Derek said, rolling his eyes.

Duga chuckled. "Good, so now it's your job to figure it out."

"Yeah, thanks for nothing."

"Mari." Duga said. "I've got a specific Project Dojo job for you."

"I was starting to think you didn't want me on this mission."

Derek raised his brows. "She's not gonna like it."

"Aww, don't taint her, you never know," Duga argued. "I need someone strong willed, preferably tall, preferably female, preferably attractive—"

"If this has anything even remotely to do with Ivan, forget it." I liked hearing them laugh at my protest. "Glad to provide tonight's entertainment. Can't I have a more important job? I know I can't be on point right now, but geez. A babysitter?"

"Sorry, everything else is covered. Enjoy your dinner, guys."

"See ya," Derek said. Duga disconnected.

"So, what about the journalist?" Derek asked, spooning some of my Imperial Shrimp into his now empty Kung Pao 3 box. He noticed my eyes on him. "Yes, I'm eating your dinner. Why aren't you hungry tonight?"

"I don't know. My brain's on overdrive right now." I stabbed a shrimp with chopsticks and popped it in my mouth. Delicious.

"Wallace," I said, then paused to chew properly. "We were right. Wallace McCoy at the Chronicle and I had a short but civilized conversation today."

"Oh?"

"Well, somewhat civilized. He hung up on me when I mentioned Val Sharma."

"Telling." Derek smiled. "I'd like to go with you when you talk to him."

I bristled, annoyed. "You think I need protection, Detective?" I asked, knowing how he felt about my calling him that. His history as a detective had been short, too short, so it was a sore subject.

"I'm curious about this guy's role in Val Sharma's death. And yes, I think you do sometimes need protection."

I stared him down.

"Because of the accident, sure. Definitely because of that. But in general, too."

"Are you serious?"

"Look, isn't that why two people form a partnership?" he asked, brows knitted.

I put down my chopsticks and let it play out.

"What?" he asked.

"Nothing, I'm listening. I'm not interrupting you, I'm not gonna present your arguments for you like I usually do, even though I know full well what they are. Yes, we're partners. And yes, we support each other as much as we can."

Derek folded his arms and rested his elbows on the table.

"Okay, go ahead. What's your argument? I'll shut up."

He wiped his mouth on a napkin. "Just that if Wallace McCoy was Val Sharma's whistleblowing link, and now Sharma's dead, McCoy had to have had something to do with how Sharma's killers found out what he was about to reveal. And maybe he's in danger now, too."

"You think he'll run if I approach him? I wasn't gonna knock on his door if that's what you think."

"I was just thinking he'd likely be talking to one of his editors about the potential for a story."

Reasonable assertion, I had to admit. "What else?"

"Whoever offed Val Sharma, don't you think Wallace McCoy might be next? I mean, if they want to eliminate the people who know whatever he was gonna expose, that would be the smart thing to do."

I didn't tell Derek what I had in mind for Wallace McCoy. I liked the feeling of keeping a few details close to the vest, partners or not. Plus I didn't like his comment that I needed protection. My phone buzzed again from Duga.

"What'd you forget?" I asked, picking up.

"Remember when I told you what Traeger was doing at the dojo?" Duga asked.

"Jujitsu class I think, right?" I put him on speaker again. Derek dragged the phone closer to him.

"That, and I just found out he's also studying 1:1 with a master, learning a very controversial technique." Duga was speaking more slowly than a minute ago. Something was up.

"What kind of technique?"

"Something called *dim mak*. It's an ancient and controversial series of maneuvers that has two or three moves known as the death touch, where if you strike in a particular spot, the blows are lethal."

I breathed deeply, as an idea formed in my head. "I guess I don't have to ask whether ST9 is one of the locations of that death touch move?"

"It's interesting. We should talk in person. But there are one or two points on the body where a variation of this move, if done a certain way, can cause what's called a delayed death touch. See where I'm going with this?"

"Delayed," Derek said. "Like how much of a delay are we talking about? An hour, a week? If so, that's genius because how could you ever identify the killer?"

"Exactly, though it depends on a lot of variables, and much of the research on this is dubious at best."

None of us spoke for a few seconds, allowing new thoughts to form. "Whoever killed Val Sharma may have wanted his death to look like strangulation—" I started.

"And you're thinking someone else knew the secret of how he died and left the ST9 in the victim's mouth as a clue for the Medical Examiner?" Derek cut in.

"Someone who had access to the body, that is," I said, thinking it through.

"And the red dot on the throat," Duga said, "seems to have been in the exact spot of the point that would have been struck as part of a dim mak maneuver."

"So, if Val Sharma's killer arranged for someone else to tattoo ligature marks on his neck as a false clue," I said twisting my hair, "looks like someone else wanted us to know the truth, enough to leave a treasure map of how to find it."

"An associate no longer loyal to the cause."

Chapter
Thirty-Four

I spent an hour propped in bed reading about the historic shroud of secrecy surrounding *dim mak*. The vibrating palm technique seemed logical based on my readings of how *qi*, or energy, either moves or stagnates in the body. So I understood the concept of pressure points located along the different meridians or qi pathways. What I didn't yet understand was delayed death caused by the infliction of a *dim mak* move. Maybe in a comic book or a fantasy novel. But the reality seemed medically inconceivable. I needed an expert.

I found a website for a school in Los Angeles, which listed the extensive training involved in dim mak, referred to as combat neuroscience. Interesting to see those two words back-to-back. The protocol, broken down into 18 chambers, takes students through the rigors of anatomy, physiology, Chinese medicine, weaponry, and psychological training. It seemed like the nexus of acupuncture, martial arts, and psychology. Fascinating.

As I absorbed details of this new science, a thought began to solidify: a connection between Traeger and Val Sharma. Traeger's dim mak training made it possible that he also understood Chinese acupuncture points, which related to the ST9 point on Sharma's neck.

Lately I'd been wondering if maybe we'd been chasing the wrong man, thinking Traeger was someone else's soldier and the real perpetrator of the chain of bank heists was someone higher up in his food chain. Or maybe we'd been chasing the right man all along but for the wrong crime. Were the bank robberies keeping law enforcement focused on something other than his real crime? That slight-of-hand was more of a Jacques Martel tactic. But as a former profiler, it still didn't fit. We had to be missing something.

My lids were heavy. I leaned over to pull the chain on my bedside lamp as another truth began to emerge. The SUV that had slowed and watched me closely earlier tonight was the same car that tried to kill me at the warehouse. I didn't think so at the time but I now realized I recognized the face of that driver. They were close tonight. Too goddamn close.

<hr />

Morning came way too fast. I was grumbly on the phone with Derek as he reminded me of our scheduled meeting with Jo Kramer at 9:00 a.m. Shit.

"If you hurry up, I'll make it worth your while," he said, his voice painfully chipper.

"In what way exactly?" I was pulling on yoga pants and a sweatshirt. I know this was a professional meeting with an important witness, but right now every part of my body hurt. Besides, I was still reeling from the shock of last night's epiphany. So hell yeah I was dressing comfortably today and the world would just have to deal with it. I was sure Derek meant a vanilla oat milk latte with cinnamon, my new obsession. Fine, I needed it. Unfortunately, I also needed enough caffeine to get me out the door. I hated short cuts when it came to precious things like coffee. Today was an exception. Fully dressed, hair in a ponytail with bare minimum makeup, I made a Keurig Starbucks dark roast, poured it in a travel mug, and took it with me.

I still had the address of Jo Kramer's father's house, more like a villa, in the exclusive Pierpont Bay subdivision of Ventura Keys, a waterfront community in the southern part of Ventura. I typed the address into Waze and headed out, dreaming of my latte, planning my approach. Jo Kramer was friendlier than I expected she'd be. She also worked for a mathematics research firm and likely had an advanced degree. I really had no idea how I would approach my question. I took three large gulps of the disappointing brew and turned off 101 to get on East Harbor Boulevard. I caught sight of Derek's Land Rover parked twenty feet from the entrance. I pulled up right behind him and gave two swift knocks as I opened his door.

"Oh my God, that smell!" I closed my eyes and inhaled to the top of my lungs. "Breakfast burritos?" I asked like I hadn't eaten in a week.

"Are you crying?" he laughed.

"Almost."

We'd started getting them lately from Corrales Mexican Food on Thompson. He handed one to me wrapped in foil, just how I liked it, and sat hilariously in his driver's seat with a bib-napkin tucked into his collar, fork, and this gigantic, messy platter on his lap. I watched him, shaking my head.

"And your far superior hand-held burrito will be dry. Why would you want to eat it like that?"

"Because it's practical," I argued. "It's neat and portable. I barely even need a napkin. And look at you, King Henry VIII."

"It's a snack. Mine's a meal."

"Whatever." I unwrapped the foil and took a huge bite. Glancing down at the cup holder, I was delighted to see a large, double shot, to-go coffee cup. "Is this mine?" I mumbled with my mouth full, then stifled a laugh.

He nodded.

"You have no idea what this means to me today."

He smiled, checking me out. "Are you okay?"

"Kind of a rough night sleeping," I said, saying nothing of the SUV and its alarming connection to my diminished life expectancy.

Derek turned the radio to a news station. I turned it off.

"Excuse me, whose car is this?"

"Please, no radio today." We ate silently, alone in our thoughts for a few minutes. I paused to sip the latte and didn't tell him they'd put almond milk in it instead of oat. I could tell the difference.

"Ready?" he asked, wiping his mouth over an empty container that five minutes ago was literally filled with food.

I cracked up. "You're unbelievable."

Derek passed me my handbag from the backseat and we walked side-by-side down the long pathway approaching the gleam of the morning sea up ahead. Kelsey Jo Kramer's front door was wide open.

"Something's happened," I whispered, I could feel it.

162

Derek took the lead and motioned for me to stay behind him. He reached down to unsnap his holster.

"Kelsey? Are you in there?" he shouted into the cavernous foyer, fit for royalty.

"If we hadn't stopped to eat, we would've gotten here on time," I hissed.

"Don't start," he mumbled, moving closer to the doorway.

"Jo? It's Mari Ellwyn. I sent you a text this morning but didn't hear back. Are you alright in there?"

I saw her soft, blonde hair through the window in another room. She had to have been standing there silently listening to us call to her. She moved into the doorway. Her eyes were red and swollen.

"You'd better come in," she said. Derek and I stood in the foyer at attention, watching pain weave wrinkles in her young face.

"Why's the door wide open, Jo?"

Her gaze looked hazy, like she wasn't quite awake yet. "I, um, get claustrophobic sometimes."

"Close her door," I whispered to Derek.

I hadn't realized how slight she was the last time we saw her. Today she was wearing a tight, all-black outfit, five foot eight and looked like she'd fall if I blew on her. Her arms were wrapped around body, showing the tips of dark nail polish.

"Do you mind if we sit down? I'm a little sore today," I said.

"Of course, follow me." She took us into a study with four sturdy club chairs. Derek remained at attention in the doorway and I folded into one of the chairs.

"What's going on, Jo?"

She looked up and smiled, then that smile quickly faded to tears. She ran out of the room and returned with a box of tissues. "Bit of a rough morning over here, I'm afraid." She sat in the chair opposite me, Derek still in the doorway.

"What happened?" he asked, leaning on the door frame.

"Now someone else at our company's disappeared."

Chapter Thirty-Five

"Who?" I asked.

Jo Kramer sniffed, grabbed a mangled tissue from her pocket and stared at it. "Adam," her voice cracked. She lowered her head and wept, blotting her eyes. "Forgive me. Adam Matusik."

"What does he do there?" Derek this time.

"Director of Operations and Public Relations."

"You don't usually see those two areas lumped together like that," I commented.

"I know. Small company, people wear lots of hats. Adam does other things too." More tears. "Sorry."

I'm sure Derek and I were thinking the same thing.

"How did you find out?" I asked her.

"I've got a friend in HR, she called me this morning. Well..."

"Are you in love with Adam? Are you seeing each other?" I asked.

"Funny, isn't it, how the heart has its own agenda? I suppose y'all are thinking there's some connection, now, between Adam and Val."

"Isn't there?" I asked. "If not, that would be quite a coincidence."

"I don't know. None of it makes sense, and the whole team's freaking going crazy. Adam's one of the pillars at our company, you know." She smiled. "Someone who's always got a plan, everything under control."

"So, Val Sharma," Derek cut in. "He was the Marketing Director, right?"

She nodded, looking up at him.

"And now Adam Matusik, who's missing, was the Director of Operations and PR."

I angled my head back to get a good look at Derek's face, watching his eyes piece together a scenario. "You're wondering if it's a coincidence that Marketing and PR are now offline at this small company?" I asked him, still thinking about the bigger fish in this equation - Praxis.

"It makes me wonder what they were working on," Derek replied, looking at Jo for an answer. "When was Adam reported missing? And are the police involved yet?"

"Today," she answered quickly. "And I don't know a thing about the police. Adam's wife, ex-wife I mean, who also works for AEI, told HR that he hadn't come home from work last night and he's been unreachable by phone since lunch yesterday."

"Ex-wife, and they live together?"

"Yeah. Long story."

"Did you see Adam yesterday?" I asked.

"In the morning, and only in passing. He was running upstairs."

"Running."

Her lips formed into a sly smile. "He's always late. His brother's always complaining about it."

"Adam's ex-wife and brother work at AEI? What's his brother's role?" Derek asked, moving closer to the chairs.

Jo raised her brows. "Adam's brother *is* the company. Horace," she shrugged like we should have known that. "Horace Matusik is VP of Engineering. It's his research that put us on the map."

I blinked through this new series of facts. Adam Matusik and his ex-wife both worked at AEI, along with his brother. I wanted to follow up on Horace Matusik's research, but we needed to get to the witness interview about Val Sharma. I glanced at Derek and he nodded back. I loved our nonverbal communication.

"Jo, how closely did you and Val work together, like on a day-to-day basis?"

"Not at all from a professional standpoint. He's a marketing leader and I'm a mathematician. Nothing we did in our daily work caused our paths to cross, other than monthly marketing presentations to, sort of," she chuckled, "remind the technical staff that there's an outside world and they need to talk to them on occasion."

"What was Val working on just before he...disappeared?" I asked, careful with my words.

She stopped to look around the room. "You're thinking his death wasn't an accident, then." She wasn't asking. I watched her fumble with her hands, obviously making some sort of tacit decision.

"Well, considering the recent disappearance of your PR Director, it's a logical question at this point."

"I need to explain something. We all signed NDAs when we were hired, and last year some of us were *asked*—" she made air quotes, "to sign a separate NDA."

"For what?" I asked her.

"Special project."

"You were forced to sign?"

"Not that they'd ever admit. They made it seem like we were being invited into a secret club or something."

Derek was seated in the chair next to Jo with the three of us in a semi-circle, Jo with her back to the front entrance. "We're not asking you to break any confidentiality agreements," he said. "But if the police question you about Adam Matusik, or Val Sharma, they might require you to do just that to enable their investigation."

"I'm not being coy, for real. I don't know what Val was working on because we didn't talk about work. We were buddies. We sat in the kitchen during lunch and ate hotdogs while playing chess."

"Any contact outside of work?" Derek asked.

Jo pointed to the fireplace. "He painted this room with me, along with another work friend." She rose. "I'm sorry I can't help you further."

Derek had five fresh questions on his lips, I could see it. I eyed the door, while Jo crouched over a little table in the entry writing something.

"I hope everything turns out alright with Mr. Matusik," I said. When Jo shook my hand, she placed a folded bit of paper in my palm. Derek was walking to the door. I waited till we got in the car to tell him.

"She gave you that?" he asked, eyes wide.

I ignored the question and read aloud. "They've probably bugged the house. Star Lounge, 7:00 p.m., outside the ladies room. We can talk there."

Chapter Thirty-Six

Ten hours later, I was standing in a cramped, smelly passage holding a beer I didn't intend to drink. "Do you want this?" I asked Derek, who loomed over me outside the ladies room of Star Lounge.

"You love beer. You don't want it?"

"Not tonight."

"Sure, I'll drink it. I can't say no to beer. It's like saying no to sex."

"Do we know if she's even in there?" I asked just as the door opened.

"I was making sure it was empty and the door had a lock." Jo Kramer smiled back at us and peered into the main room. "Good evening. Come on in."

Jo had changed into baggy jeans, a long t-shirt and old sneakers. She looked rough, eyes still puffy.

"Interesting place for a meeting," Derek said.

We huddled near the sink. Music was playing loud, but there were no bands till the weekend.

"Are we gonna talk or what?" I asked with a sigh. It came out harsher than I would have liked.

"Well, what do you want to know?" Jo's tone of annoyance made it seem like she was doing us a favor. But she'd asked us here. I tried to reserve judgment.

"Val was a whistleblower, wasn't he?" I asked the rhetorical question.

Jo nodded and bit the inside of her lip. Shifted her feet.

"What was the second NDA for?" Derek asked.

"That," she said. And we stood there together, hanging on the words she hadn't yet said, holding our full glasses of beer with the smell of urine on the air.

"Jo?" I asked.

Her eyes widened.

"What are we doing here? Do you need us to guess so you can't be blamed for violating your NDA?"

Lips pinched, Jo shook her head. I could tell she was a loyal person. Maybe this conversation felt like a necessary breach only because of desperate circumstances. I could see the war going on in her face.

"You all work for AEI. So, what's Praxis? Do you work for them, too? Did Val?"

Her blue eyes widened and her mouth opened. "Where in the hell did you hear that name?" she asked.

Now it was my turn to be coy, not ready to mention my conversation with Wallace McCoy.

She took a long breath, held it, then exhaled with her eyes closed. "Okay, you've been doing your research obviously. So yeah, we all work for Praxis," she said, finally. "They're the mother ship. AEI's just one of its many, how shall I say, investments, you could call it."

Derek set his beer on the grimy sink. I felt his impatience building. "Was the second NDA you signed about the existence of Praxis?" he asked.

"No. The mother ship wasn't a huge secret, or not to everyone. We get our paychecks from AEI. But when you see your bank statement, you see that AEI is a d/b/a for Praxis. The issue isn't that the company exists. A number of people know about it already."

I watched her glance at the ceiling. Was she looking for surveillance equipment? Had it come to that? I looked too, but only found stained, grimy ceiling tiles.

"The issue is what they're doing."

"Keep going, Jo."

She leaned against one of the stalls and crossed her arms, eyes

169

locked on Derek. "The NDA had a bunch of legal mumbo jumbo about how we were legally prohibited from talking about something called Project Mercury." She laughed. "No one knew what the hell it was about. I'd never even heard the term Mercury before. Or not in that context."

"Val Sharma knew, obviously," Derek said. "He never spoke to you about it?"

"He did and he didn't. He talked to me but I didn't realize, you know, until he was - gone, that's what he was talking about. Sometimes we both worked late and we'd stand out in the empty parking lot for a while hanging out, chatting, sitting on our cars, sometimes for an hour. Val started asking me hypothetical questions, like would I take a risk and tell a secret even if I knew it might hurt someone. I told him it was entirely context-sensitive and hard to answer without having the details."

"Did he tell you anything specific about Praxis?"

"No. But after that night, this would have been over a month ago now, our lunchtime chess games stopped. We never left work at the same time anymore, which meant no more parking lot chit chat. I think he changed his hours to avoid having to talk to me. He was at work, but he sort of broke contact. I tried to talk to him about it, but he said he was fine and just busy."

"That must have hurt you," I said as a question.

"I knew it wasn't personal, and I had a feeling he wasn't allowed to tell me."

"Meaning?" Derek pushed.

"Meaning he was being forced into something he didn't want to do and was threatened if he talked. Whoever threatened him probably knew we were close."

"What else?" Derek asked. "Any other details about Val you can share from that particular week? That would have been the week before he disappeared."

Jo sighed and bent forward with her hands on her knees.

Someone jiggled the door handle from the outside. Time was running out.

"He looked skinny," she whispered, "like he was losing weight. And he was traveling a lot. I saw him with a suitcase a few times. He'd be gone for three or four days at a time."

This was by far the most important witness interview we'd done recently and neither of us had recording equipment. I hadn't brought my handheld recorder, my phone recorder wasn't turned on and, at this point, it was probably too late. What was wrong with my brain?

I took a perfunctory sip of the cheap beer, sacrilege. "NDA or not, you brought us here to tell us something about Project Mercury."

"I don't know much," Jo countered. "Praxis is run out of the Caymans. Val did share that much. He called it a shell company created by lawyers with a post office box and no digital footprint whatsoever. Guess that was the point. When I asked about its mission, he said 'you don't want to know'."

Derek and I exchanged quick looks, watching Jo nervously tap her fingers on her hip. "But you do know, don't you?" he asked.

Another set of three knocks at the door, followed by someone jiggling the handle. Jo's blonde head shook. "Praxis is secretly building a quantum computer." She paused to allow us time to make the right assumptions.

"To do what exactly?" I asked, remembering one of my first assignments as an intelligence analyst. "And isn't that like ten-billion-dollar hardware?"

Derek's eyes flashed, wondering how I knew about this. I winked back in our secret language.

"At least, depending on the number of qubits, and not including software or the cost of research or a facility," Jo clarified. I recalled the term *qubits* as being the quantum computing version of a classical computing bit.

Derek was nodding. "That's the purpose of the shell company, I imagine. The only way you could essentially hide billions of dollars of expenses and keep them off your balance sheet."

Jo nodded.

"By now there are many companies building quantum computers," I said. "Not just IBM and Google anymore. What's the endgame? And has AEI been involved in this?"

"Primarily anyway, AEI's been focused on mathematics applications from the beginning, and still today."

"Something in the equation, not trying to be funny here, must have changed though," Derek said. "If we confirm that Val is indeed dead, his death was not likely accidental, and now Adam is missing. We need more information."

"Quantum computing's mainly used for cryptography," Jo

explained. "Praxis is using it for integer factorization for encryption."

My mind raced. "So, they're developing an encryption algorithm to give them market dominance—" Jo nodded as I was talking— "over IBM and Google or something?"

"Why?" Derek asked. "I mean, what's the payoff?"

I remembered a similar case from my previous life, a corrupt executive at a tech giant funneling illegal funds into a similar project.

"What?" Derek asked, watching me.

"The term is quantum supremacy, right? All these companies vying to outdo each other." I looked at Jo.

"That's right. It's all about speed. The number of qubits you have allows you faster computational speed, vastly faster, unfathomably faster than classical computing models. It's mind-boggling."

"How are there competitors if no one's supposed to even know about Praxis?" Derek asked, practical as always. "Is that what was about to happen? Val found out about Project Mercury, or he was brought into the fold and was gonna go public with it?"

Jo gave a curt nod. "They've been able to hide the fact that their investors have been moving billions of dollars in and out of that company to build this beast."

I looked at Derek. "Wallace McCoy," I whispered.

"That's what I was thinking."

"Who's that?" Jo asked.

"A journalist, someone Val called repeatedly in the days right before he disappeared."

"How would you know that?"

I closed my eyes. "We have his cell phone," I replied with not just a little bit of shame.

"Okay, that explains something. I saw them," Jo said. "Adam and Val arguing one night in the lobby by the elevators. It was dark and no one else was there. I was walking downstairs and heard them. It was pretty heated. Adam was shouting 'Never! Never in a million years.' He said it several times. And Val said something like 'I have no choice now.'"

"Adam would have opposed the idea of going public about Praxis?"

"He's one of the principals. Look what he'd have to lose. He answers to Horace, and Sebas—"

Our heads simultaneous jerked to the door in response to a

banging. "I don't think anyone's in there, it's been locked for a while," a woman said outside the ladies room door.

"Who's Sebastian?" I asked.

"Well, Horace, VP of Engineering, answers to Sebastian, the CEO, and to Daniel, who's a sort of mentor."

"Who wears the pants, though?" Derek asked.

Jo tipped her head and thought about it. "Val thought Sebastian was Daniel's puppet."

"Is Daniel a principal of Praxis?"

"I don't have that answer, probably because I'm not in the inner circle. And someone's waiting for this room."

Chapter Thirty-Seven

June
Santa Barbara

I woke early the next morning feeling utterly lost. Coffee wasn't helping. With all the details and complexity around our meeting with Jo, it came down to just one question: how much did I actually believe of her story? I took my time getting dressed, and an hour later I was headed north on 101 toward Pismo Beach. I'd arranged surveillance of Wallace McCoy through Jazmin, who discovered that he hides out in an ocean-front condo writing on his balcony on the weekends. Famous, she'd said of him. Everybody knew him down there. Well, I had about two hours to devise a plan to draw him out.

I loved the oceanfront running trails in Pismo Beach, especially Dinosaur Caves Park that took you over a long wall of bluffs overlooking the crashing waves. But there was no time for running today even though my lungs were dying for the endorphins. Who was I kidding? My body wasn't ready for that anyway.

The water to my left looked as bewitching as the aqua sea in Tortola. That all felt like a world away. My phone rang, Derek, probably checking to see if I'd left yet.

"Hey partner."

"How's it going?"

"Just checking in on you," he said. We churned through the details of our meeting with Jo. "Something's bothering me about what she said about that NDA. She was asked to sign it, but she also said she wasn't in the inner circle. That doesn't make sense."

"Inner enough, I should think," I replied. "Or maybe she's in as far as she wants to be. She seemed pretty rattled by everything that's happened."

"I saw some resolve from her, though, like she needs to know the truth now."

"Do you have time to run down this Daniel fellow?" I asked.

"Yeah, I'll see what I can find out about him and also Sebastian, starting of course with Praxis."

"Sounds good."

"Be safe up there today."

•———••••———•

101 traffic was surprisingly light. Ninety minutes later, I rolled slowly past 367 Ocean View Avenue, as Jazmin had directed me. Light, terracotta stucco with a tile roof, two mature palm trees out front and turquoise tinted glass – facing the water. Beautiful. Either Wallace McCoy came from money, he knew someone and got a deal, or he had alternative income sources. Probably the latter, but good for him. He lived well. I parked on a side street and crept slowly up the stairs. His front door had a mail slot next to it, perfect. I knocked four times, medium-hard, medium-fast. Of course he was home. He was writing. Where else would he be?

"Yes, who is it?" someone said from behind the closed door. It was the same voice as the man I'd spoken to.

I stepped back two paces so he could see me through the peek hole. "Marissa Ellwyn. We spoke on the phone?"

Five second pause. Then, "I'm sorry, I'm rather busy. And I have nothing to say."

Prepared for this, I pulled two 8-1/2 x 11 photographs out of my bag. One of Val Sharma from the AEI company masthead, the other a morgue photo of his body before autopsy. Ruthless, I know. For now, I held them between my fingers, waiting.

"How did you find me?" the man asked with irritation.

I couldn't help but smile. "I told you on the phone, I'm a private investigator. That's what we do. We investigate. You come down here to write every weekend."

"What do you want from me?"

I pulled open the mail slot and slid the first of two pages through. I heard it swish onto the floor. "I think you know this man."

I heard a long sigh. It was a small triumph, but I'd take it. He knew him. Of course he knew him. So that meant Wallace McCoy had met Val Sharma in person too. Strike one.

"When was the last time you saw him?" I asked.

"Look, I've got nothing to tell you. I honestly know nothing that could possibly be useful to you about this man. I barely know him. We had one, maybe two—"

"Phone conversations?" I asked. "Try thirty over a two week period." I dropped the other photo into the mail slot.

"Oh my God," he moaned and took a step back.

"As you could have been one of the last people who saw him alive, I think the police might be interested in asking you a few questions. Have they already?"

The lock clicked. The door opened into a broad foyer. The man wore black slacks and a V-neck sweater with nothing underneath but skin. I moved slowly through the doorway. He stood about an inch over me, mostly bald with a scruff of grey on the sides. Late forties, handsome, good bone structure and a nice tan. Fake? Maybe. He wore black reading glasses on his forehead, and I'd bet he forgot he even put them up there. He rubbed his face with both hands while staring at the images on the floor. I picked them up and returned them to my bag.

"Wallace McCoy?" I asked, gently.

He nodded and looked up, this time taking a moment to appraise me. "Tall *and* a redhead. Are you trying to kill me? Come in."

I followed him to an outdoor terrace in the back of the house, unable to contain my smile at his comment. I found a pristine, white-cushioned furniture set on a terrace that faced a private garden—a separate terrace from the one out front facing the ocean. He brought me here because it was private and no one would hear us. Or at least I told myself that was the reason. I had my gun in its holster on my hip, covered by my jacket. I'm sure he suspected as much.

I pulled my phone out of my purse and searched through my apps.

"Do you mind if I record our conversation? It's standard when—"

His palms went up, face flushed. "I'll only talk to you if you don't."

"Fine, no problem." It was a fun ploy I'd used before. Useful because it made the witness feel like they'd gotten their way, putting them in control and, simultaneously creating an atmosphere that now they owed me something. I tucked my phone back in my purse and contained my grin.

"Look, I'm sorry about the shock therapy," I said. "The photographs. You needed to know how urgent this is."

"How did he die?" the man asked, perched on the edge of a chair leaning his elbows on his knees.

I shook my head, deciding in that moment how much I was prepared to reveal about this case, reminding myself that I was here to data-mine, not to let Wallace McCoy do the same to me. "I don't know. But we're pretty sure it wasn't accidental, as you could surmise by the photo."

"Do you work for the family? I assume the police are involved."

"No and yes. I'm trying to piece together a picture of the final days leading to Val Sharma's death. Your phone number showed up on his phone with a number of calls in the two weeks preceding his death."

He sat back in the chair with his feet on the ottoman. White tennis shoes that looked like they'd never stepped outside. No socks. I liked the look. Very European.

"What did you talk about?" I asked.

"You must know something about it or you wouldn't be here. Why don't you tell me what you know and I'll either confirm or deny."

I hung my head and sighed. "I honestly have no patience for this cat and mouse nonsense." I bent to pick up my purse and something creaked in my lower back. "Ouch."

"Bad back?"

"No, I'm fine. I'm gonna just—"

"How about we switch it up then," he said.

I stared, studying the faint lines in his face, the fixed position of his mouth, and the bright white of his eyes offsetting the dark blue irises. "What did you have in mind?"

"Well, I may have a few questions of my own."

"About?"

Wallace tilted his head sideways, and smiled in a way I never expected of a stranger. It felt warm. Fondness almost. An odd feeling came over me in that moment, pregnant with anticipation. Of what, though, I wasn't sure. He'd made a comment about my hair earlier. Was he just attracted, or was it something else? I kept staring, analyzing him in my facial database. Did I know him from somewhere, had I met him before? I reached behind me and rubbed the lower right side of my back. Something had gotten pinched the way I was cushioned in the puffy chair. I shifted, pulling out so my feet were flat on the floor.

"Preparing for a fast getaway?" he asked.

"Always."

"I would think with your background you'd have all kinds of resources available."

"Sorry?"

"You know, for investigating Val Sharma."

The tiny smirk on his mouth told me he was enjoying this, having information I didn't, using it to manipulate my interest. I had neither time nor tolerance right now for these games. I needed to connect with Jazmin and Derek on the Traeger robbery case. I rewound his words a few seconds and shook my head.

"Background. Have you been doing research on me, Mr. McCoy?"

He didn't answer.

My heart rate rose and my mind started spinning. "What, my website? I'm not important enough to have a Wikipedia page, if that's what you mean."

"I was always curious what it would be like to spend years under deep cover and then come out into the open with a more legitimate, visible profession."

Everything got very still. I felt like a teenager who'd just been caught creeping back into the house smelling of marijuana at three in the morning.

"I imagine that would be hard, yes," I said, keenly aware of his every micro-movement and glad to keep things hypothetical.

"Well, especially, as I've often thought, when your career in the intelligence community gets you shot on a container ship in the middle of the ocean."

Jacques Martel. How could this stranger possibly know this? I stared, unblinking. Who the hell was this guy?

Wallace McCoy, who had just become my adversary, sat back and crossed his arms, smug son-of-a-bitch. I felt naked while some part of me cried inside. The gun on my belt dug into my skin. Thank God. He obviously knew I'd been shot by the notorious Interpol "red notice" criminal and my lifelong nemesis. I marveled at how I hadn't even thought of his name lately. And here he was, worming his way into my life and work again.

"Are you gonna tell me who you are?" I asked. "I'm guessing you're either not really a journalist, or maybe just not only a journalist."

He didn't move right away, so I bent down to grab my purse as a gesture of the end of our conversation.

"Oh no, I am a journalist and I have no other official profession. As a journalist, I analyze facts, lies, details, and put them into stories."

"Have we met before, Mr. McCoy?"

"Perhaps not in the traditional sense." He rose and motioned me with two fingers to follow him into his house.

"What do you want from me?" My voice cracked and I didn't care how unglued I sounded now. I wanted to get out of there to call Derek. Something had told me I shouldn't have come here alone. Why hadn't I learned the lesson about backup, and why was I always without it when I needed it? I checked in with my internal danger radar. Nothing about Wallace McCoy, save what he'd just said, felt dangerous. In fact, loathe to admit it, I felt drawn to him. Something I couldn't put my finger on. It's true, I'd been shot by Jacques Martel himself, not one of his army of underlings, because my team and I had gotten too close to one of his scams. If McCoy knew these details, he or one of his associates had to have been on that ship at the same time or knew someone who had.

"I need to show you something, so you understand."

Right. Nothing creepy about that. We moved down one hallway and he pointed to another. Time seemed to slow in that moment, like in the basement scene of *Silence of the Lambs* when Jodi Foster finds herself in the dark, knowing the fate that was about to befall her. Was this man, this stranger, about to harm me? I consulted my sixth sense. The jury was out.

"Please," he whispered, standing directly over me now. "I would never hurt you."

Chapter Thirty-Eight

Wallace McCoy led me down another hallway, then turned right into an awkwardly small bedroom. I stopped outside the door, watching, reminding myself how to find the front door from here. Would he motion me in first, or ask me to follow him? I checked my inner radar again; something in me knew I was safe with this man, despite the contradictory signs. I followed him, watching him flip a wall switch that turned on about ten small art-lamps positioned all over the perimeter of the room. The walls were covered with paper, clippings, notes, interspersed with small white boards with black writing on them.

"What is all this?" I moved a few steps toward the wall, squinting. "Is there an overhead light?"

"A terrible one." He flipped it. It was terrible - too dim and turned everything yellow. He turned it off.

I nodded and inched closer, now recognizing something. Hair. The shape of a head, cheekbone. Jesus. Was I seeing what I thought I was seeing? I grabbed onto the lip of a glass desk. It felt cold. Fucking Jacques Martel. Would I ever be rid of him?

"Here, sit. I know you're still not recovered." The man helped me lower my suddenly weak body into a desk chair with wheels.

I looked up, searching. "Recovered. That's two, Mr. McCoy. Two things you know but shouldn't know about me. You have exactly ten seconds to tell me what's going on or I'm out of here."

"Alright, fine. Martel, as you know, is a crime boss. Not mafia, but independent. With vast means, resources, and genius wit." He started pacing in lecture mode. "He disguised his profession early on, as you well know, as an international art dealer, but this was a front."

I shook my head, trying to puzzle out the possible reason behind his obsession with my nemesis. "Why are you telling me this, and how do you know of my connection?"

"He has a veritable army of underlings who are carefully vetted, expertly trained, most of them ex-military. To say highly paid is an understatement. Martel inherited billions of stolen cash from his father and he's made his own billions from two decades of his well-oiled crime machine. They're a family of criminals going back generations. Most of this you knew already."

I nodded, blinking back.

"But he's careful what he invests in," the man added, and crossed his arms to wait for my response.

"Invests," I said, to which he raised a brow and smiled. "Interesting word."

I got up and walked the length of the room, looking more closely now to the wall art. Jacques Martel photographed on a boat, in a living room, standing in a circle with several other men, fifty or more long-range photographs of one of the most notorious criminals the CIA had ever studied.

"All he cares about is money. And power," I said.

"Rarely seen outside, he's said to be somewhat agoraphobic. He never married but supposedly," he paused to watch my face. "He has a son. Somewhere."

Again, he let another word hang in the air like a million-dollar quiz question.

A son. Okay. We'd been talking about Val Sharma, who was East Indian. Martel was white, so not likely. I moved back to the chair when my lower back pulsed again. A son. Wallace knew I'd been shot by Martel three years ago, and obviously he knew about my more recent accident. The accident where Traeger and his men rammed an SUV into my body to stop me from investigating their cache of stolen bank booty. My God, it couldn't be.

"Traeger?" I said in a dreamy voice. "You think he might be... Martel's son?"

Wallace gave a single nod.

I felt sick. "How could you know this? Conclusively?"

Now he sighed. "I don't, conclusively. But we think he's the son. We suspect he is."

"Who's we?"

"A team of us—"

"Team?" I cut in. "Who?"

"Analysts, investigators, field ops, profilers who have studied the legacy and track record of Jacques Martel for twenty years. And you," he pointed. "You're an indelible part of the Martel story. And now you're on Traeger's radar. You need to be very careful."

"So Traeger killed Val Sharma?" I asked, only thinking it as the words came out of my mouth. "The dojo." I put my palm over my mouth.

"What dojo?"

"Traeger works out at a dojo where my associate teaches. He's studying an ancient martial arts technique."

The man nodded and looked at the floor. "Dim mak maneuvers provide fatal blows to a victim and are virtually undetectable by law enforcement or forensic pathology."

"Nothing's undetectable nowadays," I argued.

He tipped his head. "This is. It's called delayed death and it's not a myth."

I was remembering what Duga had said about it. "Okay...why Val?"

He moved his index finger in a circular motion.

Me figure it out? Okay. Let's see how much I've been paying attention. "Val Sharma was a whistleblower about to blow the top off of a company called Praxis."

The man nodded.

"But did Val have a connection to that dojo?" I asked.

He didn't reply. The dark blue eyes blinked back.

"I guess the fact that they exist, their relationship with AEI, and the fact that they've built a quantum computer is... I don't understand. Why would Traeger or Martel care about Praxis?"

"Think about it."

Was Martel the bank behind the Praxis quantum enterprise? He certainly had the means, from what I remembered, and from what Wallace had just confirmed. "Are you saying Martel wants to own the crypto market? How can he do that?"

"I'm not saying you're right, but others on my team have had the same speculation. He can do it by creating a rock solid, unhackable crypto hash algorithm."

I was remembering how Jo described this.

"It's like a super secure blender that turns any information—"

"Wait, like what kinds of information?" I asked.

"Anything you'd want to protect. Files, data, financial transactions. It turns them into this unique, unbreakable code that has this magic property." The man's eyes widened. "It's nearly impossible to ever figure out what went into that blender to create the code."

"So it can't be reverse engineered, then." I nodded.

"Right, and you'll never be able to replicate it, either. No other pieces of data will ever be able to create that same code. So this hash algorithm, or code, protects sensitive information, ensures it will never be compromised, and keeps your data safe. And when it comes to crypto, this feature is more important than ever."

"Praxis has done this?" I asked. "Conclusively?"

"With Martel's money, resources, hardware, and staff. We think so, yes."

"Jesus." My mind went to Jo Kramer, wondering how her lover, Adam Matusik, might be involved. "Wait, what about the robberies?" I asked. "And what about my—" My voice caught in my throat, thinking about the cold rebar I'd been rammed into by Traeger's car. I felt McCoy's hand on my shoulder. When I turned my head, I saw a tall vase holding an exact replica of the yellow roses that were on my dresser when I came home from the hospital. Had Wallace McCoy, this stranger, sent them to me? How could he have known?

"That was you?" I asked, pointing to the vase.

"Guilty."

His eyes were open wide, watching my reaction. "They tried to kill me. That was Traeger, right?"

"Yes."

"Does he know who I am?"

"Yes of course."

"I mean—"

"I know what you mean. Traeger knows about you because your

team is working with Ivan Dent and LAPD to try to take him down. But more than that, he knows you're entangled with his father, and that entanglement goes way back. Listen to me." He crouched so he was eye level to me. "Don't underestimate Traeger. Your team might get him, but you'll never have him long. Martel's network is too vast."

I laughed. "What, they'll break him out of prison?"

"James Traeger will never set foot inside a prison cell."

I got up and started pacing again. I needed to call Derek. "What are we supposed to do? He needs to be prosecuted. He's stolen millions of dollars. And he's still doing it!"

"I know. But you can't touch him."

More pacing, this time outside of the room. I examined the hallway and moved to a small room directly across from the room with the Martel wall.

"Please, don't go in there. It's a sort of –"

I stopped short, catching sight of something familiar on one of the walls. I couldn't breathe.

I flipped on the light switch and marched to the wall. "What the hell is this?" I couldn't stop my involuntary tears. I was all over this wall.

My heart pounded. My lungs couldn't find air. It was my face, hair, profile, alone and with other people. Walking, working, driving.

The man slid his arm around my shoulder. "I'm –"

I shrugged it off with a violence that surprised me. I turned and pushed him with open palms. He fell back onto the floor. "What the fuck is going on?"

He rose and blocked the doorway.

My hand moved toward my gun. "What are you doing?" The boom of my emotion-ravaged voice bounced off the walls. "I came here to fucking interview you. You!" I wiped my eyes seeing pictures of me with Derek, me with Duga, alone sitting in my car, a vintage CIA photo with Roger McGuin, my former boss. My eyes kept scanning the wall. One with my father. Jesus. "I want an explanation, now, or I'll have you arrested for stalking."

I watched him, this man Wallace McCoy, as he prepared to speak. His face, his eyes, and his body looked respectful but not contrite. He wasn't sorry he'd illegally spied on me for years, maybe decades. Motherfucker.

"You were part of the research I was doing to investigate Martel," he said quietly. "I was following him while you were hunting him with your team, so at some point it was natural that I also followed you and your activities. It was my job, Mari. My job, do you hear me?"

"Right." I wiped my eyes.

"At first, anyway. I guess I got a little smitten and sort of went overboard." He stood back, straightened his shoulders. "I'm very sorry, Ms. Ellwyn," he said as a formal declaration. "I feel like I know you by now. I know I've breached your privacy in the vilest way possible. It's unforgivable. Maybe someday I'll convince you that I meant you no harm."

Chin lowered and eyes on the floor, it wasn't a bad apology, really, except I knew he wasn't sorry. I thought about tearing down the photographs, but they might be glued on instead of taped, proving difficult and time-consuming, maybe keeping me here even longer. Forget it.

"What's your connection with Martel?" It was a question I should've asked an hour ago.

"Interpol."

"Interpol?" I laughed but felt like crying. "I knew you weren't just a journalist."

"I am, sort of. I'm French. Actually, I have dual citizenship. My job title is Forensic Police Data Management Official, but essentially I'm a journalist who does research all day and never publishes a thing."

"You learned of Martel through that post?"

"Learned? Martel's exploits catalyzed the majority of offices and roles there. He's the organization's greatest embarrassment."

"They never found him?"

"They're hoping to through Traeger. He's his Achilles heel. But no. Not yet. Jacques Martel is still, and may be, forever at large."

Chapter Thirty-Nine

Still shaken from my meeting, I followed Derek's instructions and parked in a bank lot across the street from the Akido Center and Dojo. The air felt warm and thick, stagnant almost, the sun mockingly bright overhead. I would have preferred to go home and crawl into bed for the next hour, pretending the world didn't exist.

With everything else going on, it wasn't difficult to compartmentalize the melodrama with Wallace McCoy. I guess I was used to marginalizing my emotions, as one therapist put it, pretending I didn't feel rage, violation, horror. And God help McCoy if Derek, or worse, Ivan, found out about his creepy little shrine.

But in that tense encounter, I'd learned some interesting facts about my nemesis, Martel. Because of my accident recovery, and because Derek had always babied me when it came to personal safety, I was the backup's backup in the Traeger operation, relegated to a lookout post across the street. At least I knew what Traeger's team drove, from having observed their fleet for so long now. I texted Derek and relayed my position and that I'd seen no sign of Traeger's team so far.

How'd your journalist interview go? he texted back.

I gave a curt *long story* reply and quickly changed the subject to ask about timing. But I knew he wouldn't drop it.

He's in class right now, three people plus the instructor. Duga's got Francone and Jazmin watching out front, and Ivan's team is in position.

Where are you now? I asked.

Smoothie shop next door. Stand by.

I'm watching, I wrote, pulling binoculars up to my eyes.

From this distance, I could see inside the dojo from the large, front windows. Three younger men, one could possibly be Traeger, listening to an old man talking. I texted Derek as much. The men bowed to each other. Before the students walked away, I moved my view to the right and saw Derek walking out with a smoothie in one hand. Behind him, I recognized one of the officers on Ivan's team. Back in the dojo, the four men remained in a circle. Traeger, I could see him clearly now, was the tallest. The one in the middle turned his head left and right, then pulled back two paces and walked toward the locker rooms on the east side of the building.

I've seen him, Traeger, standing with three other men inside, confirmed. Be careful.

When I picked up my binoculars again, my view was blocked. I headed down the street partially hidden by parked cars, binocs in hand. I couldn't see anything now but heard raised voices.

"On the ground, on the ground, now!" The sound bellowed out from an open window in the building.

I froze, waiting, staring. The door to the dojo sprung open from the inside. I saw Traeger emerge, hands cuffed behind him, with Duga glued like his shadow and Derek behind him. I watched Traeger's face and he hadn't so much as flinched. He didn't smile, smirk, eyeroll, nothing. Almost like he'd expected this all along. Ivan's team filed in from the east side on the sidewalk, guiding the cluster to a squad car parked at the curb a few doors down. One officer opened the door and two others, whom I didn't recognize, took custody of Traeger, one on each arm, and mirandized him. I watched it in slow motion, remembering what Wallace McCoy said. With that thought, I texted Derek.

I wrote *Wallace McCoy said Traeger will never see a prison cell.*

Done deal at this point.

Too easy, I typed back.

We'll see.

My eyes glued to the scene diagonally across the street, I took a few more paces toward the dojo eyeing traffic in both directions. No black SUVs, vans, or even trucks in the past few minutes. I called Derek and watched him pick up, standing across the street from me now.

"Hey, nice job," I admitted, yet still waiting.

"Yeah, I think we're good. They're about to—"

"Listen to me," I cut in. He saw me now and nodded.

"What's up?"

"Something you don't know about him. Can you hear me?"

"Yeah…I hear you. What?"

"Traeger's Jacques Martel's son."

He paused. "Are you fucking kidding me?"

"I learned this from Wallace McCoy. Just passing it—"

Before I even got all my words out, the ground rumbled. The vibration and the sound bounced me off the sidewalk and crumpled me against a parked car. Still facing the street, I opened my eyes and saw a blue sedan emerging from a cloud of black smoke driving away from the dojo, and behind that car was another vehicle engulfed in flames. I tried to stand. My ears were blocked.

A car bomb had gone off just after we lowered Traeger into the squad car no more than twenty feet from the dojo's front door. No, please no. I pulled myself to my feet to look for Derek, thinking the worst. He was leaning against a storefront looking at me and pointing at the ground. He bent low and picked up a set of handcuffs. Fuck.

I jogged across the street. "Are you alright?" I asked, out of breath. Derek shook his head and pointed at Duga, who was stumbling across the sidewalk toward us.

"Hey," Derek went to him. "You okay?"

"Still breathing if that's what you mean," Duga replied.

"So he was tipped off," I said.

"I saw the getaway car, but no plates," Duga added.

"I think I did too, a blue sedan?"

Duga nodded. I could see defeat in his eyes. Twice, now. First my accident, and now this. The black smoke wasn't clearing. My eyes were on fire but I knew rubbing them would make it worse. I heard an ambulance finally several blocks away.

"Was anyone in the dojo hurt?" Derek asked.

Duga pointed. "I was headed there next, I'll let you know."

I pulled out my phone and called Ivan. "Please tell me your team's okay."

"Alpha Team's accounted for, yes. You okay? Your team?"

"Do you know about the blue--"

"We're on it," he cut in. "We have the plate number. It won't be long now."

I hung up without answering him and gave the report to Derek.

"Won't be long now, good one," Derek mocked. "And now Ivan's team will be setting up roadblocks everywhere, assuming he'll be leaving town."

"He's not leaving town," I said. "That would be too obvious. He's gonna hole up somewhere planning his next bank heist."

There had to be ten car alarms going off at the same time, no doubt triggered by the rocking vibration of the blast. The block was lit up by police cars and fire trucks snaking their way through. Derek, Duga, and several dojo students were on the ground against the building, helping each other up.

"Ma'am, please back away from the car," an officer said with his arms outstretched.

"She's with our team." Derek motioned me forward. The man reluctantly stood aside. "Are you alright?"

Derek's hair and clothes were disheveled. Black ash had splattered on his left cheek. "Did I hear you say, not one minute ago, that Traeger would never see the inside of a cell?"

I raised a brow and nodded. "McCoy."

"What does he know about Traeger?"

"More than we do," I answered, soberly, reminding myself of right-timing and how this wasn't it.

I checked on Duga one more time, got text replies from Jazmin and Francone, then I left my car parked in the bank lot and drove Derek's car back to my house. I'd pick mine up later – if it wasn't towed. I asked Jazmin to meet me at home if she was available.

"Nice of you to drive," Derek said, as I helped him into the passenger seat.

"Take it slow, okay?"

"My ear's a little blocked and my head feels funny."

"Mine too," I said. "And I was across the street. You should've waited for the ambulance and gotten checked out."

"Pot calling the kettle black maybe?"

"Funny."

"Nothing a beer and a steak dinner won't cure."

"Are you ever not hungry?"

Derek winced as he pulled the seat belt across his chest.

"Let me help you with that."

"Stop stalling and tell me what happened with Wallace McCoy."

I clipped his seat belt and put mine on. "What's the issue?" I asked, genuinely curious since I hadn't told him a thing about it.

"Just a feeling that I shouldn't have let you go there alone."

I didn't like the word *let*, but honestly I had bigger problems right now. I debated whether to tell him about McCoy's obsession. My little voice told me to not mention it. But wasn't this why I wanted a partner in the first place? To help me understand things, interpret clues, draw conclusions. Okay fine, here we go. Probably a bad idea to do it while I was driving, or maybe that was advantageous. "Remember the yellow roses someone sent me in the hospital?" I asked.

"He sent them? How—"

"Precisely my question as well. How did he know I'd been in an accident? Turns out he's been following my career ever since I first started following Martel." It was a strategic way of saying stalking, though not completely untrue. He had definitely been following my career.

"Former CIA?"

"Interpol."

Derek nodded. "So he sent the flowers to let you know someone was watching you? Or to warn you about Traeger?"

"Are you sure you don't need to go to an Urgent Care? I'm serious. You don't look well." I glanced at him peripherally but didn't dare look because he knew all my tricks.

"No urgent care. And don't think I didn't catch that slick redirect. Fine, keep your secrets."

"He's harmless," I said, wishing I could believe it myself.

"We'll see."

Chapter Forty

I chilled for a long time on my sofa in complete silence while Derek cleaned up. Yoga breathing always calmed me down and was a good opportunity to check in with myself. Psychologists called it self-regulating. To me, it always felt like an unnecessary indulgence, but tonight I knew I needed it. Maybe the McCoy problem would just go away and I'd never need to see him again. A text from Lin Hagen interrupted me.

Val Sharma's tox screen came back negative for drugs, nothing out of the ordinary.

Interesting, and that may be true. But then why would the body still be missing? Nothing about Sharma made any sense. I didn't bother replying, because I knew Dr. Hagen wouldn't tell me where he was, what he was doing, or confirm any wild theories about what he'd really been doing in my foyer that night. The tox screen results were a notable detail, but made me wonder what specifically had been tested.

I served Derek prison rations of bread and water, then hovered, observing him closely. A car bomb had just exploded a few feet from him. The human body, as I knew too well, was unpredictable. An hour later, he seemed okay, so we drove to the bank where I picked up my car. On the way, I told him what I'd learned about Praxis from my new Interpol connection.

"So far, that seems to track with what Jo Kramer told us," he mumbled, rubbing his temples.

"Did you take the ibuprofen I left out for you?"

"Yes, doctor. Waiting for it to kick in."

"I want to see her again, Jo. I think I should go alone this time, too. She's afraid. She might feel more comfortable talking just to me."

"Am I that scary?" he asked.

"Hell yeah you are. Look, I've asked Francone to see what he can dig up on the two names Jo Kramer gave us: Sebastian and Daniel. I'll talk to Jo and see if there are any developments with her Director of Operations who disappeared."

"Nothing from Hagen?" Derek asked, as I climbed out of his car.

"I don't like leaving you alone right now," I said.

He walked around the back of the car to the driver's side. "Now you know how I feel most of the time."

Standoff. We just paused there, six feet away, letting the words fill the space between us. "Hagen said Val Sharma's tox screen came back clean. And that's another one."

"Another what?" he asked.

I let out a long exhale. "Exactly how many people connected with Val Sharma are either missing or dead?"

"Camille, Hagen, Adam Matusik," he said. "But now that you put Martel at the head of the table…"

"I know. Things look a bit different, don't they? Wallace thinks it's Martel's money that's financing the whole Praxis operation. Whether AEI is involved in research for quantum computing, we don't know yet. Are you sure you're all right? I hope you're going home now."

"Yes, straight home."

"You'll feel better tomorrow," I said.

"I'll feel better when we've tracked down our escapee."

Between Ivan's team at LAPD and officers from Ventura, three teams of trained law enforcement were scouring the area around the bank for James Traeger. Something about his connection to Martel made him instantly more important and less attainable. We had to find him; traditional means would get us nowhere. If Wallace was right and Traeger was Martel's weakness, it was my job to find Traeger's weakness. And Jazmin was the perfect trump card.

In the time Derek was at my house, the temperature had dropped about fifteen degrees. I stopped home to grab one of my long sweaters, calling Jazmin when I pulled in. Jazmin's background, for a woman of twenty-five, still blew me away, considering myself at her age. As if MIT as a sixteen-year-old wasn't enough, she'd used her hacking skills, disguised as IT prowess, and turned them into marketable, highly paid commodities prized by various government entities. She never told me who she'd worked for specifically, maybe the Department of Defense, doing ethical hacking work to help companies build unhackable software. I parked and started up the walkway, and found her sitting on the front steps.

"You startled me."

"Hey. How are you feeling?" she asked, smiling for some reason.

"You were closer to that car bomb than I was. Are you okay?"

"You know me, I'm indestructible. What's up?" she asked.

"Did I miss a joke?" I'd stopped ten feet from my front entry. Leaning against the door was a tall vase of yellow, long-stemmed roses with a white ribbon, a tiny card, and a small box the size of a hardcover book. It hadn't been mailed; a delivery person wouldn't likely leave the flowers and box unattended.

He'd been here. Wallace McCoy, at my house. Jesus.

"Mari? You okay?"

"Sorry, someone left me something at my front door."

"Yes, I see that," she said, eyes wide waiting for an explanation.

"I need your clandestine IT skills," I said, not wanting to deal with the explanation and knowing this job would more than just pique her interest.

"Clandestine. You mean dark web? Oooh, fun," she said and rubbed her hands together.

"Not necessarily, but we need to uncover Traeger's weakness, as well as who busted him out. I'll just say look wherever you can. And watch your back."

"You got it."

Armed with my favorite dove grey, cashmere sweater, I grabbed a thin scarf from the coat closet and coiled it around my neck before pulling the flowers and package inside the door. I'd deal with them later.

I headed back to AEI to ask Jo Kramer some follow-up questions. I knew I was on her shit list after our ladies room meeting, but I needed my pound of flesh before she completely shut down. And who knows, I might be comforting to her right now. I sent her a text first asking to meet outside for a quick question, then realized it was late and she might have left work. I found her waiting at the curb, standing in flat shoes, skinny jeans, and an oversized jacket wrapped around her thin frame. Her blonde hair gave her otherwise bookish looks a lightness, fooling the world.

I parked and rolled my window all the way down. "Jo. Working late tonight?"

"What are you doing?" she asked, eyes stern in disapproval. "We can't meet here like this, out in the open. Pull around there." She pointed to the right. "Drive past the parking garage, don't go in but drive past it and park in one of the spots back there. I'll walk down."

She looked paranoid, biting her lip, glancing left and right. I did what she suggested, resisting the urge to look up into the windows towering over us in the only skyscraper in Ventura. Who might have been watching us, wondering who I was and if I was likely to get in the way of their plans? Watching her move down the decline toward the parking garage, I tried to imagine Jo Kramer's world. Recent college graduate working as a software developer, maybe one of the only women in her department and very likely the youngest.

She approached the driver's side window.

"What's so urgent?" she asked, glancing behind her.

"Did something else happen?"

She looked up and shook her head. "I'm scared. Shit's going down right now."

"Why are you here then?"

"Where do you suggest I go?" she asked, sighing, leaning on one hip.

"Jo? Talk to me."

She gave an anxious laugh and glanced behind her.

"Where's Adam Matusik?" I asked, diving head-first into the deep end. I watched her face as I said his name. Her eyes filled up.

"There's been no news. I haven't seen him since the last time I saw you." She raised her brow. "No one has."

"Are the police involved? Have they come around interviewing you yet?"

Jo's eyes rose. A guilty pose.

"You're hiding from them? Wow, that's not gonna make you look guilty or anything."

"I've got nothing to hide! I'm just here showing up for work, dealing with all this crap myself."

"I know you're in a difficult spot."

"They warned me not to talk to the police," she whispered. "Or anybody else."

"Who? Who warned you?" I leaned in.

"Work. You know. HR, other people I hadn't met before."

"Did they say they were with HR?"

"Not exactly."

"AEI employees?" I pressed.

"Maybe. Or maybe Praxis. I have no idea."

So they were already silencing her. "What do you think Val was about to expose when he disappeared?"

She peered at me, deciding something. Her eyes looked strange. It was a risky question because she'd answered it the last time we saw her. But I felt in my bones that she'd only given us a crumb. She was agitated about the situation, annoyed with me showing up here. But I had to move this investigation along faster because now, according to Wallace McCoy, this was a Martel operation. And ultimately that meant that my life was in danger. Again.

"Praxis. I told you," she whispered.

"You mean the fact that they exist? Had the principals been concealing that?" It seemed illogical to hide a ten-billion-dollar company.

"That's what the shell company was," she said. "A cover. The idea was that no one would be able to trace the activities of the shell back to AEI."

"Or at least not anytime soon, I guess. And when you say activities, do you mean buying the computer hardware, or software development, or what?"

Jo went silent but kept staring, indicating yes, I was on the right track, and she was only willing to confirm certain details of my questions. I had to think fast. That invisible door was already starting to close.

"Could be either of those. But what Val was about to expose wasn't that. The IRS might be slow but eventually the trail of money would be discovered."

"Look Jo, I'm trying to figure out why you lost your friend and, as it's looking now, possibly another co-worker. I don't think Val was killed just because he was about to expose the development of a quantum computer."

She blinked her long lashes, watching me piece it together.

"What, you think they can hear you ten stories up?" I asked.

"Nothing surprises me up there anymore. I need to get back."

"Wait—"

"Okay, you're right." She nodded. "And it's not just a quantum computer."

"What do you mean?"

"It's *the* quantum computer," she clarified. "Faster than any of the other quantum computers in existence today. Or that's the prevailing notion anyway. Arrogant bastards. They were already full of themselves before this."

"Even still," I said, as I thought. "Would revealing that to the world be enough to kill for?"

"Maybe not, unless Val was also about to reveal what they're planning to do with it."

"Was he?"

"Only one person can answer that now. The journalist Val had been talking to."

That meant another discussion with Wallace McCoy. Fabulous.

Chapter Forty-One

I got home from my meeting with Jo and collapsed into the arms of my cushy sofa, the kind you melt into and then can't get back up. Out the vertical living room windows, slivers of night sky peeked through the dense trees; beautiful, yet even now I longed for my old view from Ocean Park. Duga picked up Trevor and took him for a walk earlier and was keeping him overnight. Trevor loved sleepovers at Uncle Duga's house. Of course he did; Duga had a gigantic doggie bed and gave him too many treats. Even without barking, Trevor's quiet presence could fill up a room. Tonight, there was emptiness, blessed perfect emptiness that my mind had been craving.

I paced the creaky floors to quell my restless energy, thinking, then plopped into my dad's chair in the library. I could still picture his brawny shoulders sticking out past the edges of the frame, legs crossed like an intellectual, eyes narrowed in defiance of all that was wrong with the world. My mind had so much to sift through, I needed more than just peace and quiet. I needed a full-on retreat. When was that ever gonna happen?

I went to the kitchen, poured myself a glass of pinot grigio, and returned to the front foyer, ignoring the yellow roses while cautiously eyeing the box left by Wallace McCoy. I shook it, it was light with what sounded like paper inside. Probably a love note. It would have to wait.

No sooner did I return to the thinking chair when my phone buzzed, interrupting my space. Derek. *I'm with Duga and Robert. We have some news about AEI. Thinking about bringing dinner over. Are you up for some annoying houseguests?*

God help me. These were people I considered family, who took care of me after my accident. No, I sure as hell wasn't entertaining houseguests right now. *I can Zoom in about fifteen minutes. Will that work?* I typed.

I brought the flowers to the kitchen, resisted the urge to throw them in the trash and set them on the counter near the sink instead of in the middle of the table. I wouldn't give Wallace-the-Admirer the satisfaction. Would wondering if it had a surveillance bug in it make me seem paranoid? Of course he'd know that I'd be suspicious. I drummed my fingers on the sink, then grabbed the flowers from the stems, no thorns thank God, emptied the water, refilled the vase and felt every part of the surface. I inspected the flowers themselves. Unless a bug has been pushed down into the petals, they were clean. Get a grip, girl.

I sat at the table with my nearly empty wineglass now, fondling the flat, cardboard box with fingers still scarred from my accident. What did I think it was, a ransom note? I pulled it open on one end, half expecting a handwritten note, or maybe a marriage proposal, to pop into my lap. I pulled out a large sheet of paper, which turned out to be thick, glossy photo paper. My God…where did…

Tears filled my eyes, I couldn't stop them. After all this time. Richard Ellwyn—my weak spot.

I stared at the 8 x 10 inch black and white image of my father and me standing together talking on the Santa Monica Pier, leaning back against the railings facing the water and half-facing each other. The photographer must have been on the other side no more than eight feet away from us. I hadn't noticed him because I didn't know him, until now anyway. I remembered that day, about two years ago. After our contentious dinner in Tortola, my father came back with me and stayed in Santa Monica for a week. Before sunset, I'd go running on the beach and he'd take Trevor for walks on the pier, then we'd get coffee down the street at Philz. Did that memorable week make up for how he was absent for most of my childhood? Odd—in some ways maybe it did.

I knew I had a spare 8 x 10 portrait frame in my bedroom closet because the last one I bought online came in a two-pack. I flipped over the picture and saw some hand-written script:

Can I see you?

The question was signed WM. Without thinking, I took a pen and wrote *yes* under it and texted a picture of it back to Wallace. Why was I willing to see him? That wall, it made me feel targeted and vulnerable. But the truth is, I felt sort of drawn to him, a truth that made me feel even worse. What had I just agreed to exactly? Great job, Mari, as usual asking the right question too late.

"Hello, hello," I said with too much exuberance, computer on my lap on my bedroom chaise with my favorite picture of 18th century-era watercolor cranes behind my head. It was a perfect video background. Thank God I'd wiped my eyes and dabbed depuffing solution under them, followed by a dot of concealer and some lip color. Passable, at least.

"Looks like happy hour's already started," Derek commented from one of the Zoom squares.

I raised my glass and took the last sip but no longer felt festive. I tucked the forbidden picture back into the cardboard box and kept it on my lap out of view of the screen.

"Duga and Robert with you?"

"Coming," Duga bellowed in the background.

"Jazmin?" I asked.

Duga angled his head toward the upper part of the screen. "I heard she has a date."

Derek's brow rose and he looked behind him. "Duga knows all, apparently."

I liked hearing this, often wondering who she was leaving behind when I called her at all hours. "Good for her."

"So, Sebastian Wainwright," Derek said, moving his face closer to his laptop screen.

"He's the CEO," I recalled from their website.

"How would you know that?"

"She never sleeps. She never did in college either." Robert Francone peeked at the screen from behind Derek.

"Hey handsome, nice to see you." I winked.

Derek made a pouty face. "You never call me handsome."

199

I eyerolled him. "Robert, tell me about Mr. Wainwright. Sounds like a British name."

"Not a bad guess. He's South African, and one of the AEI founders," Derek said.

"And in his spare time he…" I let my voice trail off with a raised brow.

"That's where it gets interesting," Derek cut in.

I suspected as much. "Sebastian Wainwright is the CEO of AEI and on the Board of Directors of Praxis. Correct?"

Derek nodded.

"Do we know who else is on that board?" I asked.

"Horace Matusik, who also works at AEI." Derek's brow stretched, waiting for my brain to kick in.

Jo Kramer had mentioned him. "The brother of Adam Matusik, the Operations Director."

"The one Jo Kramer's in love with?" he replied.

"That's an unproven theory at this point. Anyone else of interest?"

"Yes. Daniel Ito. Mr. Wainwright's mentor."

"Yep, Jo mentioned him, too. Do we know where they live?"

Derek looked back at Robert, who was sitting on Derek's sofa behind his desk chair. "East Coast," Robert confirmed. "Is that important?"

"Just curious if they spend their time here or overseas. Like the Caymans."

"More than likely," Robert said, "if Praxis has a physical location at all in the Caymans, it's a rented storage unit paid by the month without gas or electricity. More likely just a PO box."

I sighed and set my glass on the table next to my chaise. "So, where's the payload? We're talking about hundreds of millions of dollars to build a gigantic and highly sophisticated piece of technology."

"Working on it," Robert said, tight-lipped.

"You must have a few ideas."

Robert nodded, but wasn't willing to commit yet. "I've heard about similar operations like this in Eastern Europe, like Albania, but for hardware as finicky and sensitive as this, you'd need to control literally every variable. More likely Western Europe. My guess would be Germany. Munich. I'll know more on that soon."

Derek got up and Duga took his seat.

"You look tired. How are you holding up?" I asked.

"Tired's not the word. There's a detail Robert came across in his AEI and Praxis research."

"Another board member?" I asked.

"Right."

"Well, I might have guessed Dr. Hagen, or even Wallace McCoy, but for the look on your face..."

Duga stared back and shook his head slightly.

No, I thought. Please. "Not...Traeger?"

"Traeger."

"No! He can't. My God."

"Which essentially confirms," Derek said from behind Duga, "that Jacques Martel, Traeger's father, has funded the construction of a quantum computer."

Wallace McCoy had intimated this when we spoke. I felt sick, suddenly.

"Why though?" Duga shook his head. We all took a beat to breathe and take that in. "It's an incredibly complex and expensive proposition, with no immediate return and the potential for massive financial loss."

"Maybe he's funding AEI's research to develop a quantum algorithm to claim it's the fastest quantum computer in the world," Derek added.

I stared. "And when did you become—"

"Are you kidding? It's a well-known tech innovation race, but it still doesn't answer the larger why. Mari, you know him better than anyone."

Loathe to hear it, he was right. I did know him. "Well, besides his grandiose tendencies and adoration of humiliating law enforcement, Jacques Martel cares about money. So there's only one reason I can think of why he'd be doing this: to take down the crypto market. The question is, what are we going to do about it?"

Chapter Forty-Two

We stayed on Zoom for another few minutes talking logistics about hunting down the two AEI top dogs, Wainwright and Ito. I had no intention of traveling to New York where they both lived, but Robert agreed to fly out for a quick 2-day trip while Derek and I hit up our primary witness again.

Duga dropped off Trevor with two new squeaky toys—comforting on his teeth and gums, and a great relaxation tool for high strung Great Danes. I knew the thuds and squeaks on the stairs would likely keep me up, but I was glad to have him back home, never quite at ease alone in the Frankenstein manor.

Chew toys or not, I wasn't sleeping. I was horizontal at least in my favorite white silk pajamas, eyes closed, under the covers, my mind running in circles. I kept going back to the notes I'd found in Camille's car with her observations about Val Sharma. With so much time considering the red dots on his body, I may have ignored the most important detail.

I grabbed my phone and found the photos I'd taken of those pages. Running through crime scene photos, the bank, Wallace McCoy's house, Trevor, there. There were five, and I think the notation I needed was on page one. There it was again.

Tox, standard, non?

Hagen texted me yesterday, out of nowhere, to inform me that Val's toxicology screen came back normal with nothing out of the ordinary. What I needed to know was what Camille meant by the word "non".

I opened Chrome and typed in "non-standard toxicology tests" and found articles on non-DOT, or Department of Transportation drug tests, typically used in pre-employment testing. No, not what I was looking for. I knew from previous cases that things like psychedelic drugs were difficult to detect on a standard tox panel. I knew there was something here, something beyond my reach. My eye lids felt heavy but energy – maybe anxiety – buzzed in my chest.

Derek was picking me up at eight tomorrow morning, as Jo Kramer said she'd grant us five minutes at 9:00 a.m. How bloody generous of her. I leaned over to look at the bedside clock, 1:30 a.m.

I had three options. Alcohol, warm milk, or just get up and pretend it was morning. I'd done it before. My body felt tired, though. I knew it would eventually surrender to sleep. Trevor's huge head popped up when I swung my legs to the floor.

"Did you miss me, big guy? Alright fine, tiny snack. Come on."

Coming down the staircase, all I could think about was the night Lin Hagen first broke in, and the shock I felt looking at a part of the wall that seemed to be undeniably glowing. I paused at the bottom of the stairs, but the wall still looked as it should. I had to have been dreaming it. Trevor nuzzled my hand to remind me of my priorities. Thankful my nightlights were working, I found my way to the kitchen and grabbed two maple bacon treats, feeding Trevor out of my hand. He put both pieces in his mouth and reclined prostrate on the kitchen floor to enjoy, chew, and swallow properly. Expert eater.

I tiptoed around the corner, crouched to the floor and peered upwards to scan for the strange bluish aura I'd seen coming from behind the wood-paneled wall. Even from this angle, nothing. Still not satisfied, I moved slowly to the foyer with my back to the mudroom door.

The barely detectable light was green now, not blue. Holy shit, there it was. Maybe I wasn't crazy after all.

Palms sweating, I needed time to investigate without distractions. Summoning Trevor back to the kitchen, I tossed a few more treats in his dish, then resumed my vigil before the glowing wall, up close this time.

A tiny, pinhole light that looked like it came from an LED night-vision camera device looked me in the eye, reminding me of an old sense of dread, of intrusion, that what I thought was privacy actually wasn't. I'd read about these devices on spygadgets.com, if it was the same device. They were supposed to be night-activated, so if I turned on a light or used a flash beam, the device would sense it and the light would go out. Now crouching so it was eye level, I put my forehead on the millwork and saw a tiny screwhead with a mini bulb in the middle. It was that bulb that emitted the green LED light. I shuddered. Jesus.

My heart raced. I ran upstairs to grab my phone, with the padding of footsteps trailing me, my loyal sentry. I texted Francone. Would he kill me for waking him this time of night? What time was it, anyway? I counted to five; he was calling me back already.

"What happened?" was how he always started conversations at 2:00 a.m.

I snapped a photo and texted it to him. "Check your texts. Is this what I think it is?"

"Lemme see," he said.

"Wait, I'll call you right back." I disconnected and called him back on Facetime. "Here we go." I aimed the phone at the wall, almost touching it. "Too close?"

"Back up three inches," he said, rubbing his eyes.

I retreated. "Now?"

"I can see it."

I felt like crying. "Is it—"

"Looks like a mini screw nanny cam. Video and audio. Very high quality considering the cost. Probably a Tadi, 360-degree streaming camera with DVR. About $3k."

"Who the fuck… How would—" My voice cut and I paused, took two long breaths trying to think logically, tabling my emotions for later.

"Can I meet you there first thing in the morning? I'll take it all apart and find out what's connected to it, you know."

"What do you mean? I assumed someone was using an iPhone app to monitor it." Like that's not bad enough.

"Is your front door locked right now? Windows locked? Go check please."

I did it, even though I'd already checked them. "Confirmed,

everything's locked. I feel like going to a hotel."

"Not a bad idea. Okay, don't freak out when I tell you this, but there's probably a laptop back there somewhere," Robert said, softly.

"Oh for fuck's sake. Seriously? A laptop?" I felt nauseous. My brain flooded with questions one after the other. Who was watching and listening to me, and why? Somehow, I knew it had something to do with Jacques Martel and Traeger. I wondered if maybe Wallace might know something about it, not that he'd installed it but he might be aware of it. Or had he installed it himself as a voyeur? Oh my God. "I seriously might get sick right now."

"I would too. Look, I've texted Jazmin. She's on her way over there now. I recommend you go upstairs to bed and try to forget about it for a few hours. I'll be there by eight and—"

"Don't bother sending Jazmin. I'm going out to sleep in my car." I hung up.

I didn't come close to either sleeping or going out to my car. I thought about one of my favorite scenes in the original Tomb Raider movie, where Lara Croft hears something ticking inside the wall of her house under a staircase. She just happens to have a hatchet handy—of course, she's a Tomb Raider—and crashes it into the wall, splinters flying everywhere. She discovers a tiny room beneath a staircase containing a crate with a ticking orb. Unfortunately, in my case, the ticking orb wasn't likely to be an ancient artifact with a note from my father. More likely a laptop showing that someone has been spying on me, watching me parade around the house in my silk pajamas, or a towel, watching and hoping for some specific piece of information I apparently had in my head.

I didn't dare touch the wall or the device facing the foyer, though I'd already revealed my knowledge of it and called Robert. Whoever was watching me knew that I knew, or they would soon enough. But right now, at 2:30 a.m., I was more interested in what the device was connected to.

First things first: I texted Jazmin trying to get her to go back to bed, but she was already on her way.

Next, I sat on the bottom step of the grand staircase in the dark. My initial inclination had been to go outside and walk around back. There was the basement window, the bulkhead doors, which had been rusted closed for over a decade, and a large, steel, side door in the back that only Tran and I had keys to. But the perpetrator…I shivered. Even the word made my back tingle sitting here alone in the dark. Whoever had installed this elaborate system was likely nearby so they could monitor their installation. That meant they could be outside watching the house right now. I crept over the creaky floors from the foyer to the kitchen, where Trevor sat at attention, watching me closely, curious but more interested in more treats appearing in his dish.

"No, Mommy's not okay," I said, pulling open the basement door.

My finger instinctively touched the wall switch. I needed to see, somehow, what was attached to the tiny screw camera in the foyer without revealing my movements to anyone watching outside. From the basement, the only view in was from the single set of horizontal ceiling windows facing the back yard to the east. Still standing on the top step, a shudder of terror shot through me like lightning: what if they were already in the basement?

Starting my rhythmic breathing, I climbed back up the two stairs, closed the door to prevent Trevor from following, then ran upstairs to get my gun and holster. Belt on with my Beretta M9, I headed for the staircase again. I had my phone in one hand with the brightness set to about 30%. The basement was pitch black. I used the flashlight on my phone kept to a low setting to light my way down the stairs.

I wondered if my new washing machine had been installed yet. It was supposed to have been last Friday; I hadn't had time to check. Good thing it wasn't my primary means of washing my clothes. Come to think of it, my last two texts to Tran about arranging payment had gone unanswered. Was he traveling? It was too risky to be surveying appliances right now. I sat in silence on the bottom stair, phone pressed to my chest, listening, letting my eyes adjust to the dark.

What was that odd smell? Tran had found a couple of dead mice down here last summer and we'd had a disturbing conversation about all the ways they could have died without a trap. He never determined the cause. I suddenly longed for the safety of my kitchen.

Not a sound now, I couldn't sense any human presence down here, but that assessment was of course inconclusive. Even so, I had to know where that screw camera led. I craned my neck to look back up the stairs to gauge the geometry of the foyer compared to where I now sat. The other side of that foyer wall panel would be around to the left side of the staircase and up pretty high. There was literally nothing over there though. No ladder, no way of getting enough elevation to even install it.

Or there wasn't the last time I was down here.

Maybe the camera installation happened recently. After all, had I ever noticed a glowing wall in the foyer when I'd lived here before? No, but I'd only been back for just over a year. I gathered my courage the way I'd been trained—to focus on the mission and block out every other thought from my head. I knew what I had to do. Get up, now.

I craned my neck and shoulders to peer behind me to the left. Seeing only darkness, I stayed there, breathing, for a full minute. As my eyes adjusted, I saw what looked like intersecting lines in the dark. Squinting now, I could make out a kind of scaffolding positioned against the back wall. How in God's name would someone be able to get that piece of heavy, complicated, and loud equipment into my basement and put it together without my knowing?

The only person who had outdoor access to this basement besides me was Tran.

Could he have seen something down here, or someone?

Chapter
Forty-Three

Dogs just know things. Trevor woke from his food coma and started nuzzling the basement door in the kitchen, making his agitated whimpers. The door thunked every time it pushed against the frame. I came back up and sat on the floor with him, taking stock. It was 3:05 a.m. and I was alone here. Despite my vibe test and what my eyes had seen, some tiny speck in my brain told me there was someone in my basement. Of course, the logical thing to do would be to a) call the police or b) wait till morning, call Derek and, with he and Robert, figure out the truth of how the nanny cam was installed in my foyer. I could also bring Trevor down there with me. But if I found anything, he could lick or sniff something that might later contaminate a crime scene. Three deep breaths.

Phone in one hand with the flashlight engaged, why was my can of mace never within reach when I needed it? I no longer cared if someone outside saw the beam. Armed with the false bravado that comes with curiosity and desperation, I moved down three steps and stopped to assess. The smell I'd noticed was stronger on the right side, but my intuition was leading me left to see the scaffolding. I reached the bottom step, breathing steadily to stay focused. The scaffolding equipment extended about eight feet up. It had to have been constructed here in the basement, but how, when, and why install something so elaborate? It didn't make sense. I tried to remember the last time I was down here and in particular this corner of the room. Ten months, a year, maybe longer?

The scaffolding materials were made of heavy steel bars and rods. They looked sturdy enough to hold a thousand pounds of weight. So... why? I moved the light beam upward and stopped when I caught sight of a small laptop perched on a sort of shelf. My back felt cold suddenly. I rotated left and right to make sure I was alone. Nothing else looked out of order. Moving closer to the scaffold deck, I shined the light behind the laptop. A wire connected it to the back wall, looking like someone had drilled into the concrete block walls. What were they looking for that would necessitate going through so much trouble and expense to watch me? They could have used a ladder, but needed a flat surface for the laptop. This can't be happening.

I stepped carefully toward the right side of the staircase. The odd smell got stronger with each step. All I could think about was growing up here and all the lies I told my parents to avoid coming down here. Illness, nervous conditions, almost like I knew back then that something like this might happen someday and that truth had glimpsed my adolescent brain twenty-five years before it happened. I reserved judgement and kept going, one agonizing step per second.

The flashlight landed on something shiny—the new washer. This was bad. Why? Because it meant Tran definitely had come down here to install it after all. Three steps later I had definitive evidence of what I was looking for. Tran never left.

• ——— • • • ——— •

Without thinking, my fingers found my phone and pressed Derek's number. "Hey. Can you do a crime scene intake?" I'd whispered the words as if Tran might hear me. I heard Derek groaning and rustling his bedsheets on the other end of the line.

"Are you crying? Where are you?"

I just stood there, stunned. I couldn't move, one hand over my eyes, then covering my mouth. The smell I'd detected, oh my God. If I had magical powers, I'd transport myself out of here, literally anywhere.

"Hey, answer me. What's going on at 3:45 in the morning?"

I sniffed and swallowed, blinking to make sure I was seeing clearly.

"I'm in my basement."

"Are you alone?" he asked.

"Interesting question. Not exactly." It was so quiet down here, too quiet. "Tran is dead."

"I'm so sorry." I knew Derek would be carefully calibrating his questions and tone of voice. "You discovered him?"

"Yeah."

"He's in your basement?"

"Yeah, I'm looking right at him."

"Have you called it in?" Derek asked in his investigator voice, more awake now.

"Yeah, that's what I'm doing. Can you do the intake?"

Long sigh. "Sure, go ahead."

That meant I would narrate a series of details, which he would record for me. I started with the obvious facts. "I'm in the basement of my home in Santa Barbara. There appears to be a dead man lying on the floor clutching something."

"Are you certain no one else is down there? Are you safe right now?"

"I honestly have no idea. But I think so."

Short pause. "Okay. What's in his hand?" Derek asked.

"I don't know yet."

"Miraculous you didn't grab it out of his fingers. And that means please don't," he emphasized.

"I won't."

"And you recognize him, right?"

"Yeah, it's Tran, my landscaper. The poor guy."

"Do you know his last name?"

"I think that is his last name." I was shocked by my composure and ability to simply report the facts of what I was seeing in this grotesque scene in my family home. I was trained for this sort of thing, but still. "I've been standing in one spot in the basement since you picked up your phone. My legs don't seem to want to move."

"Do you have a flashlight?"

"On my phone."

"What do you see? Go head to toe."

"Jesus." I paused and breathed, unable to prevent the putrid stench from entering my lungs. I needed air right now to keep me from passing out. "Professional hit, one shot in the middle of the forehead, small caliber, maybe a .38, maybe smaller, I can't tell from here."

"How far are you from the body right now?" Derek asked.

"About two feet. Nothing else noteworthy, eyes are closed." Thank God for small miracles. "He's wearing what he usually wears. Loose fitting jeans and a plaid flannel shirt, work boots. No jacket. Judging by the smell, I'd say he's been dead about two days."

"You told me you'd been trying to reach him," Derek said. "I'm sorry. What a shock. Listen, I texted Jazmin. She's outside right now and she's gonna come in and wait for you in the kitchen. Okay? I didn't want you to freak out when you heard noises upstairs."

"Thank you. Tell her to distract Trevor if she can," I answered. Suddenly, sobs came barreling up my chest. I held the phone away from me a foot or so and I let myself cry through the shock, letting it run its natural cycle, all the while realizing what Tran was holding. I knew Derek could hear me.

"Hey, stay with me, I'm right here. Okay?"

I mumbled something inaudible and wiped my eyes with the back of one hand, still standing frozen in a spot in my basement next to a brand-new washing machine I now would never use, and two feet from a man who made the best tea I'd ever had. Poor Tran.

"You okay over there? Do you want Jazmin to come down?" Derek asked. He hated when I cried.

"No, I'll be right up. I don't want to add any forensic complications down here anyway."

"Mari, listen to me, please don't to—"

"What, touch the book he's clutching in his hands? I don't have to. I know what it is."

"It's a book? You can see it now? Where did it come from?"

"From behind the old washer. It's my father's missing diary."

Chapter
Forty-Four

As if a dead man in my basement wasn't bad enough, my friend no less, I had the excruciating pleasure of sitting in my kitchen while a team of law enforcement paraded through my house. I locked Trevor in my bedroom to protect him from the disturbance of our routine. Great Danes were so sensitive to that. And now I had to wait for a decision to be made about my father's diary, which was now evidence. What could be worse? Sitting here with Ivan Dent.

Derek, Jazmin and Robert Francone were in the living room talking too loud for this time of night, starting with Traeger then quickly transitioning to the names I'd just learned of last night: Sebastian Wainwright of AEI; Daniel Ito, his mentor; and Horace Matusik, VP of Engineering. I can't say I was disappointed to see Ivan, tonight of all nights, but any comfort his presence initially brought faded to irritation after two minutes of nonstop talking. A plate of Pepperidge Farms Sausalito cookies kept his mouth closed, at least, while I pulled my thoughts together.

Team A in the living room was puzzling out the leadership relationships of AEI and Praxis based on data from Jo Kramer and what they had researched on their own. Shouting, play-arguing, and coffee, and every few minutes Derek leaned back in his chair to peer at me through the doorway, making sure either Ivan hadn't talked me to death or I hadn't killed him.

Team B in the basement consisted of three police officers, another outside the basement side door protecting the scene from the neighborhood, the Sherriff-Coroner from Santa Barbara County, and two pathologists from the Coroner's Bureau.

"They're gonna need your gun so they can run a ballistics check on it," Ivan said.

I knew the drill. Tran was killed, or probably killed, from a gunshot wound to the forehead. I owned the house where he was killed, and I owned a gun, so of course it had to be checked out.

I watched Ivan biting into cookie number three. "Dude, seriously? You're diabetic," I warned.

"You're the one who put a plate of my favorite cookies in front of me. What do you want me to do?" He took two more bites then sadly pushed the empty plate across the table. "They'll either question you and take an official statement, or I can take that statement now. It's up to you."

Lord. I sipped from the glass of water I'd poured and composed myself. Standing at the sink, I could see Tran's truck across the street. "Sure, take it now. What do you want to know?"

Chief of Police Ivan Dent, my former lover of three years, clicked the pen and wrote something on a legal pad in front of him at my kitchen table. Then he pressed a button on his recorder. He asked what made me go down to the basement.

"To investigate the audio surveillance device I discovered in my foyer earlier tonight," I replied, reminding myself not to embellish my answers.

"When was the last time you saw Mr. Tran before tonight?"

"Just Tran," I corrected. "I saw him about three weeks ago getting into his car after he did some yard cleanup and landscaping for me. I waved to him but didn't talk to him."

"Is it typical that you wouldn't talk to him?" Ivan asked.

I shrugged, remembering again about the need for exactitude in this type of interview, knowing what I said right now would very likely end up on typed pages in a future deposition or in a trial. "He seemed to be in a hurry."

"Did you ask him about it? Did you find out why?"

Come to think of it, no, I hadn't. "No," I replied. "The next time we communicated was via text when I asked if he could come over and check my washing machine. It turned on but stopped when the tub was filled with water and wasn't cycling through."

"Did he replace it?" Ivan asked.

I raised a brow, remembering the smell in the basement. I'd probably remember that smell for the rest of my life. "Yes, two days ago but I didn't have a chance to go down there and look at it until tonight. I texted Tran yesterday and the day before to see if he'd had a chance to do the install and to try to meetup so I could pay him. But I got nothing back."

"Obviously he came here for something," Ivan suggested with a question in his voice.

"He did the install," I clarified. "The new washer is down there and looks like he's already taken my old one out to his truck."

"Where's his truck now?"

"Parked across the street," I pointed, and felt so negligent for not noticing it sooner. Not that it would have helped.

"Okay." Ivan read through his handwritten notes. "What did you find in the basement related to your surveillance device?"

I raised a brow again. "You haven't been down there?"

"No, I've been up here trying to keep you calm while there's chaos in your house." Ivan's face always got red when he was upset. "And eating cookies I shouldn't be eating."

"Thank you. For being here, I mean. So yes, there's a fucking scaffold taking up the whole wall down there, and a laptop propped on a shelf. Someone drilled a hole in the wall and the laptop is connected to the device."

"Okay." I watched Ivan doodling in the margins of the legal pad. That meant he was preparing to say something he thought might not be well received. I caught sight of Derek leaning back to look into the kitchen. "How well did you get along with Tran? Were you friends, or just friendly?"

I kept my voice completely calm. "I've known him for years. He worked here while my mother lived here. We've always been friendly. I respect his expertise, and he's trustworthy so I never worry that I'm getting screwed." I scratched my head. "Was trustworthy, I guess."

"Who do you think did this to him?" An impartial police investigator would never have asked that. But Ivan knew me, trusted

214

my judgment.

"I think it's suggestive that the same night I detect a clandestine surveillance device in the wall of my foyer, Tran is found dead in the basement where there's more surveillance equipment installed. I think my wiretappers were here two days ago, and Tran came in through the side door. He probably saw—"

"He had a key?"

"Yes, Tran had the only other key besides my own." It was a lie; Duga had one and so did Derek. Maybe not the best time to volunteer that. "Tran came in to remove the old washer and install the new one. He probably saw that someone else was there after the job was complete. So, he was a witness and a loose end that would compromise their operation."

"Whose operation?" Ivan asked.

I shrugged. "Who do you think for God's sake? Whoever's watching me."

Ivan turned off the recorder, eyed the cookie plate one last time, and headed downstairs to check on Team B.

I went to the living room and sat next to Robert, resting my head on his shoulder. "What a night," I moaned.

"Are you done?" Derek asked, referring to the official statement.

"Almost." I returned to the kitchen and texted Ivan, who was in the basement, to come back up for a quick second.

I took away the cookie plate away in a gesture of respect, then pulled my bottle of limoncello from the bottom rack of the refrigerator door and set it on the table with one small, juice glass. Ivan climbed the stairs as I was pouring.

"Yes, thank you, I'd love some."

"Oh sorry, I thought you wouldn't want any because you're on duty," I lied, knowing limoncello, despite how it was mostly sugar, was his weakness. He has so many. I needed a favor, so I also needed any leverage I could get. I grabbed another juice glass, poured him a splash, touched his glass with mine, and said "Salud."

He toasted, sipped, but watched my eyes the whole time. Damn him.

"What?" I asked.

"Ooookay, I get it."

"What do you get exactly?"

"You want the diary," he snickered. "You're gonna ask, cajole, and manipulate me any way you can so you can keep the diary without us taking it away."

Nature is always the best revenge, I realized, when tears flowed from my eyes unexpectedly.

"Oh no, not that," Ivan groaned. "I can't do this now, for God's sake."

"They're not crocodile tears. See for yourself," I leaned forward.

Derek heard the raised voices. He came in and stood behind me with his hands on my shoulders. "Everything alright in here?"

Ivan flung back his head. "Your boss is trying to kill me."

Of course. It was my father's diary, the father I hadn't seen for most of my adult life and half my childhood. And this was, or I believed it was, the secret diary I always knew he kept somewhere in the house. He didn't deny he had one, but he never told me where it was. Now I knew. I'd seen it in poor Tran's rigor-frozen hands. And now it would be taken to headquarters, logged, photographed, dusted for prints, probably analyzed by a forensic team, and who knows what would be left of it after that. So, I asked Ivan for the next best thing.

"I'm not preventing you from doing your job. I just wanna know what's in there. So, my request isn't to tamper with the evidence. But I'd like to photograph a few of the pages before you take it away. Would you permit me to do just that?"

Ivan sat back and crossed his arms, alternating his glance from me to Derek, then nodded. "Let me get it."

Chapter
Forty-Five

Maybe Chief of Police Ivan Dent had less influence than he thought, or maybe rational thinking took over. But I wasn't allowed to touch let alone photograph the diary until it had been entered into evidence. The crime scene team removed Tran from my basement around 5:30 a.m.

I asked one of the officers for permission to collect the laptop on top of the scaffold, no go. Someone in gloved hands brought it down, taped it closed, packed it in a plastic bag and deemed it untouchable for the foreseeable future. I understood the drill certainly. I'd seen plenty of trials go sideways because of mishandled evidence and, as a result, killers left to roam the streets. And it was really just curiosity about the laptop. But my heart and soul needed that diary. Bastards.

Next challenge: Wallace. A nagging sense of dread told me he knew something about the surveillance device stuck in the wall of my foyer. That was tomorrow. For now, I locked all the doors, double-checking every window again on the bottom floor, and clicked the new deadbolt they'd just installed on the kitchen door leading to the basement. Why exactly was that even necessary? At some point, when you've been awake for twenty-three hours, you just keep saying "okay" until people leave you alone.

I found Trevor asleep in the center of my bed on top of the comforter, where he knew he was never allowed. It was a familiar power play with us. I'd ignored him for hours and my punishment was having his dog germs on my white, jacquard, satin-trimmed duvet. Dry clean only, that'll teach me. That's fine, I had one more *okay* left in me. I plopped down on the bed, resting my head on his back and allowed myself to drift.

• ———— • • • ———— •

By ten o'clock, the sun was high and made the room too bright to sleep. I fed and watered Trevor, hoping last night's commotion didn't set him too far off his routine. I'd try feeding him again at noon, dinner at six. Fingers crossed.

A text from Francone had come in while I was asleep: *Call me, found something of interest.*

I made a mental note to do that, but first, coffee. Lacking the patience for French press perfection, Keurig would do just fine. I guzzled the first cup, then brewed and sipped a second while I decided what to do about Wallace. Another in-person visit was too risky, but over the phone I had much less chance of being able to manipulate him. Wallace looked and lived like a man who had it together. But some part of him seemed unstable. I should bring Derek with me down there, in the same way that I should have learned from my mistakes by now. Would I ever?

I felt too drained to leave the house today and might stay in my sleep pants all day. Like Sherlock Holmes said in *The Final Problem*, after surviving three assassination attempts in one day, "I have been using myself rather too freely." I too had been pushing myself with too little regard for my health and wellness, physical and otherwise.

Trevor looked up from his now empty bowl with those soulful eyes telling me I hadn't had enough sleep-pants-days since the accident. I felt his vibe of neediness, or maybe it was my own. Fact is, I didn't want to sit idle in this big house and ruminate. Here alone in the mornings, I always remembered my parents and the ugly truths of my family—a father leading a double life using the CIA as his excuse, a runaway mother, and a half-brother I only just met. I'd essentially been alone all this time and could spin a lifetime of stories about all the holes they left in my heart. Maybe now I wanted something else. Something more.

I could move back to my house in Santa Monica anytime I wanted.

I'd thought about it lately, even dreamed about it. This yard was sized for a castle, the grounds were too hard to keep up, Trevor never liked walking here and I knew he felt no emotional connection to the estate. Maybe it was too quiet and we'd lived together in the city all his life. Maybe it was time. Besides, I desperately missed Cognoscenti's lattes and the reassuring sight of the beloved Santa Monica Pier. Had the time come for me to stop pretending, to stop preparing for a future that would never come? Food for thought.

I decided to text Wallace before calling him, because I had an agenda. I remembered how adored I felt when I opened the picture he sent of my father and me, and his flirty little "Can I see you?" scrawled on the back. I needed to recapture that feeling now so he heard a hint of flirt in my voice. *Can you talk?* I typed and while I waited for his response, I went back upstairs to get my bathrobe.

A minute later, my phone buzzed.

To you? Of course.

What's your schedule today? I asked, counting the seconds. Five...six... *Wide open after lunch. What'd you have in mind?*

Send me your email and I'll send over a Zoom link, I wrote. Perfect bait.

• ⸻ • • • ⸻ •

Finally, around 2:00 p.m. I got properly dressed. Derek showed up right on time for my Zoom call with Wallace. I wanted him here with me so he could witness anything inappropriate, but I needed him out of view. I answered the door wearing a slick, black pants suit and a silk crepe blouse.

"Wow. You look great," Derek beamed, nodding slowly, wondering. "Do you have a date?"

"Yeah, with you."

"Cool. Where are we going?"

"Follow me." I walked him to the living room and pointed at the sofa. "I need you there. I'll be on Zoom here. I'm gonna try not to make eye contact with you because you're not supposed to be here."

"Ah, Mr. McCoy."

I nodded, averting my eyes.

"What are you not telling me? Does he have a thing for you?" Derek leaned his head down and crossed his arms, brows furrowed. Normally I take offense at his overprotectiveness. Today, I didn't mind.

I laughed and shook my head, remembering the photo wall in his house. "You could say that. And that's fine. I'm using it to my advantage. Sit," I commanded, "and no moving, talking, clearing your throat. Okay?"

"Understood."

I logged into Zoom and opened the meeting, waiting for Wallace to pop up on the screen. He was probably running to a mirror.

Chapter
Forty-Six

"Good afternoon," Wallace McCoy said, his expression grim, eyes half-closed.

"Hey." I smiled. "Are you feeling okay?"

"Actually I'm sick. Fever."

"How did that happen?"

"You know, same as you I suspect. Working too hard, never relaxing even when you're not working. You, on the other hand, look like a magazine cover."

I gave a demure smile. *Don't look at Derek. Don't look at Derek.* "Sorry you're sick. I had a question I wanted to ask, but if you're not feeling up to it, we can reschedule."

"I'm fine. I'm sitting comfortably. What can I do for you?"

In a game time decision, I started on a different interrogation track than I'd planned. "Remember when you said Traeger would never see the inside of a prison cell?"

Wallace looked down and rubbed the bridge of his nose, exhaling an audible groan. "I heard about the car bomb."

"He was tipped off," I said, brows high, head tilted. "He knew we were coming. He knew when, and he had a plan in place."

"You think I –"

"You knew about the sting, didn't you? When I talked to you, you knew about it already."

"My team," he said and paused for effect, "is watching every aspect of Martel's operations literally twenty-four seven. That includes Traeger." His tone was defensive.

I glanced at Derek and my jaw tightened. "You could have warned me. My partner was injured. People could have died."

"I can't compromise the security of surveillance channels that have taken decades to put in place. Look, you were right. I'm tired. Can we continue this interrogation later?"

"Sure," I said. "I have a different question I was going to ask you anyway. I was wondering why you bugged my house." I clenched my jaw when I said it, leaving no room for back-pedaling or misinterpretation. I was outright accusing him of breaking and entering and illegally installing surveillance equipment in my foyer.

Wallace's eyes opened wide but he didn't speak at first. He swallowed and took a deep breath. "Installations aren't part of my role."

Well, that was an interesting response, which made me wish I was recording this conversation. "But you know who did it."

"Of course," he said quickly.

I was shaking my head, knowing he'd never tell me who did it. I tried a different tact. "What are they looking for?"

"I gave it to you," Wallace argued, turned back to look at something then moved closer to the screen. "You have it."

"Um…I have what? What are you talking about?"

"The flowers. The picture?" he asked. I couldn't help but glance at Derek now, who was moving to the foyer toward the bouquet of flowers. I'd placed the picture, after handling it at my kitchen table the other night, back in the foyer on the console table next to the flowers. Derek picked up the photograph and studied it, then held it out so I could see. I tried not to look at him.

"They've been watching me ever since you came here, to my house. I had to get rid of it."

I combed my fingers through my hair, thinking. Stimulating my scalp helped get my brain in gear. What had he given me? Flowers, and a photograph.

Wallace's face looked tight, and he was whispering.

"Who's watching you?" I asked him.

He looked down at something, and his chin lit up. His phone. Now my phone buzzed with a text. *Look at what I gave you,* he wrote. *Look closely.*

"Derek," I said aloud, no longer caring about appearances. "There's something on the flowers, or in the flowers. Check the vase."

Wallace shook his head.

"Okay. Not the vase?"

What else did I give you? he typed.

"The picture?" I asked. Derek held it up in the other room. "There's nothing on the picture, if that's what you mean."

I watched Derek flip the picture over and read the back. His eyes widened. Yeah, I'd have to explain that one later.

"Wallace, there's nothing on the picture. Besides, I was asking you about the device someone installed in my foyer."

"Who's been in your foyer besides you?" Wallace asked. So now he was talking in riddles and texting.

I looked at Derek. "My partner." I pointed at Derek. "Some other folks on my team. Duga. Jazmin. Ivan Dent."

Wallace shook his head. "Who else?"

"Jesus," I put my hand over my mouth. "Lin. Dr. Lin Hagen broke in here a few weeks ago and was skulking around in my foyer."

Wallace stared back, silent. Oh no. Derek shook his head.

"Lin Hagen works for you?" I laughed at the irony. Derek came into the room and stood beside me.

"Mr. Abernathy. Nice to meet you, finally," Wallace said. Derek stared at the screen unmoved. "My associate is right. You two do look like a wedding cake." How could he know Derek's name? "And I never said Hagen worked for me."

"Maybe not for you. With you?" I asked.

No answer.

"Camille Bota? She as well?" I asked with a bite to my voice. "My neighbors? How far does this go?" I felt Derek's hands on my shoulders, calming my paranoid brain.

Wallace shook his head, his deep blue eyes blinking back in the silence, marking time as he waited for me to piece it together. Hagen yes, Camille no. Maybe that whole posturing thing with Declan Fergus was more than just him acting as Hagen's boss at the Medical Examiner's Office. Were Hagen and Fergus caught up in Wallace's organization, whatever that was? A good theory anyway. If so, did that mean Camille found out about it? But why would anyone care if she had? And that still didn't explain the connection to Val Sharma. If Wallace really did work for Interpol or some watchdog agency, was Hagen involved in that?

"Declan Fergus?" I asked.

Wallace gave a single, curt nod.

"Okay. Lin Hagen, and then Camille found out about…what?" I asked. "She must have found out about Val and whatever he uncovered. Is that why she's been missing and is now on the run?"

Wallace pointed down. That meant my phone. It buzzed again. *Photo box.*

"Photo box," I read aloud to Derek.

"It came in a box?" he asked.

"Stay here," I said, leaving Derek holding my phone facing the screen. I'd dropped it in a trash can and thank God hadn't emptied it yet. I'd set the photo Wallace sent of my father and me on the table, quietly keeping me company over the past few days. It felt nice to look at it. Like he was here with me in some way while I agonized over the fraying strands of my life. An accident, two unsolvable cases, not to mention my dead friend Tran now. There it was, on top of a bunch of crumpled bags and junk mail, partially covered with dirty paper towels. As I pulled it out, I again felt like the weight was all wrong, yet that hadn't registered until right now, holding the cardboard between my fingers. I looked inside while I moved slowly back to the living room. My fingers dug inside and felt tape at first, then the shape of something hard.

"Jump drive." I pulled it free and handed it to Derek. "Do you agree?"

"That's what it looks like," Derek said.

It held it up to my laptop screen. "Is it safe?" I asked Wallace.

He shook his head soberly.

"Okay, not safe. So, there's incriminating material on this. Evidence? About what, or whom?" I asked.

Wallace blinked back. I was loathe to admit that I liked looking at him. Did he feel safe somehow? He certainly shouldn't. But I think in some way he did.

"Traeger? Martel?" I pushed.

Blink blink.

"Files? A video? What's on here?"

He looked down, texting a response. *A facility tour in Germany.* Praxis! Had to be.

LISA TOWLES

Chapter
Forty-Seven

"Did Val Sharma take this video?" I asked Wallace.

He shook his head and looked down at his phone, then started typing. *He told me about it, where he thought the facility was. Val came to me because he started hearing about a secret project around the same time some financial irregularities surfaced. When he asked Adam Matusik about it, Adam silenced him. Val wanted someone impartial to investigate it because it wasn't safe for him to do so.*

I held up my phone so Derek could read the text.

"Impartial?" Derek snorted. "You're a journalist."

I hadn't told Derek yet about Wallace's Interpol connection and high-profile background.

"You're right of course," Wallace replied, back in speak-mode. "Corporate corruption is sort of one of my areas of expertise, or at least interest. So yes, I was intrigued by his claims and his story of secret projects, missing staff members, multiple NDAs. Then, when he started reporting large amounts of money vanishing from the operating expenses account, I stepped in."

"Sharma was the Marketing Director," Derek argued. "How would he have been privy to financial irregularities?"

Wallace shrugged. "It was hearsay on his part. He'd heard it from someone in finance."

"Back up a minute," I said. "What do you mean by silenced? You said Adam silenced Val. In what way?"

Wallace blinked back, looked at the floor, then the ceiling. Deciding something. The glow from his phone lit up his chin again.

Adam told him his job and his life depended on him dropping it completely.

Derek and I looked at each other and nodded. "And look where he ended up." Just like Tran, stumbling upon something in my basement that he shouldn't have. "You went to Germany?" I asked Wallace.

"Someone from my team did. They found the facility in Munich, based on Val's intel, and were determined to make Val's untimely death meaningful by exposing what was going on."

"So I'm guessing you don't think Val's death was an accident," Derek said.

Wallace cleared his throat and took a sip of water. "Does anyone? No. And neither of you ever met him so I can understand your suspicion. But I did. I sat with him several times. He was strong, strapping almost, a healthy young man full of passion with an exciting future ahead of him." I watched him as he spoke, his bitterness, and his admiration for Val. "One never knows about medical history and such, or about mental illness when you think of potential suicide. But I'll say this—given the details of this case so far, I think Praxis potentially had a lot to lose if their plan got exposed."

"But you haven't exposed anything yet," I said. "What happened?"

"Horace," Wallace said, with a heavy sigh.

I looked at Derek. "Horace Matusik, Kelsey Jo Kramer told us about him. He's the head of engineering, right?"

Wallace nodded. "Among other things. He's got his fingers in a lot of pies."

"And he's the brother of Adam Matusik," I added, "Director of Ops and PR, who disappeared two months ago. Do I have that right?"

Wallace's jaw tightened. He leaned back in his chair and crossed his arms over his chest, waiting for us to reach our own conclusion.

"Is Horace threatening you?" I asked him.

He blinked once. According to spy craft, one blink was yes, two blinks no.

Derek now, leaning closer to the screen. "What kind of relationship does, or did, Horace Matusik have with Adam?"

A tiny smile crept onto Wallace's mouth, then he controlled the movement and tightened his jaw again, still staring. No blinks. Wallace raised his brows looking at me now.

"Shit, I just remembered I got a text from Francone last night, I was supposed to call him back," I said, mostly to Derek, then looked at Wallace. "Francone is my security—" I stopped when his eyes looked sheepish. "Oh, but of course you know that already. Don't you?"

I watched Wallace's face and felt my own grow hot. "Okay, so I guess you know why my security officer was contacting me?"

"No. Why don't you call him. I'll wait. Mr. Abernathy and I can get to know each other a bit more perhaps."

"I'm good, actually," Derek replied. I was surprised he didn't jump at the opportunity for posturing.

I left the two of them alone and sat in one of the East Lake velvet chairs I kept along the perimeter of the foyer, like my parents had when I was growing up. As a child, I'd always had this idea that my grandparents, and other relatives who'd passed away, visited us at night and sat talking, laughing, smoking cigars in those chairs, watching over us. It was a childish thought, or maybe just child-like. And in this moment, it felt comforting to sit in one of them and imagine my ancestors watching over us while Trevor and I slept upstairs. I'd take all the help I could get.

I called Francone from my landline, since my mobile was still in use in the other room. I got his voicemail after the first ring. I left him a message and a minute later my phone rang.

"You never call me from this line," Francone said.

"Robby hey, I'm sorry I'm just now getting back to you. Too many things going on. How are you doing?" I asked, remembering he hated being called Robby, my college name for him.

"Ready for this?" he asked, ceremoniously. "Adam and Horace Matusik are more than just brothers. They're identical twins."

Chapter Forty-Eight

I filled Derek in when I got back to the sitting room. His mouth contracted, considering all the implications. "Well that's an interesting wrinkle."

"I'd say more than just interesting. I can think of all kinds of possibilities." My mind raced.

"Like?" Derek asked.

"Matusik," Wallace said. Was there anything he didn't hear? "Did you learn something?" he asked.

"The two brothers. My security officer discovered something," I said. "They're twins. Identical twins apparently. I'll brace up Kelsey Jo Kramer about that." I looked at Derek. "Can you come with me on that errand?"

"I'll meet you there. I've got something to do first."

Something to do usually meant one of his other cases, the kind he doesn't typically like to share with me. But I had no energy for pulling the truth out of him or anyone else today.

"So, our next task," I said, returning my attention to the intriguing blue eyes on the screen, "is to find a safe computer on which to view the video you sent me. And hopefully stay alive long enough to do that."

"Take every precaution," Wallace whispered.

"I can't help but ask…" Derek shrugged. "Do you have any other surveillance devices installed in this house? Or our cars, office, anywhere else?"

Wallace stared back, at both of us. "For clarification, I'll reiterate that I didn't install the one in the foyer," he confirmed. "I know Dr. Hagen, but I'm afraid I knew nothing about that agenda. If a camera was installed, I suspect they're looking for that video, and you should know they won't stop looking. Even though you've removed the device from your wall, the video I sent you is a liability because it creates a variable of exposure they hadn't planned on."

"My going public?" I asked.

"It's certainly a possibility, and that's the outcome these people will do anything to prevent. Be careful, and please stay in touch," Wallace said, nodded, and then disconnected the call.

Derek sighed and handed me my phone. I returned to the foyer chair sinking all my body weight into it. Derek paced in front of me. I didn't know what to make of the detail Francone had shared, and there was little room in my brain for managing another layer of deception.

"What do you think?" Derek asked.

"Could you please sit? You're making me even more anxious."

"Sorry." He took the chair beside me stretching out his long legs.

"Right now, I'd like nothing more than to be able to talk to my dad."

Derek tipped his head. We'd talked so much about our fathers over the years we'd been working together. I looked down and fiddled with my watch, Derek's father's watch. That connection meant something, though I was never sure what.

"What would you ask him if he was here right now?"

I let out a long exhale, remembering. "We had this game we used to play when I was little."

"Let me guess, a spy game. Wouldn't that be ironic."

I smiled. "At the time I don't think I really knew what a spy was, nor did I have any idea he was one himself. He just taught me what he called brain games. Things like memorizing details of a room and saying them back once you went in another room. Memorizing license plates while driving on the freeway."

"No wonder you have such a good memory," Derek replied.

"There was this other one where he taught me how to summon him if he wasn't around and I needed help."

"Must have been handy, because wasn't he away a lot when you were little? In Moorhead?"

Moorhead, Minnesota, that one-horse town on the border of North Dakota. Hearing him say it bulleted me back to the dusty roads, empty spaces, and open sky. Then in the layer below that, isolation, loneliness, and abandonment.

"He must've had someone watching the house while he was out of town, because every time I did this trick, there was a response within an hour or two. And that's impressive because Moorhead's in the middle of nowhere."

Derek, still lounging in the foyer chair, crossed his arms and smiled. "I'm intrigued. What's the trick?"

"You know the thing about putting a plant or something on your balcony as a sort of SOS?"

"I thought it was a red scarf or a flag or something."

"For us it was... Hold on." I jumped out of the chair, remembering that I kept a memento of him in the back of the kitchen utility drawer, something that got moved and knocked around every time I reached back there for the potato peeler or whetstone. I extended the drawer as far as it would go, my fingers feeling for the familiar, round shape. Got it. I fumbled with it on the way back to the foyer.

"Yellow tape," Derek said. "I've heard of blue masking tape for paint jobs."

"This was our proverbial balcony plant. I'd rip off six inches of tape," I tore off a piece for a demonstration, "or the distance from my thumb to my pinky, and I'd stick it longways on the mailbox post, like this." I stuck the tape to the foyer wall over the console table. "And I now realize he must have had a camera installed on the telephone pole across the street that was programmed to detect the tape." I couldn't wipe the grin off my face thinking about it.

"And? What if he was out of town or out of the country?"

"Well, after I stuck the tape on the mailbox post, I'd leave a note for him inside the mailbox but with the flag down. Usually within an hour or so, one of his minions would remove the tape and stick it on the back of the envelope with a note from him, or someone who worked for him."

"Man, my family was boring."

"Believe me, I would have taken boring any day to have him home with us for dinner."

"So do it."

I stared back. "Do what?"

Derek gestured toward the roll of yellow tape with his eyes. "I mean, if he's still an active operative like you suspect, and he's got access to resources and technology, don't you think it's possible he's still got you on some kind of surveillance? You're his only daughter, for God's sake."

I nodded. It was worth a try. I pulled a sheet of my good, monogrammed stationery and matching envelope from the console table drawer, plus a Waterman ballpoint I hadn't used in years.

"Traeger?" he asked, wondering what I was scribbling. I didn't answer because my phone buzzed with a text.

"Must be your new boyfriend," he mumbled.

I picked up the phone. "Shit. It's from Camille." I read the text, read it again, and a third time trying to process the riddle. Derek rose to read it over my shoulder.

"It's too late. I know, and now they've found me. 1+1=1," he read. "1+1=1, what the hell does that mean?"

I shook my head, absently folding the sheet. I stuffed it in the envelope then folded the flap in. I wrote nothing on the outside of the envelope, as had been our custom so long ago. I headed out front to the mailbox, realizing my eyes were wet. Wow. How many years before that pain subsided? Maybe that wasn't how it worked.

Chapter Forty-Nine

The familiar line-up of stars hid behind thick gray clouds over the Santa Barbara hills. Of course I stuck the yellow tape on the mailbox post and slipped the letter inside. And of course I tiptoed out to the mailbox three more times in the middle of the night, in my robe and slippers, only to find the same envelope with my note inside, and the tape unmoved. How was it that one action could so instantly transform me back into an eight-year-old girl desperate for her father? In some way, I was standing again on the hot summer dirt of Moorhead. No school, nothing but heat, sky, and the sad click of time. Something was pulling me back there, I felt it.

I'd called Francone and Duga when I got Camille's text to have them stake out her house and report anything suspicious, even though she was on the run. I couldn't get the 1+1=1 out of my mind. But they reported it was dark over there with no car in the driveway. *They found me*, she'd written. Her abductors? I checked my phone one more time before going back to bed and thought about the family farm in Moorhead as my lids snapped down for the third time tonight. How many secrets were still buried on those lonely grounds?

Derek picked me up at 9:30 a.m. the next morning, despite what he'd originally said about meeting me at Jo Kramer's.

"Didn't you have something to take care of?" I jibed. "One of your other cases?"

"I called," he said. "Nothing's needed today." Which meant he didn't want me asking about it. And I had no right to, per our agreement. Even so, it bothered me when other cases took his attention. The word partner, in my mind anyway, had an expectation of priority, and I wasn't always at the top of the list. And the controlling part of me hated how I was intrinsically locked out of all the juicy details of those cases so he could maintain confidentiality to his clients.

We both allowed some silence to fill the car for a while, losing ourselves in the slow throb of morning traffic, my eyes pinned toward the horizon.

"So?" he said by the time we got on 101 toward Ventura Keys.

"Sorry. What?"

"The mailbox. Did you check it?" he asked, like it should be obvious.

"Not this morning."

He smiled and looked back to the freeway.

"Something funny?"

"That's your 'not enough coffee' voice. Didn't sleep much?"

"I've had two cups so far, and yes, if you must know, I checked the mailbox three times in the middle of the night. The tape was still there at 3:00 a.m. No idea if it'll be there when I get back." I glanced at his face again. Another grin. "Okay what, for God's sake?"

He turned his gaze from the road to look at me. "The tape's gone. I looked."

He watched me carefully, while occasionally watching the road. It was a common problem whenever we drove together, so I'd gotten used to keeping my phone in my purse and my eyes glued to traffic in front of us. The tape was gone? And a note for me in the mailbox? How could I possibly keep my attention on anything else today?

"So, what does that mean exactly? The tape gone indicates... what?"

"Can we talk about something else? Like Kelsey?"

"That's not her name, don't forget."

"Okay, Jo. Whatever."

"Do you wish I hadn't looked?"

"At the mailbox? I don't know," I admitted. "Look, the idea that my father's been watching me all this time is no surprise, really. There were times when he sent me furniture deliveries if he thought my apartment looked too sparse, with cryptic notes that made me realize he'd been roaming around my place shaking his head when I wasn't there. Occasionally filling the fridge with food, leaving fresh produce on the counters."

"That makes sense," he said. "After getting shot by one of Europe's most notorious crime bosses, I can see why he'd want to keep an eye on you and ensure your safety. You're lucky, in that sense."

He meant well, I guess, with no idea what it meant to be raised by a single, resentful parent. What I didn't tell him was that I dreaded whatever was waiting for me in that mailbox. What would be worse – having his help or not?

"What's your plan with respect to Jo?" Derek asked, changing the subject.

"She leaves at 9:30 on Wednesdays for a meeting that starts at ten."

"Duga?" Derek smiled. I'd had Duga watching her movements for the past week, knowing we'd need to shake her down again for more details. Today was the day.

"Yep, creature of habit."

We parked diagonally across the street.

"Wait," he whispered. "What are you doing? She'll—"

"I don't care. I'm not waiting anymore."

Derek hung back at the car, probably a good idea in case she ran or took off suddenly. I stayed on the opposite sidewalk so she had a complete view of my approach, then cut across the street to her front walkway. The front door was still open a crack.

"Jo? It's Mari. We need to talk." Twenty feet from her front door now, I could see the shape of her head and body in the doorway, unturned in response to my voice but also unmoving. She was deciding. Did she even have time to talk to us before her meeting? Or was it a different deliberation: how much had she told us already, and what would we be asking today? I was two feet from her front porch now. The door opened another inch.

"I know you're probably leaving for work soon. We only need a few minutes."

Now she emerged fully into the doorframe, arms flanked at her sides, eyes on fire. "We?" She glanced at Derek quickly returning to me. "Have you been watching me?" Her voice was tight and pointed.

I didn't move.

"Don't you realize what your being here means?" She was about to cry but the tears hadn't fallen yet. I felt them coming.

"Means to who?" I heard Derek ask behind me. "Who's watching you, Jo?"

Thank God he'd remembered to call her Jo. Derek approached quietly with his hands at his sides, obviously practiced at the art of calming wild animals.

"Who's Horace, Jo?" he asked.

I liked how it was him doing the talking, so I could be the empathetic partner standing by, eight feet from her, offering quiet reassurance while we tore down her defenses.

Her wide, watery eyes scanned the street on both sides. "Not here." She waved us inside. I saw her blue fingernail polish. "Go through to the back. I'll meet you on the patio."

Derek followed me in. I wondered who was watching her but didn't dare speak a word till we got outside.

Chapter Fifty

Jo Kramer arrived on the patio wearing a jacket three sizes too big, and way too heavy for the warm climate. Probably her father's. Did she need a security blanket before speaking her truth? Derek and I sat on wooden deck chairs. She crouched on a low, flat touchstone marking the end of a rock wall along the property's rear perimeter. It was a beautiful yard with well-tended foliage, lighting, a fire pit.

"What are y'all investigating, really?" she asked.

"It should be obvious," I said.

"Not to me. You're sort of quietly sniffing around the edges of—"

"Val Sharma," I shot back. "That's where it all started. His body was discovered and brought to the medical examiner's office as a John Doe. Before we even knew who he was, we found out about it by someone from that office who wanted to keep it all quiet."

"Why?" Jo asked, pulling the jacket close around her body.

"You tell me." I sat back on the uncomfortable chair, watching Derek observe her.

"Who's Horace?" Derek asked again, in a low tone of voice I only hear him use during our most tense interrogations. He typically lets me be the bad cop while he's the one who smooths things over. Jo could run out of here any minute, changing her mind. I felt pins and needles in my hands.

She scrunched her eyes in response. "You know who he is," she whined. "I've told you. He's Adam Matusik's brother. The—"

"VP of Engineering, we know that," he answered, cutting her off gently with his palm up. "Something else you want to tell us about him? About his relationship with Adam maybe?"

Jo rose and pulled a single cigarette and lighter out of the jacket pocket, fondled it thoughtfully, then lit it and took a long drag. She walked around the slate courtyard smoking and watching us.

Derek frowned at this like a judgmental parent.

"Give me a break, it's the first smoke I've had all week," Jo said, and returned to our makeshift seating area. "Well obviously you know they're—twins, right?" She watched both of us.

"I thought it was of particular interest to learn that they're identical twins," I commented.

She nodded in agreement. "It's...I don't know. It didn't start out this way. But in the past year I've watched this weird pattern emerge between Adam and Horace." She paused to tap ash into a glass dish. "There were rumors, back in the day, about how they traded places during college because one was a better test taker than the other and cheating was alleged, passing themselves off as the other. Then Horace, I think it was Horace, got kicked out of MIT because of it. Their childhood mentor, Daniel Ito, was used to cleaning up their messes and supposedly bought his way back in. There were rumors that the boys were best friends and roommates all through school, other rumors that they secretly hated each other and slept with each other's girlfriends."

"Yikes," I said.

"Switching places when taking exams. That's a big deal," Derek said.

Jo raised a brow.

"What?" I asked her.

"That's the code word, and that's what this whole mess is about." Jo stubbed out the cigarette and bit her fingernail.

"Code word? For what?" Derek asked.

It seemed so obvious now. My God, I'd been so blind. Switching identities, but it was more than that. "Switch..." I mumbled under my breath. "That's the name of the Praxis quantum computer. Isn't it?"

Jo stared at the floor. That was her answer.

"Why that name?" Derek asked her.

Jo exhaled a plume of smoke that blew back in our direction. "You get a significant performance gain," she replied, "well, potentially anyway, by using what's called a quantum switch in entanglement distribution within quantum computing. So, in quantum teleportation, which is used in the super-positioning of qubits in quantum circuits, the use of this switch allows for noise reduction within quantum computations. That means less errors and higher data integrity. Their use of a quantum switch is their superpower. It's gonna revolutionize crypto, banking. Literally everything we know."

"So quantum noise means computational errors?" Derek asked.

"Yeah, well, disturbances that could lead to errors in results, in a type of technology that requires ultra precision."

"You said revolutionize everything we know," I said. "How? Val Sharma was your Marketing Director and look what happened to him. And Adam—"

She rose again, pacing this time, in a slow circle, wiping her eyes with the jacket sleeve.

"Jo? People are disappearing because of this project. People are dying. I don't want to see you get so far in that you can't find your way out. We can help you, but you need to come with us and talk to the police about what you know. About Adam, about Val, and Horace. Praxis may have started out as a tech company, but they've apparently got so much to lose now, they're willing to kill to protect their secrets. I'm worried about you."

Derek's phone buzzed in his pocket. He looked down and pulled it out. "This is yours, I grabbed it from the car console."

He handed it to me, showing an SOS text from Duga in our code. I pressed the button to call him back.

"Hey, what's up?"

I heard nothing.

"Duga, you there?"

"I'm here." Pause. "I'm so sorry."

"What?"

"Camille's body was found this morning. She's dead."

I grabbed Derek's elbow to steady myself. Camille. Good lord.

"What?" he asked, reading my eyes.

"Camille," I whispered, then returned my attention to Jo. "We, um, need to attend to something. Jo, you be careful. When you're ready to talk to the police, text me and we'll go with you."

"Or are you ready to come with us right now?" Derek asked her.

She shook her head. "I've got a meeting I'm gonna be late for. I need to keep playing the game and try to trust that they're not bugging my phone or my car. Funny, I used to love this job."

• ⸺ • • • ⬛ ⸺ •

I called Duga on Bluetooth when we got back to Derek's car. He gave us details of Camille's body being found in the same place as Val's, by Lake Piru. What about this location made it ideal for dumping bodies? My hands shook. Derek's warm fingers grabbed them while he drove.

"Her text last night," I said remembering what she'd sent during our Zoom with Wallace. I might have been one of the last people to see her alive, on my street the other night. "I assumed the word *they* meant whoever had kidnapped her in the first place. But what about the 1+1=1?"

"What is that?" Duga asked. I'd forgotten to tell him about the text. Never enough time.

"We don't know yet."

"Something related to Project Switch?" Derek asked. "When does 1+1 equal one?"

"When one of the ones is actually a zero," Duga answered.

"Or when one of the ones overtakes the other," Derek countered. "Are they talking about one as in binary? Or one as in—"

"I think the ones are the two brothers," I said, telling Duga what Francone told me about identical twins. We drove in silence for a few seconds letting that theory form. "If one twin plus one twin still equals one, maybe that means one twin killed the other. I think Horace Matusik might have had a motive to kill Adam to prevent him or Val from going public about the Praxis project. Val worked for Adam."

"Nice theory," Derek replied. "But where's Adam's body, and now where's Horace?"

We disconnected from Duga, still contemplating Derek's rhetorical question. "I need more coffee."

Chapter
Fifty-One

Right now, we desperately needed to see that video from Wallace, and Duga had just the machine. I decided meeting at our office, or any familiar location for that matter, wouldn't be prudent, all things considered. After all, someone—maybe Hagen or one of his shady associates, had taken great pains and great risk to install a surveillance device in my foyer and then break into my basement to install their own private viewing gallery. Fuckers. My hands still formed into fists when I thought about it. I had to believe whoever did this was also involved in the killing of Val Sharma, and now one of my oldest friends. Poor Camille.

It was too hard to believe right now. And my bitterness didn't touch the pain I still felt in my heart over Tran. He must have seen them breaking into my basement. Who else would they kill to protect their ten-billion-dollar secret?

We decided that hiding in plain sight was the best idea. We chose Dune Coffee Roasters in downtown Santa Barbara for our movie-viewing, using Duga's super-powerful gaming laptop with Derek and I sharing a set of AirPods sitting out on the patio. I knew it would be loud, but we'd be better able to see anyone approaching us. I had my

Beretta on me in a belt holster, covered by my leather jacket.

It was one of those crisp early spring days. Technically too cold and windy to sit outside, but occasionally the wind stopped, the sun spilling out through the clouds reminding me that as a kid, I'd spend all day every day outside. Funny.

Derek had scored an unthinkable parking space ten steps from the café. In between the sound of traffic, my ears picked up a bird song I swear I heard right before I woke this morning. Or had I dreamt it?

Derek returned with two coffees and set them on the table. "Did Duga already load it in?" he asked, taking the lid off his cup.

"It's an MP4 on the desktop. Turn the volume all the way up."

"It's up."

I watched Derek use the touchpad to double click on an MP4 file called "PS". Did that mean Project Switch? He handed me one of the AirPods. The video player opened, showing a vertical orientation, of a long, gray hallway with what sounded like two sets of footsteps. The volume must have been up high when this was recorded. One of the walkers was obviously holding an iPhone. No talking so far. The footsteps stopped, someone turned the phone inward, then facing out again toward the same hallway but we heard no sound. Had they muted the phone? The movements were jagged, like the phone was in someone's hand while they were talking or arguing. Derek and I glanced at one another but kept an eye on the zigzagging screen, waiting. The video showed the two walkers moving forward again with the sound on, but slower now, and stopping when they got to a door. The camera showed a keypad. I heard whispering, more emphatic whispering, then again the phone went to mute.

"Not what you were expecting?" Derek smirked, nodding at the screen.

"Well, I wasn't expecting an infomercial if that's what you mean. I have a feeling we're about to witness a security hack."

We kept watching, while the iPhone camera angle straightened to show a numeric keypad with a key card slot along the right edge.

"Ready?" someone said on the screen.

The other person, neither of which had been visible yet, snapped a small, black box onto the keypad. We saw a series of green, LED-lit numbers cycling quickly through what looked like an encryption password-breaking loop, stopping on one number, then another, then another number every twenty seconds or so. We watched and waited till seven numbers were visible on the small device. The person holding the iPhone then angled it so it clearly showed all seven numbers: 5719803 and landed on the keypad long enough to watch someone's finger inputting that number sequence, which resulted in a larger green light showing on the keypad.

The videographers wanted us to see the code. "This is an exposé. Jesus."

Next, a red light blinked along the right edge of the keypad, prompting the user to slide a Cryptocard, I remembered them from my former life, with the electronic stripe facing down. One of the iPhone operators slid a card across the edge and the red light turned green, matching the green keypad light. A loud, metallic click sounded and the doors in front of the two iPhone operators opened six inches, wide enough to show a security guard standing on the other side. I had a bad feeling about that guard.

Chapter Fifty-Two

"Wait." I wagged my finger to the left.

"Rewind?"

"Just a little."

"Ten seconds?" Derek asked.

"About that."

Derek dragged the horizontal scroll bar slightly left so we could see the frames as he cascaded back.

"There, the keypad."

"Run it?" he asked.

I nodded, pointing at the frozen frame. "What do you see?"

He looked closer. "A hand, a woman's hand. That's interesting."

"Interesting why?" I asked.

"I don't know. For some reason I thought it was two men walking. I just had that impression."

"Blue nail polish," I mumbled.

"I'm not getting the significance."

"Jo Kramer. That's Jo Kramer's hand." My heart pounded.

"How do you know that?"

"She was wearing blue nail polish, dark blue nail polish the first time we met her. It's an unusual shade so I made note of it. Do you realize—"

"Couldn't it be someone else with blue nail polish?" he asked. Good question.

"Not who's so deeply connected with this case, no."

Derek's hand went up. "Let's keep watching and see where this goes. But if you're right, Jo Kramer's one of the videographers in this operation and her playing the victim all this time has been a ploy. I should've known. I'm going forward now."

I took a moment to scan our surroundings, then returned my attention to the screen. The camera showed a quick movement and then the screen went gray, like the phone was moved to someone's pocket. I heard footsteps and three voices: two men, one woman. The vocal tones revealed a calm conversation of back and forths, questions and answers, an exchange of information, then footsteps down a corridor.

"Now?" I heard Jo Kramer ask, certain it was her voice.

"No," the male voice answered. "After we get through this door."

Another door clicked open, this time with no keypad, and now we could see again. A tall white door leading to another hallway, then a door to the right leading to a flight of stairs. I could hear talking but couldn't make out the words under the thud of shoes on clanky steel steps.

"Shit," I heard Jo Kramer say. "What now?"

The iPhone was held up to show another keypad.

"Try it again?"

"Go ahead," the man replied. I watched the blue fingernails typing in the same numeric code as the last keypad. Something clicked and a slot along the right side glowed green again. The man ran the white card through the slot and the door opened, same as the last time. "This is it," he said. "You sure?"

The phone bounced slightly. "Go," Jo replied. "It's dark," she said, holding the phone up to scan the room.

Derek uncrossed his legs under the outdoor table and sipped his coffee. "Look, I'm gonna fast forward so—"

"No don't!" I shouted. "Sorry. We need to—"

Derek glanced over his left shoulder. "I don't like being out in the open here."

"I thought we were hiding in plain sight. What's the issue?"

He sighed. "No issue. I'm pretty sure where this is going anyway."

I pointed to the laptop. They were aiming the iPhone at a window in a steel door. They moved closer, revealing what looked like a clean room with a huge, cylindrical, gold object hanging in the middle.

"Someone's using their iPhone flashlight," I said. "Good idea, except I can hardly see anything."

"So that's it, I guess." Derek moved closer to the screen. "Amazing. I've been reading about the architecture of these things. The hardware is incredibly complex."

"And apparently it needs to be kept in a room with a climate as cold as deep space."

I leaned in, squinting. Jo was holding her phone up to the glass and rotating it slowly left and right, showing what resembled an enormous, multi-tiered chandelier, gold, held together with an intricate array of thin wiring.

Jo nodded, pointing ahead. "Four levels," she narrated. "Quantum data plane on the bottom, control and measurement, and control and host processors." Jo pinched the iPhone screen to zoom in closer to the extraordinary device. Sometimes referred to as a chandelier, it had that overall shape, with shiny gold discs, boards, pipes, and clusters of wire arranged in an incredibly intricate, precise design. It was beautiful in a way.

The man with Jo cleared his throat. "We're employees of AEI," he narrated, "here on an international mission to expose one of the biggest lies of the modern business landscape. My associate and I are in Munich, Germany at the headquarters of a company called Praxis, and this is their secret, a project designated as Mercury. The computer we're looking at has been designated as Switch because it utilizes a quantum switch in its circuit architecture. And the best definition I know of a quantum switch is a digital switch that can be in the on and off positions at the same time. The purpose of this technology is to utilize a unique algorithm in combination with the quantum switch, to essentially eliminate quantum noise or errors, bringing next generation validation, data integrity and most importantly speed to its quantum operations."

"What about—" Jo Kramer asked in a meek voice.

The man cleared his voice. "Right. As an employee of AEI, I confirm the truth that all the principals of AEI know about the Praxis mission, and know that ultimately this machine was developed to create unhackable authentication keys that are used in crypto trading. Why? Unhackable authentication keys would reduce crypto theft, create greater investment from pension and hedge funds, boost investor confidence, thus increasing market participation. It would be a major step towards making crypto safe and accessible enough for mainstream individual adoption, with potentially significant—very significant—capital inflows. In short, we believe this device was built to take down the US economy."

I reached out to pause the video and turned toward Derek. "Holy shit. This is a whistleblowing video. If this is Jo Kramer, that other person has to be Val Sharma."

Derek advanced the video again, but the screen image jumped to the floor, with grunts, the squeak of shoes on a floor. A scuffle. Raised voices. Someone was trying to stop them.

"Adam, no!" Jo cried out. Adam? Where had he come from?

"Jo, it's Horace. Watch out." That sounded like Val's voice.

"No, it's not. It's Adam."

"What did you hope to gain by doing this?" The voice of a third man, either Adam or Horace Matusik.

"You can't do this. I'm gonna expose this, this project, all of you. I've already—"

"Oh really?" The voice of the third man snickered. "How exactly had you planned to get out of this building in one piece? Both of you? Do you have a magic carpet, or a Star Trek transporter?"

"Adam no, please," Jo said. "Val, give him your phone."

"No way! This is our only leverage."

"Val," Jo again, now in a lower tone. "He's going to kill us. Give him the—"

The camera still aimed at the floor, we could see a dark-haired, dark-skinned man's head and shoulders, someone's hand stretching his shirt collar, and a syringe injecting something into his shoulder.

"Please," Jo now, sobbing. "Don't do this."

"It's already done."

Chapter Fifty-Three

The wind came out of nowhere, flapping my jacket, nearly tipping over Derek's half-filled coffee cup. A dark gray cloud canopy hovered at a low ceiling, no rain yet but promising. Neither of us moved, stunned by the thud of Val Sharma's crumpled body visible on the white tile floor. The video ended there, either because somebody stopped the recording or it ran out of battery. Did that really just happen, or were my eyes deceiving me? I wanted to rewind and re-watch it, paying more attention to the details I might have missed, but the gusts were too strong now. I felt a few cold droplets on the top of my head. Get my hair wet? No way.

We quickly packed up and slipped into Derek's car. He started the engine, pulled on his seat belt, and froze, hands on the steering wheel.

"Are you okay?" he asked.

"No."

"Did we just witness a murder?"

"Where's the jump drive?" I asked, feeling the weight of that question vibrating in my chest.

"I got it."

"Where?" In my haste to shut down the computer and pack up, I hadn't seen what he did with it.

"In my holster."

That made no sense because of course there wouldn't be room for it if his gun was in there properly. I glanced at him and he winked back, which told me he suspected his car was bugged, scary thought. He'd probably hidden it in his wallet. He'd done it before with larger things than a jump drive. I still had a hundred other questions, like how they got Val Sharma's body back from Munich, the legal ramifications, was it done through back channels, a private jet maybe?

Finally, we drove off heading toward the AEI office, where we'd camp out and wait for Jo to exit the building, giving me a few minutes to calm my pounding heart.

I rolled down the passenger window to feel air on my face. I pulled it into my lungs and held it there for too long, then coughed till my eyes watered.

"Bet you a hundred bucks you're thinking about your mailbox right now," Derek said, breaking the silence.

"We missed it," I said, curious how he could even think about anything else right now.

"What?"

"Her."

"Jo?"

We'd missed the signs, missed what she'd been hiding from us all this time. I remembered Jacques Martel's bullet piercing my right shoulder, after the task force I'd been leading finally tracked him down, through my intel no less, after a two-year search. I found him, we collectively cornered him. But he shot me before I got to him and he got away, a truth that had since taken residence in the pit of my heart as a tiny icicle. Because we failed, he got to me first. And Jo Kramer had just outsmarted us and it was happening again. I was dying inside.

"Hey." Derek reached to grab my elbow. "Where are you right now?"

"I don't know," I whined. "We're seers. Or we're supposed to be."

"Don't do that. I know where you are right now. You're in the Martel place, aren't you?"

I exhaled slowly.

"That was an extraordinary case and set of circumstances, in which you almost died."

"Yeah, but…" I sighed. "This is what we do. We observe,

extrapolate, dig out the wretched, hidden truths under layers of fear and shame. We pull it out of people. We're truth-finders and we blew it. I blew it."

"Go ahead, take ownership of this if you want to make yourself suffer, but frankly that's a cop-out because it's not that simple."

I looked at him, sullen. "Why not?"

"Because first of all, you're the one who—"

"What?" My voice cracked. "What have I done here but been led around by people like Lin Hagen and Camille?" I wiped my running nose with my hand and didn't care. "I'm not detecting. Detecting is about listening and synthesis, making order from chaos. I'm not doing that. I'm just following the chaos around with a fucking dustpan." I wiped my eyes now. "I've lost my edge and my focus."

I didn't realize at first that Derek had pulled the car to the shoulder and turned off the engine, allowing me to rage on.

"Look, this case is way bigger than Jo and Val Sharma," he said. "If nothing else, that video just confirmed it."

"Understatement."

"Let me just come out and ask you. Do you think Jo killed Val?"

I was about to say no, but I stopped to remember the scene in my head. "If she had, why would she have screamed? She's quite an actress, we've seen that, but her scream didn't sound fake. I don't think so." I pointed to the AEI door. "We'll know in a minute, there she is."

"You think she's gonna run?"

"She might," I said, my eyes glued to her. She was standing hunched over, walking close to the building, laying low. "Oh yeah."

"Okay. How do you want to play it?"

Chapter
Fifty-Four

In extraction situations like this, lying was always the best policy. Derek and I, still undetected, communicated via eye contact and hand signals, backing off from the car, eyes glued to Jo who had, by now, almost slinked her way to the parking lot.

"We going in big or small?" Derek asked, waiting for my cue.

"Let's go quiet." I ran towards the parking lot steps, ducking behind cars as much as possible for someone six feet tall. Derek walked up with his self-assured long strides, catching Jo's eye as her hand rose with her electronic car door opener.

"Hey, Jo," he said in a disarming tone. She looked to her right, caught sight of him, and completely froze. I watched Derek raise his hands high and tip his head to the right, looking behind her at an invisible team of law enforcement officers. He waved his hands slightly. "No no, guys, back up. We're good here. All friendly." Then to Jo, "Right, Jo? Are we good? Mari and I need a minute to talk. And I'm not asking."

Jo Kramer's head was turned toward the woods behind the AEI office, looking for the police officers or squad cars we knew didn't exist, while I moved up toward Derek and stood beside him, closer to

251

Jo's car.

"We've seen the video, Jo. We know what you've done." I watched her upper body crumple forward in sobs, still standing with hands on her knees, now holding onto the edge of another car. I kept my voice calm and neutral. "We've got some backup with us." I gestured toward the woods. "And if you run, that'll be bad for you. Now, if you're smart, you'll walk with us over here so we can have a calm conversation without anybody getting hurt. I know that's what you want, Jo."

Her eyes looked literally twice their normal size. She gave me a single nod and took two steps toward me, pausing to lock the car that she hadn't actually unlocked. Funny the things we do to secure one part of our lives when another part unravels. I opened my arms to corral her toward Derek; he kept his hands strategically in his pockets. I loved the symbolism of trust, there, and I could tell that was putting Jo Kramer, a practiced manipulator, at ease. We walked her across the street to stand near Derek's car. I picked up my phone and spoke into it like it was a police radio and looked back at the woods.

"Yeah, we're good here, stand by," I said to the invisible officers. "No, no, I don't think that'll be necessary." Jo looked as if she might faint. I remembered to breathe. "Would you be more comfortable sitting?" I asked her, raising my hand toward the car.

"Yes, please," she said, and climbed in the passenger side of the backseat.

I motioned for Derek to sit with her in the back, and I'd take the front driver's seat so I could see her. I didn't say anything at first allowing a few beats of silence to fill the gravity of this moment of truth, or what I hoped would be so. Kelsey Jo Kramer rested her head against the door and closed her eyes.

"I think you may have left out a few details," Derek said.

She shook her head too fast, betraying her frenzied state. "I know. I had—I—couldn't."

"How about taking us through the org chart again," I suggested. "Horace is the VP of Engineering."

"VP of Technology, actually," she corrected.

"And Adam?" I asked, tuned in to observe every nuance.

She cleared her throat. "Adam." Her lids closed and her chest moved, containing the fire flaming in her heart. "Director of Operations and Public Relations. Then Val, as you know, was the Marketing Director. I've told you this already so many times."

"He reported to Adam?" Derek asked.

"Mmm hmmm," she confirmed, looking swallowed up by the backseat. "Everyone thought Adam and his protégé, Val, were pushing to reveal the truth about Praxis, about how they'd created quantum supremacy."

"We know all this," I cut in. "Horace wanted to be a geeky engineer and sit behind his computer all day and not tell anyone about what they were doing under the hood."

"Where's Adam, Jo?" Derek asked.

Her face sank, the eyes half closed, mouth contracted.

"He disappeared three weeks ago now," I added. "You know where he is, don't you?"

"Everyone thought—" She stopped and cleared her throat. "Everyone thought Horace had somehow silenced him," she said now, finding a spot on the seat to focus her eyes.

"You mean they thought Horace killed him?" I asked, exchanging looks with Derek, knowing we were getting into interrogation mode. We needed to decide who was who. I was in no mood for bullshit so I guess I was gonna be bad cop today.

"What happened?" I demanded.

Without looking up, she shook her head. "Horace was standing in Adam's way, blocking his path to fame, public acclaim being associated with the world's fastest quantum computer. Adam wanted the press and the association with that story. Of course he did, he was a PR guy. He loved the media and all it brought him." She shook her head quickly, as if willing away demons she wasn't strong enough to face.

The windows were starting to fog. I pressed the ignition button and rolled one of them down two inches, then turned off the motor again. "So, you think Horace killed Adam to protect the Praxis secret?"

More head shaking and a long sigh. She met our eyes now, both of us. "It was the other way around." Jo leaned forward and rested her head in her palms between her knees. Her body shook with sobs.

"We're right here." Derek placed his palm on her back.

"Adam killed Horace to get him out of his way. He—"

"Wait," I cut in. "Adam killed Horace? Don't you mean—how do you know that?"

"He pretended to be him! Don't you understand? They were identical twins for God's sake."

Jo had an innocent face, open and searching, the kind of face you wanted to dry with a soft towel when tears flooded her cheeks. I checked the street, making sure nothing would disturb her.

"How do you know Adam killed Horace?" Derek asked now.

"Adam started wearing Horace's drab clothes, drove his boring car, stayed at his house. Even me! He tried to pass himself off as Horace to me." More sobbing. "I'm in love with him! Didn't he think I would know him well enough? For fuck's sake they have different hairstyles, they even smell different. What the fuck do I do now?"

"We've talked to you four times before today, Jo. Why didn't you tell us any of this before?"

She opened her palm and contracted her brows in disbelief. "They were threatening me. They thought I was gonna pick up where Val left off, with that reporter he was talking to. They said I'd never work again in the tech industry and I'd be ruined, or worse."

"Have they been watching your house?" I asked her. "If so, I'm sure they've seen us coming and going."

"I suspect they have bigger problems right now."

"Who's they?" Derek asked. "Who specifically?"

She paused and reached up to rub her temples. "Daniel and Sebastian."

"Do they know about the video?" I asked.

She nodded. "They said if I tried to do anything with it, it would be in violation of the NDA I signed, violation of my employment agreement, and would put the lives of hundreds of employees in danger."

Something didn't sit right here. "Why didn't they try to physically take it from you? Seems like that would've been easy enough if you went there every day."

"That would be too obvious."

She was holding back, I could feel it. I stared her down. "They never broke into your house, tried to find it?"

Single nod. "They did once. I keep my laptops out of sight so they didn't find it."

They searched for her laptop, didn't find it, and just gave up? That seemed unlikely. "Wow, blackmail. Does Adam know that *you know* he's not Horace?" I asked.

"Not sure. I can't get far enough away from him." She looked at the building in front of us. "From all of them."

I smiled at the double entendre. Project Switch wasn't just the name of the quantum computer, but Adam's little project of taking over the identity of his twin. $1 + 1 = 0$.

"So, when you thought Adam disappeared three weeks ago, you're saying that was actually Horace?" Derek asked.

She nodded. "I think that's when Adam stopped being Adam and became Horace."

"When was the video taken at Praxis?" Derek asked.

"Shortly before Adam and Val disappeared. A few months ago now."

"So, where's the body? Where's Horace? The real Horace?" I asked.

Jo's eyes widened, blinking, looking around, deciding something. "I started following him last weekend."

"Adam?" Derek asked, scratching his head.

"Adam posing as Horace, yeah. One night, Sunday I think, it was late, after eleven. He left and drove to a storage facility in Camarillo, parked, left his car there, and walked off."

"You followed him? Pretty risky."

"I was more interested in his car."

"Don't those places usually have key card access?"

"I was on foot so I slipped under the barrier. I found his car parked in a space, and—" more sobs now. "It smelled so foul!" Her wail turned to sobs, her body rocking back and forth. "It smelled like death. He left him in there. He left him!"

"In the car?" Derek asked. "Seems like that'd be easy to find."

"Trunk."

It still seemed careless, maybe even reckless. She told us the final details of Adam's black Lexus, and gazed back with a scared rabbit look, asking what we were going to do with her. I moved clumsily from the driver's to the passenger seat in front so I could see Derek.

"Are you arresting me?" she said to Derek this time.

"We're not the police, so we have no authority to arrest you. We'll check out the Lexus and your story. The police will want to talk to you in connection with the video, because you witnessed Val's murder."

More tears now. "Don't you get it? It's more than just my career on the line. I'm dead, even if I didn't go to that reporter. Which I didn't. They'll kill me. You know the truth. You can't leave me alone now. Please."

Chapter
Fifty-Five

After two hours of waiting in an underground parking lot, for cover, I had Duga pick up Jo and drive her to LA to stay with him at his monastery. It was safer than a hotel, and far enough away that it might slow down the Praxis machine for a day or so.

Derek and I called in Jo's story of stolen identities and murder to our contacts at the Santa Barbara Police Department then waited for them at One Stop Storage. The way she described it, I half expected to smell the body from the front entrance. Nothing of the sort, but the black Lexus was exactly where she said it would be, parked against a short row of units that lined the west side of the property. First, two police officers showed up to meet with us and verify the presence of the car to validate Jo's story. When a pair of homicide detectives arrived, those initial two officers left to find Jo Kramer, not realizing she was on her way south. First, the two detectives interviewed both of us, briefly, then jimmied open the trunk of the car. I was about fifty feet away at that point and it was all I could do to cover my nose before the stench bowled me over. Next, they contacted the property owner. Third, they called in a crime scene investigation team.

Photographs were taken of the car, the facility and, shortly thereafter, the trunk. I asked the ME, later, how long they thought the victim had been dead. The ME's office representative said we'd have to wait for the official report, but the estimate was 2-3 days, which didn't answer the question of where he'd been for the past three weeks. I did the math. Adam had killed Horace three days ago, an act that required significant planning to execute without being detected right away. The question was, where was Adam now, and did he know what we'd learned from Jo? She was our link to not only Adam but to the truth about Val. How many people would have to die at the hands of Praxis to keep their secret safe?

They let us leave after the crime team finally transported Horace Matusik's body to the morgue. I went home and slept for a while, ate some crackers and cheese, paced my bedroom floors for two more hours, untangling the threads of a convoluted mess of details. I wondered if they'd perform a DNA test to verify that this was indeed Horace and not Adam. It had been so long since I'd had a full night's sleep and hadn't woken up with a headache, I could no longer even remember feeling well. Derek and I had done our due diligence by calling in the police, providing details of Jo Kramer's theory, and leaving the rest to the experts, as Ivan typically reminded me. Ivan would likely know about this already but he deserved a call from me anyway.

I don't know why, but I made myself wait to visit the mailbox again till after I'd reached out to Ivan, maybe some throwback pattern of finishing chores before playtime. The mailbox wasn't what I'd consider play, but it was a childhood game that helped me cope with things I couldn't understand or control. Fitting.

Sometimes I felt like Derek and I were connected telepathically. There had been times when I found myself in a bad neighborhood, tracking down some lead, and he just appeared two cars behind me, waving in my rearview mirror, watching out for me like the universe sent him or something. I'd never believed much in things like that before I met him. Not sure if I was dreaming or not, having been up literally all night, I padded downstairs, Trevor trailing me, and opened my front door knowing I'd find him there. Maybe he was checking up on me, or maybe he couldn't sleep either.

"I knew you'd be up," he said. He looked terrible. I'm sure I looked worse. I didn't let him in, despite the chill in the air. I hadn't worn my robe. He took off his jacket and slid it over my shoulders. "Walk?" he asked.

"I'm glad you're here." I hooked my arm in his, and we took off at a turtle's pace down my darkened, tree-lined street. Sometimes I wondered if, in a parallel universe, Derek and I were married. And other times it seemed as if we were too familiar even for that, like maybe we were family instead, brother and sister in a previous life. Something.

"Tell me what that big brain of yours is churning through right now."

"Why." I let out a long breath.

"Why what?"

"Why everything. It was my first word, my mother told me. I drove her insane when I was little, asking why this, why that. Today, I guess I'm wondering why we investigate. Why do you do what you do?"

"Justice is the draw for me. I tried being a detective, as you know."

I snickered, but in a friendly way.

"Law enforcement is too frustrating, too hobbled by rules and constraints. What we do has more freedom. I don't know. I do miss actual police work sometimes. What about you?"

"My *why*, you mean?" I asked.

"Yeah."

We walked like that down my street, turned right and went downhill a ways, the night sky devoid of answers. "I always needed to know why people did the things they did. Like I needed some profession that gave me an opportunity to lift the veil and study the motivations behind human behavior."

"Criminal behavior?"

"Not specifically, or not at first."

"Why, though?" Derek asked with a smirk. "I mean, why do you need to know?"

I looked at the sky behind the trees as we walked past them on my darkened street. So nice out here. "There was a man who died on our ranch when I was eight years old," I said, randomly.

"You never told me. Who was he?"

"I don't know. I was home alone one morning and something sort of drew me outside, this was in Moorhead. I'd slept late, which I never did, so everything felt strange. The house was so quiet, and it was blazing hot out. I walked outside sort of following my instincts. I thought I saw something out in the hills. When I got closer, I saw it was a broken motorcycle with some parts on the ground around it. What scared me was a circle of crows flying overhead. That's when I looked down and found a body about twenty feet away, half buried in the dirt. Dig," I mumbled.

"Dig?" Derek asked.

"I sort of heard the word in my head. Something made me do it. I crawled up to the body and started digging dirt away from the man's face and neck. I saw his chest move so he was still alive, barely. I dug him out far enough for him to cough and sputter. Then I ran back to the house to get him some water and came right back, expecting him to be dead. He wouldn't drink because he was in too much pain. I saw where someone had shot him. There was a big hole with blood in it just above his navel and below his ribcage. I asked him questions, tapped his face to get him to open his eyes and talk to me. He opened them, but I knew he was a goner. And there I was, alone on the ranch, overwhelmed by the fact that I was the last face this man would take with him to the afterlife. I sat with him there, with my hands on his chest, for a long time. I tried talking to him but he only moaned and winced. At one point I did get him to drink some water, and afterward he wrapped my tiny hand in his. He put something in it, and then he sort of slumped over. It was a .12-gauge shotgun shell."

We stopped walking and were standing in the middle of the street near where I'd seen Camille the other night.

"That's something to behold for an eight-year-old. What happened?" Derek asked. We started walking again.

"My mother was at a neighbor's house. The police came and took away the man and his bike. When my father got home a week later, I asked him about it. I told him about the shell casing. My young brain had to know why a man would be shot like that, right off his bike, and obviously on purpose, right? What other explanation could there be for such a thing to happen? And it obviously happened nearby, or else why would he end up in the middle of our ranch? I had a thousand questions, no one to answer them, and a shell casing that would no doubt solve the mystery."

"Did you turn it in?"

"My father asked me to give it to him and said he'd give it to the police. But I knew in my heart he wouldn't. So I lied to my father and told him I lost it. I've kept it all these years, never knowing who he was, or why he died, and knowing in my bones that my father had all those

259

answers and would never tell a thing."

Chapter Fifty-Six

And there I was, standing alone after Derek left, eight years old again with my toes digging in the hot dirt under the mailbox on Oakport Street that ran alongside Red River in Moorhead. Our mailbox had been slightly too tall for me, back then, but still within reach.

Now a grownup wearing Derek's jacket and shearling-trimmed slippers, my hand pulled open my mailbox on Holly Loop. Thirty years through time, waiting for the father who never came home, solving and perpetrating crimes all over the world instead of where I needed him to be. By my side, on the porch with my lonely mother, pretending to be interested in her mundane stories of the neighbors and our small-town world. But that wasn't the father I ended up with. The fantasy that replayed in my dreams was much more normal, like other fathers who showed up at 4H events and little league.

"Sparrow," he called me back then, which I later learned was a code name for female spies. "Keep looking for clues and never stop asking why."

I still remember the first note from him, after his first ever trip abroad. Once a week, after I put tape on the mailbox post, the tape would disappear and there'd be a single, white index card in the

261

mailbox, but the flag was still down. Our code. I knew he didn't write the notes himself, though they were handwritten by someone, one of his associates, who cared enough to capitalize the word Sparrow and sign them "Love, D".

Tonight, an owl broke the blanket of silence, maybe the same one I heard most nights if I opened the kitchen window. Was he watching me? I knew owls had amazing vision, but mostly to help them find prey. Was I one of his curiosities? I pulled down the mailbox door and peered inside. It was empty, save for a single index card with one word on it.

Sophie

The night air was cold but without wind. It felt crisp and clean when I dragged it deep in my lungs. Sophie. Okay.

Back inside, I marveled at how this house never felt warm. It never felt comforting, not like my house in Ocean Park, because that was *my* house. I'd bought it with my own money, got my own mortgage, and I lived there alone. If Dad had written Sophie on an index card, that had to have something to do with our former client, Sophie Michaud, the French art student who was killed on campus in San Diego by her therapist, Adam Bouvet. Her final project before she died was an art installation of the famous Renoir painting, La Parisienne, a portrait of a demure young woman in a beautiful cobalt dress. A print of that painting hung in my living room in Ocean Park, in memory of Sophie. It was a little over ninety miles away and it was midnight. Maybe I could make it in an hour. What was I even looking for?

I left quietly, masking the sound of my car keys, which always rattled Trevor. I'd be back in time to give him breakfast. I locked the door, slipped out, and drove the whole way with all the windows down. It was freezing at first but I wanted it that way. I wanted the cold to wake me up, not just keep me alert for the drive but wake up all the sleeping parts of me, the parts I'd been hiding from. I could feel my father close. I cried at one point, not sure if it was from acute stress from this case, delayed stress from my accident, or repressed pain. There were so many layers of grief.

I got there at 6:15 a.m. The kitchen door was still stuck, and I had to nudge it with my toe while pushing with my hands. It had been on my list of repairs before moving north. It smelled musty so all the windows got opened immediately, in every room. My eyes had adjusted to the dark, so I kept all the lights off for a while and opened a bottle of wine. Wow, my own kitchen. My mother wasn't coming back to Santa Barbara. It was time to come home.

I sat there in the dark, cold silence for a while. Crickets, cars, the groan of a motorcycle far off, and the laugh track of someone's TV next door. I didn't care. I needed the change of venue, the escape. I hadn't realized that my face was angled directly up at the La Parisienne painting. The index card in my mailbox had said Sophie, and this was her painting in a way.

My wineglass clanked on the coffee table, breaking the silence. I pulled down the small painting and brought it to the kitchen table, where I placed it face-up under the hanging pendant light. What was I even looking for?

First, I scanned the painting itself—a quintessential Renoir. I flipped it over to see the back side and my head bounced back an inch when I saw a piece of paper taped to the back of the frame. *My father had been in my house.* I wanted to check the fridge to see if he'd filled it with groceries like he did sometimes, partial penance for the sin of violating my home and my trust. I carefully unfolded the page, purposely not removing the tape. Wow. I stepped back to take it in. It was a very thin paper, ripped from one of those old *Time Life* magazines, about ten by fourteen inches, black and white, dated 1979. I pulled out a chair and sat, using the flashlight on my phone to light up the tiny print of an article under a large photo of a tall man with his hand on the shoulder of a small boy. I didn't recognize the boy but I recognized the man, the face I'd take to my grave. Handsome, gaunt almost, sculpted nose and cheekbones.

It was an old photograph of Jacques Martel.

I had to get back because Trevor was waiting for me, and because my father had just given me the missing piece I needed to arrange for the extraction of Europe's most notorious crime boss and, possibly, his son, James Traeger.

◆ ——— • • • ━ •

"Hello?" Derek answered after three rings.
"Hey partner, sorry to bother you."
"No bother. Are you driving? What time is it?"
"Early, 7:30. I'm driving back from Ocean Park."

I heard fabric rustling, probably propping up a pillow. "What were you doing there?"

I told him about the mailbox note, the reference to Sophie, and the page tacked to the back of the painting.

"Read it," he said, clearing his throat.

"Well, I can't right now, obviously, but it was a *Time Life* Magazine story on the nostalgia of vintage cars. Martel was apparently a collector back then of vintage Porsche 911s. This was late seventies. And the nostalgia is about how Martel's girlfriend bought him the car, then she died and he gifted it to his son. Then the car disappeared."

It was quiet on the other end. I waited, hoping I wouldn't hear him snoring.

"Interesting. So, stolen?"

"I guess. The quote in the article had Martel saying he'd give anything in the world to get that car back. This is what my father wanted me to know."

"I see where you're going with this. Do you know where it is?"

"I don't, but apparently my father's been busy all these years. Leverage always was his secret weapon. There's an address handwritten in the margin of the page. I texted you a picture of it."

"You think the car's there?"

"I don't know, but he does. So it might be worth a try."

"What's your plan?"

I thought about this for a minute, watching the road in front of me, scant cars on either side, feeling the cold wind on my face through the open window. Based on my vast experience with Martel, this had to be done right the first time. There was only one chance, and one way.

"I think the plan is Wallace."

Chapter Fifty-Seven

I went home, fed Trevor, took him for a quick walk, then slept for four hours. Before going to sleep, I texted Duga to meet at my house with Derek at one o'clock. They arrived ten minutes early. All I did lately was make coffee.

"Hello again," I said to Derek, and gave Duga a half-hug.

"It's afternoon," Derek edged in beside me. "Do you have any of those—"

"Cinnamon rolls?" I smiled. "You're so predictable. I saved you some." We huddled around the kitchen table. "Thanks for coming."

"Are you kidding?" Duga said. "This is a once in a lifetime opportunity."

Derek poured coffee for himself and refilled my cup. "Do you get the feeling your father's been holding this clue for decades, just waiting for the right time and circumstances to use it?"

"Probably. What'd you find out about that address?" I said to Duga.

"It's a residence in Beverly Glen."

I raised my brows. "Full circle," I said, another reference to the Sophie Michaud case.

265

"A guy named Anton Davies, a collector, owns about twelve vintage cars, seems totally above board, owns several of the local smaller airports around LA and SoCal. Seems like a legit businessman from what I can tell so far."

"With a passion for Porsche 911s?" I asked.

"Not just, but including those, yes. He's got a few of them from the 60s and 70s, an Alpha, a Karmann Ghia."

"And *the* 911 is confirmed to be in his collection?" I asked. "I don't mean to hammer you with details, but we need to be sure."

"Parts of his collection are publicized."

"Here we go," Derek said, grabbing the last cinnamon roll.

Duga smiled. "I have a friend in the insurance business and his policy lists the make, model, and details of each of his cars. The specs match what you read to me from the magazine article. 1979 Porsche 911G, dark green."

"Well done," I said. "How do we know it's *that* Porsche 911G though?"

Four bleary eyes stared back at me.

"Okay. Why would Martel say he'd give anything in the world to get that car back? He's a millionaire, not to mention a thief. Just buy one or steal one, for God's sake."

Derek nodded. "You think it's that particular car he wants because he stashed something in there? And that's why it was stolen?"

"That's what I'm thinking," I said. "So, we need to play it right."

"How do we do it?' Derek asked.

"I think we get a message to Martel and his goons that his long-lost Porsche may have been found."

Derek was shaking his head.

"What?" I asked.

"I know what you're doing. You're gonna suggest the car in exchange for Traeger. He'd never go for it."

"We're just gonna give him the address of where the car was seen at Anton Davies' property." I shrugged. "He'll know it's a trap of course. But if he wants that car bad enough..."

Derek thought about this, sipping and chewing like he hadn't eaten in a week.

"Davies lives alone," Duga added, reading notes from his phone. "Divorced, no kids, works all the time. Travels a lot too, obviously. He owns planes and airports. Find out his schedule and a time when he'll be out of town. We could send someone to the house to do some repairs, and someone could pose as Davies for the purpose of a meeting." Duga stared at Derek.

"Me?" Derek wiped icing from his mouth.

"Does Martel know your face?"

"No," Derek and I answered in unison. "But I might need you," I said to him. "I think Francone might be a good choice."

Both of them smiled and nodded. Time to call Wallace.

◆ ── ◆◆◆◆ ── ◆

I love my team. We were a motley crew but we worked off of each other's strengths, and in three hours we had a viable plan, assumptions were at a minimum, the logistics were sound, and the universe was cooperating because Anton Davies would be in London till the end of the week. That meant his estate was being looked after by a team of four servants, who were all permanent residents. A personal assistant, who was also the butler, a four-star chef, housekeeper, and groundskeeper. Duga's job was to get the servants out of the house for at least two hours. At the same time, though? And how would Duga prevent them from alerting their employer? My job was to get word to Martel's network about the discovery of the car he'd been hunting for forty years.

I'd already talked to Wallace twice this morning about this. Thank God Derek and Duga were gone by then. I opened FaceTime and pressed his number.

"This must be my lucky day getting to see your face three times already. To what do I owe the pleasure?"

"You're a shameless flirt, Wallace."

"I can't help it."

"Where are we? Can you get word to his—"

"Already done," he interrupted. "I've planted the seed. His people will do the research and get back to me if there's interest in pursuing it. In the meantime, work your plan and get everything in place."

"Okay. When might we hear something?" I pressed.

"For this? The car? And this is what he considers *the* car of all the cars he's owned. Probably soon. Tomorrow, if I'm right."

Duga texted me to meet him and Francone at a Starbucks in

downtown Ventura. They already had a table with half-empty coffee cups, looking like two bank robbers conspiring over a blueprint the size of a place mat.

"Boys."

"Hey boss," Francone stood and bear-hugged me."

I flinched, more out of habit at this point. The slight rib compression from his squeeze barely hurt now. I guess that was progress.

"What are you cooking up over here?" I went from one face to the other. "Someone gonna tell me?"

"It's good," Duga said. "You tell her," he said to Francone.

Our heads hovered over a white page nearly touching. "Luckily, Davies' security system has a sensor to detect carbon monoxide poisoning. We can rig that so it triggers an alarm, showing a dangerously high level, way too high for human safety limits."

"What would naturally cause that?" I asked.

"Leaks in fuel burning appliances, like dryers, water heaters, generators—"

"Good. That's good. Now how long would someone have to be out of the house after it's detected?"

"Five hours minimum," Duga answered.

"That's perfect. That'll realistically get his staff out of the house. So, if Martel actually does come to see this car, Davies won't be here."

"I'll be posing as his assistant," Francone said. Risky.

I nodded, thinking. "I told Wallace to float a story about how the owner was considering selling it for the right price. So, if you meet him, you would say what about that?"

"A misunderstanding. Mr. Davies would never sell that car but that we have other cars we're considering selling."

"That's good, except Martel would never come here himself. He'd send one of his men." My heart sank as I said the words.

"That's fine," Francone said, "because whoever he sends will be on surveillance, and that will lead us right to him."

"In theory, yes."

Chapter
Fifty-Eight

"Anton Davies."

The voice was cool, aloof, and clipped. He was obviously busy, so I was surprised he answered a call from an unknown number. The carbon monoxide scam seemed well-planned but just didn't feel right to me. My father always taught me that if something felt too complicated, it wasn't meant to be. So instead, I explained to Davies who I was, explained Martel, and said he was in a unique position to do the world a huge public service by flushing out a criminal mastermind. No response. One, two, three seconds...

"I'm listening," he said, finally. He was playing it cool, but I heard the energy through the phone, heard him reverting to a young boy playing spy games in the backyard on a summer night. He was all for it, danger and all. This way, if Martel showed up, he'd meet Anton Davies directly. He could see the car, hear about how it had been legitimately acquired, and when asked why he was selling it, Davies would show him the magazine clipping. It seemed reasonable that Davies might read that and wonder if it was time to unload part of his collection. Apparently, the intel Duga had pulled about Davies' schedule was correct, except Davies hadn't left yet.

269

It all moved very quickly from that point. Wallace heard back almost immediately from the Martel insider network, and of course we agreed to keep off the Interpol radar for now. Once we got the feds and Interpol involved, that plan could take six months requiring ninety-seven approvals. Wallace texted that there was not only interest but urgency, based on some family details. He understood, from the research his network had been doing on Martel for years, that he cared about power and family, in that order. To me, that meant Martel wanted the car back to use it to re-open his relationship with his estranged son, James.

The time had been set by Wallace's insider contact for 6:00 p.m. tomorrow. It was a smart tactic doing it at dusk, allowing the cover of darkness for both parties. Derek and I had a video call with Davies to hammer out some last-minute details. He and I sat together at the large desk in my office, on the bottom floor of the Santa Barbara estate, as I'd started calling it, knowing my real home was Ocean Park.

Davies said he had a number of concerns he needed us to address.

"Go ahead, Mr. Davies, fire away," I said. Derek adjusted the laptop position so it showed both of us on the Zoom call we'd arranged.

"Will Mr. Martel come himself or send a representative?" Davies asked.

"We don't know. More likely a representative," I said.

The man paused and looked down. I pictured him drawing an asterisk beside that item on his bulleted list.

"What about the newspaper clipping? Will you give that to me beforehand?"

"It's a photo of a picture in *Time Life* Magazine. I've just texted it to you. Let me know if you have any questions."

Davies looked down at his phone swiping to get the picture up.

"Address?" Derek whispered to me, referring to the address my father had hand-written in the margin.

"I cropped it out of the photo so Martel won't see it."

Davies sighed and looked up. "The biggest concern is what to do if he actually wants to make a purchase." He gave an exasperated eye roll. "Much as I'd like to help you, I'd never sell this car. Not to a stranger off the street and not to your notorious crime boss."

"We know," Derek said, man to man, showing his palm to calm him down. "No one's asking you to sell your prized car, just to simulate

270

a typical buying experience. He might make you an offer. If he does, do what you'd normally do."

The man's eyes narrowed. "Which is what?"

"Tell him you'll think about it and ask for his card. Hopefully he'll be in our custody before it ever reaches the next step."

"Who else will be here on-site during the meeting?"

Derek and I exchanged a quick glance, knowing Davies was watching our every move. I suspected the initial allure of the plan had waned after hearing the reality of the logistics. And maybe now he wasn't interested in helping the police.

"Two officers on-site," I said. "One inside the house, one in the backyard, while you and your buyer will be in the garage. That's standard, minimum complement for basic safety." Under the desk, Derek lifted the toe of his shoe and tapped it twice. Okay sure, it might be more like 5-6 members of a SWAT team, needing their tactical expertise.

"What about the son? Will he be wanting to see the car at some point as well?" Davies asked.

"I doubt it," Derek answered, which was true. There was no way Traeger would come out of hiding for a car I knew he didn't want in the first place. But my hope was if Martel bought the car for Traeger, at some point he'd need to make arrangements to get it to him. Our operation, if it worked, could save the global law enforcement community millions of dollars of time, manpower, and resources. The old article about Martel's love of vintage cars was a powerful detail for his casefile, no doubt, thanks to my father. Though it might not be enough to pull him out of his lair.

Chapter Fifty-Nine

July

I woke up early the next morning listening to the world. To Trevor breathing on the floor, wind whistling through the sycamore leaves, and to the messages in my heart, all the while fumbling with the bullet the dead man gave me on our ranch when I was eight. Maybe now was the right time to look it up on ATF's national ballistic information network. Even the thought of it brought back the dark, sick feeling to my insides, and this unspoken knowing that it would somehow lead back to my family.

It was earlier than I thought. In the old days before I moved up here, before the Traeger case ate every moment of my consciousness, I used to be able to sleep till eight o'clock on a weekend no problem. Now I was lucky to make it to five.

And honestly, I had no business going down there in person—I'd promised Derek I wouldn't. Maybe he knew better. But Jacques Martel and I had a kind of karmic entanglement that connected to my past, my father, and probably my future. I had to be there because of my stake in the game.

So, I would have to be smart about it.

We were ready. Everything was in place, everyone knew their parts. Davies' estate was in Montecito, an exclusive suburb of Santa Barbara known as a celebrity enclave, on the edge of the Santa Ynez mountains. I drove in the dark of early dawn, using Waze to find the neighborhood, and parked three streets away under the shade of a huge oak, turned off the motor and opened my laptop. Derek, Duga and Francone were on point, and there was no sign of anyone yet. I was hours ahead of our scheduled meeting, but everyone should have been scouting the place out. The latte I'd gotten at a 24-hour convenience store was still hot, and still weak. You get what you pay for, if you're lucky.

I hid my laptop under the seat, climbed out and walked the neighborhood to get a feel for the place. Most of the homes in Montecito were close to the front of the property with tall trees, so it was easy to stay under the radar. I explored West Park Lane, Park Lane, and Park Hill Lane. They all looked similar, with $8M estates towering over the landscape, accentuating the significance of this operation and how ill-equipped I felt to run it. Davies' home was out in the open at the corner of West Park and Park Hill, with easy access in and out. His garage was on the right side of the home and a three-car-wide driveway. I knew Derek. He would be wondering where I was. I called his number with my story ready.

"Early bird," he said.

"Yeah, I felt like a walk," I replied. At least that part wasn't a lie. "No Trevor, just me chasing away the cobwebs, you know."

I heard no sounds on the other end.

I could see my car parked ahead under the trees, and me the only pedestrian. "It's even too early for dog walkers," I added, listening to my footsteps on the street. "Are you driving?"

"Nope, just checking on something."

"I think we've got everything covered," I argued, then saw a shape emerge from the front of my car. The shape of Derek Abernathy. "Shit."

"Ohhh, something the matter?" he said aloud, disconnecting his call, coming toward me. Why did I suddenly have an urge to run?

"You don't trust me," I grumbled.

"Because you're not trustworthy."

"That hurts."

Derek crossed his arms. "Okay, sure. Let's talk about trust. Why have a team if you don't trust them to do their jobs? You think you're the only one who can find Traeger. Don't you?"

"Yes. No. I don't know."

"And don't you also think you're putting the operation in jeopardy by being here, given your history?"

Damn him. He came closer, but carefully.

"You don't have to go far and we need you to monitor us. But," he sighed and stopped. "Could you please cooperate just once in your life? And drive home and monitor us from there?"

"Geez, am I that bad?"

"Yeah. You are. Now go."

———— • • • ————

I needed coffee anyway, so I returned to the convenience store two exits away, then realized they'd have surveillance cameras on-site. I opted for a McDonalds drive-through, which had just opened. I drank it in my car as I headed to Coast Village Road, which had some shops and a nicely paved walkway. I parked in the back lot behind Montecito Bank and Trust and walked through the lot to the next street over. There was a darkened alleyway between two buildings that reminded me of alleys in East Coast cities like Boston and New York. California alleys were nothing of the sort, this one framed by trellises on each side boasting the full bloom of fuchsia bougainvillea. Stunning. It was peaceful here and smelled oddly like incense. I recalled a hippie Tibetan store used to be in the village, but it had closed during the pandemic.

My coffee was hot, a little stronger brew than the last one, and frothy.

I stopped walking to take a deep swallow, tilting my head back. Without a sound to prepare me, a man's silhouette darkened the other end of the alley. He was walking in my direction, slowly. Was it Derek? Had he followed me? Maybe, but for the rock in my stomach and dread in my chest. Sometimes the world does this, I'd discovered, turned itself upside down in the space of a single breath.

Jacques Martel stared back at me. A few more wrinkles than last time, but the clear blue eyes as sharp as ever, clad in a light blue dress shirt tucked into his pants, no jacket. Did that mean no gun?

I'd only seen him in the flesh once or twice, and always from far away. He was twenty, maybe twenty-five feet ahead, just the two of us on each end of a cloistered vestibule, no one else up yet, out of view of my team or local law enforcement. Some moments define your life. Holmes versus Moriarty. Here we go.

"Long time, Ms. Ellwyn."

Scant shags of hair at the temples, his face looked oddly younger than I would have expected, given he'd been on the run for the past thirty years. The skin around his eyes drooped like someone his age, early seventies I'd guess, but his mouth and jaw were set in a form that seemed natural, like that face had never smiled on its own, like a genuine smile of joy. It was the face of a con. Shocking after all this time, my nemesis in the flesh.

"Not long enough."

"What do you want?"

"You know." I shrugged, my eyes locking onto his hands. They almost looked too large and meaty for his thin, wiry frame but for the size twelve or thirteen shoes. How many throats had those hands squeezed in his seventy-something years, how many triggers pulled? I should be afraid of him, I should care more about my safety. "What all law enforcement wants. To bring you in and see you pay for your crimes against humanity."

His face didn't move.

"How about you, what do you want?"

"To be left alone."

"Yeah, well, the apple doesn't fall far from the tree."

The mouth stretched on one side. The same eye aimed low to join it as he stifled a laugh. "James? You'll never find him."

"We did find him. We had him."

"Yes, alright, for a while maybe, a few seconds, but you were sloppy," he replied quickly in one breath "You never used to be sloppy. You got too close to me, once before, and look what happened." The hands outstretched. Posturing.

"Yeah, I got shot, thank you very much."

"Sorry. I never meant to injure you."

I checked the cold, stone eyes.

"I meant to kill you."

I could tell myself I didn't care, but my belly began to tremble inside. I felt it, felt *him* in there, in my spine, my body.

"That's what you want? To kill me in this alley?" I shouldn't be taunting someone like him. Maybe it kept me from asking about crypto, about his connection to Praxis, if he'd been behind all of it like I suspected.

"I'm not armed right now. Go ahead, call your team," he said. "Tell them. What you don't see, though, is one of my snipers aiming a long-range rifle at your partner's head. He's in the driver's seat of a black pickup truck with binoculars trained on Mr. Abernathy right now. He's, my man, wearing an absurd cowboy hat, no less. The hat doesn't work on him. I told him so."

"Doesn't meet your dress code?" He watched but didn't react, no doubt curious how quickly I could grab the gun in my purse. "So how's the art theft business these days?" I asked, fear or recklessness causing me to keep talking. It was through stolen art, after all, that I first learned of him in my former life.

"Yes, you used to own an art gallery in LA I recall."

I shouldn't be surprised that he remembered that. "You've moved onto more profitable enterprises, I see. I remember when art used to mean a great deal to you. A long time ago."

His eyes squinted, sizing me up, like he was visualizing us standing on a chessboard imagining the next five moves. I considered taking a step toward him, then thought better of it. I liked my proximity to the parking lot. I also liked the feeling of being alive and would like to keep it that way a while longer.

"Well, meaning depends on a lot of factors. I'm old now. 72, can you believe it?"

"Some things change," I said.

"And some things never change."

"Your son's stolen a lot of money. That's an understatement."

"Yes," he gave a theatrical sigh. "He does like money. Like me, I suppose. That's his racket."

"If you give him to us, I'll pretend I never saw you today."

"You have nothing I want," he shrugged. "So how can you make a deal?"

"Oh, I have something you want."

"Is that so?"

I was dying to mention the car, but didn't dare ruin our operation. "A piece of evidence you and your goons have been looking for, maybe for decades." I did take a step closer at that point. And he followed my lead. We came within about eight feet of each other, me with the cooling coffee in one hand. I set the cup on the ground at my feet and took out my phone. I navigated to the picture of a shell casing on a long-range rifle. I held out the phone so he could see, then picked up the coffee again and sipped, mostly to pretend like I was feeling comfortable. He looked curious, but not the least bit threatened. "See, I think there was another time when you and your network were looking for a guy, found him on our ranch in Minnesota, and shot him probably from across the street. He rode his motorcycle onto our ranch, crashed it in the dirt and died there."

"Where is it?"

"The shell? I've got it. Go ahead, search me, I don't care. I've already run it through the database."

"Really? And what did you discover from this...artifact?" he asked.

"It pinged your case file, for one thing. What did he do, this man? And don't pretend you don't know what I'm talking about."

"I've been told I have a memory like an elephant. I remember him. He embezzled from me. Tried to get away with fifty thousand dollars. That was thirty-five years ago, too, when that was a lot of money. What I don't understand is why that shell casing would be of interest to you and your team." His eyes blinked back, studying me. He tipped his head and raised a brow.

"What?"

"Oh, it's nothing really. Just that he wasn't acting alone, this man. He had an accomplice, who also worked for me back then. Now *he's* the one I really want. He's the one who kept the money. Now. If you had him to trade for James, that'd be something different. I might consider allowing James to serve a little bit of time in that case."

"Wow, close family." I took another sip of the coffee.

"James is a punk. He's my flesh and blood, but he's still a punk. Spoiled, like his mother."

"Who is this mystery man you speak of? Who was working with the man who died on my ranch? He pretty much died in my arms."

"Is that right? You make it sound so, I don't know, cinematic. Well, your father of course. Richard Ellwyn."

He knew exactly what buttons to push. "You're a sick son of a bitch, you know that?"

"Truth hurts, does it? You think this is a joke?" His voice got louder and echoed off the alley walls. "What do you think he's been doing all these years? What do you think I've been doing?"

It would explain why he hid out in BVI all those years, escaping from Martel. And it would explain where he got the money to set up his own enterprise, but the explanation seemed too easy. I wasn't sure I believed him, not conclusively. But it seemed at least possible. Maybe Martel was on the right side of the law back then. I covered my mouth to keep from throwing up.

"Now him, Richard Ellwyn," Martel said, drawing out the syllables in the name. "I would trade him for baby James. Certainly yes."

"I don't know where he is," I said, which was true of course. "I've never known. Sometimes he shows up, then I don't see him for two years or a decade."

"You can contact him," he countered.

"It's not how it works."

"No? How does it work, then? You realize, Ms. Ellwyn, that I could kill you and every member your entire team right now with a single command."

"I know."

"Do you?"

"You won't kill me here, not right now."

"You seem so sure."

Now it was me who smiled. "Because it's too easy, and I know you. Jacques Martel not only likes but needs a challenge or it's not meaningful to you. And you've had so few worthy adversaries."

The man tipped his head. "Wish I could say you were wrong. Maybe you and I have more in common than you'd like to admit."

"I have coffee in one hand. You could easily grab the gun out of my purse, shoot me, disappear, and no one would ever know it was you."

"But what's the fun in that?"

"Exactly," I said. "Here's the thing. Someone's got to pay for your crimes, at least for what your son has inflicted on the state of California. I told you once, I'll tell you again. Give back the money your son stole, or give us James, and I won't say a word about seeing you here. Not to anyone. If I did, you could find me and kill me."

"One of these days, you're going to lead me to him."

My father. I heard a sound behind me in the parking lot. I turned my head but saw nothing.

When I turned back toward Martel, he was gone.

Chapter Sixty

Jacques Martel had let me go. Why?

There was still so much to do. I needed to follow up with Jo Kramer and find Adam Matusik, certain as I was that she'd been hiding him—probably out of love—all this time, deceiving us.

I obeyed Derek's request and drove to the estate, camping out with my laptop so I could take advantage of the 17-inch monitor in my office. It was also closer to the front door in case I needed to run. I don't know what I was expecting, as it was still too early for any action. Anton Davies had set the meeting for late morning. For now, I needed to sit quietly and come down from the adrenaline rush of my encounter. Had that really just happened? Had I survived a chance meeting with a lifelong adversary on nothing more than my wits? Yes, I had, and I knew now I could do it again if needed. I think I'd wondered, all this time, whether I was really cut out for this type of work. I wondered the same thing when I'd worked for the Company, knowing the intelligence community was filled with accidental misfits like me.

But I survived those desperate days and so maybe I could keep doing this work, close the Ventura Office if Derek agreed, return to our grungy little office trailer in Fashion City and my beloved Ocean Park. I'd been the happiest of my life there, and I know Derek loved his place in Glendale. Maybe it was time to cut my ties to Santa Barbara and make a decision about my mother. Change comes at a price far less than the cost of standing still.

I heard a car door out front. Kneeling on the sofa, I could see Jo Kramer's hair from behind the curtain sheers. I moved to the front door and pulled it open, waiting. She took a few steps toward me. She still had some explaining to do.

"I'm sorry it took me so long."

"For what?" I asked.

"You were kind to let me stay with your friend, and you gave me your address and phone number a while ago as someone I could trust. And I need that right now."

"Were you followed?" I shifted my eyes to the backseat of her car. Something was moving, someone opened the passenger door and rose to stand beside her. Crew cut, bald on the very top, earnest dark eyes, oval face. Jo loved this man, the same man who killed his brother Horace as well as Val Sharma, because of what he discovered about Praxis. Before she took another step toward me, I sent a group text to Derek and Jazmin, asking them to call the PD and send a squad car immediately to the house to arrest two fugitives.

"Adam?" I called from the front door.

Jo's eyes were wide and wild, like she could take off any second.

"You'd better come in."

We moved to the foyer, the three of us, where I was careful to close and lock the door behind me. Trevor was upstairs in the bedroom, hopefully he'd stay there. I wondered about Anton Davies and my team. I wondered if Martel was watching me right now.

They sat next to each other on the couch. I was still in the doorway, watching their hands, another trick my father taught me. Adam had on black pants, a white shirt, and a black sport coat. He wiped his palms on his pants. Jo was monitoring both of us.

"Look," she started.

"You're both in a lot of trouble," I said calmly. "You know that, right?"

Adam looked at the floor. I came into the room further. "How about I go through it all and you correct me if I'm wrong."

Jo rested her head in her hands. Adam was a practiced strategist; I could see it.

"Val Sharma, Marketing Director for AEI, was a whistleblower who discovered and tried to expose the relationship between AEI's secret funding mission and the development of a shiny, new toy."

"Toy?" Adam now. "That's what you're calling the world's fastest computer? An innovation that could change the future in ways that nothing else has?"

"Developed by a private, shadow enterprise with dubious funding." I looked at Jo now. "Do I have that right?"

Adam contained a chuckle. "Praxis is a recognized AEI business partner."

"Now you're defending them?" Jo asked him.

"I'm not clear on what's so illegal about building a quantum computer," I asked as bait. "If someone has ten million dollars, it's my understanding that in this country anyway, they can spend it on whatever they want as long as they disclose their spending. Can't they?"

"Not if they're developing it to take down the crypto market and destabilize the US economy," Jo said, shifting her position. She'd moved a few inches away from Adam and turned to face him. "You killed Val to keep him from exposing your secret project, didn't you?"

"How did he kill Val, Jo?" I asked. I needed her to say the words, to have a verifiable record of this conversation. I remembered the Praxis video, and I also remembered Camille's autopsy notes of Val. I hadn't finished my research into non-standard toxicology tests, but I knew there were a number of substances that were extremely hard to detect by even non-standard tests. Adam Matusik was smart, crafty, and desperate. He could have easily gotten this information and used one of these lethal substances on Val.

I looked at Adam now. "I think you injected Val with something in the front of his shoulder, and another injection in his neck. Am I right? Some kind of toxic substance that would be unlikely to show up in a standard autopsy report or toxicology screen?"

He was looking at the ceiling. And if I was right, the tattoos on his neck were just a distraction.

"Jo, anything you'd like to add?" I asked.

"Answer her!" The words came out as a sudden shriek. "And you also killed your brother because he was blocking you."

Adam Matusik got up from the sofa and wrapped his arms around his body. I thought I heard a motor on the street. Maybe the police.

"And now you're both going to jail."

"I don't think so." Adam reached down and pulled a pistol out of an ankle holster. Crafty. My gun was close, within reach, but I knew enough to not make any sudden moves.

"You can go," I said calmly. "No one's stopping you. But they'll find you eventually and you've got a lot to answer for."

Jo was a deer in headlights, frozen with her arms outstretched, reaching for Adam but afraid to move, no longer trusting the man she loved. "Adam, let's go. Now." Jo backed up toward the front door still facing me. Adam glanced left toward her and did the same. One step, two. Two more and they were out the door. I didn't move. One one-thousand, two one-thousand. I could hear their steps.

A car door shut outside. Then, "Put the gun down!" An officer's voice cut the tense silence. Then, "He's running. Circle around, cut him off on the next street." I went to the doorway as another officer was cuffing Jo in the driveway. What a mess.

<hr />

I rested for a while, not intending to sleep but to just catch my breath. Jacques Martel and Adam Matusik in one day felt like too much excitement, even for me. I'd been texting Derek, asking about the operation and so far everything had gone as planned. But Martel had to have known of our plan and sabotaged it after his run-in with me in the alley. He'd said he had a sniper watching Derek. All I wanted to know was if we had Traeger or not so I could finally take a deep breath.

Lin Hagen had been bothering me. Camille Bota, my old friend, died unnecessarily and I still think Lin was in love with her. He'd probably gone into hiding after learning of Camille's death. And like before, my new friend Wallace McCoy seemed to read my mind.

Call me please, was all his text said. A man of few words. I liked that about him. I hated admitting that I liked a lot of things about him. I should have been appalled by the Mari wall, and I was, really. But there was something about him, I couldn't put my finger on it. Destiny?

I dialed Wallace's number as a FaceTime call by accident.

"Hello beautiful."

"Sorry, I meant to just do an audio call. I can call you back if you want."

"I've missed you," he said. I had to admit I liked his voice. "Okay, got it. You haven't missed me."

I laughed. "Do you have information to share?"

"Unfortunately, yes." His smile vanished.

"What is it?"

"Dr. Hagen was the one who planted the wiretap in your foyer."

I knew this already, remembering that night. "He was in here, so he had access. But I appreciate you confirming that. Why?" I asked.

"I found out he works for the same watchdog organization I do."

"What? He's a fucking operative?"

"Not Interpol, but I also work for a corporate watchdog organization and Hagen works for them."

I stayed quiet, thinking. "But—"

"There's more."

"Great."

"I'm sorry to drop this in your lap, but you need to know. Are you at home right now?"

"I'm in Santa Barbara." I exhaled.

"You need to get out of there, now."

"Why?" I asked, annoyed at another sudden imperative.

Wallace was walking around. It got dark behind him. He was outside and now sheltered under an awning of something, with a brick wall behind him. "Lin Hagen works for Martel. He's been infiltrating both organizations, playing them off each other."

"When did you discover this?"

"Only recently. Martel's hired Hagen to kill you."

"Wait a minute—"

"No, Mari. Get out of there, now. I live too far away. I can't protect you."

"I don't need protecting, for God's sake." I liked the way the words sounded, but I felt a thud in the front yard. Could that be Lin, posing again as a lovesick doctor? Son of a bitch. The layers of treachery were unrelenting.

Another thud. Maybe a car door?

Wallace was shouting something into the phone.

I sort of checked out, mentally and emotionally, dissociating myself from the drama and scandal, from betrayal after betrayal. Everything seemed in slow motion.

My front door opened. Hadn't I locked it after the police took Jo and Adam away? No. I hadn't. I saw the round shape of Lin Hagen's head darkening the doorway. I took three steps to the console table and reached in to grab my gun and holster.

"Hold right there. Don't move." Hagen's voice.

"Who's there?" I asked, the sun in my eyes, feigning confusion. It had worked before. Maybe it could work again.

"It's Lin. Lin Hagen."

I wasn't sure how well he could see me from across the foyer. I set down the holster, hoping he'd maybe think I was putting down my gun. "Oh, thank God, doctor," I said, pretending I hadn't just heard Wallace's warning. The call was still connected. I could see Wallace's face flattened to my phone as it lay on the table beside my purse, and now my holster.

"Doctor, I can hardly see you. Open the door further." I don't know what I was doing, other than following my instincts. Something told me there was someone else out there, behind him. Maybe looking for him. If Hagen was a double agent, no wonder he'd been so paranoid. No one moved an inch, Hagen still standing in the doorway, me in the middle of the foyer with the table right behind me, gun in hand.

"I heard about Camille," I said gently. "I know she was important to you. I'm sorry for your loss."

"Yes. Well, things happen," Hagen replied quickly. He was obviously here to kill me. "She knew things."

"Yes," I said, more animated now. "I think Camille knew what was in Val Sharma's blood because of the non-standard toxicology tests she ordered. Am I right? And you stopped her from getting those results."

Hagen chuckled, aiming his head at the floor. I saw a shadow move behind him. I shouldn't be here alone right now, Wallace was right.

"I think you loved her."

"You've got a lot of theories, Ms. Ellwyn, I'll give you that."

"Oh, they're more than just theories. I think the tox screens on Val Sharma would show a high dose of thallium in his urine," I said before I'd even had a chance to fully think it through. I'd read somewhere about Martel using thallium to incapacitate victims. Clear, odorless, and very difficult to detect post mortem. "I think Camille suspected this and that's why she ordered those additional tests. Who are you people? This is like Game of Thrones."

"You're right, Camille was curious, too curious. She went too far."

"And so did you, doctor." It was someone else's voice now, a man's voice. I knew that voice because I'd heard it this morning.

Lin whipped his head back and froze.

"Mari, get out of there, now!" Wallace shouted from my iPhone.

"Don't—move." The grainy voice again of Jacques Martel, standing just outside my doorway. Wait a minute. Was he here for me, or for Lin?

"Yes, you," he said to Lin. "You know too much about my organization, doctor. And now you've become a liability."

The shot came from a pistol with a silencer on it, I recognized that sound. It hit Hagen in the back of the head. He wobbled on his feet a second, then his knees gave out and he crumpled forward onto my floor, leaving me standing facing a dead body, a pool of blood, and the notorious Jacques Martel for the second time today. Without warning, Martel vanished into thin air again. Earlier he'd spared my life. And now he'd just saved it.

Chapter
Sixty-One

My phone rang at 6:00 a.m., which I should have been well-accustomed to. Especially lately. I rolled left and stretched my arm out to grab it. My thumb pressed something, I wasn't sure what.

"Yes?"

"Good morning, Sunshine. I'm sorry to wake you."

Ivan. I could just hang up and pretend it was an accident. "Has somebody died?"

"No," he answered, without the usual banter. Good, it was too early anyway.

"What's up?"

"I have something for you."

"At your office?"

"No, I'm out front."

Lord. I tried to hide my long sigh, secretly hoping he was in Santa Barbara and didn't realize I'd driven back to Ocean Park again.

"It's six o'clock in the morning."

"It's important," he said.

"I'm not home, actually. Can you just leave it outside for me?"

"Nice try. I know you went back to Santa Monica."

SWITCH

One – one thousand. Two – one thousand. "Fine, give me a minute."

I left him out there for ten long minutes, while I brushed my hair, my teeth, and put on my robe and slippers.

"Ivan's here," I said to Trevor, who followed me to the kitchen door and whined. Maybe he could smell Ivan's cologne. I unlocked the door and opened it a crack. "Come on in."

While Trevor welcomed Ivan, I ground coffee and boiled water, taking out two mugs. I knew he'd know about what happened with Jo and Adam, and I'd already told Derek via text. But I hadn't shared anything yet about Lin. One minute after Martel disappeared, two suited men arrived in a van, picked up Lin Hagen's body and drove off with it, leaving me alone in my foyer. There was blood on the floor. My hands were still shaking.

"No half-and-half, sorry."

Ivan patted his stomach. "I'm skim milk now, can you believe it?"

"Yeah, whatever. What's going on so early?"

Ivan sat at my kitchen table, wearing his uniform, completely awake and chipper at 6:15. I hated people like him. I read his face.

"What is it?"

"You should be happy, actually."

"That means I'll be anything but."

"We picked up Traeger and we've got him in custody."

I just stared for a minute, waiting for the however, but it didn't come. "Your team picked him up?" I asked with disbelief.

"The feds, actually. They took over surveillance and they got him at a gas station."

"Where?"

"Anaheim."

"Casualties?"

"Two officers."

I closed my eyes. We aborted the car scam with Davies after my encounter with Martel. If they'd known about the dojo, they would have known about that too. I looked back at Ivan, deciding.

"They're injured but they'll recover."

"Thank God."

He shook his head and looked at the table.

I grabbed his hand and held it. It felt like a strange thing to do, but also human. I still didn't believe Traeger was in custody.

287

He tapped my forearm and nodded, pulling out his chair. He set something on the table next to me.

"Oh my God." I held my fist to my mouth for a moment. "I don't know what to say." I picked up the diary and held it to my chest, suddenly out of breath. Ivan was legally obligated to confiscate it after they removed Tran's body. "Thank you," I said and half-hugged him, laying my head on his shoulder.

An hour and two coffees later, Trevor and I were walking our beloved route on the Santa Monica Pier, first down below on the soft sand by the chess park, then on the pier itself up to Pacific Park. The water was glassy today, still early, hardly any of the morning joggers showing up. I kept my hand on Trevor's leash and leaned against one of the posts. My father's diary, which I'd waited to look at, naturally opened to a page in the middle. A small slip of folded, yellowed paper slipped out and almost fell on the pier. My hand caught the top edge of it.

May she become a flourishing hidden tree,
That all her thoughts may like the linnet be,
And have no business but dispensing round
Their magnanimities of sound;
Nor but in merriment begin a chase,
Nor but in merriment a quarrel.
Oh, may she live like some green laurel
Rooted in one dear perpetual place.

A Prayer For My Daughter, WB Yeats, 1919

I read it twice. The second time, I caught sight of a man walking toward me with a hungry smile and the most beautiful blue eyes.

"There you are," Wallace McCoy said with his hands strategically behind his back, leaning down to bow to Trevor. Seemed like the right approach. Trevor blinked back. "Ready for breakfast?"

"Yeah, I'm starving."

Chapter Sixty-Two

THE CROWN COURT CASE THAT COULD RESHAPE GLOBAL TECH: AEI AND PRAXIS UNDER FIRE IN ESPIONAGE PROBE

Wallace McCoy, Senior Correspondent, Crypto Analyst [London]

A British Crown Court convened a closed-door hearing on Tuesday to consider preliminary testimony in a sweeping industrial espionage case implicating American tech startup AEI (Abacus Enterprises, Inc.) and its Munich-based parent company, Praxis Research. The transnational investigation—now attracting attention from federal authorities and Interpol—follows the suspicious death of AEI Marketing Director Val Sharma, whose personal investigation unearthed evidence of unethical business practices tied to the development of quantum computing technologies.

The defendants, Sebastian Wainwright, AEI's CEO, and Daniel Ito, AEI Corporate Advisor, Board Member, and cybersecurity expert, stand accused of conspiring to steal proprietary algorithms from rival tech firms across Europe and North America. Both men deny the allegations, claiming they are victims of an internal sabotage campaign orchestrated by former colleagues and rival entities threatened by AEI's rapid ascent in the high-stakes race toward quantum supremacy.

Judge Eleanor Havers, presiding over the case, issued a preliminary statement—her first since penning a critical legal brief on the erosion of ethical boundaries in transnational technology development. "Bilateral research accords were meant to spur innovation," she wrote, "but have instead become fertile ground for corruption, espionage, and corporate brinkmanship."

Quantum Supremacy: The New Arms Race

At the center of the legal storm is AEI's breakthrough work in quantum computing—an arena widely regarded as the next great technological revolution. Quantum supremacy, the theoretical threshold where quantum processors outperform classical supercomputers, has vast implications for cybersecurity, AI, and financial markets, particularly the volatile crypto sector.

AEI's stated mission centers on democratizing encryption tools and developing secure communications systems. However, Praxis—a shadowy entity with no public office outside of a Munich post office box—is suspected of darker motives. With little to no digital footprint and hidden financial records, former employees have described its internal operations as "clandestine", with one anonymous source likening it to "a government research lab without the government".

"The quantum race is no longer about speed—it's about control," said digital economist and crypto activist Troy Naylor in a viral TikTok exposé. "If companies like Praxis dominate this space, we're talking about the potential privatization of the future's most powerful technology."

Death of a Whistleblower

The death of Val Sharma, initially ruled accidental, has been reclassified as a suspicious death following new forensic evidence submitted by investigators. Sharma, known internally as a rising star at AEI, reportedly discovered missing funds and accounting irregularities related to a classified project, anomalies he intended to report to the press and the Senate Oversight Committee before his untimely demise.

"Val loved this company," said Kelsey Jo Kramer, AEI employee, in an emotional statement. "He believed in innovation as a public good.

And he was silenced in the most brutal way possible. Now those secrets may be buried forever."

The Twins Who Tore a Company Apart

In an extraordinary twist, sources confirm that AEI's founding team included identical twin brothers—Adam and Horace Matusik—who held opposing visions for the company's future. Adam, Director of Operations and PR, advocated for open-source development and decentralized networks. Horace, Senior VP of Engineering, worked in classified defense research, pushing for proprietary systems and high-security contracts, vying for more testing and research.

"It's like something out of scripture," said Professor Anna Lins, a technology ethics expert at the University of Cambridge. "One twin wanted to give fire to the people, the other to sell it to the highest bidder."

Horace Matusik was found shot dead three weeks ago under mysterious circumstances. His case is under further review with significant interest from the FBI.

Adam Matusik is currently at large.

A Tipping Point

The British High Court is now weighing a motion to suspend Praxis European R&D operations pending the outcome of the criminal trial. Activists warn that such a move could destabilize an already fragile tech economy.

"Slamming the brakes on Praxis would rattle global innovation markets," said Naylor, referencing recent crypto volatility tied to uncertainty in the quantum sector. His viral TikTok video features a superimposed EKG chart of the cryptocurrency market's dramatic fluctuations, now widely circulated among policy forums.

As the investigation unfolds, AEI and Praxis have become lightning rods for a broader cultural and economic reckoning—one that asks not just who owns the future, but who is willing to kill for it.

This story is developing.

Chapter
Sixty-Three

August
Los Angeles

"Attention Flight 885 passengers flying from LAX to Dallas Fort Worth. This flight will continue to Fargo, North Dakota and Alberta, Canada. We've got four extra legroom seats still available and we'll begin boarding at 8:20."

I looked down at the scratched, gold face of the timekeeper that had led Derek's father around so many years ago.

"Time is entirely up to you, Sparrow," my father used to say, that name, his special name for me. Sparrows always seemed sort of nervous and vulnerable in the grand scheme of avian politics, but the metaphysical sparrow totem symbolized hard work, persistence, and empowerment. Time is up to me, in a way, or at least I have a choice about its influence.

"There's plenty of time, once you stop running," he also said, when we connected in Tortola in March. My father will never stop running, I knew that now. As for me, look what I was doing at this moment— about to board a plane heading backward in time to the home of my

Midwest childhood, to a house that had once been filled with sorrow and emptiness—my mother's, and mine. I didn't know if I'd find her there, alone or with her lover Mason Middleton, or if another family was living there now, cooking, sleeping, ranching, living like we had once. And I wasn't prepared to do research and call first.

I was going back to 770 Oakport Street to ring the doorbell and stand on the threshold of past and future. I didn't want to deal with my father's abandonment. I still don't. Nor did I feel strong enough to face the decades of feelings I'd suppressed about that time in my life. I guess what's changed since then was that I had support now. Jaden my half-brother, and of course Derek and Duga—my other family. Moorhead...wow. Was I really doing this?

"Passengers of Flight 885 to Dallas Fort Worth and Fargo, we will begin boarding momentarily beginning with our first-class passengers and anyone needing special accommodation. Please have your boarding passes or smartphone app ready."

It was real now. My fingers fumbled for the phone in my pocket.

Hey partner, about to board, I wrote to Derek.

The typing indicator dots moved. *Why didn't you let me go with you?*

I don't know. Maybe shame. Some kind of quickening for me I guess.

You're a glutton for punishment.

Maybe.

Well, I'm only a phone call away, you know. Do you think she'll be there? Your mother?

I hated the pragmatism of his question, of course zoning in on the whole purpose of this fated trip. Do I think she'll be there? In our last interaction she said she had a story to tell. The question was whether I was even the intended recipient of that story. Maybe. But since I hadn't announced my visit beforehand, maybe not. I would have been happy for an explanation of where the hell she'd been all this time. But the other question knocking around my heart was if—and how much—she knew of the man who died on our ranch that day, when I was eight, completely alone. Martel knew of him immediately, and his ability to spin a tale of my father's involvement was just like him.

I rose, grabbing the handle on my small suitcase, which was filled with an odd assortment of random items I'd selected with the care of choosing food for your last meal on earth. While my left hand unzipped the outer compartment with my father's diary, my right hand dug low in the pocket of my jacket holding the single bullet casing gifted to me by the dead man on our ranch. Our blue and white plane stared back from the large airport windows, ready for action. Ready for deliverance. I walked down the skybridge, thankful I'd found my AirPods so I could listen to my favorite Sam Tinnesz song, "When the Truth Hunts You Down".

Does it ever.

Bring it.

About the Author

Lisa Towles is a bestselling, award-winning Bay Area crime novelist and a frequent speaker on the topics of writing, marketing, and creativity. She writes standalone thrillers as well as her E&A Investigations thriller series. Lisa attributes part of her success to the fellowship and support she receives from membership in Mystery Writers of America and Sisters in Crime, and from her trusted relationships with local, independent bookstores. In addition to writing, Lisa also hosts an author interview video series called Story Impact. She has an MBA in IT Management and works full time in the tech industry. Learn more at lisatowles.com or indiesunited.net/lisa-towles.

Acknowledgements

Writing a complex crime thriller is not unlike living through one. You begin with a spark, and then spend the next six months searching for clues, pulling on threads to find a way, to find your truth. Sometimes the answers come quickly, other times they're hiding in the darkness and silence of 1am. And more often than not, they were with me all along. But like any good investigation, a novel is never written alone. This book came to life through the insight, encouragement, and support of many people. My deepest thanks goes to the following kind souls who provided love, time, care, and expertise to improve this book:

My publisher, Lisa and the Indies United Publishing team—your extraordinary vision in creating such a vibrant, supportive community is nothing short of inspiring. Your tireless energy in promoting and marketing my work continues to amaze me.

My editors, Cindy Davis and Jennie Rosenblum—your sharp eyes, expert guidance, and thoughtful suggestions have shaped this book into something worthy of its readers. I am so grateful for your insight and care.

My generous beta readers—Ana, Max, Ron, Leslie, Melissa, Lee, and Nikki—thank you for your time, honesty, and thoughtful feedback. Your perspectives and careful eyes made this book stronger in every way.

My talented cover designer Tatiana at Viladesign.net. Thank you for creating such striking, memorable covers for all three books in the E&A Investigations series. Your artistry captures the spirit of the story with impact and elegance.

My husband, Lee—your fire, your passion, your creative insight, and your unwavering belief in me fuel everything I do. Your love is my greatest blessing.

My parents, who continue to surprise me with their strength and fortitude, especially this year. You are my inspiration, thank you for believing in me.

My sister, literally the smartest woman I know. You joined me on a research trip exploring the settings that breathed life into this series, and you were an amazing beta reader who flagged several key passages that led to important changes. This book is better because of you.

My amazing nieces, Olivia and Cassidy—you are brilliant, fearless, classy, and so kind. I'm so proud of the energy you are bringing to our world.

My SinC NorCal and MWA friends—thank you for being on this journey with me.

And finally, to my beloved readers—your engagement, messages, kind reviews, follows, and continuous support mean more than words can express.

Salt Island

Book 2, E&A Investigations Series
Indies United Publishing, 2023

Winner – Reader's Favorite Award
Winner – Reader's Choice Award
Winner – Pencraft Award
Winner – The BookFest Award
Winner - Literary Titan Award

"A masterpiece of a crime thriller"
- *Nigel Adams, Book Reviewer*

"An Intoxicating read, hugely entertaining"
- *The Book Commentary*

"An exceptional thriller"
- *Midwest Book Review*

Excerpt:
https://tinyurl.com/ax7ebeuy

Book Trailer:
https://tinyurl.com/bd6bt7v4

Available in Kindle, Paperback,
Hardcover, and Audiobook

Hot House

Book 1, E&A Investigations Series
Indies United Publishing, 2022

Winner - The Book Fest Award
Winner - NYC Big Book Award

"The page-turning twists keep coming as do welcome doses of humor.
Fans of bantering sleuth duos will be eager for the next book."
- *Publishers Weekly*

"Memorable characters make for a winsome, absorbing detective tale."
- *Kirkus Reviews*

"Towles does a fantastic job of pacing the storyline so that the reader
hangs on to every clue as it is discovered. Recommended for
fans of Baldacci, Slaughter, and Gardner."
- *San Francisco Book Review*

Excerpt:
https://tinyurl.com/2ez53dca

Book Trailer:
https://tinyurl.com/5a5wjctr

Available in Kindle, Paperback,
Hardcover, and Audiobook

www.ingramcontent.com/pod-product-compliance
Lightning Source LLC
Chambersburg PA
CBHW021503110726
47899CB00001BA/274